Trust Me On This One, Emily

Kathryn Barnett

Arizona USA

TRUST ME ON THIS ONE, EMILY

Published by Cactus Rain Publishing, LLC
San Tan Valley, Arizona, USA
www.CactusRainPublishing.com

ISBN: 978-1-9476460-6-3

Cover Design by Deb McEachern-Burton, Studio 19
Certified Proofreader Anita Beery

Published August 15, 2019
Published in the United States of America

Trust Me On This One, Emily

Kathryn Barnett

DEDICATION

To all the 'Thalidomiders' and their families,
this novel wouldn't have come about without them,
and for my mum for believing in my writing.

ACKNOWLEDGEMENT

My special thanks go to Nadine Laman and her team at Cactus Rain Publishing for believing in Emily.

My heartfelt thanks go to two brave Thalidomide women, Louise Medus and Rosaleen Moriarty-Simmonds, for having the courage to share their stories.

To the Sunday Times Insight Team for the facts behind the Thalidomide story. Also, BBC's *Call the Midwife* which first inspired me to take the Thalidomide story further.

Final thanks go to my friends and family for supporting me through the process of becoming an author.

PART ONE

'More the knowledge lesser the Ego,
lesser the knowledge more the Ego.'
Albert Einstein

Chapter One
March 1960

I rushed to the bathroom and knelt upon the lino floor. A wave of nausea swept over me. A painful retch reminded me that today would result in the same pattern of sickness and fatigue.

Taking a deep breath, I anticipated missing out on a bright March morning and not being able to take a walk by the River Thames. At two months pregnant, I could only estimate when I would feel better.

Slowly, I rose and splashed water onto my cheeks, watching in fascination as a stream of water gushed down the plughole. It wasn't until I heard movement from the bedroom that I turned off the tap.

At the sound of footsteps I opened the door and came face-to-face with my husband, Laurence.

'Emily, you have been sick again.' His brown eyes regarded me with sympathy.

I stepped into the bedroom eager to touch him, but he was dressed in a new grey suit, and remembering my vomiting, I kept my hands to my sides, for fear of soiling his clothes without warning. He had recently taken a new job as a pharmaceutical salesman with the biochemical company Distillers, and he looked sharp.

I glanced despondently towards the stack of paper on my desk and was reminded of the enormous task still ahead of me, if only my sickness would subside. Maybe I could take some more of my father's homeopathic remedies, and there was my mother's suggestion that lemon and ginger could help—anything that would allow me to get my novel written before the baby arrived and we became a family of three.

'It's all right.' I took a breath against his probing gaze and pushed aside all thoughts of self-doubt. 'It will pass soon. This is how it is supposed to be.'

His hand reached over to cup my face tenderly.

'The remedies are taking awhile to kick in—'

'Emily, think about it: If these remedies haven't worked yet, they are unlikely to resolve the symptoms at all. I know you like to believe in the old ways, but you need to look ahead and accept that medicine has moved on.'

He brushed a lock of my auburn hair behind my ear. 'It's time to put the health of our child first, that's why you need to see the doctor and ask for Distaval. It's an amazing drug, and I promise it will rid you of this sickness. There's no reason for you to suffer like this anymore. Medicine is entering a new dawn, allowing us to be free of pain, so we can live the life we want.'

I glanced again at my unfinished work, thinking I would probably be unable to continue once the baby was born.

'Always the salesman.' I smiled.

'You can trust me on this one, Emily,' he said, and after the gentle squeeze of my hand, he left for work.

Months went by, and I was in the later stages of pregnancy when one afternoon I bumped into Laurence at hospital after my antenatal visit.

'Emily,' he said, gesturing for me to join him in the quiet alcove, where he had been speaking privately with my doctor.

I took a deep breath, anticipating what might happen next.

'Tell the doctor about your experience with Distaval.'

I gazed at the doctor who had just assured me that, despite my earlier bout of morning sickness, everything was going well with my pregnancy.

'It did help me,' I almost whispered and wiped at my forehead, feeling the heat of a glorious summer's day without a cloud in sight.

'Excuse my wife's modesty, but take a look at her glow. Only a few months ago she was plagued with morning sickness that kept her housebound. Now she couldn't look healthier. That's the Distaval effect.' Laurence beamed and wrapped his arm around my waist. The baby kicked vigorously as I shifted my weight from one foot to another.

I placed my hand over Laurence's and gathered together what strength my pregnancy would allow. 'I couldn't have completed my manuscript without Distaval,' I added.

'That's another reason why you can trust Distaval, a drug that allows women to carve out a career whilst pregnant, whatever next.' Laurence winked at me.

'But what of its safety?' the doctor interjected.

'Its absolute safety is the reason why I recommended it to my wife.' Laurence patted my stomach.

'But can it be taken safely without the risk of overdose?'

'It's so safe it couldn't kill a rat,' Laurence laughed.

'You do present a compelling argument, Mr Alexander.'

'I trust in Distaval 100 percent. Now my wife is looking tired, so why don't you arrange her ride home and we can discuss the matter further in your office?'

'I didn't cry outwardly, but inside I screamed.'
A parent

Chapter Two
September 1960

I bore down and gave a final push. The nurses had drawn the curtains, and on the last day of summer there was just the twinkle of a reddish-gold sunset. I felt the baby slip out between my thighs. A wave of fatigue hit me and I leaned hard over the bed. I wondered if they would offer me any more pain relief as my insides surrendered to defeat.

'It's a boy!'

'My husband will be happy,' I panted. *Maybe next time it will be a girl.*

It was then that the midwives crowded around me in silence. One of the younger midwives offered me a hug and helped me back onto the bed. But as I glanced at her, she looked set to cry. I saw the baby's head peek out from his blue blanket. He had almond-shaped brown eyes, set in a ruddy face. I looked to the midwives, hoping they would allow me to hold him briefly.

'We are going to take the baby to the nursery, for he seems a little unwell,' another, older midwife, piped up.

'When will I see him?' I cried, as one of the midwives hurried from the room with my baby.

'You are quite tired yourself, Mrs Alexander. I think rest is in order,' the older midwife said, and not having the strength to argue any further I leant back against my pillow and fell asleep.

***

I awoke several hours later, desperate to hold my baby.

When Laurence came to visit me that evening, I turned to him and asked, 'Have you seen the baby yet?'

'No, they told me he is a little unwell, so I have come to see how you are.'

When one of the nurses approached my bedside, I asked more firmly if we could see the baby now.

What followed seemed like the longest hour of my life as the nurse hurried off to the nursery. When the doctor finally came, I couldn't mistake his grim expression, even as the baby cooed contently in the nurse's arms. I stole a gaze at my baby and found it hard to believe that he had been unwell at all, as his long eyelashes fluttered from all the attention he was receiving. I held out my arms for him, just as Laurence leaned in close to stroke his rosy cheeks.

It happened quite fast then as I folded back the blanket. A shrill cry lodged deep into my throat, silencing me, even before I realised what was wrong with my baby. I took in his long tapered fingers and absent thumbs, his legs that finished at the knees and his tiny crooked feet. I counted his thirteen toes.

Then I heard Laurence scream from behind. 'Take it away, for goodness sake, someone! How did this happen?' he demanded.

The doctor stepped in, relieving me of my baby and passing him to the nurse. I was offered pain relief in the form of a tiny white pill that held the promise of taking all my sadness away. Once again, I was convinced by the healing power of the prescription drug and was relieved to lean my head onto my pillow. Laurence's lips quivered against mine as he bid me good night, and then I felt my sorrow slip away in my longed-for sleep.

✻✻✻

When I next opened my eyes, it was to a dull ache in my head, and I wondered how many days had passed since coming to the hospital. I glanced around the room towards the heavily drawn curtains that gave no clue as to the time of day. I lay there for a few moments longer before finding the strength to push myself up in bed. It took me just as long to remember why I was here. Tears sprung to my eyes as the memory of my baby with his poor short legs and too many toes came rushing back to me in an instant.

I waited for the sound of footsteps to pass outside the door before I swung my feet to the floor. Taking my first tentative steps as a mother, I tied the sash of my dressing gown tightly around my waist and left the room. I wandered undetected down the corridor until I reached the nursery.

I sauntered amongst the bassinettes searching for my baby. It was then that a terrible thought went through my mind: *How easy would it be to switch babies? I could give Laurence the son he craved for.*

At the sound of a newborn's howl, my gaze met with that of a young nurse in a crisp blue uniform attempting to bottle feed an infant, who I recognised as my son. The baby wriggled in her arms and pursed his lips against the intrusion of the bottle's rubber teat.

'Mrs Alexander, you should be resting,' the nurse said with a firm gaze that made me wonder what the nurses had been saying about the baby in secret.

'What's wrong with him?' I asked, approaching his bassinette and closing the gap between us. The baby let out another howl as the nurse teased his lips with the rubber teat.

'The doctors are not sure why this has happened to your baby, Mrs Alexander. Perhaps his deformities are the result of some genetic disease in the family?'

Not being able to recall my father mentioning any such incident, I shook my head emphatically to the answer of 'No.'

'Well, it is probably too soon for us to know the reason for his deformities. Perhaps, we will know more once we transfer him to Great Ormond Street Hospital for tests.'

I felt my body shudder at the thought of his tiny body being violated by needles and undergoing what I thought of as unnecessary tests. It took me several minutes to calm myself enough to ask if I could hold my baby at last.

'Yes, of course,' she said, eager to be relieved of a difficult baby. His head fitted easily into the crook of my shoulder, but still, I felt my body shudder at the realisation of how unprepared I was for motherhood.

'You could try feeding him yourself,' suggested the nurse, taking her clipboard and heading towards the next bassinette.

I eased my back into the comfort of the nursing chair and felt my breasts heavy with milk for him. The nurse helped to position the baby inside my nightgown, so his lips could rest upon my nipple. He released a cry in exchange for her effort before I felt him take his first suckle of milk.

'When Alex was born, I was frightfully brave.
I cut off all my feelings.
That was a terrible mistake.
I didn't come alive again for seven years.'
A parent

Chapter Three

The following morning, feeling the first chill of autumn blow through the open window, I sat in bed cradling my baby. Laurence strolled into my room, and without a word he took a seat at my bedside and crossed his legs, just as the nurse entered the room.

'Is he latching on all right?' The nurse edged nearer, but averted her gaze to scribble down some notes in my file.

'Yes, we seem to be getting the knack of this,' I said.

'That's good,' the nurse added, before closing the door behind her.

Still feeling numb about everything, I somehow found the strength to touch Laurence's arm.

'We've missed you,' I said.

He winced.

'Emily, I'm sorry I didn't stay longer the other day.'

'I don't know what they gave me after the birth, but when I woke up it felt as though I had been asleep for a week. Unbelievable, isn't it?' I offered a silly laugh.

He looked deeply into my eyes, without offering any clue as to how he felt about our son.

'You don't have to do this, Emily.'

'Laurence—'

'You could leave the hospital alone. No one would expect you to be his mother. We could tell everyone that the baby died, and try again for another child.' He paused, allowing the thought to sink in. 'Think about it, darling. What kind of life would it be for you with him?'

'He's our son,' I whispered, feeling the baby shift in my arms.

'Imagine how it will be, with everyone staring and pointing at him. I want to protect you from that.'

'By denying he's our son?' I cried.

'The hospital will take care of him, and afterwards there are institutions suitable for him.'

'He would grow up thinking he was never loved,' I said, stroking my baby's soft head against a wave of rising anger.

'How would we explain him to our friends and family? Have you thought about that?'

'Without me feeding him, he won't survive.'

'Maybe he won't, anyway. I didn't want to tell you this, but I spoke to the doctor today. He thinks that because the baby's legs are deformed, the same could have happened with his internal organs.'

I blinked numbly. 'If that's the case, then he should be with his family.'

'Please, Emily, be practical.'

'I can't give up on him!'

'Do you even know what you're doing?'

Laurence returned to the hospital that evening and suggested a walk in the grounds to clear my head. He took my hand and led me down the three flights of stairs and out into the garden. The wind whipped against my cheeks as I glanced up towards the third floor where our baby slept in the nursery. Ahead lay the ten-acre boundary between the hospital and nearby Richmond Park.

I felt his fingers grip mine in urgency and guide me towards the bench. Taking a seat beside him, I wondered if his sorrow was the same as mine. How did he feel when remembering our son? Leaning my body into his, I rested my head upon his shoulder against a wave of exhaustion.

His lips pressed on my forehead, causing a lump to rise in my throat.

He threw an arm around my waist and pulled me tight against his chest. I breathed hard, fighting against what I wanted and what I knew I had to do. He didn't release me for a few minutes, and when he did, I caught sight of his single, lingering tear.

'Maybe the words came out wrong earlier, but I need you home, Emily. For everything that I've done wrong, please give me a chance to make it right.'

'Our son needs someone to fight for him, and as his mother, that has to be me. But I want it to be you, too, Laurence.'

'We don't know the first thing about looking after a baby with his difficulties. What if we got it wrong? Life is going to be hard enough for him as it is. That's why we must hand him over to the authorities, who can offer him the best chance,' he said; and despite having let me go, I felt his brown eyes implore me to consider his point of view.

'How can I abandon him after holding him in my arms and hearing his cry? If you love me as much as I love you, then you'll find it in your heart to be a father to our child. But if you can't, then I am willing to do this alone, because that little boy up there,' I nodded towards the hospital, 'he comes home with me, no matter what.'

✳✳✳

I waited much of the next day for Laurence to visit, and delayed my packing until the evening. I was sure that if I lingered at the hospital for too much longer, the doctors would arrange for my baby's transfer to Great Ormond Street Hospital.

That evening, having given up on an appearance from Laurence, I telephoned my father.

'Daddy,' my voice croaked with tears.

'Emily,' he soothed. I took a deep intake of breath, and after an absence of five years, I asked to come home.

The following afternoon I went to the nursery, but only managed to give him a half feed before he fell asleep. I scooped him into my arms, thinking that late afternoon was the best time to flee the hospital, when I assumed most of the nurses would be busy with their district duties.

I managed to get to the front door before I was approached by one of the nurses. I turned to face the older midwife who had helped me give birth.

'Mrs Alexander, you're leaving us already?'

'I'm taking the baby to my parents. It's all been arranged,' I said. I had never done anything like this before.

'I see, and your husband will meet you there?'

I shook my head, taking a deep breath against my fluttering heart with more deep breaths needed. This was going to be harder than I thought.

'Then, perhaps I can offer you a lift somewhere.'

'The station,' I said softly.

I followed her outside the hospital and onto the driveway, where behind the brown-brick building, parked under the cupola was a green Morris Minor.

She drove the two-mile journey in silence. The only sound to be heard was that of the baby's steady breath.

When we arrived at Richmond Station, she offered me my suitcase.

'Good luck with everything,' she said, touching my arm briefly. I waved her off before hurrying into the ticket hall.

I found an empty seat by the window, and at quarter to five, the train was starting to fill up with weary commuters heading home to Brighton for the weekend.

The baby was drifting off to sleep as the train pulled out of the station. His eyes rolled as we went over Richmond Bridge. He let out a whimper, and I was reminded that if I had any doubts, it was now too late to go back.

I tried to ease my mind by listening to the sound of the train trundling through the Surrey countryside. My thoughts turned to Laurence, almost anticipating him boarding the train bound for the opposite direction.

I allowed a tear to drip down my cheek at the thought of my poor baby. I adjusted him in my arms. He gurgled as I changed trains at Clapham Junction. I sighed, well aware that we still had an hour to go before reaching Brighton. I hoped he wouldn't need feeding before we got to my parents' home.

A ruffle of cotton brushed against my knee, and I looked up as a flurry of commuters rushed into the carriage. A young woman with lacquered blonde hair clung to the arm of her suited male companion. They took a seat opposite me.

The woman's gaze fell to my baby.

'Beautiful baby,' said the lady.

'Yes, he is.' Another tear escaped. I cursed my hormones.

'What is his name?'

'Rex,' I said, to my surprise.

'After the actor?' she gushed, leaning forward to get a closer look at him.

I held him tighter to shield him from their stares.

'No,' I replied, dreamily. 'He is named after his grandfather.'

By the time the train pulled into Brighton, the station was swamped with the Friday evening crowd. I started to wonder about my decision to keep Rex. What if Laurence had been right and he would be better off in a home? But I didn't have much time to consider that thought when I felt a tap on my shoulder.

My father was dressed in an open-necked shirt and navy trousers. His green eyes regarded me from behind his thick-rimmed glasses. His hand went to his auburn hair as unruly as Rex's.

'Emily,' my father greeted me with a kiss on the cheek, followed by a quick hug. I felt myself shudder, not sure if it was from relief or terror.

'Come, let's get you both home, and you can tell me everything.'

His gentle hand guided me out of the station and to his awaiting black Rover.

The short journey home was punctuated with silence. I noticed several glances from my father and guessed that he was keen to know what had happened between Laurence and me. But I wasn't ready to tell him.

We arrived at Regency Square and the sun-bleached lawn that I had known as a child. It was surrounded on three sides by a development of townhouses. The painted walls were complete with stucco and divided by wrought railings.

My father helped me out of the car and petted Rex's head for the first time. Then he went to the boot for my suitcase.

The front door opened before we reached the top of the steps. There stood a tall, lean woman in a green paisley dress with blonde hair that had been whipped into a stern bun.

'Emily,' my mother said, 'I'm glad you came to us.' She looked behind us, before ushering us into the black-and-white hallway.

Rex let out a cry, and I knew I didn't have long before his next feed. I hurried after my parents into my father's study.

The room contained little more than a high desk and a row of bookcases, with the overriding aroma of cigar smoke.

'Well,' my father said, this time with a firm gaze.

I approached his desk and laid Rex onto the tabletop, and only then did I unfold his blanket. Rex's arms flung open and he let out a howl. My parents stood behind me and took in Rex's deformed legs and multiple toes.

My father examined Rex's feet in curiosity. My mother joined in by looking Rex over for vital signs of health.

'This is most unusual. I don't think I have come across this before,' my father said.

I took a deep breath. 'What do you think? Can you help Rex? Can you make him strong and heal his soul?'

There was a moment of silence as I felt the room spin and thought momentarily of Rex. Milk coursed through my breasts for him. My parents' voices drifted into the background. I swayed awkwardly and noticed my mother reach out for me—too late as my body hit the parquet floor. I felt a splitting pain in my head, almost like tiny sparks of electric current, and then I felt my world dissolve into darkness.

'I thought at first I couldn't cope.
I did, but it's changed my life.'
A parent

Chapter Four

I was awakened from what seemed like a long sleep by the drawing back of curtains. The shock of the sunlight meant that it took me a few minutes before I could look out onto the patio, where amidst the pots of geraniums stood a black pram that I assumed held Rex.

My mother reached over to puff up my pillows. She took out a vial of Aconite, a homeopathic remedy for anxiety and headaches, from her pocket. Unscrewing the top, she shook out a single sugar pill to pass to me. Without asking her what it was, I leant my head back against my pillow and sucked on the pill easily.

'The neighbours had a whip-round for Rex. I even managed to persuade some of the local children to decorate one of the rooms in the basement for him.'

'Did they see him?' I asked in shock.

'No, they didn't,' she said, reprimanding my selfishness with a stern gaze.

'Why didn't I notice?'

'Your father and I have talked at length about you, Emily, and little Rex. We want to offer you the basement floor as your home. We appreciate that as a young woman and mother you will need that space to flourish.'

'Mummy.' My hand found hers and I held it tight.

'Rex has been pretty awful, refusing the formula milk. He's bit of a stubborn one, isn't he?'

I let out a nervous laugh.

'Emily, it will take time, but at some point you must come to terms with what has happened and accept that Rex's disability is lifelong. It's likely that you will never truly get over this. You'll just have to find a way of coming to terms with what has happened, that way you will learn quicker to bond with your son.'

I released a sob that had been lodged in my throat since I first saw Rex. My body rocked and I gave in to my grief wholeheartedly, for the little boy who I feared would never walk, and for the father who was afraid of loving him.

My mother wrapped an arm around my shoulder and helped me to my feet.

'The instinct is there, Emily, you just need to channel that into positive energy. Let me show you how,' my mother said.

She left me to get dressed, and with Rex still asleep, she took my hand and led me along the basement hallway and into an adjacent room that had once been used as a lounge.

The room was sparse, with boxes of old belongings from my childhood. There was a single brown sofa and a couple of worn side cabinets. Yellow curtains had been tied back with matching ribbons to reveal a sash window looking out onto the garden.

'This is going to be Rex's playroom. I thought we could start with a wall mural. I was thinking Winnie the Pooh and the Hundred Acre Wood.'

'I don't know much about painting,' I sighed.

'Lucky for you that I do. Come on, Emily, grab a brush and I'll show you how to get started.'

My life in the basement flat started as simply as that. Mesmerised by my mother's enthusiasm for Rex, and after spending the morning painting, we sat down together and developed a plan for Rex's education. The plan was based on some of her child development books that, apart from basic childcare, also endorsed the theories of Freud and the German psychologist, Erikson. He believed as part of his theory that the child's environment was essential for the growth, development, and identity of the child.

'Independence, Emily, that's the way forward for Rex.'

Together we took out a plan of activities for Rex and highlighted the areas of his development: physical, social and emotional, language, and intellectual. I surveyed Rex's room, glancing at my old rocking horse, abacus, and basket of rattles, and thought of ways to introduce those toys to Rex to help his development. A glance at a peaceful, sleeping Rex told me what I hoped to be the truth: That despite his difficulties, he still stood a chance of enjoying a happy childhood.

*'The highest ideal of cure is the speedy, gentle,
and enduring restoration of health by the most trustworthy
and least harmful way.'
Samuel Hahnemann, founder of homeopathy*

Chapter Five

A few days passed before Rex and I were summoned upstairs to see my father. I kept Rex in his white vest and terry-towelling nappy and held him close to my body. Breathing in the aroma of baby lotion and talcum powder, I climbed the main staircase, but found myself pushing against the will to remain downstairs with Rex.

Reaching the second floor, I slid my hand along the banister and approached a series of rooms. My childhood memory told me to choose the middle room. Knocking on the door, I adjusted Rex in my arms.

'Come in,' my father called.

I turned the handle and walked inside the room. As a child, I had rarely been allowed into my father's consulting room. Stolen glimpses had allowed me to only guess at what the medicine cabinet contained, and to wonder about the remedies within the strange blue bottles imprinted with Latin labels.

'Emily.' My father smiled tenderly from behind his desk.

The room smelt of lavender and camphor oil. On the desk sat a Moses basket. I laid Rex into the basket, before realising that we had a guest. An Indian gentleman dressed in a three-piece suit stood to my father's right.

'Allow me to introduce you to Dr Dhillon, who I have been consulting with on Rex's treatment.'

I offered my hand to the doctor. 'It's a pleasure to meet you.'

'The pleasure is mine, Mrs Alexander. Your son presents a fascinating case for us homeopaths.'

'Take a seat, Emily,' my father instructed.

'So, what do you think?' I asked.

Rex cooed and his little hands pushed against the basket.

'His vitals seem encouraging,' my father said, offering Rex his finger, which he curled tightly into his palm.

'Good grasp reflex.' My father nodded, turning to the doctor.

'Dr Dhillon and I have been discussing some remedies for Rex. We thought of Syphilinum.'

'It's not all bad.' Dr Dhillon laughed at what must have been my astonished stare. I knew that this was frequently used in the treatment of syphilis. 'A lot of it is about utilizing creativity and coming out of the shadow of darkness.'

I nodded, liking the doctor already. I didn't know much about India, but understood it was the reason my father had changed from orthodox medicine to homeopathy, and it was where he had met my mother.

'We also considered Anacardium. His little legs have shortening of the bone, but his arms are unaffected. There's a sense of disconnection about him. In fact, if you look closely, one leg is slightly shorter than the other.'

A tear escaped my eye, forcing me to look away.

'Mrs Alexander, forgive us with our medical talk. We forget our sensitivities.'

'It's all right, really. I should be stronger.' I took a deep breath. My father reached across the desk to squeeze my hand.

'Apart from offering him Calcarea phosphorica for his bones, we considered Hydrogen for the unification of body and soul. Think of it as a coming-together remedy, offering the basic element of oneness with the world.'

'I know you want to help. But what if he can never walk or lead a normal life? What then?'

'Homeopathy won't make his legs grow. We must accept the limitations placed on us by medicine, but we can work with what nature has given and help Rex fulfil his potential—and maybe even beyond,' my father said.

I traced his strange toes. There was no denying that he was different. But as he responded to my touch with a smile, I knew I must give homeopathy a chance to help him.

'He is mine. God gave him to me.
And if he had nothing, he was still my baby.'
A parent

Chapter Six

The following afternoon, I was giving Rex his two o'clock feed when I heard voices from the hallway.

'Are you here to see your son?' my mother asked.

'No, I'm here to see my wife,' I heard Laurence reply.

Rex suckled greedily at my breast and I leant back in my chair. I was relieved that he took my milk so easily, for I had learnt these last few days that a good feed often meant a long afternoon nap.

Rex's room was a tranquil place with sky-blue walls, a white crib, and a nursing chair. The large window looked out onto the walled garden and at the herbaceous border interwoven with Calendula.

Rex let out a whimper. I eased him off my breast and caressed his back gently, waiting a few minutes before laying him down to sleep.

Then, buttoning my blouse, I left the room and headed for the hallway.

'Emily, thank goodness you're all right,' Laurence said, pulling me into his arms quickly. I felt his suit buttons press against my swollen breasts.

'I will leave the two of you to talk,' my mother said. I turned to her, imploring her to stay, but she simply nodded at me and retreated upstairs.

'What were you thinking, Emily, going off like that without telling anyone? The doctor was furious that you didn't wait to be discharged first.'

'And if I had waited, what would you have done? Sent Rex away to London without my consent?'

'Do you know what a risk you took, coming down here by train on your own? What if you had collapsed halfway? Did you give your health any consideration at all?'

'We couldn't have that, could we? What if the passengers had discovered I was carrying your disabled child? Imagine the shame!'

He pressed his hands flat against my shoulders, and I felt him shudder.

'Why did you even come here today?'

I glanced at his suit. Distillers' business. Why had I thought otherwise?

'There's a hospital down here that's on my list.'

'Well, you should go and impress the doctors there with your wonder pills. Don't let me stop you. Better that you are seen with some glowing pregnant woman and perfect baby, than Rex and me.'

'It's not too late. You could still come home with me. We could forget everything else that happened. I love you, Emily, my life is nothing without you.'

'Then take us both with you. At least give it a try.'

'I can't do that.' He cupped my face and I saw his tears. I embraced him, desperate to show him that it was possible to love Rex.

Hearing Rex's cry, Laurence pulled away. He looked at me one last time, imploring with his eyes, but I shook my head and then watched him open the door and leave without a backward glance.

Chapter Seven

Winter brought icy showers that kept us inside the house. One afternoon, I sat playing with Rex in his bedroom. I was offering him a small silver rattle to shake when I heard a loud tap on the door.

Rex's room had evolved over the last six months, as my mother had encouraged me to discard the crib for a mattress on the floor, and there had been the addition of a long mirror and low shelf that my father had erected for his toys. The shelf included, amongst other toys, a wooden box with a hole in the top for a ball that Rex had to practise pushing through to help him develop his hand-eye coordination.

Rex shook the rattle with excitement as I laid him down on his bed. I went to open the door and was surprised to see my father with another gentleman who was dressed in a dark blue suit.

'Emily,' my father said, 'this is Mr Roberts. He's an orthopaedic surgeon, and he's come to take a look at Rex's feet.'

My heart quickened, not having given much thought to the moment when I would have to allow Rex to undergo medical treatment.

'It's wonderful to meet you,' I said, offering him my hand to shake. All three of us went to surround Rex's bed to the sound of tinkling bells from Rex's rattle.

Kneeling down, Mr Roberts examined Rex's crooked feet.

'Mr Miles, are you familiar with the Kite method for correcting club foot?'

'Tell us what we have to do to help Rex.'

'The procedure will require a lot of manipulation and keeping his feet in a cast.'

Feeling overwhelmed by their medical talk, I glanced at the window, listening to the rattle and the pouring rain. It took me a few more minutes to return to their conversation.

'Do you think it will be successful?' my father asked.

'That's difficult to say. The other option is surgery.'

'We want to try your method, no surgery,' I interjected.

'It will involve gentle nursing,' Mr Roberts added and handed the fallen rattle back to Rex.

'We can do that.' I crouched down and brushed away a lock of Rex's blond hair from his eye.

'Very well, I will schedule another visit with Rex for next week.' Mr Roberts paused, and as he did so, his hand touched my arm. 'You're doing very well, Mrs Alexander. You should be proud.'

I nodded, before watching my father accompany Mr Roberts to the door.

✳✳✳

That evening after the rain had stopped, I dressed Rex in a warm coat and blue woollen hat, and laying him in his pram, I took him for a walk. I bypassed the gardens and walked aimlessly for a while before heading down a side street that I remembered from childhood. There, I approached Our Lady of Lourdes Church, where I used to worship regularly when I lived at home. I entered the nave with Rex. I crossed myself and went to light a candle. Sensing footsteps behind me, I turned around and saw Laurence.

'I'm sorry, Emily,' he whispered, and crossed himself.

'How did you know we were here?'

'I followed you.' He held up a hand. 'Please let me explain. I want to help Rex, and I have thought about what I need to do.' He reached inside his pocket to hand me a cheque. 'I want to support you both financially by sending you a cheque each month.'

'What about being a proper father, Laurence?' I whispered.

'I can't do that Emily, I'm sorry,' he said backing away from us and hurrying out of the church.

I felt the flicker of candlelight and my tears mingle in disappointment. I fell to my knees to say a prayer for Rex. Then, I placed Rex back in his pram and returned home to my parents.

'Any man can be a father,
but it takes someone special to be a dad.'
Anne Geddes

Chapter Eight
September 1961

Rex leaned forward in his pushchair to clasp a handful of red material to the din of 'Coming 'round the mountain.' At various strategic points stood the children ranging in age from toddlers to nine-year-olds. My mother had seconded a couple of the mothers to supervise the activity, while the rest stood to one side clasping glasses of lemonade.

Fanning myself with my straw hat, I surveyed the scene. Our garden was heaving with women and children. I watched Rex teeter precariously on the edge of his pushchair and exchange yelps of delight with his honoured guests.

Rex was dressed in a sun hat over his baby blond hair which was now turning auburn to match mine, and dungarees that had been cut to accommodate his cast. His little hands reached out to catch the pink-and-blue ball as it bounced between the children and Nylon with vigour.

I skirted the perimeter to watch my mother take control of the game by removing the ball in exchange for beanbags. Edging nearer to Rex, my back leaned against the wall interwoven with honeysuckle. My hand brushed his as I turned to hear him utter, 'Mama.'

A smile broke on my lips, believing that this was the sign we had been waiting for. I leaned over the Nylon and hugged him tight. His little body wriggled in protest.

'Emily,' my mother reprimanded. 'You're spoiling the game. Either you watch, or join in.'

'Did you hear Rex? He can talk!'

'Of course he can. What have we been doing this past year? He's going to turn out fine, Emily, just wait and see.' Her hand rested on my shoulder, and I looked to see several children disappear under the Nylon, only to emerge a few minutes later and brush past me in curiosity.

By late afternoon, I wandered inside the house and found my mother in the kitchen, lighting the candle on Rex's cake.

'Who are these people, Mummy? How do they know Rex?'

She placed the matchbox down on the counter and looked at me pointedly.

'Your father has recently been elected president of the Rotary Club.'

'So these children?'

'Their fathers are members of the club.' She sighed. 'We want Rex to feel like any other child, Emily.'

I followed her into the hallway to the garden door. 'Look at him out there. This is just the beginning for him.'

'He still won't have a father. How do we make up for that?' I said, feeling tears well in my eyes.

My mother offered me a brief hug before opening the door. She left with the birthday cake to the sound of joyous cheer from the garden.

'Happy birthday to you.'

I followed the chorus into the garden.

'Happy birthday, dear Rex.'

I knelt before him and took his spongy hand into mine.

'Happy birthday to you!'

He smiled at me, a toothy grin that made me want to hug him close.

'Hip, hip hooray!'

I scanned the crowd, thinking that just for a moment Laurence had remembered.

'Time for a wish.' My father embraced me, blocking my view of the side entrance. I closed my eyes and stole Rex's wish.

✳✳✳

Later, needing some fresh air, I went to the front door and saw that a present had been left on the top step.

Bending down, I retrieved the gift and searched for a label, but found none. I took the present inside and sat on the staircase and ripped open the brown paper to reveal a child's sailing boat

with blue sails. Attached to the rudder was a label that read:
Dear Rex,
Happy birthday!
From,
Your father

I held the present to my chest as tears trickled down my cheek at last. Then I took the boat to Rex's room, and hearing his contented snore, I placed it on the middle shelf beside the silver-framed photograph of Laurence.

'Learn from yesterday, live for today, hope for tomorrow.'
Albert Einstein

Chapter Nine
October 1961

Rex was halfway through his vegetable curry when I turned away from him to mix up a couple of pots of red and green paint for him to do hand prints later. I heard the click of the basement gate and saw Laurence briefly before he disappeared down the steps.

Casting the paint pots aside, I went to the kitchen door and turned the handle. Laurence breezed into the kitchen, toting what could only be described as a white bucket seat under his arm.

I offered him a smile and took the contraption from him, placing it on the floor out of Rex's way.

Laurence's attention drifted to Rex. Our son was sitting at his own little table that camouflaged his feet, which had improved somewhat with treatment.

Rex, upon noticing Laurence, offered his spoon to be fed, resulting in a spoonful of curried cauliflower landing on the wooden tabletop.

'Rex, you can feed yourself,' I said.

'He looks so young,' Laurence commented. At thirteen months, Rex was easily the size of a six-month-old baby.

'My mother's a stickler for independence,' I sighed, grabbing a cloth to wipe Rex's table.

'I've come at a bad time.'

'No, not at all.' I nodded towards a chair, but Laurence shook his head. 'We could take Rex outside for a bit, before his nap?'

'Sure,' Laurence said, grinning.

I leant over and lifted Rex out of his chair. His small hands pummelled my back gently. I turned to see Laurence watching us in fascination, before heading down the hallway and out into the garden.

On the patio was a tartan blanket strewn with Rex's toys, building blocks, an abacus, and dozens of hard-backed books from his morning lesson.

I tidied a space for Rex and sat him down on the blanket, then surrounded him by cushions in case of a fall. His little body rocked, and I wondered how long it would be before he resorted to his favourite position of lying on his tummy.

Laurence came up to me and placed the strange white apparatus on the flagstones. Rex chose a pink cube and began tracing its edges with interest.

I knelt down with Laurence and examined the bucket seat.

'It's called a flowerpot, and it's supposed to help babies like Rex to sit better.' Curious about Laurence's newfound interest in Rex, I picked up my son and slid him into the seat.

Rex was clapping his hands in appreciation at his new toy, when my mother approached us.

'Hello, Laurence, this is unexpected,' she said, with a cordial smile.

'Mrs Miles, I know I probably should have called first.'

My mother breezed past him to approach Rex. She knelt down to his level. 'It's just about time for his afternoon nap, isn't it, Emily?'

'We were just about to take him inside,' I explained.

'I'm sorry if my visit has caused any problems. I thought with it being a Saturday afternoon...'

'Rex follows a strict routine here.'

'Look at him, Mummy. He hasn't taken his eyes off Laurence. He's probably bored of the same faces.'

'Um,' she replied.

'Meeting new people must be good for his emotional development.'

'So, how useful is this contraption?' My mother glanced at the bucket seat.

'It could prevent accidents, at least until he masters the balancing act.'

'It was good of you, Laurence, to think of Rex and come out of your way to drop by the house this afternoon.'

'I just wanted to help.'

'I shall leave it to the pair of you to put him down for his sleep,' my mother said, departing before we had the chance to respond.

'Never know what she really thinks of me.'

'She's quite protective of Rex.'

'Yes, I got that impression.'

'I'm glad you came today.'

'So am I.' He squeezed my hand.

'Let's take him inside,' I said. After pulling Rex out of the bucket seat, I heard Laurence follow me inside the house. I laid our son down gently on his bed, but saw Laurence creep away, filling me with disappointment that yet again he was cutting his visit short.

*'Every doctor, every hospital has been notified,
every woman in this country must be aware that it is important
they check their medicine cabinet
and they do not take this drug.'
President John F Kennedy, August 1962*

Chapter Ten
November 1961

Laurence strode into my living room sporting a tieless shirt and creased navy trousers. Approaching me, his open collar seeped with perspiration, and without warning he pulled me into his arms.

'Have you heard the news?'

I shook my head. It was hard to explain life at the house, how we did things differently here and that I didn't even have a television in the basement.

'It's important that you don't hate me for what I'm about to tell you.'

'This is about Rex, isn't it?'

'I'm so sorry.' I listened to his chest heave and tried to comfort him as best as I could.

'It's been all over the news about, about Thalidomide.' His words tumbled out as a way of explanation.

He looked to me for understanding. But it didn't make sense. I had never even taken an aspirin as a child. Whenever I had a fever, I was sent to bed with a dose of Belladonna, so analysing how Thalidomide had damaged Rex was just as much a mystery as why I had taken it in the first place.

'They were deformed like Rex, some even worse. It is all in Dr McBride's report,' said Laurence. 'There's still no definite way of proving that Thalidomide was to blame. We conducted the tests. We did everything they asked of us.'

'Then how did it happen?'

Together we walked down the hallway to the door that spelt out REX in blue and green.

'You can go inside, if you like. He's probably still asleep,' I said, watching Laurence's hand clasp the handle.

'He's grown a little since your last visit,' I said, and placing my hand over his, we entered Rex's room together to watch him for a moment as he stirred in his sleep.

'Taking a drug to make oneself feel better is not essential.'
A doctor, discussing the public view of Thalidomide
as the scandal came to light

Chapter Eleven

I was tucking Rex into bed the following evening when my mother came into the room and lingered behind me. I reached for Rex's nightlight and swayed between leaving it on and switching it off. I felt Rex's fingers comb my hair, hinting that he wasn't ready for the dark yet.

'Good night, Mummy,' he said. I leaned over his bed and allowed him to wrap his arms around my neck. His hands squeezed my cheeks and he planted a kiss on my lips. As he pulled away from me, I felt compelled to stay by his bed and watch him curl his small body into the mattress.

'Let's talk in your room,' my mother whispered, and I followed her out of the room.

'This is about Laurence, isn't it?' I asked, watching her pace the room.

'I'm going to ask you a question and I want a truthful answer. Did you take Thalidomide when you were pregnant with Rex?'

'No,' I lied.

'Emily,' she coaxed.

I went to the window. 'I had a dream once. For a short while, I did something that mattered to me that didn't involve Laurence or Rex, and I was happy. That's right, give me that look. Tell me how selfish I was and what a terrible mother I must have been to put my dream before that of my unborn baby. When Laurence suggested Distaval, I didn't think twice. After all, what damage could two tablets do to my baby, when everyone was telling me it was safe? Yes, I bartered my son's legs so I could pursue a dream—Imagine!'

The following morning, my mother suggested that we take Rex for a walk to the park. It was another bright, crisp day, which fooled us into believing that it wasn't quite winter yet. I dressed Rex in a light coat, but tucked a blanket inside his pushchair.

We approached a tree-lined street of whitewashed Regency houses, and I wondered about the families inside. Were they also going through the same experience as us? I knew there was no way of estimating how many other toddlers out there were affected the same as Rex.

A gaggle of children rushed on ahead and made for the iron gate that separated the street from the grassland of the park. After watching the children, I looked down at Rex. He had pulled the blanket to one side, revealing his leg casts.

Tucking the blanket back over his knees, I felt my mother grab my arm and guide me towards a low brick wall, which divided the row of terrace houses from the sloping pavement.

'What are you doing?' she asked. 'You are reinforcing the message that he should feel ashamed of his body.'

I bit down on my lip. 'I just find it hard sometimes.'

'Of course you do, but you must have known it would be difficult when you brought Rex home. You could have left him at the hospital, yet you chose to be his mother.'

'Mummy,' Rex interrupted, and I took that as a cue to go to the front of his pushchair and lift him out of the seat.

'Swings today?' Rex asked.

'Of course.' I hugged him tightly and felt his casts bump against my hip.

'I want so much for Rex to be happy.'

'And he is. You are doing so well, my darling, and with our plan in hand, he will continue to flourish. We will take Rex to the park every day, as part of his outdoor play sessions. We will ignore the stares because we believe in Rex. Thalidomide will empower us, not destroy us,' my mother said, joining our hug.

'Every great tragedy forms a fertile soil in which a great recovery can take root and blossom, but only if you plant the seeds.'
Steve Maraboli

Chapter Twelve
September 1962

I was in the garden with Rex the first time the doctor came to visit. I had just pulled Rex's feet through the bars of the swing, when I heard a clearing of breath and turned to glance at the middle-aged gentleman dressed in a navy suit.

'Hello, can I help at all?' I asked, thinking he must have been one of my father's patients who had been waylaid from the house.

'Please, allow me to introduce myself. I'm Dr Donahue.' He offered me his hand, and I let go of the swing to shake it.

'May I?' Dr Donahue asked, glancing at Rex.

I nodded and stepped aside. He gave a big push, causing Rex to soar into the air. Rex squealed in delight, and we laughed simultaneously.

I led him to the wrought-iron table, where I had placed a warm teapot and cups for an afternoon break, and we took a seat opposite each other.

'So what brings you here?' I asked, pouring him a cup of tea.

'Thank you.' He smiled and took the cup and saucer, holding them close to his chest. 'It's about Rex.'

I poured myself a cup of tea.

'I haven't come here to upset you or Rex. I just want to help,' he explained.

'Rex is doing well. He's had a two-year treatment for club foot, and as a result, his feet are no longer crooked. If you understand a little about homeopathy, you would see that being here has helped Rex so much already, and this is just the start for him.'

'We are concerned that Rex hasn't received proper hospital treatment or been assessed for limb-fitting.'

I glanced towards Rex, at his bare feet that poked out from his cut-down trousers.

'Let me help him. I know Thalidomide let him down badly, and we can never make up for what happened. But there is something which science can offer that you can't.'

'You don't approve of our ways?'

'I believe there is still a lot we don't understand about the body or how medicines work.'

'We can't go back to London.'

'You wouldn't need to. I could take you both to the limb-fitting centre at Roehampton, although it would mean him staying there for assessment and fitting.'

'I don't know,' I said, going to the swing and placing my hand upon Rex's shoulder. Rex's head turned to gaze up at me, expectantly.

'It would only be for a week at the most. I would personally make sure that he was home for the weekend. I'm based at Chailey Heritage Hospital here in Sussex. I have been conducting some pioneering work with the Thalidomide children. I have to tell you that so far, the practice of limb-fitting has proven to be extremely beneficial for children like Rex. Science did enough to damage him; let it do its best to help him by offering him the opportunity of learning to walk.'

Rex's arm dangled free and the doctor took hold of his long fingers.

'Do this now, while he's still young,' said the doctor, scribbling down his telephone number and handing it to me, before departing through the side entrance.

✳✳✳

'They have opened up discussions about a compensation deal,' said my father the following evening, as I helped Rex onto the tower of cushions that allowed his arms to reach the top of the long dining room table in the upstairs parlour.

'Let's not talk about this in front of the child,' my mother interjected.

I took my place and waited for her to serve the red-bean stew.

'What does this mean for us, Daddy?' I shifted in my chair, feeling the chill from a mid-September evening.

'Last month there was a meeting in Southampton, resulting in the decision to sue Distillers for damages.'

I forked the carrots with interest, before glancing to my right at Rex. Holding his fork between his fingers, he was able to demonstrate a basic hand to mouth movement that allowed him to enjoy small mouthfuls of vegetables.

My mother had yet to start eating the dinner that she had spent the afternoon preparing.

I turned back to Rex too late as his stiff little fingers dropped his fork into the thick sauce. I reached over to rescue the fork for him.

'Leave him!' my mother yelled. 'Let him try himself.'

'He can't, that's the point. Because of Distillers.'

'We can help him overcome these difficulties to a degree. We don't need outside help,' she said.

'You mean Dr Donahue?' I said.

'There have been letters and adverts in the newspapers about Thalidomide. Rex isn't alone,' said my father gently.

My mother reached for the bottle of Sauterne and filled her glass. 'What do they want with this letter writing? What do they hope to achieve?'

'They want to establish a society for the Thalidomide children,' said my father. 'The society has the support of Lady Hoare and Sir Frederick. This is an important step forward, Celia,' he said, winking at me. 'Sir Frederick's a banker. That means the right support for the appeal.'

My mother took a sip of her wine. 'I know I prefer to keep little Rex's care private, but—'

'Dr Donahue doesn't appear to oppose our ways, and it's important for Rex's development that he starts limb-fitting sessions soon, Mummy.'

'Careful, Emily, about trying to sound too much like Laurence.'

'This isn't about pleasing Laurence as much as giving my son the best opportunities for success,' I answered quickly.

Glancing over at the window at the kaleidoscope of sea and sky, I thought a little more about Dr Donahue's proposition.

'No friendship is an accident.'
–O Henry, Heart of The West

Chapter Thirteen
March 1963

A little more than a year had passed when I read of a local Thalidomide support group being held here in Brighton, so it was during one spring morning that I navigated my way through Brighton's lanes in search of the Regency Bookshop. I had left Rex at home with my mother, so I had only a spare couple of hours at the most to attend the meeting.

I spotted the green awning and wandered into the shop. Drifting into the antique section, I found myself amongst the grandfather clocks, Welsh dressers and brass lamps, making me think that I had come to the wrong place. I glanced down at the scribbled address from the *Brighton Echo*. The meeting had to be here.

A woman approached me then. She wore a beige tweed dress and red kid boots and was blessed with honey-blonde hair. It was with her free hand that she clutched a matching red handbag.

'Are you here for the Pollyanna Club?' she asked gently. I nodded and gazed down at my scuffed black patent shoes, which I had put on in a hurry so as not to be late.

'Then follow me downstairs. I'm Sylvia, by the way.'

'Emily,' I replied. I followed Sylvia down the spiral staircase, taking each step carefully before entering the basement.

The room was crammed from ceiling to floor with antiquarian books. I had to fight the temptation to browse, not remembering the last time that I had been allowed this much freedom.

In the middle of the room, a round table had been set up with several velvet-backed chairs. All but one of the chairs was taken by the time of my arrival. Amongst the drawn faces, I recognised

Dr Donahue. Dressed in a casual suit, he stood up and offered me his outstretched hand.

'Hello again, Mrs Alexander. Welcome to the group.'

'It's good to see you,' I said taking a seat opposite Sylvia.

'So how are we all getting on?' asked the doctor.

A low mumble resounded around the room.

'What are our concerns for our Thalidomide children?'

'My son never gaining bladder control,' one father shot out. The audience nodded in sympathy.

'I understand, sir. Let us have a conversation about how we can help our children gain independence. Has your son been offered surgery? Catheterisation? Do you receive support from the local authorities?'

'He's in hospital at the moment.' The man shook his head.

'We wish him all the best, and remember that this is a place where we can share our experiences. There is no need to feel isolated, support is available.'

My gaze went to Sylvia as she crossed and uncrossed her legs. Her eyes caught mine and she offered me a smile.

The doctor dug into his briefcase and pulled out a long stick with an S-shaped hook on the end. 'How have we found the dressing sticks?'

'Why aren't we talking about compensation? That would help us more than wacky gadgets,' Sylvia said, rising to her feet. 'Who else agrees?' The remaining parents got to their feet as a sign of solidarity. I was the last to stand.

'This is not what we are here to discuss,' the doctor said.

'Why shouldn't they be held accountable for what they did to our children?' Sylvia shot back.

'It isn't as simple as that. Any legal action would prove futile. Please, I implore you to focus on the needs of your children first.'

'Without compensation, how can we continue to provide our children with the help they so desperately need?' Sylvia asked, getting louder with each question.

'Here, here,' chorused the parents.

For the next half-hour I listened to the parents share their concerns. I drifted between hearing their worries and giving in to my own sense of fatigue from being Rex's mother.

'Let us conclude the meeting with information on occupational therapy. I have some leaflets here. Please take one before you leave.'

The doctor placed a stack of leaflets onto the table. One by one the parents reached for a copy before filing out of the room. I heard the thunder of footsteps on the staircase.

'I'm sorry about that,' said Dr Donahue, approaching my side. 'I want to help, but this talk of compensation won't do any good.'

'Why?'

'It would be almost impossible to prove Distillers' negligence, and any lawsuit would cost more money than the parents could ever afford.'

'Of course, it would be difficult.'

'Shall I pick up you and Rex at eight tomorrow morning?'

I gazed at him in confusion.

'For his limb-fitting session, remember?'

'Yes, of course, I'm sorry. I should have remembered.'

'Is everything all right, Mrs Alexander?' He touched my arm.

'Oh, it's just the usual. Me, trying to do my best for Rex.'

'Looks like you are doing very well.' I caught his smile before heading for the staircase.

Outside the shop, I saw Sylvia and a blond-haired gentleman, who I presumed to be her husband. He wrapped his arm around her waist as she broke down.

'I'm trying, Chris, but I don't know if I can do it anymore. It's just too difficult,' she said.

Glancing their way, I wondered if there was something I could say to help. But before I had a chance to approach them, they had disappeared into the crowd.

'It's the little moments that make life big.'
Unknown

Chapter Fourteen

The following day, having agreed to Dr Donahue's proposition, he arrived at the house to take Rex and me to London. I dressed Rex in a white shirt and red shorts. There was a familiar seaside breeze to the morning air, so I grabbed my green jacket to wear over my blouse.

'Here's some Arnica for Rex to protect him from the X-rays and some Argentum nitricum for your peace of mind,' my father said, offering me two vials of pills, as he accompanied me out of the house.

'Thank you.' I touched his arm as we stood waiting for the doctor on the front step.

'Do take a moment to think about what the process will mean for Rex, and be sure about everything before making a decision. Rex is still young and has plenty of time ahead for this.'

Dr Donahue arrived and I followed my father to the doctor's car.

'Look after them both.' My father leaned into the rear window of Dr Donahue's cream Ford Consul and kissed my cheek.

'Bye, bye, Gramps, we're going to London!' Rex clapped his hands in excitement.

The car pulled away from the kerb. Rex and I waved at my father until he was a distant figure on Regency Square. Then I cuddled Rex close to me and felt my heart pound in anticipation.

'Don't worry. This is just the beginning for Rex. In a few months' time, you'll look back on today with no regrets. You are only doing what any mother would.'

I offered Rex his colouring book and watched him lodge the blue crayon between his fingers and press down on the outline of a peacock.

Gradually, the scenery changed from the coastline to one of heaving city traffic. I was back in London. I waited until our car slowed before I pushed myself up in my seat.

We had arrived at a three-storey villa with a sign that read Queen Mary's Hospital. I looked ahead at the sweeping driveway that must have once been part of a country estate. Rex gripped his book and gazed at his new surroundings in curiosity.

'It looks impressive,' I said, with a nervous laugh.

'It will be fine, Mrs Alexander,' Dr Donahue said, regarding me in the mirror.

We entered the hospital, and wheeling Rex in his pushchair, the doctor guided us down the corridor and into one of the side rooms. There, a nurse in a navy uniform and white cap approached us and extended her hand to greet us.

'I'm Sister Williams. Dr Donahue has told me about Rex.' Her eyes swept over Rex casually. 'It's good to meet you, Mrs Alexander. Please take a seat.'

'I'll be back shortly,' the doctor said before heading for the door.

'How has everything been going? What problems have you been experiencing?'

'It's been difficult. But we have been trying hard to make a go of it.' I plastered a smile on my face, and Rex's hand reached for mine. He held it tightly, not wanting to let me go.

'Let me take a closer look at Rex,' said the nurse, getting up from behind her desk to kneel in front of us.

'His feet appear to have had some treatment, but he has no surgical scars. We will need to take some X-rays.'

I nodded, and with my free hand I reached inside my handbag and took out a vial of Argentum nitricum, sensing that today would be a lot harder than I thought.

'Why don't we go into the nursery? You will probably feel more relaxed there.'

I gave Rex some Arnica and wheeled him down the corridor to the nursery.

The room had several half-moon-shaped tables set up with Play-Doh and paints for the children. In the centre of the room and aside from the paddling pools was a built-in sandpit.

I took Rex out of his pushchair and sat him amongst the sand. He reached for a spade. It was then that I heard a clearing of breath and turned to see Laurence watching us. He was dressed in a navy suit, similar to the doctor's. Casting his briefcase aside, he approached me and pulled me into his arms.

Over his shoulder, I saw Sister Williams drift from the room. We knelt on the floor together, inches from our son, watching as Rex scooped sand into a yellow bucket.

'I heard that you were bringing Rex here today,' Laurence said.

'I am doing the right thing, aren't I?'

'Yes, of course.'

'So what brings you here?'

'Work, actually, supplying steroids to the hospital, and I wanted to see you both,' Laurence said.

I traced the sand with my fingertips. 'Can you stay for a bit?'

'All right,' Laurence said, just as Dr Donahue returned with Sister Williams.

'We need to go through what happens next,' said the doctor.

I lifted Rex from the sandpit and put him back into his pushchair, and then Laurence and I followed the doctor and Sister Williams into another room. This one was filled with plaster casts and variously sized artificial limbs, constructed from leather and metal, and made to fit the tiny bodies of a generation of Thalidomide-impaired children. Again, my hand went to the vial of Argentum nitricum, and I held it tight.

They undressed Rex to his underpants, and catching my stare, he offered me one of his customary smiles as the team surrounded him to examine his shortened legs.

One of the therapists approached us to introduce herself as Miss Kelly, saying she was one of the many occupational therapists based at the hospital. I took in her neat brown bun and navy-and-white uniform. Glimpsing kindness in her dark eyes, I was convinced that, despite the awkwardness of the situation, she was here to help us.

It was decided to observe him at play one final time before the limb-fitting began. I watched Miss Kelly help dress Rex and slide him into a wheelchair. This time they wanted Rex to play in the

Wendy House, which contained, amongst other toys, several brooms of varying heights, a play oven complete with saucepans and utensils, and a child's ironing board and small iron. Rex crawled in and pulled himself up onto the toy oven. Worried that it would topple over on him, we stepped forward, but Miss Kelly shook her head. The test here was to see how he coped in different situations.

'I understand how difficult this must be for you both,' she said, scribbling into her notebook. 'But think of the benefits of the procedure and how, in the long run, this is the right decision for Rex,' she continued, just as the doctors returned to tell us that it was time to get started.

They undressed Rex once more and covered his small body in Vaseline before fitting him into a Tubigrip suit. Suspending him slightly above the table, they fitted paper under his arms to prevent chaffing of his skin from the straps.

A memory of his birth flooded my mind, causing me to turn away in fear. I felt Laurence pull me into his arms. Taking a few deep breaths and promising I would be brave, I pulled away from Laurence to turn my attention back to Rex. They had him wrapped from the waist down in plaster-soaked bandages.

'It takes fifteen to twenty minutes to dry. Perhaps you'd like to have a breath of air and cup of tea?' said Dr Donahue, and he glanced at Laurence and me in commiseration. Seeing pity in his eyes, I knew he must hate this procedure just as much as we did. But if it was the only way to allow Rex to walk, we had to allow them to carry on.

Rex, despite what was happening to him, still found a way to have that grin on his face that told us he wasn't taking it nearly as seriously as we were.

'All right,' I said, and we followed Dr Donahue out of the hospital. We found a bench to sit on for a breath of fresh air. The doctor left us briefly, only to return with the promised cup of tea for Laurence and me.

'It's not just Rex who is glad to see you today,' I said, taking a sip of my tea.

'I know I should do more. I have treated you both terribly, and I am sorry.'

'Well, today's a start for all of us,' I said, placing my cup and saucer down to touch his hand.

By the time we returned to the hospital room, they were cutting Rex free from his cast, and hearing the thump of plaster of Paris steadied my nerves. Already, I was feeling the fatigue of experiencing something quite awful through my son's eyes.

From then on the procedure seemed less intrusive, as out of the casts they were able to make a bucket shape from the leather for the buttock sockets. Rex sat in this and his little legs dangled through, attached to which were straps that fitted around his feet and worked to hold the artificial legs on.

'Now Rex, how do you feel about wearing these new legs?' Dr Donahue asked.

I caught my breath, realising that no one had asked Rex if he wanted to be fitted for the legs. We just assumed he would be happy to do so out of a desire for him to feel like any other child, but perhaps he was sufficiently content to get around by crawling and shuffling.

Rex looked down at the bolts and wiring and frowned, encircled by the team of doctors, nurses and his parents who were all waiting on his response.

'Will I be able to walk in them?' Rex asked.

'That's the plan,' Dr Donahue replied.

'Will they make me big and tall?'

Dr Donahue smiled. 'The legs will give you the necessary height that you lack naturally,' he explained.

'I want to run and kick.'

'The important thing to remember, Rex, is that we are learning something new all the time that can help you to move around better. You just have to be patient and willing to give it a try.'

Rex's lips curled into a smile, perhaps already thinking of what he could achieve with these new limbs of his. He had survived so far on floor level, and very soon he would outgrow his pushchair. So I held his gaze and said what I felt he needed to hear from me.

'Dr Donahue is right. You should give these new legs a try. Remember, nothing is ever gained from holding back, Rex.'

'Nanny?' Rex uttered.

'Yes, she would want you to try, too,' I said, thinking of my mother eagerly waiting at home for us. She'd be keen to know how it was going. Feeling the glow of success, I was glad to have come alone with the doctor and even better for Laurence to have been here today to experience it with me. As I took Laurence's hand we stepped forward at last, watching as the doctors fastened Rex into his new legs.

'Our first aim is the welfare of the child, nothing else matters.'
-Peter Tinniswood, 'The Thalidomide Tragedy,' 1965

Chapter Fifteen

I returned to Queen Mary's Hospital on Friday afternoon with Dr Donahue to collect Rex, without any prior knowledge of what the term 'limb-fitting' truly meant.

I was led to a regular ward and, as such, anticipated a long session ahead of us. Noticing Rex's bed surrounded by a whole team of doctors, nurses, and other therapists, I had a moment of doubt, fearing that my mother had been right about keeping Rex's care private. But so far I hadn't any reason to question Dr Donahue's motives for wanting to bring my son here. I had to believe that all the discomfort Rex would suffer would be worth the chance of him being able to walk. With that single thought in mind, I kept back and allowed the doctors to do their work.

The doctors helped Rex into the bucket-shaped knickers contraption. It had two pieces at the bottom and four feet coming out of them, one set went forward and one backwards.

Rex grimaced from the sensation of metal and leather digging into his tender skin, and I thought of voicing my objections. But as they helped Rex to stand on his new legs, and with the offering of a crash helmet and crutches, I saw his eyes brighten at being transformed from a small toddler into a child. I folded my arms across my chest and turned to Dr Donahue. From his encouraging gaze I knew the procedure had been a success.

Free at last, Rex squealed in delight as he leaned on his crutches and took his first step. 'Look at me, Mummy!' he exclaimed, as tears of joy coursed down my cheeks.

✳✳✳

By the time I took Rex home from the hospital, a level of curiosity had developed between the doctors and us about our different view of treating Rex. I was dubious about their methods, but worried that I didn't possess enough knowledge to care for him completely without their support, as my parents wanted me to do.

Rex was a naturally stubborn child, and remembering the difficulties I had with him as a baby over his feeding, I wondered how he would adapt to his new limbs once we were home. I still had to convince my parents on the merits of limb-fitting. Aside from regular hospital visits, that meant shifting the furniture around in the basement to give Rex ample space to walk—or more accurately, cruise—as he was doing during his first few days at home.

Rex's first pair of artificial legs coincided with a new phase in our lives, eagerly embraced by even my doubtful mother. Together, we helped Rex each morning to fasten on his legs, and, following advice from the hospital in those early days, he wore them from early in the morning until teatime weekdays and for half of the day on Saturday.

It wasn't easy for Rex, as this new advancement in his life brought on a new series of issues and left a trail of red marks on his skin from where the sockets of the limbs began and ended. Worried about the impact on his body, we had to change his routine to include periods when he didn't wear the legs at all. It was then that we watched him revel in the freedom of crawling around as he used to do. But one thing we were both loath to do was to insist upon Rex wearing a crash helmet.

'All children have accidents; wearing a helmet won't make him any less clumsy,' my mother insisted, relegating the crash helmet to a shelf in the cupboard, never to be brought out, not even for the doctor's visits.

'The crutches, however, will be useful,' she commented, and she was right.

Rather than it being an easy transition as we had hoped, it would take Rex awhile to become a confident walker, probably because much of what he enjoyed could be done at the tabletop, needing only an arrangement of cushions for him to sit at the table for mealtimes and play.

One particular afternoon, as Dr Donahue came to visit, I positioned Rex into a corner of the garden in full view of us. We watched him alternate between leaning on his crutches and splashing paint onto the easel. I was slightly dubious about this, as he had several accidents already when he had toppled over and had needed our help to pick him up. He had scabs on his chin and forehead to show for this; but, as always, my father prescribed him Arnica and Calendula, and we watched him continue to adapt to these new devices in his own way.

I poured tea for the doctor, hoping for an accident-free session.

'I see he has a few grazes to show for his effort—that is to be expected. It will take time for him to be proficient with his walking. In the meantime, there is something else for us to show him that will help,' the doctor said, reaching to position a small black wheelchair in front of our table. I had been dreading this moment more than the trauma of seeing Rex midair and being fitted for his artificial legs.

I took a sip of my tea and avoided the doctor's eyes.

'It is for his benefit that he works between the artificial limbs and the wheelchair.'

I turned to Rex, noticing him too absorbed with his painting to acknowledge this milestone moment when he officially became disabled in the eyes of the world.

'I leave it up to you to choose how to introduce the wheelchair to Rex, but we could do it today if that helps,' Dr Donahue suggested.

'I was hoping for Laurence to be around for this moment, but I think he is leaving Rex to adjust to everything first before visiting us, which makes sense,' I said.

'I spoke to your husband yesterday and filled him in on all of the developments.'

I wanted to tell Laurence about how much Rex wanted to make him proud. It wasn't easy for him, wearing those awful legs that hurt him so much, and now the wheelchair. I had hoped his weight and size would have prolonged this moment a little longer, but I had been wrong.

'Allow me to help, Mrs Alexander. I have assisted many of the children at Chailey through this transition. It's never easy, but after the initial shock passes, it feels less traumatic for everyone.'

'Does it really?' I asked incredulously.

My gaze went to Rex wobbling on his legs, and I wondered which of the two scenarios was worse: the pain of wearing legs never meant for his tiny body, or succumbing to a disability that left him seeing the world from his chair.

I rose from the table and followed the doctor to Rex's side.

Upon noticing us at last, my son smiled proudly and leaned on his crutches to steady himself.

Waiting for the doctor to bring the wheelchair to our side, it took all of my strength to remain silent, watching Rex as he took one look at the wheelchair and screamed, 'No!'

*'Friendship is born of the moment one person
says to another,
"What, you too? I thought I was the only one."'*
C S Lewis

Chapter Sixteen
April 1963

The following month, as I was leaving the Regency Bookshop after my second meeting of the Pollyanna Club, Sylvia approached me.

'Hello, you're Emily, aren't you?'

I nodded.

'I'm Sylvia. We met briefly last month, before the meeting.'

'Yes, of course.' I thought back to last month and of Sylvia's emotional encounter with a blond gentleman called Chris.

'I'm sorry we didn't get a chance to talk last time. How about a cup of tea, if you're not in too much of a hurry that is,' Sylvia said and reached inside her handbag for a packet of cigarettes.

I looked over my shoulder, but I couldn't see Chris here today.

'My husband didn't come. He's at home with Pollyanna.' Her hand brushed mine as she struck a match.

'I hope it's nothing too serious.'

Ignoring my comment, Sylvia took a puff of her cigarette, and we headed down the lane in silence. She stubbed out her cigarette near the entrance of the Steaming Mug Café.

'Shall we?' she said, and gestured with the wave of her hand. 'I wanted to talk to you, but I didn't have your number.'

The café offered an eclectic mix of cakes, chocolates, and other sweet treats across two floors. The waitress took us upstairs to the Empire Room, complete with a tiger's-head throne. Taking a seat, I glanced around the room at the crowd of day-trippers from London, who were too busy examining the throne to place their orders.

'So tell me about your Thalidomide child,' asked Sylvia, forcing my attention to her at last.

'I have a son, Rex. His legs finish at the knees. He has thirteen toes.' I paused, feeling the urge to speak more slowly. 'He had club foot as a baby, but the treatment has corrected it.'

'I have a daughter, Pollyanna, and she was born without arms,' she said. 'That's the worst bit over. Now tell me, how difficult has it been for you?' She took my hand in hers, and it was tender and reassuring.

'Rex is my only child.'

'Are you living with your husband?'

'We're separated. I'm living with my parents at the moment.'

The waitress set down the tea tray.

'Chris and I are still together, if you can call it that.' She shook her head. 'That's the secret of Thalidomide,' she replied bitterly.

'I'm sorry,' I whispered.

'May I pour your tea?' she said, debating between the teapot and the jug before finally pouring a dash of milk into my cup.

'Do you ever cry about Rex?' She exchanged the jug for the teapot and filled my cup with steaming liquid, then set about doing her own in the same fashion.

'I try not to. It's best for Rex that he doesn't see me upset,' I said, turning away from her.

'What about you, Emily? Aren't you angry about what happened to Rex?'

'What good would that do? It wouldn't change anything. I still would have taken those pills.' Feeling a deep sigh rise in my chest, I took the cup to my lips.

'That's what they want you to believe, unless you take a stand.' Sylvia's blue eyes glowered.

'You're talking about compensation?'

Sylvia took a sip of her tea and looked at me squarely. 'Emily, when was the last time you thought independently for yourself? Pollyanna was my third child, and after having two sons, I was so excited to have a little girl. What should have been a happy time for Chris and I was cruelly snatched away. That's why we have to fight back; not let them pretend it didn't happen or that they weren't in the wrong.'

'I don't know, Sylvia. I just want Rex to be happy and to feel like any other child.' I paused. 'I don't want a fuss.'

'Don't play into their hands. Think of everything you have lost, and start seeing that none of this was your fault.'

'Tell me about Chris,' I probed, eagerly changing the subject.

'He's an art dealer. I was a model in Paris when I met him. We married quickly, and the babies started coming. Then, almost four years ago, my father died and everything changed. The doctor prescribed Distaval to help me sleep. I didn't even realise I was pregnant at the time; and after Pollyanna was born, Chris worked away from home and it all became difficult—' She blinked away her tears. We didn't say anything for the longest moment.

'That's why we have to fight, Emily, because we didn't know.'

'If God is all you have, you have all you need.'
John 14.8

Chapter Seventeen
May 1963

In the days that followed, I found myself thinking more about what Sylvia had said at the café. Why hadn't I put up more of a fight about Thalidomide and what it had done to Rex? What did that say about me? Those thoughts lingered in my mind as Sylvia's brief touch came back to me again. That lump in my throat felt a little less painful than a few weeks ago.

I feared disappointment—of course I did, of not getting things right with Rex. Was my judgement so bad that my mother had to do all my thinking for me? And what of Laurence, who thought it was all right to abandon me whenever he liked? I breathed deeply. Don't let it get to you, I admonished myself; but still, Laurence had freedom which had been denied to me because of Rex. Sylvia's glower came back to me as a reminder that anger served no real purpose except the creation of more heartache.

I bit down on my thumbnail in contemplation of a trip that was being organised by my local church to Lourdes. Admittedly, before I had Rex I would never have considered going on the pilgrimage. Laurence and I had been lax about such things. I hated crowds, and being packed onto coaches, trains and ferries filled me with equal trepidation.

I wasn't like Laurence, I thought. I couldn't have left like he did after Rex's birth and still think it was all right to come back, whenever he liked. Nor could I have reinvented myself, as Sylvia had done, from a model to a housewife. I wasn't much good at anything, not a good enough writer and without the courage to convince Laurence that our situation was becoming intolerable.

Tears welled in my eyes. I wanted to cry, but if I let go, when would it stop? Does the pain ever leave you? Would I ever feel myself again, and what did that mean anymore?

With the early morning breeze I turned my thoughts back to Lourdes again. I should make the trip with Rex. He needed the blessing for his own health. A tear broke. I allowed myself that privilege. After all, it was early enough for no one to see me cry.

I should go to Lourdes. I would take Rex with me, and there would be no time then for useless emotions to invade my thoughts. Rex, God and I would have to be enough.

✳✳✳

The cost of the trip convinced me to hold off for a couple of days before presenting my father with Rex's invitation for the annual pilgrimage to Lourdes.

'Rex is doing remarkably well as he is,' was my father's reply.

'We don't know the extent of internal damage that Thalidomide caused him,' I pointed out, but that wasn't the reason I wanted to go.

'That's true; but I'm not sure if the pilgrimage will offer us any more answers, if that's what you are looking for, Emily,' he said with a probing gaze.

'You said he was a curious case.'

'Not so much now. They estimate there to be hundreds of cases of Thalidomide children in Britain.'

'Still, I should go with Rex to Lourdes,' I responded, struggling to justify my motives for the trip.

My father got up from behind his desk and approached my side. I hesitated at revealing more than I should as Sylvia's words crept back into my thoughts. 'If it is about you being a good mother, Emily, you have nothing to reproach yourself for, but if you want to go, I won't stand in your way.'

✳✳✳

On the morning of our departure to Lourdes, a few weeks after presenting the invitation, my mother sat with us in Rex's playroom. She took a seat next to me and cleared her throat.

'Emily, going to Lourdes is something special for us as a family, so I think we should make an affirmation to Rex. Please repeat after me: I am a very special child. I am loved and wanted. I will achieve great things. There is no such word as can't,' we chorused, and I heard the echo of Rex's little voice beside me.

Later, as we waited for the minibus to arrive to take us to London, I was surprised to receive a visit from Laurence.

'Your father told me about your trip to Lourdes, I couldn't let you go without saying goodbye,' he said, and we wandered into my little kitchen.

'Rex is upstairs with my father. Do you want to see him?'

He shook his head. *But why not?* I thought as he buried his face in my hair. I held on to him when I shouldn't, and it was only the chime of the doorbell that redeemed me of my weakness.

We travelled with the rest of the pilgrims, stopping first in London, before continuing our journey down to Portsmouth, where we boarded the ferry to France. Despite the blustery sea air, I wheeled Rex up onto the upper deck, and the memories of Laurence and Sylvia slipped further from my mind. It felt good to have a little bit of freedom for a change; but as I leaned closer to the edge and glanced down at the open sea below, that niggling feeling of wanting to give up on life flashed through my mind with horror.

Arriving in France, I cast that thought aside as we took the train to Paris and another one towards Lourdes. Approaching the foothills of the Pyrenees resplendent with wild flowers, I lifted Rex from his wheelchair to give him a view of the meadowlands that lay below the viaduct. Rex, being on a train for the first time in his life, couldn't resist a squeal of excitement. I hushed him to the stares of the other passengers, but deep down I was happy. This was the kind of experience that I wanted for Rex.

Lourdes was a citadel of white and gold, teeming with pilgrims from all over the world. But I was determined to make our time here in the mountains as special as possible for Rex. So we spent the next five days between the hospital with the children and the dormitory room at our hillside hotel. Children, who had never met before, shared beds and stories of the pilgrimage, encouraging Rex, the youngest and healthiest of the group, to stay awake long into the night. I prayed by my bedside, but seeing Rex, I was confused. He was in a better shape than most of the other children here. So what had motivated me to take him on this journey? Was it to strengthen his soul, reinforce the teachings of the Catholic faith, or for my own selfish advantage?

The echo of choral voices from the steady stream of new and departing pilgrims tormented me again with questions about life.

One night as I was closing my eyes, a vision came to answer my prayers. I saw Our Lady dressed in a white nun's habit. But instead of going to one of the children whose rattled breath had stopped me from falling asleep, she came to me to stand over my bed.

'It's all right, Emily, Rex is going to be just fine,' she said, filling me with the feeling of peace. Holding on to my moment of serenity, I closed my eyes and thought what a beautiful dream I must have been having.

On the fifth and final day, we went to the chapel to receive our blessing, which started with us touching the Massabielle stone, and I stood there feeling all my doubts lift from my shoulder. I was good enough. I thought again of the other night, certain that this time it had been an apparition, a message to me that my prayers about Rex had been answered and that I had nothing to fear about my life ahead.

I heard the shuffle of pilgrims around me as they left gifts and photographs for the Virgin Mary. Wheeling Rex along, my mind was dreamy like never before, and it was only when we took the water that I started to think deeply about my experience here. I was hopeful for Rex, convinced that he just needed to find his own place in the world; and as for myself, I was on a journey of discovery, too, curious as to where it would take me next.

Afterwards, clutching our candles and zigzagging down the hill, I felt sure that I was taking home with us a tiny piece of the miracle of Lourdes, meaning that Rex and I were going to be all right.

'Coming together is a beginning.
Keeping together is progress.
Working together is success.'
Henry Ford

Chapter Eighteen
July 1963

The lawn was already heaving with guests by the time my father and I arrived with Rex for Lady Hoare's garden party in Hampstead, London, in aid of the Thalidomide children. We each held Rex's hands, guiding him between the picnic blankets as he rocked precariously on his artificial legs.

I looked ahead to the marquee, watching the flurry of guests with curiosity. Ladies fashioned in matching hats and heels leaned on their suited, gentlemen companions. I searched the crowd and thought maybe I would see Laurence here today.

A white-gloved waiter strolled by, breaking my chain of thought. He offered us each a martini. The alcohol tantalised my lips as I felt Rex pull on my hand. I gazed down at my feet. Two little girls without arms passed each other wooden giraffes with their feet, and by curling their toes they could easily deposit the animals back into the Noah's ark.

'Mummy, can I play, too?' asked Rex.

A balloon flew ahead and landed on the blonde girl without arms, bouncing onto her knees. My eyes settled on Sylvia, crouched behind the blonde girl. The little girl shuffled forward on her bottom and the balloon finally rested in her lap.

'Emily!' Sylvia gushed upon noticing me.

'Can I?' Rex repeated.

'Yes, of course.' I turned to my father and he set Rex down on the blanket. Rex's eyes brightened at the sight of the beautiful blonde girl.

'Hello, Sylvia. Please allow me to introduce you to my father.'

My father leaned over and shook Sylvia's gloved hand.

'I'm glad to meet you. I have heard all about your medical practice, quite revolutionary.'

My father smiled. 'How did the two of you meet?'

'I suppose you could say Emily and I are comrades. We met at the Thalidomide support group, of all places.' Sylvia laughed.

Sylvia turned to me as the little blonde girl shuffled up close to Rex.

'They are quite a match, aren't they?'

'She's a stunner,' I said.

'I sure hope so, but then again she's my little girl. This is my daughter, Pollyanna.'

'She's amazing,' I said, watching Pollyanna's toes curl around a wooden lion. Rex held out his hands. But Pollyanna shook her head and chose instead to pass the animal with her feet to a brown-haired girl, also without arms.

I heard a clearing of breath and looked up into Dr Donahue's blue eyes. He held a martini and gazed at us with interest.

'How is Rex getting on with his artificial legs?' asked the doctor, kneeling down beside me.

I stifled a laugh, thinking how my life had changed when social conversation now revolved around limb-fitting.

'He still needs our support, but I suppose he will grow more confident in time,' I answered.

The doctor nodded. 'Don't suppose I could borrow you for a bit?'

I gazed at my father.

'You go and enjoy yourself. I think Rex is quite content here with the girls.'

'Thank you, Daddy.' I got to my feet and caught Sylvia's curious gaze.

'Watch yourself, Emily,' she said, grabbing my hand briefly.

I felt myself frown but followed the doctor, bypassing an arm-deficient girl in a baby walker, who used the device to rotate on the grass. Moving on, I watched a little boy about Rex's age enjoying a donkey ride, and with hooks for hands, he was able to grip on to the reins. Approaching the marquee, a little black girl with doll-like arms was being cuddled by a young white nurse.

Glancing down at the platters of assorted canapés, I chose a salmon one and devoured it quickly. The doctor edged closer and his arm brushed my bare skin.

'I expect you hoped to see your husband here.'

'I'm learning not to expect too much when it comes to Laurence.'

'I'm sorry to hear that.'

'I was glad of your support with Rex. I don't think I could have gotten through those hospital visits without you.'

'He's an incredible child; they all are in a way. We doctors didn't have any expectations, and yet we continue to be amazed by their courage and fortitude. In fact, that's what I wanted to talk to you about today.'

'The Thalidomide children?' I asked.

'Rex's education, and I know you only want the best for him.'

'What are you asking, Doctor?'

'Would you ever consider placing Rex at Chailey?'

'I don't think so. Rex belongs with his family.'

'But for how long? You won't have that many options when it comes to schooling. He's a bright boy, and there is a lot more we can do to help him.'

'I won't consent to Rex being placed in a home.'

'Can't you see I'm trying to help Rex?'

'I think you've said enough,' said my father, stepping in between the doctor and me, before wheeling Rex to my side.

'I meant no harm,' Dr Donahue protested, but seeing my father's stern gaze, he strode out of the marquee.

My hand reached for Rex's, squeezing it tight. 'I shouldn't have left you, my darling, I'm sorry,' I said.

'Come,' my father said. 'Let's go and enjoy the party.'

Outside the marquee, the crowd had swelled as able-bodied children darted amongst the Thalidomide ones. A young boy in a wheelchair demonstrated the hooks and pincers of his robotic arm, to the amusement of his family.

We reached the children's play area, and Lady Hoare approached us with a smile.

'Mr Miles.' She extended a hand. 'I've heard all about your practice. This must be Rex.' She kneeled down to Rex.

'How would you like to have a go on the swings?' She touched Rex's hand.

'Yes, please!' he answered.

My father lifted him out of his wheelchair and carried him to the metal frame. There, he slid him into the fabric contraption. Lady Hoare's dark hair brushed his cheeks as she gave him a bounce. Pollyanna's head turned to regard Rex with interest.

'I'm sorry I haven't been in touch,' said Sylvia, glancing at me. 'It's been pretty awful lately. We must meet up and talk.'

My father took over with Rex, and the excited yelps of the children mingled with that of a harmonica being played nearby. Above the din, Lady Hoare reached for the microphone to announce the cake-cutting ceremony.

'Better join in,' Sylvia said, pulling Pollyanna out of the swing. The little girl wriggled in her mother's arms, content only when her feet touched the grass.

My father passed Rex to me. 'Don't worry about anything,' he soothed. I nodded, and as the crowd gathered close, I was glad not to see the doctor.

Surrounding the table, Sylvia took my hand and pulled us to the front, where Lady Hoare's eyes settled on Rex.

'Would you like to help me cut the cake?' she asked.

'Of course he would,' I said and passed Rex to Lady Hoare.

In her arms, his hands covered hers and the knife sliced through the fondant icing. Sylvia edged in, holding Pollyanna around her waist. The little girl's feet danced upon the table, and as Lady Hoare offered the first slice to Rex, he broke some of his cake to share with Pollyanna.

'Prejudice is the child of ignorance.'
Samuel Hoffenstein

Chapter Nineteen
1964

It was half past three on a Friday afternoon when we ushered the mothers into the house. Clutching tightly to their children's hands, they looked around our black-and-white hallway in apprehension.

Rex's shoes tapped against the floor as he approached them. My mother touched my shoulder before drifting upstairs, leaving me to face them alone.

I took in their belted coats and lacquered hair and the way they turned to each other conspiratorially.

Tom was the first child to step forward. Gazing at the young boy, I noticed that, unlike Rex, Tom's hair had been neatly combed: the result, I imagined, of this carefully planned visit.

'Hello Rex, do you have a Brio train set?'

'My dad bought me one for my last birthday,' Rex beamed.

Tom's mother raised an eyebrow.

Maisie broke free from her mother to approach Rex. 'Have you got any colouring pencils?' The girl's blonde hair had been pulled back from her round face into a bun and secured tightly with pins and a white ribbon.

'I have a huge blackboard,' Rex gushed.

'Don't tell me — from his father?' Maisie's mother shuffled her weight from one foot to another in agitation.

'No, that was a gift from his grandfather,' I said, offering them a smile of pure satisfaction.

'Shall I take the children down to Rex's playroom? Then perhaps I could take your coats and offer you a drink, lemonade, or martini?'

'Tea would suffice,' replied Maisie's mother.

'Can we hold Rex's hand?' asked Tom. The children watched as Rex rocked precariously on his legs like a small tin soldier.

'Yes, of course you can. That would be kind of you both,' I said, enjoying their mothers' mortified gaze as the children took hold of Rex's hands and helped guide him down the steps to the basement.

I led the children into Rex's playroom. The room had developed over the past four years to include a wall-length blackboard. The brown sideboards had been replaced with low shelves, making it easy for Rex to access his favourite toys, including his Brio trains, planes, and wild animals. There was also a low bookshelf, complete with some Dr Seuss books.

I watched Maisie run to the blackboard and reach for the pink chalk, while Rex and Tom sat at a low table and compared trains.

'I've got Thomas,' said Rex, gripping tightly to the blue locomotive.

'I prefer Percy.' Tom shrugged, reaching for the green one.

I drifted from the room and headed back to the hallway. 'They're fine for the moment,' I said. 'Let me take your coats and I'll show you downstairs.'

'You live downstairs with Rex?' asked Maisie's mother.

'I do, and do you know what? It was the best decision I ever made for Rex. My family has been wonderful, and I couldn't have got through it without them,' I said, stopping to open the bedroom door to lay their coats on my bed. Then I guided them into the kitchen and filled the kettle.

Later that day when everyone had left, Rex went upstairs to my father's consulting room. I watched my father lift Rex onto his chair, and with the addition of cushions, the little boy reached the desk. My father passed him an embossed reference book.

'This is my *Kent's Repertory*. In here are the details of all the important homeopathic remedies.'

'Wow!' Rex's brown eyes widened. With his small hands he opened the cover and turned the first page.

'Dr Dhillon and I decided that you are doing very well on homeopathy, and you need Sulphur, a constitutional remedy, because you are a strong, healthy boy. Remember that, Rex.'

'What's constitutional?' Rex frowned.

'It's how your body is made up, and although you are a little different from most, homeopathy can still be based around you.' My father ruffled Rex's curls and the little boy let out a laugh.

'You know he's far too young to understand big words like constitutional,' I said, strolling into the room.

'Hanging around doorways now, are we, Emily? I thought you'd be busy with your mothers' meeting,' my father teased.

'You know they don't like us, Daddy.'

'That's because we live in a better house than they do.'

I laughed. 'That's true enough.'

'Why don't you and Rex have dinner upstairs tonight? Your mother is cooking her famous nut roast.'

'Sounds good,' I said, and my father hugged me before whispering into my ear. 'Don't worry, I'll make a homeopath out of him yet, and that's sure to rile the community even further.'

I giggled, having forgotten how good it felt to laugh.

'A child can ask questions that a wise man cannot answer.'
Unknown

Chapter Twenty

Every Sunday, my mother and I took Rex to church for morning Mass. One particular Sunday morning, as I helped Rex get dressed for church, and his fingers pulled at his buttonholes, the same tirade began.

'Why doesn't Gramps go to church?'

'Because he is more attuned to nature than to God,' I said, helping him into his navy trousers. He discarded the last shirt button to pull haphazardly at his zip.

'I like nature, too,' he said.

'Yes, but it's important for you to understand spiritual matters,' I said, finishing his zip and reaching for his socks.

He shook his head. 'Why?'

'It's what Nanny and I want for you.'

'What about Gramps?'

I passed Rex his coat, watching as he pushed his arms through the sleeves before grabbing at his buttons.

'He has patient cases to look over before tomorrow,' I sighed, wondering why I had taught him to be so inquisitive.

'I could help him, I could.'

'No, Rex.'

'I could hold his big books open for him. I'm good at that.'

'Nanny is waiting for us. We don't want to be late,' I said, as he slid off the bed and into his wheelchair. 'And Tom and Maisie will be there. You wouldn't want to miss them.' I smiled in satisfaction at having the last word. I heard him sigh as I wheeled him to the front door where my mother was waiting for us, dressed in a powder-blue suit.

We walked to the church and took our place in the middle pews to the echo of 'Enter, Rejoice' being sung by the choir. In those days we were afforded plenty of space, for the parishioners, upon noticing Rex, would often opt for another pew.

Father Fitzgerald entered the church, carrying the Book of Gospels, which he placed at the altar. The servers carried a processional cross, candles, and sprinkled incense. A chant resounded in the church. Then Father Fitzgerald went to his chair at the altar.

'In the name of the Father, and of the Son, and of the Holy Spirit.' All together we made the Sign of the Cross.

'Amen,' we chorused and took our seats.

'The grace and peace of God our Father and the Lord Jesus Christ be with you.'

'And also with you.'

'Now let us turn to a reading from Matthew 19:14,' began Father Fitzgerald, opening the Book of Gospels.

'Then were there brought unto him little children that he should put his hands on them, and pray: and the disciples rebuked them. But Jesus said, suffer little children and forbid them not, to come unto me: for of such is the kingdom of heaven.'

Later, after the service, I followed the long line of parishioners into the churchyard. And not yet ready to go home, I wheeled Rex into the garden, where Tom and Maisie approached us.

'Can Rex play with us?' asked Tom.

I nodded and watched the freckled boy whisk my son away to the grassland by the apple tree, where a group of schoolchildren had eagerly gathered. Just a short distance away stood a collection of mothers, who were busy catching up on local news before going home to prepare their Sunday roast.

'You have to admire Emily. She's brave to want to raise the child by herself,' said one parent, whose voice I recognised to be that of Maisie's mother.

'Poor child, from what I gather he has been abandoned by his father. It's good of you to take your children around to their house,' said another young mother.

'Tom insists upon it, says Rex has been teaching him to play noughts and crosses. He knows how to make all the marks despite having no thumbs.'

'Well, he can't very well run away, can he? I wish Maisie could colour as neatly as Rex. He knows his primary colours, too. I'm going to take her around to Rex's more often. He is a nice, mannered boy; must take after his grandfather.'

'No one knows much about his father,' the young mother interrupted.

'I heard he worked for Distillers,' Tom's mother piped up.

Unable to bear their talk any longer, I strode to the circle of women. 'Yes, imagine that: thinking you are responsible for your son's disability, and what of the countless other Thalidomide children—let's not forget about them. Don't you think my husband has suffered enough without your mindless gossip?'

The congregation crowded around to form a tighter circle. 'Emily, we're sorry, it's just—'

'I know Rex is different. But his differences are the reason why your children, unlike yourselves, do not feel the need to discriminate.'

There was a hushed silence, followed by a shuffle of heels on the flagstones. I knew it would take time for the world to understand children like Rex. But what was Rex supposed to do in the meantime?

I turned and saw a ten-year-old choirboy race Rex up and down the garden in his wheelchair.

'What's the time, Mr Wolf?' called Rex.

'Eight o'clock!' yelled Maisie from her post under the apple tree.

My son screamed in delight as each spin propelled him closer to Maisie.

'You shouldn't let them get to you,' my mother said, approaching me to place her hand on my shoulder.

'I just want to protect Rex and Laurence.'

'You see the best in everyone, Emily, but the world isn't like that.'

'Then what am I supposed to do?'

'Listen to Rex's laughter, and appreciate how far we have come already.'

'What's the time, Mr Wolf?'

'Lunchtime!'

Rex's wheels thumped against the tree trunk.

'I better rescue him, before he has an accident,' I sighed.

'Leave him, Emily, let him enjoy this moment a bit longer,' she counselled.

Maisie spun Rex's wheelchair around, and on noticing us, he waved. I waved back, and for once I let myself go and allowed tears to moisten my cheeks without regret.

*'Free the child's potential
and you will transform him into the world.'
Maria Montessori*

Chapter Twenty-One
1965

My search for a suitable school for Rex led me to a private Montessori establishment in Hove. We had been unsuccessful in trying to persuade the local infant school to enrol Rex, and the option of a special school hadn't appealed to us. But the idea of incorporating independence into education, which I took to be the foundation of the Montessori Method, did interest us. So, when the Montessori directress called to invite us for a school visit, I couldn't help but feel optimistic for Rex.

On the morning of the visit, and with three months to go before he was due to start school, I supervised Rex's dressing. By now he was able to master buttons and zips with ease. The most help he needed was with his toileting, and that was more to do with his wheelchair than his physical development.

'I want to wear my legs,' said Rex, pulling a comb through his stubborn curls.

'All right, Rex,' I said, and positioned the artificial legs by his bed. I eased him into the bucket knickers contraption and tightened the waistband, so his little feet dangled inside the blocked leather open-ended sockets. I helped him pull on his trousers, which skirted the black imitation leather shoes and cordovan socks.

He grinned. 'I want to show the teacher that I can do things myself. I'm not a baby.'

'I've explained to the teacher about your difficulties. They will understand and help you, but you can also show them what you've learnt so far,' I said, offering Rex a light sweater. He pulled it over his head with ease.

'I'm not difficult,' he grumbled.

'I know you're not, Rex. It's just that you appear a little different from other children, but to us that's what makes you unique.'

'Will Tom and Maisie be there?'

'You know they won't, but you will make new friends. Now come, your grandfather is waiting for us.'

'Can I go upstairs to his special room later?'

'If you're good and polite to the teacher, then yes.' I held Rex's hand and we made for the hallway. A smile formed on his lips. Who out of the two of us were the best at blackmail, I wondered?

My father was waiting for us by the kerb; he eased Rex onto the back seat of his car before turning to me. 'It will be all right, Emily. I know it's a big step, but think of all he has achieved so far. Today is proof that he is like any other child.' He offered me a hug and I took a seat beside Rex.

'The school's in Hove,' I said to Rex.

'Is that a long way away?'

'No,' my father laughed, 'just on the other side of Brighton.'

'Oh.' He released a sigh of disappointment and looked out of the window as we passed the seafront and headed into suburbia.

***

The Montessori School was housed in a semi-detached, three-storey Victorian dwelling in the centre of Hove. The rectangular sign declared that the establishment educated children in the Montessori Method from two and a half years to seven years.

Entering the school, I was greeted by a white-haired American lady. She was dressed in a high-necked white blouse and navy skirt. She shook my hand and guided us inside.

'Welcome to the Children's House. I'm Miss Ferguson, and you must be Mrs Alexander and—'

'I'm Mr Miles, Rex's grandfather.'

'Yes, of course,' said Miss Ferguson, before ushering us through the long hallway and into the classroom.

A single glance around the room convinced me that I was entering a laboratory rather than a schoolroom, with the rows of wooden shelves complete with an array of unusual objects for children, such as glass jugs, china bowls and implements which had been arranged neatly onto tiny trays.

'This must be Master Rex, who I have heard all about.' She smiled. My father squeezed my hand. It would be all right.

'Is this going to be my classroom?' asked Rex, rocking from side to side on his legs.

'This is the nursery class. Your classroom is next door, but as this is your first visit, you can stay and play here if you like,' Miss Ferguson said, turning back to me. 'Why don't I get one of my teachers to show Rex around the room while we have a talk in my office?'

I looked at Rex as his eyes darted around the room in curiosity.

'It won't take long, and then perhaps we can arrange a follow-up visit?'

Miss Ferguson swung the hand bell, and a young woman in her early twenties entered the room. She hesitated a moment before approaching Rex.

'Hello, I'm Miss Weston. Would you like me to show you the planets?'

Rex offered his hand, and she guided him to the other side of the room, where she took out a red papier-mâché-enclosed balloon.

'This is planet Mars...'

'That's part of the cultural curriculum,' said Miss Ferguson. She escorted us from the classroom back to the hallway and into another smaller room, complete with a mahogany desk and floor-to-ceiling bookshelves.

'Please take a seat. Tea, anyone?' We shook our heads.

'I know it is a lot to ask, but Rex is a healthy child, and my mother and I have been doing our best to educate him at home. But he's gotten to the point where he needs to start school.'

'Mrs Alexander, from what I have seen already, Rex shows promise; and with some support I feel he would do well at the Children's House. I would be only too happy to welcome Rex into the school. He can start in September.' She smiled, and I realised then that I had just taken another big step towards being Rex's greatest advocate.

'When one door closes, another opens.'
Alexander Graham Bell

Chapter Twenty-Two
1967

Two years passed, and in that time Rex had settled into his Montessori School. But as he approached his seventh birthday, I was faced with the difficult decision of which school to send him to next.

One afternoon, while waiting for Rex to arrive home by taxi, I received a visit from Laurence. He strode into the kitchen with his suit jacket slung over his shoulder and took a chair from around the kitchen table to sit down beside me.

'I can offer you tea. We have some time before Rex is due home from school,' I said, glancing at the clock, which read five to two.

'I do need to talk to you about Rex.'

I filled the kettle and struck a match to ignite the gas.

'He can't remain at the Montessori School much longer; he's almost seven. He'll need to continue his education elsewhere. Have you thought about where you are going to send him next?'

'Of course. There is a special school that Rex could attend, but we are not sure that would be the best option for him.' I spooned tea into a china teapot.

'Dr Donahue tells me you turned down a place at Chailey.' The kettle let out a whistling sound. 'Rex would be amongst other Thalidomide children. He wouldn't feel so alone.'

'He's not alone, he has friends and family,' I pointed out.

'Emily,' Laurence coaxed, coming up behind me to wrap his arms around my waist. 'I only want to help.'

'If you wanted to help Rex, you'd come to the house more often and visit your son.'

'Let me help with his education. The school at Chailey is very good; they encourage independence in the children, and it's not too far away. He would be able to come home for the weekend.'

I pulled away from Laurence to fill the teapot with boiling water, before going to the fridge for a jug of milk, which I placed on the counter. Turning around to face Laurence, I noticed his brown eyes had turned glassy.

'I'm sorry,' I said, and touched his cheek.

'It's all right, Emily. I'm such a coward, a better husband and father would have stayed and found the courage to understand his son. But I wasn't that man.'

'As I keep telling you, it's not too late to change.'

Later, when Rex arrived home from school, and wanting some fresh air to clear my head after Laurence's visit, I wheeled Rex down the street and made for the local park. I was expecting the playground to be deserted at just before three, so I was surprised to notice the solitary figure of a mother and child. From a distance, the woman appeared to be of similar age to me. Her blonde hair had been pulled back from her face with a green bandana, and up ahead of her was a girl of Rex's age. The girl had blonde hair to match her mother's, except hers hung all the way down to the small of her back.

It was a hot afternoon, and I was able to glimpse the girl's long legs, partially hidden by her polka-dot cotton dress. As the girl turned and stepped forward, I drew in my breath. I was gazing at a Thalidomide girl, and for some reason she was familiar.

The girl scowled at me in response.

The mother turned towards me, and I recognised her to be Sylvia. She approached Rex's wheelchair. The girl, who by now I remembered as Pollyanna, observed Rex and fled to the climbing frame.

'The park is normally quiet at this time of day before the schools empty out, so we don't have to worry about the gawkers,' said Sylvia, folding her arms under her breasts, protectively.

'We didn't mean to intrude. I just can't face going home yet,' I said, feeling Rex's hand squeeze mine in support.

71

'How have you been? We don't seem to be very good at keeping in touch,' Sylvia said, guiding me to the bench. Taking a seat, I gazed into her aquamarine eyes.

'Mummy, are we going on the swings?' I offered Sylvia a knowing smile and went to the front of Rex's wheelchair.

'How are you, Rex?' asked Sylvia, coming up behind me.

'My dad came to our house today, when I was at school.'

I watched Pollyanna dangle precariously from the monkey bars.

'Is everything all right?' Sylvia touched my arm. I put Rex onto the ground and watched him shuffle on his bottom, before going into a crawl.

'Laurence wants to send Rex away to Chailey.'

We stood up and made for the swings. I watched Rex use his arms to heave his tummy onto the swing and move up and down gently. I took the middle swing between Rex and Sylvia and pushed myself into the air, as tears ran down my cheeks.

'Sometimes I think about sending Pollyanna away.'

Pollyanna had managed to navigate her body to the end of the climbing frame, and with a final flip, her feet touched the ground. She ran over to us and took the swing next to Rex. Her long legs propelled her high into the air, and it was only when she touched the ground that she leaned over to Rex. 'Bet I could get you to join me on the climbing frame.'

'Please don't, Rex, or we'll both be in trouble with Nanny.'

'Ah, Mummy,' he sulked. Pollyanna got off the swing and sat down on the ground, gazing up at Rex.

'I have never known a child like her,' said Sylvia, turning to me. 'She doesn't need me for anything. She just gets on with it.'

'She needs you,' I replied.

'How do you hug your daughter when she has no arms?'

I watched Rex's arms dangle over the swing to touch the space where Pollyanna's arms should have been.

'Do it like this, silly,' Pollyanna laughed and shuffled closer still. She curled her right leg around her neck. That way Rex could touch her toes with his fingertips.

'Anytime you can't face going home, you can come over to mine. We would like that, wouldn't we, Pollyanna?' Sylvia placed a hand on her daughter's narrow shoulder. Pollyanna uncurled her leg and got to her feet.

'Of course, and then I could show Rex how I play the piano with my feet.'

'Pollyanna's into music,' Sylvia said, followed by a flicker of a smile.

'We'll look forward to that, won't we, Rex?'

Hearing the creak of the gate, Sylvia quickly scribbled down her house number on Regency Square, and Pollyanna used her feet to pass it to me.

The able-bodied children descended upon the playground, causing Pollyanna and Sylvia to dart away without a backwards glance, leaving Rex and me to face the gawkers alone.

'The only thing we have to fear, is fear itself.'
Franklin D Roosevelt

Chapter Twenty-Three

Rex's wheels crunched over the pebbles as we made our way along the beach the following month. I wished for once that Rex had worn his legs as I struggled with his wheelchair against the midday heat. With the sun beating down on us, we found a vacant spot close to the pier. After a quick glance at Rex, the other bathers shuffled aside, offering us plenty of space to hammer down our windshield in a vain attempt on our part to protect our fair and freckled skin from the voracious heat.

My mother went off to buy us ice creams, while my father set up the easel for Rex. I relaxed in one of the striped sun loungers, watching Rex lean forward in his wheelchair to apply his first swirl of blue paint onto his canvas.

'Do you think he'll understand when I finally tell him?' I asked, as my father took a seat next to me.

'You mean about Thalidomide?' He leaned his head to one side, regarding me closely. 'I think he has a big heart, and when the moment is right, he'll understand.'

'He has to forgive me,' I said.

My father reached over to squeeze my hand, just as my mother returned with the ice creams, offering one to Rex before coming to us.

'You should be careful, Emily, with your father's fair skin, that you don't burn,' she said, sitting next to my father.

I licked my ice cream. After finishing it, I reached for my copy of Emily Bronte's *Wuthering Heights*. I lay back against the lounger, and after reading only a few pages, I fell asleep.

I awoke to the sensation of someone shaking my shoulders, after what seemed like only a short nap.

'Mummy, do you like my painting?'

I looked at Rex's painting in surprise at the series of long strokes of yellow, blue and white bordered by what I thought of as little grey pebbles. 'That's amazing! Well done, Rex,' I said, leaning over his chair for a hug.

'Looks like this afternoon has been very industrious,' my mother said and smiled.

I gazed at her bare legs and loose blonde hair in fascination, unsure if I would ever understand my mother.

I turned to my father, dressed in shorts, socks and sandals. 'Good to get out of the house once in a while, isn't it, Emily? I think it's important for our skin to soak up the vitamin D.'

'Spoken like a true clinician,' I giggled and turned back to Rex. His wheelchair almost touched the wooden frame of my lounger.

'Do you know what, Rex? I think your father would like to see your painting the next time he comes to visit. Because I think he would be very impressed with you.' Rex beamed. His hand tickled my toes and a smile formed on my lips.

I looked ahead and saw a woman in a blue print dress approach us. With the camouflage of her wide-brimmed hat, I didn't recognise her at first until she came closer and I saw her red-rimmed eyes.

'Sylvia?'

'Emily,' she quivered. 'I'm so glad I found you here. It's Pollyanna. She's been taken to hospital.'

'No!' I said and gave her a hug. I held her close for a moment before pulling away. She reached for my hand.

'She's got a heart infection. What if it's Thalidomide again?' I glanced at Rex as he sat on the lounger with my parents, and I hugged her again.

'The only way to have a friend is to be one.'
Ralph Waldo Emerson

Chapter Twenty-Four

I had a dream last night that I was back at the maternity hospital in Richmond. I hadn't thought about that place for such a long time, but my memories hadn't faded all that much. I found myself wandering down the corridor, following the echo of a baby's cry that led me to a room that I hadn't discovered before. I felt the gentle breeze from the open window.

A doctor and several nurses surrounded a baby.

'There's a definite sign of bowel malformation in the infant. I'm sorry to say that I have had a few cases like this recently, and the outcome has always been grave,' the doctor said to the nurses.

'There isn't anything we can do. It's all just a matter of time.' I watched as they gazed down at the baby.

'A matter of time,' I said.

Upon hearing my voice, the doctor turned around, and I saw that it was Dr Donahue holding the conference. 'You shouldn't be seeing this, Mrs Alexander. This isn't the place for you.'

The nurses shrouded the baby from sight as he let out a shrill cry. I covered my ears for a minute until my curiosity propelled me forward to stand by his bassinette.

'Mrs Alexander,' Dr Donahue repeated.

I saw snatches of his brown eyes that made me think it was Rex. But on second glance, I was shocked at seeing a limbless baby positioned close to an open window.

'This is not your baby,' said Dr Donahue. 'Your baby has already been discharged and placed at Chailey, under the instruction of your husband.'

I felt it again then, that lump in my throat that silenced everything else, holding me in limbo. Only this time I fought back to open my mouth and swallow hard against it, until another sound overtook my action—one of pounding footsteps and the feeling of being shaken awake.

'Emily!'

Pushing open my eyes, I saw my father looking down at me in alarm.

'I heard you screaming from the hallway,' he said softly, moving to sit down on the end of my bed, as he had done every night through a spate of night terrors leading up to my eleven-plus exams.

'Where's Rex?' I breathed.

'He's with your mother. After being awoken by your screaming, he managed to crawl upstairs and find us for help.'

I shook my head. Up to now I had been so good at keeping everything in check, until hearing about Pollyanna. It was Sylvia, too. I think she must have unsettled me; just when I thought everything was under control.

'Do you want to talk about it?' my father asked.

'I'm frightened for Rex. That's all.'

'About telling him about Thalidomide?'

'No, it's more about him having other problems that we don't know about yet, like Pollyanna.'

'That could be the case, yes. Heart problems, even in healthy people, can remain undetected for years, but it's unlikely. And even if it were the case, we would cope as we've always done—by tackling it together as a family. It wouldn't change anything about Rex, he'll always be clever and strong, most of which is because of you, Emily. Now, why don't you join us upstairs for breakfast? Rex wants to help your mother cook, which could be fun.' He winked before leaving the room.

After enjoying a plate of fried eggs, mushrooms, and toast, I prepared myself for visiting Pollyanna in hospital. I still didn't know that much about her, but that was about to change. Sylvia telephoned regularly with requests for us to visit her at home. As of yet I hadn't taken her up on her offer, so, feeling guilty, I asked my father to drop me at the Royal Alexandra Children's Hospital, where Sylvia had informed me that Pollyanna was being treated for her heart infection.

Leaving Rex with my mother, I was quiet during the short car journey to hospital. I saw my father glance at me, disappointed that he hadn't said enough to reassure me about Rex, and anxious that my nightmares had returned. With that in mind, he hugged me for longer than usual as we parted in the driveway by the hospital's main entrance.

The Royal Alexandra Children's Hospital was housed in a baroque-style building comprised of three storeys of the finest red brick. I hesitated outside for several minutes to admire its terra-cotta mouldings and think about what I would say to Pollyanna.

Sylvia had been brief about the cause of the infection. All she knew was that it would require Pollyanna to spend the summer in hospital. My father had suggested some homeopathic remedies that could help Pollyanna, if Sylvia was willing for her daughter to be treated with homeopathy. But I was cautious about bringing up the subject when none of us knew how serious the infection was at that point.

The thought of any such deformity developing inside Rex was still vivid in my mind as I entered the hospital and made for the girls' ward to be greeted by the swish of doors and the odour of ammonia. It was here in this place where my nightmares began and ended. I raised my head to dispel my fears, still trembling from the dream of last night that hadn't left me yet.

I found Sylvia outside the entrance to the ward. She was dressed in a pink miniskirt and spotted top, with her blonde hair neatly combed. I could have been fooled into thinking that she hadn't spent the night at Pollyanna's bedside. With impatient haste she pushed past the nurses to reach my side.

'I am so glad you came,' she said, as we stood gazing at each other for a moment, unsure of what to say to make the situation more bearable. With her aquamarine eyes, I thought of how much she looked like Pollyanna, and felt my tears break.

'Don't cry, Emily, not in this place,' Sylvia said, reaching for a cigarette to smoke. I half wished for that same habit myself to calm my nerves.

'I am sorry about Pollyanna. Out of the two of them, I'm sorry it is your child who's sick. It could have been Rex, couldn't it? At any time, who knows? I didn't take him to the hospital for the first two years of his life. He didn't have half the tests that Pollyanna had. But that's what it is about, isn't it: luck? You don't deserve any of this, Sylvia. I know how hard you try to be a good mother to Pollyanna, and you are, so don't ever let anyone tell you otherwise,' I said, watching Sylvia puff on her cigarette. The tears had reached my cheeks, but I didn't care.

'You know a lot about this, sick children—what not to do, and stay so calm about it. What's the secret? Tell me that, at least.'

'I focus totally on Rex. It is all about him, nothing else comes close.'

'Easy when you only have one child to think about, no jealousy because the older two are healthy and normal and aren't getting the attention they want. Pollyanna exploits the situation by refusing to follow even the simplest of instructions. She won't allow anyone to help her dress, so a morning is lost on her trying unsuccessfully to do it all herself. My sons are starting to gain a record at school for being late. And that's when I think about Thalidomide. I really hate Distillers.'

'Sometimes when it is late at night, and normally when I am missing Laurence, I think what if I hadn't been weak and taken those pills? I knew better than to take them, but I did anyway, to please Laurence.'

Sylvia stubbed out her cigarette. We stood side by side, and I couldn't imagine talking about this with anyone but Sylvia.

'It will be all right with Pollyanna,' I said.

'You think so?'

'She's a fighter and so is Rex. That's how they've survived up until now, and they will keep going. Even if it's to prove a point to medical science; teach them a thing or two about humanity.'

'It's so tiring being her mother. Aren't you exhausted?'

'All the time; but you're not alone, you know that. I'll sit with Pollyanna for a bit and give you a rest.'

'Would you?' She reached for my hand, and I wondered if she wanted to hug me again. She was nothing at all like what I expected her to be. Gripping my hand, a smile flickered on her lips, and I was left thinking that mine was the first offer of friendship that she'd had in a while.

I found Pollyanna awake and hooked up to an IV, with a cluster of fever spots on her cheeks to show for her struggles. Approaching the bedside, I watched the more able children being seated around wooden tables to be served lunch.

'They wouldn't let me sit around the table for lunch,' said Pollyanna by way of greeting. 'I had mine in bed as if I'm that sick.' She frowned to prove her point.

'Perhaps they'll let you join the other children tomorrow.'

'Maybe.' She turned her head to one side, concentrating on me solely. 'Where's Rex? You should have brought him.'

'They wouldn't let me. No visitors under fifteen are allowed in hospital.'

'That's a stupid rule. I can't do anything in here. They keep me in bed too much, and it stops me from being able to use my feet for doing things. Say you've brought me something to look at. My mum just sits with me and keeps looking at the nurses all the time like she's expecting bad news or something. I won't die. I'm not that sick. A child next to me died last night, but she had no hair and was really skinny.'

'You are sick, Pollyanna, but I don't think you are going to die, either.'

'Promise you won't cry. My mum does when she thinks I'm asleep. She's always here and never goes home, but my dad's gone again. I wish you'd bring Rex, but silly rules; everyone has rules, and they don't make any sense. Like why our dads are always away, and we can't do stuff that other children can. That's not fair. You think it, too. That's why you cry when no one sees you.' She nodded.

'I have a drawing for you from Rex.' I trembled, taking a few minutes to dig through my bag as Pollyanna's words sunk in. She was a strange child, but Rex liked her, and that counted for a lot with me. I placed the drawing on the table in front of her and caught my breath.

'A starfish.' Pollyanna smiled, taking in the waxy contours of Rex's blue and green sketch. 'Read me a story,' she demanded, nodding towards a bookcase in the corner of the play area.

'Visiting time is almost over,' said one of the nurses as she approached Pollyanna's bedside and proceeded to change her drip. I watched as more penicillin was pumped into Pollyanna's neck.

I waited a moment before rising to my feet. 'I have to go now, Pollyanna. Your mother will be in later to see you.'

'Will you come back tomorrow and read me a story?'

'Yes,' I promised, and meant it.

✳✳✳

The days passed quickly. I was reluctant to leave Rex with my mother to visit Pollyanna in hospital, but with Sylvia spending most of her time there, I felt obliged to offer her my company. Sometimes I saw snatches of Chris, hurrying from the ward after visiting Pollyanna or in the hospital grounds with Sylvia. They hugged emphatically, just as they had done the first time I had seen them together outside the Regency Bookshop, only now I noticed how Chris seemed eager to depart. Was he heading for London or perhaps abroad to search for new art to sell?

Increasingly, I felt drawn to Pollyanna and Sylvia, seeing them as lonely figures dealing with a terrible situation not a lot different from my own. Sylvia and I started to meet together in the hospital grounds. One glorious summer's afternoon, as we strolled through the lightened grass, we found a deserted spot under one of the oak trees.

'Pollyanna seems to be getting better,' I said.

Sylvia lit a cigarette. 'Those support groups are not nearly enough. They don't teach you anything about how to raise your Thalidomide children, and with all their medical talk, it's no wonder that most of the children have ended up in homes,' she said, blowing the perfect smoke ring. She paused to pull off her shoes. Glancing at her in interest, I wondered how much of this moment I would remember in the years to come when our lives had changed and we had forgotten about these meet-ups because the connection between us had faded into the distance.

'Where is Chris?' I asked, changing the subject.

'Away in Paris at the moment,' she said, flatly indicating that that line of discussion wasn't something she wished to pursue. And I hadn't the courage then to press her any further.

'Pollyanna likes her father, but he's not around enough to make a difference. See, you and I are not so different, are we?'

Silence fell between us as she puffed on her cigarette. Watching her curl her red toenails, on such a hot day I thought if our circumstances had been different we could have gone to the beach together, but we couldn't, not really. I noticed several mothers drift into the hospital. Were they heading for the girls' ward, too?

'We should go and see Pollyanna,' I said.

'She likes you, Emily, I can tell. Just think if Thalidomide had never happened. You'd have a daughter by now.'

'I love my son.'

'You think of how your life should have been every morning you wake up and see him; I understand that, too. We mustn't stop fighting,' she said, with her head close to my shoulder. 'We must find a way to justice; it's the only way forward. We can't give up. That's why I'm counting on your support, Emily.'

*'Sometimes the strongest among us are
the ones who smile through silent pain,
cry behind closed doors,
and fight battles nobody knows.'*
Unknown

Chapter Twenty-Five

Our car approached the rectangular sign that read 'Drive with Care, Children.' I could make out some of the sprawling hospital that was Chailey Heritage, yet the manicured grounds succeeded in protecting us from what I feared lay ahead beyond the main entrance.

The hospital was founded in 1903 by Dame Grace Kimmins to help disabled boys to learn a craft. It offered the boys the luxury of the Sussex open air; and over time came the theory of using the hospital to provide children with a range of disabilities the opportunity for physiotherapy, general education, and practical life skills all under one roof.

'If you don't want to go inside, if you have changed your mind, Rex, I could ask the driver to turn around. It's not too late to go home.' I reached for his hand.

'It's all right, Mummy, I'm not afraid. It can't be too bad, can it?'

'No, my darling, and remember that you are capable of great things. Never let them put you down.'

'There's no such word as can't,' said Rex in imitation of my mother. He broke into a fit of giggles, and I found myself smiling my tension away. It was only when the car stopped that I took a deep breath.

The driver went to the boot to retrieve Rex's wheelchair. My fingers wound through Rex's. I thought back to the hospital and of my first days with him. How I felt I had to protect him from the world.

'Mrs Alexander.' The driver bowed and helped Rex to slide himself into his wheelchair.

I climbed out of the car and went to the back of Rex's wheelchair. With my hands gripping the handles, I made the slow walk to the hospital.

A nurse in a royal blue dress with a starched white apron and matching cap greeted us. In silence, I listened to the thud from her stout black shoes. Rex stretched his arms above his head and turned to look at me. We entered the long corridor with its twelve-panel glass doors that led to an outside area. The nurse guided us to the doctor's office and knocked on the door.

The door opened and I saw Dr Donahue sitting behind his long desk.

'Mrs Alexander.' He got to his feet and approached our side. His blue eyes glanced down at Rex's shortened legs. 'That will be all, nurse.'

'Very well, Dr Donahue. Call me if you need any assistance.' She glanced at us briefly before she strode out of the room, closing the door behind her.

'Your husband isn't with you?' he probed, returning to his chair. 'It's often easier when both parents come together. It makes the transition smoother.'

'Laurence had to work.'

'Yes,' he nodded, as if that explained everything. 'Are you still living separately from his father?'

'I'm not sure what that has to do with Rex's stay here. He will only be here for a few months, until I can secure him a place at a local school.'

'Of course.' The doctor gazed at me.

'I'm not sure what to expect from Chailey.'

'Well, this is an institution for handicapped children.'

'I've never thought of Rex as that.'

'How is he getting on with his artificial legs?'

'They pinch my skin and are horribly hot,' Rex moaned.

'Yes, I admit we haven't quite perfected the engineering yet. But it's worth a try, isn't it? To feel more normal and make your mother proud?'

'I'm already proud of him.'

'At Chailey, we encourage the children to be as independent as possible. We have desks that accommodate their artificial legs. How is his education going? Any problems that we need to be aware of?'

'Rex is an intelligent child and fiercely independent.'

'Well, we will be the judge of that, Mrs Alexander. From what I understand he could do with some structure to his life.'

'Thalidomide broke my family. How I've pieced it back together is no one else's business, but mine.'

The doctor smiled. 'Perhaps we should take him to his dormitory. It might help with your goodbyes.'

We made our way to the boys' dormitory by heading down the same long corridor. There, we passed two Thalidomide children approaching us on their little trolleys. The trolleys consisted of a wooden platform elevated off the floor on each corner and supported by wheelchair wheels to the sides, allowing the children to move at a rapid speed.

I stopped for a moment and gazed at the children before touching Rex's shoulder. 'That looks like fun. We don't have anything like that at home.'

'We have a great occupational therapy department here,' said Dr Donahue, proudly.

The doctor guided us into the dormitory that consisted of a long room with rows of iron bedsteads. We stopped before a single bed where several T-shirts and shorts had been laid on top, all bearing the number 88 sewn into the label.

I wheeled Rex's chair close to the bed and he slid himself onto the mattress.

'Well, it all looks organised,' I said, glancing at the doctor.

I sat down on the bed beside Rex. 'You know, I wish you didn't have to come here, and as soon as I can, we'll find you a local school.' Then I reached for his hand and began reciting our affirmation.

'You are a very special child. You were loved and wanted. You are capable of achieving great things.' I started to cry as I pulled him into my arms. I heard Dr Donahue clear his throat.

'Now, Mrs Alexander, this won't help matters for the boy.' He rested his hand on my shoulder.

'There is no such word as can't,' I sobbed and held Rex tightly to me. 'I have to say goodbye to you now. I'm so sorry for this, my darling. I will make everything better soon, I promise.'

The doctor attempted to pull us apart, but I clung tighter to Rex. 'Let me finish, Doctor! Can't you see that I'm apologising to him?' I said, releasing Rex only to kiss his cheek before finally letting him go.

'It's all right, Mummy,' Rex whispered and his fingers brushed mine.

A nurse appeared before us as if she had been waiting in the shadows all along. As Rex offered me his brightest smile, I knew I had to go.

✳✳✳

That Friday afternoon I returned to the basement alone. It was moments like these when I realised how much my life revolved around Rex. My parents didn't come downstairs to see if I was all right. There was no invitation to join them upstairs for dinner. So I sorted through the pantry and tried to think of what to make for myself for dinner. On a Friday evening, Rex would have asked for macaroni cheese, so I took out a block of cheese, some butter, and milk. It was then that I heard footsteps behind me and turned to see Laurence. He clasped a bottle of white wine, and after removing his coat he went to the drawer. He took out a corkscrew and opened the bottle.

The butter had melted in the saucepan, so I started to fling in the onion and chopped mushroom that I had prepared that morning with Rex.

Laurence came up behind me and placed my glass down on the counter. I felt his arms brush mine and inhaled the scent of his aftershave with pleasure. His arms enveloped me, and I leant back into his chest.

'I sent our son away today. I have never felt more ashamed in my life,' I said, breaking the silence at last.

He pulled away from me as I made the cheese sauce. His hand covered mine as we stirred the ingredients together.

After dinner, we sat on the sofa with the remains of the wine. He took my glass and placed it down on the coffee table, and I glanced at the red threads of weariness in his eyes. He cupped my face and I closed my eyes. His lips pressed on mine, and he pushed me down into the sofa. I felt fingertips tickle my skin as he unbuttoned my blouse and discarded it to one side, lodged between Rex's crayons and odd bits of loose change. I surrendered easily to his kisses, taking pleasure as his lips explored my body and found places long neglected by his touch.

Tears rolled down my cheeks that I didn't attempt to rub away. Laurence's body kneaded mine, and he pushed deeper into my fleshy thighs. Dissolving into his embrace, and weak from loving Rex, I let out a final cry, ignoring the voice that was telling me I was about to make a mistake.

***

I awoke the following morning with my cheek pressed into the pillow. I felt a cool breeze blow against my back from the sash window that remained open summer and winter. I thought back to last night and of my allowing Laurence to stay over. Luckily, my head was still groggy, which stopped me from remembering too much about what happened. Thank God for wine.

I pushed myself up on my elbows and noticed the dimple in the mattress to my right. Climbing out of bed, I reached for my lace-edged dressing gown before wandering into the hallway.

The door to Rex's room was half open, allowing me to hide from Laurence and watch. His hand gripped the back of Rex's chair, and I caught his frown. He stood for a moment in deep thought, before he paced the room.

He went to Rex's desk and picked up the crayon sketch of a sailing boat. Laurence's eyes flew to the easel and my favourite painting. Cocking his head to one side, he scrutinised Rex's wild wave; an elongated swirl of yellow, blue, and white strokes that gave way to the delicate linear pebbles of the beach, which I appreciated as Rex's interpretation of the Sussex coastline.

I held my position awhile longer, eager to understand what our son meant to him. But the breeze from the sash window forced me to reveal myself to Laurence at last.

'Emily.' He turned to me with a brilliant smile, the one that I had seen many times on Rex's lips.

'I wasn't spying on you,' I confessed. My toenails grazed the contours of Rex's nought and crosses game.

'I admit I am curious about Rex, always have been. This painting is his?' He nodded towards the easel.

'Yes, I'm starting to think of this as Rex's studio rather than bedroom,' I said proudly.

'Have you shown it to anyone professional?'

I shook my head.

'Well, you should. This could earn him a place in art school or something.'

'Thalidomide children aren't easily accepted into mainstream education, Laurence.'

'Well, that's got to change. Rex is proof of what can be achieved.' He approached me and threw an arm around my waist. 'I want to help, Emily, but I don't know how.'

'Come to the school with me at the end of term, and we'll collect Rex together.'

'I haven't been a father to Rex. I don't know how to love him.'

'Rex is easy to love. You just have to look past what he's not, and once you do, he can offer you so much.' A tear escaped my eye and he kissed it away. Then his lips found mine, and I kissed him harder. As tears moistened my cheeks and we parted, I dared to hope that after all this time he was willing to change, even as history would conspire against us.

PART TWO

*'Hope is being able to see there is light
despite all of the darkness.'*
Desmond Tutu

Chapter Twenty-Six
December 1967

'Distillers says that because we didn't submit the writ within three years of the damage being done, we are out of time. It doesn't matter to them that at that time Pollyanna was sick, and we couldn't just leave her to sort matters out.'

I led Sylvia along the beach with my arm wrapped around her shoulder, listening to the sound of the breaking waves.

'I mean, after all this time and energy, it feels like we are no further on.' Our heels dug into the frosty pebbles and I listened to the sound of the sea, eager for it to steady my pounding heart.

'How's Pollyanna these days?'

Pollyanna had left the hospital at the end of the summer to convalesce at home. There had been no further invitations from Sylvia for me to bring Rex over to her house. I had to believe it was because Pollyanna wasn't sufficiently recovered yet from the infection, but part of me worried that it was because she didn't want to see me anymore.

'She's still taking drugs for her heart, but she seems to be getting better. Perhaps Rex would like to come over to my house to play with Pollyanna soon.'

I sensed Sylvia drawing in her breath and without waiting for my response, she went on. 'I spent the whole summer thinking I was going to lose her, and when that didn't happen, instead of feeling relieved I looked for faults in everyone.'

'Sometimes I blame Laurence for everything, in a silent way that makes no sense at all.'

Sylvia turned to me. 'I'm sorry—how selfish am I? You're not okay either, are you?'

She pulled away to reach inside her handbag for a cigarette. She lit it quickly and glanced away from me. Smoke and tears merged amongst the fog of a bitter winter's day.

'Talk to me about Rex. How's he doing at Chailey?'

I shook my head, wordless and frightened of another failure when already I felt there had been enough.

'Can I help you at all?' Sylvia asked, between puffs of her cigarette.

'Don't think you can.' My gaze fell to the icicles below my feet, thinking how beautiful they looked, but far too fragile to touch.

'Chris knows one of the school governors on the board of a local junior school. What if we got Pollyanna and Rex into that school? Wouldn't that be justice in itself? We would both feel better then, wouldn't we?'

I raised my head. 'Could we do that?'

The idea played on my mind, calming my heart with a newfound optimism that deep down had never left me.

'We could try.' Sylvia stubbed out her cigarette and a smile played on her lips.

'I like you,' I said and returned her smile.

'Why? Because I know the right people?'

'Yes, and for half a dozen other reasons, too.'

✳✳✳

Returning home, I found Laurence waiting for me in the kitchen. He poured us each a coffee and we sat at the table.

'How was your friend? Sylvia, isn't it?'

'How do you know about Sylvia?' I asked, taking a sip of my drink.

'I know of her husband, Chris. He has built up quite a list of business contacts in London.'

Laurence took his cup to his lips. 'They caused quite a fuss when Pollyanna was born. By making the doctor at St Thomas' go through Sylvia's medical file; although at the time no one made the connection between her taking Distaval and Pollyanna's birth defects. But once the Thalidomide story broke, they tried to bring some lawsuit against their GP.'

'Sylvia has been a good friend to me,' I said, and felt the need to defend my friend.

'Just be careful of her,' he warned.

'Why are you being like this when Sylvia only wants to help us? In fact, she thinks Chris could get Rex into a local school,' I said, allowing myself the credit for a big accomplishment.

'Do you think that's wise, Emily? After all, he has just settled into Chailey. Why disrupt his education any further?'

'I want Rex home.' I placed my cup and saucer down on the table with a thud.

'It doesn't have to be this way. Why don't we leave Rex where he is and concentrate on our marriage for a change?'

'What marriage, Laurence? Let's be honest with each other; things haven't been right between us for years.'

'Emily,' he said, and his eyes widened in surprise from my tone of voice. He reached for my hand. 'This isn't like you at all. What has Sylvia been saying to you? Don't listen to her. She's only jealous. We can work through our difficulties in our own way, as we've always done.'

I shook my head, determined that I wasn't going to resort to tears. I could do this, I knew I could.

'Not anymore, Rex is not a baby. He is starting to pick up on things. What are we teaching him?'

'That life's complicated. With his disability, he'll understand the situation between us far more than a normal child would.'

'Do you love our son?' I demanded. 'It's all right to leave birthday presents for him, but that doesn't mean anything if you can't show him that you love him. Rex and I, we come together as a joint package, so it's time for you to take responsibility, your monthly cheques are not enough. He is suffering by not having you around, and my father can only do so much to fill the gap.'

'You're tired, Emily, I understand that it's getting too much for you looking after Rex.'

'It's not,' I said, firmly. 'It's just that I've changed, but you haven't at all since Rex was born. So I am giving you an ultimatum, Laurence. If you want to visit me from now on, that's got to involve you seeing Rex. No excuses will be taken, because enough is enough!'

'And if I don't agree to these demands?' Laurence said, bringing his chair closer to mine, but refraining from touching me.

'We will have to talk about more permanent measures,' I replied.

'Are we talking divorce? Does Rex mean that much to you that you'd give up on our marriage and everything that you believe in?'

'Yes, I would,' I said without a quiver of doubt in my voice. 'So, you should go and have a think about what I said.' I nodded towards the door.

Laurence rose from the table and offered a kiss to my forehead.

'All right, Emily,' he said, leaving the house.

*'Education is the most powerful weapon
which you can use to change the world.'*
Nelson Mandela

Chapter Twenty-Seven
1968

Maple Rose Junior School was comprised of two low-slung annexes that stood parallel to the infant school and was situated down a busy residential road.

Climbing out of Sylvia's Rolls-Royce on a bitter February afternoon, children's grey duffle coats and brown leather satchels dashed past us to school. We crisscrossed the playground and found ourselves in the midst of their PE class. We watched in fascination as the children, stripped down to singlet and shorts, played a game of hockey, separated from the main road by low iron railings.

Sylvia wound her arm through mine, and I wondered how the world saw us, as sisters or friends?

'Speak confidently, Emily. Tell them how far Rex has come,' Sylvia counselled.

'Will they listen to us?' I asked as we strode inside the school.

'Chris has assured me that they will. He knows these people. They will want to help our children.'

The headmistress approached us outside the school office and introduced herself as Miss Faulks. She led us into her office, a cramped room that emitted a rather unsettling damp odour. She proceeded to regard us from behind her thick-rimmed glasses, alerting me that it was probably wise to have no expectations about this middle-aged lady, whose only redeeming feature was her mop of untidy, chestnut curls.

'The board has filled me in on your children's progress. Rex is above average,' Miss Faulks nodded at me, and I felt a half-smile form on my lips.

'But I am afraid we have some concerns about Pollyanna's progress.'

'We have relied so far on a home tutor for Pollyanna. That's the reason we want her to attend school. She needs the opportunity to be amongst other children. Hers hasn't been an easy life so far,' Sylvia interjected, dabbing at her eyes and amazing me at her quick change of emotion.

'I'm sorry to hear that, Mrs Watersmith,' Miss Faulks replied before proceeding to address me again.

'Our main concern for Rex are his mobility issues. Ours is a small, but busy school. However, with his academic record, I feel inclined to overlook his difficulties.'

'Thank you,' I replied, clutching my hands together in joy.

'Now, concerning Pollyanna, our main issues are around reading and writing. My teachers can offer support, but there are other children to consider.'

'Pollyanna can hold a pencil between her toes to write, and she can use her tongue to turn the pages.' Sylvia sat upright without a tear in sight.

'You have obviously been working hard at home with your daughter.' Miss Faulks gazed at us in amazement, clearly taken back by what Thalidomide children were capable of; although for us mothers, this was just the starting point.

'We wouldn't be here now if we didn't believe in our children, Miss Faulks,' Sylvia said.

'Both children do offer unique opportunities for the education system. It makes me feel inclined to give them both a chance.'

Miss Faulks shuffled her paperwork for a moment, propelling us into silence. Then she turned back to us again. 'They can start after the half-term break,' Miss Faulks concluded and reached for the telephone to signal that our time with her was up.

Leaving the school that day, I was filled with hope, believing this had to be the turning point in all our lives.

*'If you're doing your best, you won't have any time
to worry about failure.'
H Jackson Brown Jnr*

Chapter Twenty-Eight

The following week, I took a deep breath, feeling Dr Donahue regard me from behind his desk during my visit with him.

'So,' he began. 'You want to remove Rex from Chailey.' He took a sip of his tea.

'Rex was only here on a temporary basis. I thought we agreed on that.'

'Um,' he muttered, and got up from behind his desk. He went to his filing cabinet and returned with a brown file with the number 88 marked on top.

'I've found him a local school to attend. The headmistress is impressed with Rex's achievements.'

'What about his physiotherapy?'

'That can be done at the Royal Alexandra Hospital.'

'He'll need new limbs soon. He has grown a little since being with us. Can they provide the same as what we do here?'

'He could still come here for limb-fitting. I wouldn't object to that.'

'You're willing to allow us some intervention, then?'

'Of course.'

'Well, I'm not sure about this, Mrs Alexander. You can't just place him here one month and remove him the next, that's not what's best for Rex.'

'Rex needs to be with his family.'

'You are feeling guilty. I can sense that. But trust me; this is the right place for him.'

I shook my head. 'I have come to take my son home, Dr Donahue.'

'Rex has demonstrated a lot of promise, but in my opinion, he needs specialised care and education to reach his potential. Can you offer him the same?'

'Yes, I can.'

'Your husband doesn't agree. He wants to block Rex's release. What kind of life will it be for the boy with his parents locked in disagreement? I have to confess that some of the Thalidomide children have been released back to their parents with disastrous results. I don't want that to happen to Rex.'

'I need to have him at home. He has to know that he is loved and wanted.'

The doctor leaned across the desk to touch my hand. 'I know what this is about, Mrs Alexander.'

'You do?' I asked incredulously.

'I wish that I had the foresight to have predicted what would have happened with Thalidomide, before it was too late. Now all I can do is try to help the children. I feel your guilt, too.'

∗

I walked into the boys' dormitory and saw Rex sitting on the bed beside his brown suitcase. He had a book in his hand and was turning the pages as I approached him.

'Rex,' I said.

He looked up and I saw that flicker of a smile.

'Am I coming home with you?' he asked tenderly.

I sat down next to him, and taking the book from him, I drew him into my arms. 'Do you know the best bit?'

'Dad will be home?'

'Well, yes, he might be, but better still, you don't have to come back here after the holidays.' I smiled.

'Not ever?'

'I promise.' I held him close, hoping that was the truth.

I saw Dr Donahue glance my way as Rex rocked from side to side, making his way out of Chailey. We crossed the road and escaped to the common. There I unstrapped his legs and let him crawl freely through the grass, glistening with the February dew.

We took a taxi home. I wasn't expecting to see Laurence back so soon, so I was surprised to find him waiting for us in our little kitchen.

'They have settled the first cases,' he said with a frown, before turning his eyes to Rex with newfound interest.

'What?'

'In the High Court, Distillers has offered the families a deal.' He passed me a copy of the daily paper and I scanned the headlines.

SCANDALOUS
THE HIGH COURT AGREES TO MEAGRE COMPENSATION FOR THALIDOMIDE VICTIMS

*'A gift consists not in what is done or given,
but in the intention of the giver or doer.'*
Lucius Annaeus Seneca

Chapter Twenty-Nine

The following morning, I was awoken by the sound of footsteps down the hallway. I crept from my bedroom and went to check on Rex, only to find him and his wheelchair missing. I hurried down the hallway to be greeted by an echo of voices coming from the kitchen. I recognised the voices as belonging to Sylvia and Rex.

'That's it, Rex. You do the outside edge.' From the doorway, I saw Sylvia's hand rest on Rex's shoulder as he squeezed pink icing around the edge of the cake. Upon finishing the task, Pollyanna stepped forward and used her teeth to squirt squiggles of purple dots to the centre of the sponge with her icing bag.

'Emily,' Sylvia called out in warning, alerting me that I hadn't managed to remain incognito, as I had hoped.

I ran back to the bedroom and crawled under the covers. It seemed like only seconds later that the door was flung open and Sylvia wheeled in Rex. He held the cake in his lap that read in pink writing: 'Happy Birthday, Mummy, Love Rex.'

Pollyanna ran alongside his chair, and they all came to a halt by my bedside cabinet.

'Happy Birthday to you! Happy Birthday, dear Mummy! Happy Birthday to you!' they sang.

'Thank you, thank you!' I said, watching Sylvia take the cake from Rex and place it on the dressing table.

'Birthday cake for breakfast? Whatever is next?'

'It's for tea later, Mrs Alexander,' said Pollyanna.

'Of course it is.' I beamed at her.

Rex didn't wait. He just flung his arms around my neck and kissed my cheek. 'Did you help make the cake, Rex?'

'They both did,' said Sylvia.

'This will be my best birthday ever,' I said, and meant it.

'This is just the start. There's more planned for you, just you wait and see.' Sylvia squeezed my hand. Rex pulled away from me and got back into his wheelchair, just as Pollyanna squeezed through the gap to crawl onto my bed and lay her head on my shoulder.

'Happy birthday,' she whispered. I stroked her hair, tucking a blonde curl behind her ear.

'Sweetheart, this has been a wonderful surprise.' I imagined her wide smile and we remained like that for a moment, before hearing a clearing of breath nearby.

Pollyanna raised her head as Laurence strolled up to the end of my bed, carrying several wrapped parcels in his arms. 'Happy birthday, Emily,' he said, glancing at Sylvia and the children.

Pollyanna jumped down, and Rex's eyes widened in surprise. His hand reached out to greet his father. But Laurence remained rooted to the spot, protecting himself with the gifts.

'Come on, children, we better take the cake back to the fridge for later.' Sylvia picked up the cake and passed it to Rex. His little hands gripped the cake's perimeter as she wheeled him away from me. Pollyanna looked back at me with a wide smile, and then she turned and hurried after Rex.

I pushed up in bed, and folded my arms.

The parcels tumbled onto the bed. 'Well,' he said. 'Do you have any plans for your birthday?'

I traced the rose-embossed wrapping paper on each of the three gifts. I tore open one end of a parcel and pulled out a box from Harrods. Inside the box was a pair of mint-coloured two-inch heels. 'They're beautiful,' I said and leaned over to offer him a kiss as thanks.

'There are two more boxes for you to open.' He grinned, and snuggled in beside me, to throw an arm around my shoulder.

The following two gifts included a cameo pendant necklace and a black-lace negligee.

'I wasn't expecting any of this, Laurence,' I said.

'I know, but birthdays are for celebrating. Ours isn't a normal marriage, but that doesn't stop me from wanting to treat you and at the same time, spending a little time with Rex.'

That evening I wore a black Chanel dress, finished off with Laurence's cameo and heels. I held his hand, and we went upstairs to the dining room for my birthday dinner. Apart from my parents, there were several other guests, including Sylvia, Chris, Dr Dhillon and a couple of my father's fellow Rotarians.

'I haven't been to your gallery in London yet, much to my wife's chagrin,' said the doctor, glancing at Chris in his dress suit.

'Well, when you do, you'll find that I have incorporated a lot of modern pieces into my classical range,' Chris replied, forking a mushroom from his spiced-tomato starter.

'I'm still not completely convinced by modern art, but I can appreciate its commercial value as a collector,' the doctor said and leaned back in his chair.

Seated at the end of the table and dressed in a suit and a taffeta dress, respectively, were Rex and Pollyanna. As I finished my Mushroom á la Grecque, I saw Rex's hand graze Pollyanna's foot as she took a mouthful of her tomato sauce.

'So, what do we think about Vietnam?' asked the doctor, turning to me at last. It had been a few years since our last meeting, years that had added a scattering of grey hairs to his head.

'It presents a challenging case for us homeopaths in terms of methodology,' my father said.

'Indeed,' said the doctor.

'And a threat to world peace,' I concluded.

Rex was busy cutting Pollyanna's vegetables.

'What is your profession, Laurence?' asked a silver-haired gentleman seated to my father's left.

The guests shifted in their chairs uneasily. My father busied himself refilling our wine glasses.

'I work in the pharmaceutical industry,' Laurence said quickly, before taking a mouthful of his vegetable lasagne.

'Well,' said the gentleman. 'At least you'll never be out of work,' he chuckled.

'There is talk of drug addiction amongst the American soldiers,' Sylvia piped up from my right.

'I'm afraid that's nothing new, is it, Emily?' My mother said, fixing her gaze upon my cameo.

'No, probably not,' I mumbled, finishing the last of my main course.

'Well, as long as we acknowledge our differences, surely there's hope of finding a solution,' said Laurence, his hand enveloping mine, before I pulled away to enjoy my first forkful of fondant birthday cake.

Later, Laurence and I walked into the garden and leaned our backs against the wall, with only a few strung lanterns to keep us from darkness.

'You should come to dinner more often,' I said and took his hand in mine.

'Really?'

'It wasn't that bad, was it?'

'Rex seems to have found a friend in Pollyanna.'

'I find myself coping awfully well; never thought I would.' I felt him move, and with our bodies side by side, we shared a kiss, only pulling away when I felt that familiar thump of my heart.

'I've got to go to New York for a medical conference. I won't be able to visit you for a while,' Laurence confessed.

There was an awkward silence. 'So that was what the show of gifts was about,' I said.

'I'm sorry,' he whispered and his lips teased mine. I used my palms to push him away.

'Rather overused those words, haven't we, Laurence?'

'That doesn't give them any less meaning.'

'What do you want?'

'I want to spend the night with you, but not before I have said good night to our son.'

Entering the house, he turned the handle to Rex's room.

'Dad!' Rex squealed.

'Hello, Rex.' Laurence knelt by his bedside, but kept himself a distance from Rex's tiny frame. 'I've come to say good night because I won't see you for a while. I'm not sure what your mother normally does, but good night, Rex, sleep tight and hope the bedbugs don't bite,' he said and leaned over Rex to whisper into his hair. 'Look after your mother for me.' He rose to his feet, and as he did, Rex reached out to graze his father's face with his long fingers. Laurence was quick to pull himself away.

'Good night, Dad,' he said, turning over to signal that he was ready to go to sleep.

Laurence strode over to me at the doorway, and closing the door behind us, we retreated to my bedroom and I tried not to think of tomorrow.

*'If a child cannot learn in the way we teach,
we must teach in a way the child can learn.'*
Ignacio Estrada

Chapter Thirty
1969

I found Pollyanna crouched down behind the oak tree, a few yards from the school's playing fields. Her head was buried in her knees, and I sensed that she had wet herself even before I glanced down at her black tights. I knelt in the grass and touched her shoulder.

'It's all right, Pollyanna,' I said.

Sylvia stood a few paces away, gripping the handles of Rex's wheelchair.

'They wouldn't let her join in with their game of football, because she's a girl without arms,' Rex piped up.

'Is that true?' I asked. Pollyanna lifted her head and I saw her tear-stained cheeks.

'But Pollyanna wouldn't take no for an answer and started tackling the boys for their ball,' said Rex.

'Sounds about right,' Sylvia interjected.

'They didn't like it because I could kick the ball farther than them,' Pollyanna said.

'What happened next?' I coaxed.

'The other boys were older and stronger than me, and they pinned me down.' She shuffled in the dirt, and I noticed congealed blood stuck to the knees of her tights.

'That's not right, they could have hurt you.' I shook my head and glanced over at Sylvia.

'She fights with her brothers sometimes, but they know not to be too rough with her.'

'They piled on top of me, and I had to kick at them to get them to move, but they wouldn't.' She rocked from side to side.

'And in that time, she —'

'Wet herself,' I finished.

'Well, we better get you back to school and changed. Miss Faulks wants to speak to us, Sylvia.'

'Great. Well done, Pollyanna. This is all I need with your father away in New York,' Sylvia said in exasperation.

A short while later, all four of us found ourselves seated outside the headmistress' office. Rex's hand reached down and brushed Pollyanna's side. The girl fidgeted in the grey gymslip, two sizes too big for her.

'I don't think I have ever sat outside the headmistress' office before,' I said, trying to break the heavy atmosphere of silence.

'Why doesn't that surprise me? I received the cane when I was at school,' Sylvia confessed.

'What for?'

'Answering back at a teacher. The school thought I wouldn't get far in life because of my big mouth. Looks like Pollyanna is a chip off the old block.' Sylvia smiled.

Gazing at Sylvia I was hit with the realisation that my life could never go back to how it used to be, even if things worked out between Laurence and me.

The door opened, and we all turned to see Miss Faulks purse her lips at us in displeasure. We followed her into her office. She closed the door behind us, and I took a deep breath. Glancing towards Sylvia, I saw her eyes fill with tears and wished there was something I could do to guarantee that today wouldn't happen again.

'We can't tolerate this kind of behaviour from any pupil,' Miss Faulks said from behind her desk.

'I understand, Miss Faulks, and of course we will talk to Pollyanna about how a girl should behave around boys.'

Miss Faulks pushed her glasses back against her nose and turned to Rex.

'Did you witness this altercation, Rex?'

'Yes, Miss Faulks, and it wasn't Pollyanna's fault. There were four of them and only one of her.'

'That may have been the case, but I'm concerned that her behaviour poses a disruption to my school.'

'From what I gather, she wanted to play football, something that, despite her difficulties, she was able to do. Doesn't the school have a responsibility to provide a variety of games for the children?' I interjected.

'We're not that kind of school, Mrs Alexander. These ideas of yours do not fit our curriculum.'

'Perhaps they should. After all, education is not just about the three R's. It's about nurturing the child's soul. Pollyanna's social development will not evolve until she has the confidence to believe that she's part of the school.'

Miss Faulk's mouth opened and closed, and I felt Sylvia squeeze my hand.

'I could overlook this incident if, Mrs Alexander, you would be interested in helping out in the playground for a couple of afternoons a week.'

I thought back to 1960 and how my life with Rex had begun. Clearing my throat, I turned to Miss Faulks.

'I can't think of anything better than helping the children.'

'Every day is a new opportunity.'
Bob Feller

Chapter Thirty-One

I stood at the perimeter of the school playground. Moving gently on the spot, it was a damp May afternoon that felt more suited to late April. From the outside edge, the playground was a lonely place, symbolic of concrete and cold, flaking blue paint. Searching for Rex, I moved towards the climbing frame and awaited the lunch bell ding.

Pollyanna escaped through the double doors and rushed past me. Rex's gloved hands rotated the wheels of his chair hurriedly, and, without a word of greeting, he headed towards Pollyanna at the climbing frame.

Standing only a few paces from the climbing frame, I had a good view of Rex and was surprised when he lifted Pollyanna up and sat her down on the space where metal gave way to wood. Then he lifted himself out of his chair by grasping hold of her ankles, and his small body floated in the air.

'See? I told you there's no need to stay in that boring chair of yours all day, Rex,' Pollyanna laughed.

His frayed grey trousers whipped against his stubby little legs as he kicked out in freedom. At Rex's chuckle I stopped myself from intervening, knowing that everything else I could offer him wouldn't come close to the joy of this moment.

There was a rush of footsteps as the children emptied into the playground. A dozen or so proceeded to surround the climbing frame and watch in awe at Rex in mid-flight. The teachers filed out, searching for their young, troublesome pupils who had somehow skipped the end of class.

I pushed forward, and the able-bodied boys and girls formed a huddle around me, letting out a chorus of laughter at Rex and Pollyanna's naughtiness. Upon reaching Rex, his lips curled into a pout. My hands reached up to disentangle him from Pollyanna, and I slid him back into his wheelchair. I offered my arms to help Pollyanna down from her perch, but she gave me an emphatic shake of the head.

'Let me stay up here, Mrs Alexander. Don't let them see me.' She nodded towards the collection of fierce boys who had begun to pound the playground with their ball. Her aquamarine eyes widened in fear as I touched her shoulder.

'Don't worry, Pollyanna, I'll talk to them for you. You can't stay up here all lunchtime.'

'You don't understand anything. This is how it is for us. Just leave Rex here with me.'

'Your mother and I, we want you both to join in with the other children and have a chance at a normal childhood.'

'Look at us, we're not normal children.' She shook her head sadly.

'Listen to me, Pollyanna. I'm not giving up on you. I'll be here every lunchtime, and I will do whatever it takes to help you join in with their play. That's my promise to you, all right?'

She nodded.

'Good, because I want you to come down now. There's no need for you to hide away from anyone, understood?'

I offered her my arms, and she shuffled closer to me. Grasping her sides, I helped her to the ground. Wriggling free of me, she was beside Rex's chair in seconds.

'So what game can we play?' Pollyanna asked.

I found a ball and threw it to Rex. He caught it easily and rolled it to Pollyanna and she grabbed it with her feet. Then a few other children approached and joined in by turning ours into a game of throw, catch, and pass. Slowly, we forgot what it was that had triggered the moment in the first place, and we were disappointed when the bell rang to denote the start of afternoon class.

By the time Rex and I got home there was a letter perched on the kitchen counter with my name scrawled across the front of the envelope. I took Rex to his bedroom so he could get changed out of his school uniform and into a T-shirt and shorts, a fashion trend that he had followed since his time at Chailey. Sorting through his satchel, I settled upon his maths homework. Wheeling him back into the kitchen, I positioned him at the table. He opened his exercise book and took his pencil between his fingers, and pressing down on the page, he made a start on his multiplication sums.

I glanced again at the envelope.

Rex's hand trembled, and looking down at the exercise book, I saw his muddled scrawling. He rubbed in irritation at his forehead. I reached over to touch his burning cheeks.

'How long have you been feeling like this?'

He shrugged, and with little hesitation I wheeled him back to his room.

'I'm not that bad,' he protested as I slid him onto his bed and proceeded in stripping off his clothes. He pushed himself up to the pillow, and I pulled back the sheet to cover his semi-naked body.

I rushed upstairs and followed the trail of jazz music to my father's study. Leaning back in his chair, he took a puff of his cigar and closed his eyes. I contemplated calling for my mother, just as my father opened his eyes and smiled.

'Emily, you're home already. How's Rex?'

'I think he's running a fever,' I said, leaning against the door and wanting to tell him so much more.

He bolted upright and stubbed out his cigar. 'Right, bear with me a moment and I'll take a look at him.'

My father gave Rex some Belladonna for his fever and helped me to sponge him down. We remained with Rex for most of the afternoon, and it was only when we heard his deep intake of breath that we left his room.

Wandering back to the kitchen, I picked up the letter.

'Whatever it is, it can't be too bad, Emily,' my father said from the doorway before he disappeared back upstairs.

I turned the envelope over in my hands before making the first tear. Then, I unfolded the letter and sat down at the table.

Dear Emily,
By the time you find this letter, I will be gone from the

house and your life again. You don't need to remind me of my broken promises. I wish there was some way that I could bring myself to stay with you and Rex, and finally get to know my son. From what I have gathered, he is growing into a bright young boy with a future, and that's all down to you, Emily. You are a great mother and I am so proud of how you have coped with everything, these last eight years. You followed your heart with Rex. If only I could have done the same, but as you know I am weak and that's why I am walking out now, rather than settling down to fatherhood. There is another reason for my leaving. A boy called Richard Satherley will feature in the news. Born without arms, his case is going to the High Court. I find myself drawn to London to listen to the outcome. Bear with me, my darling, and please forgive my disappearance. I will be in touch.

Love always,
Laurence

I folded the letter and put it in my jean pocket to read again later. Then, feeling hungry, I cooked myself some spaghetti, but lost my appetite and kept most of the pasta for tomorrow's lunch.

The following morning, I went to Rex's room and touched his forehead. His fever had subsided, but even in the half-light, I took in his red rash that had spread from his face down to his neck, and I rushed upstairs for my father.

My father leaned over Rex, pulling up his vest to expose the rash that had spread to his chest and arms.

'Can you show me your tongue, Rex?' he asked.

Rex let out a hacking cough before poking out his tongue. My father nodded, as if confirming something he already knew.

'He's got measles,' my father said.

I looked at him in alarm.

'Don't worry, Emily. We will get him through this. Now you will need to keep the curtains drawn, and offer him plenty of water, but there's no reason why he shouldn't be up and about in a couple of weeks,' my father promised, offering Rex a dose of Pulsatilla. In exchange, I passed him Laurence's letter.

*'There is not one family I have seen that
you could say was reasonably adjusted.'
A doctor, discussing the impact of Thalidomide on family life*

Chapter Thirty-Two

The following evening, I strode across the green and approached a crescent of townhouses all bearing the familiar tall bay windows and cream wash. Sylvia's house was located in the middle row. I rang the doorbell and shuffled on my heels for a moment or two, before looking up into Chris' bright blue eyes.

'Hello, Emily, come in. We have been expecting you,' he said, with a wave of his hand.

Dressed in a white shirt and blue jeans, he appeared different from the Chris I knew from our brief acquaintance.

'Please, come into the lounge and Sylvia will fix you a drink,' Chris said, and I followed him into the hallway carpeted in scarlet.

I unbuttoned my coat and handed it to him to reveal a watercolour floral dress of yellow, aqua and grey. He hung my coat over the banister and then led me into the lounge, decorated in pink and white with matching sofas and crowned by an autumn-leaf chandelier. My eyes drifted to the French doors that led down into the garden before settling back on the room, where two blond-haired boys were sprawled across one of the sofas, sharing a Beano comic.

'Mark, Edward, sit up properly. We have a guest,' Chris commanded, and I watched his handsome sons act on his order. Noticing my gaze, Chris offered me a smile.

At the foot of the sofa sat Pollyanna, cross-legged on a Persian rug. She wore a sleeveless blue dress with yellow embroidered flowers. The girl looked up as I sat down on the opposite sofa, and as she shuffled slightly, I caught sight of her red toenails.

'Hello, Pollyanna. How's school?' I asked.

She leant her head onto the arm of the sofa with a faraway expression.

'Answer the question, Pollyanna,' said Chris firmly.

'Where's Rex?' she enquired, lifting her head towards me.

'He's not well. He's got measles,' I explained.

'Oh.' She rested her head back on the sofa.

'But he will be better soon,' I promised.

A tiny flicker of a smile curled on her lips.

'So, tell me about yourself, Emily. From what Sylvia has told me, you have developed quite a system for understanding Rex.' Chris took a seat beside his sons and leant towards me across the coffee table. 'To be honest,' he nodded at Pollyanna, 'we could do with all the help we can get.'

'Well,' I began, 'I suppose it started with an acknowledgement of what had happened, and that led us to take an imaginative way of thought.'

Sylvia entered the room. She wore a royal blue high-necked lace dress with long sleeves and a gathered skirt. Her hair had been whipped into a chignon.

'Emily.' She crouched down and offered me her cheek. Then she stood up slowly and regarded my dress with interest.

'Can I get you a drink? I bet you're a martini kind of girl.' Her eyes twinkled in excitement.

'I wish!' I laughed and saw Chris beam.

'I can imagine that, as a writer, creativity comes naturally to you,' Chris said, as Sylvia left to fix my drink.

'I don't know about the writing. I haven't had anything published yet,' I confessed.

'I'm not sure if Sylvia has told you much about my work, but being in the art world, I do have a few contacts. Maybe we could help each other. You have become something of a friend to Sylvia, and I appreciate that,' Chris said, as Sylvia returned with drinks for us all, two martinis and a whiskey for Chris. Taking a sip of my martini, I caught Pollyanna's watchful gaze.

Later, we strolled upstairs to the dining room. I glanced around the room and noticed a rosewood piano with interest. The walls bore the same hues of candy pink, and the table had been set for six people, with a view of the walled garden from the tall bay windows.

'We have made you a mushroom risotto, hope that's all right. I'm afraid I don't know much about vegetarian cooking, with Chris being a bit of a steak-and-chips man,' said Sylvia, passing me my dinner.

Pollyanna took her seat and placed her right foot onto the lace tablecloth. Holding the fork with her big toe, she lifted her foot and fed herself a mouthful of chicken. I forked my rice, but had only taken a few mouthfuls before the boys broke out in laughter.

I saw Pollyanna struggle with her spoon and spill cream sauce down the front of her dress. She reacted quickly to her frustration by grabbing at the dish of carrots with her feet. A swift kick caused the dish to fall onto the floor, creating a horrible cluttering sound. Then, she picked up her fork with her mouth and started to feed herself the remains of her dinner.

'Not like that, Pollyanna! Use your feet!' Sylvia cried.

'That's because she doesn't know how. Who's the baby, Pollyanna?' Mark, the elder of the boys taunted.

'That's enough, Mark. Leave your sister alone!' yelled Chris.

Pollyanna swung her legs down from the table, and in her haste to leave she caused her high-backed chair to tumble to the floor with a thud.

Chris caught Pollyanna before she could escape through the double doors and hugged her around the waist.

The girl laid her head in the nook of his shoulder, and I heard her deep intake of breath.

'It's all right, Polly,' he soothed.

'That's it, Chris. Spoil her, why don't you? I'm going outside for a cigarette,' Sylvia said and strode from the room.

Chris turned to me. 'I'm sorry about this, Emily, forgive us.'

'It's all right,' I said, feeling myself frown. 'Let me speak to Sylvia.'

'Thank you,' he said, before turning back to his children.

'Right, boys, clean up this mess now!'

I went down to the lounge and walked through the French doors. I climbed the metal staircase down to the garden. There, I found Sylvia in the patio, puffing on her cigarette.

'Don't know what you must think of us,' she said, as a way of greeting.

I stood close enough to inhale her smoke.

'Whatever you're going through, I am too.'

She turned to me and I caught the glow of her burning ember.

'I don't know how to be her mother.'

'Laurence has never touched his own son.'

Sylvia shook her head. 'I love her, but I don't know how to show her that.'

'Pollyanna thinks she's not normal and that no one will ever accept her body. We have got to prove her wrong.'

'How do we do that?'

'If she spent more time with Rex, she wouldn't feel so different. It's got to be worth a try, hasn't it?'

Sylvia reached for my hand and squeezed it tight. We remained like that until Chris came out to find us, and even then all three of us watched the stars for what seemed a long time before retreating back inside the house.

'Play is the answer to how anything new comes about.'
Jean Piaget

Chapter Thirty-Three
1971

Arriving at Sylvia's house one summer's afternoon, I rang the doorbell before skipping down the three steps and waiting on the pavement with Rex. The front door opened, and Sylvia emerged sporting a blue and yellow floral dress, slit at the thigh, and with a matching bandana. She hurried down the steps, and together we lifted Rex's wheelchair up inside the house.

I heard the sound of piano music from upstairs.

'That's Pollyanna you hear. The boys are at boarding school.'

I recognised the notes as Chopin's 'Nocturne.' I saw a smile form on Rex's lips in appreciation.

'Let's go upstairs. I've prepared us drinks and a bite to eat,' Sylvia said, and her heels dug into the red carpet as I followed her to the staircase. Leaving Rex's chair at the bottom, he mounted the first step on all fours. I glanced at Sylvia and she beamed her encouragement, then in single file we followed Rex as he crawled to the top.

In the dining room, Pollyanna was perched on a stool at the piano. With her feet poised by the keys, she used five of her toes to tap out Chopin's 'Nocturne,' cautiously.

'Pollyanna.' Sylvia placed a hand on the girl's back. Twisting on her stool, Pollyanna's feet spread across the keys. There came the thunder of several keys being played at once. Sitting only a short distance away from her, Rex held his hands over his ears in defence.

Pollyanna pouted at our intrusion. 'Look at what you made me do.' Ignoring both Rex and me, she shrugged away her mother's touch and swung her legs gracefully, so she was back in position for a practise of the scales.

'Sweetheart, we have guests, so either you stop or let Rex have a go.'

Pollyanna looked down and saw Rex beside the pedals. Her lips curled into a smirk.

'He can have a go, if he likes,' she said, dropping her legs down, causing her feet to almost collide with his face. He quickly shuffled aside and she jumped down to the floor. It took a moment for her to steady herself. Then, still a short distance apart from each other, Rex used his arms to pull himself onto the stool and twist his body around. For a moment, he gazed down at the keys as if frightened to touch the place where her toes had just been.

'Bet you won't be as good as me.' Pollyanna towered over him. Rex stretched his long fingers over the keys and began to race up and down the scales in zest.

'Come, let's leave them alone for a bit.' Sylvia took my hand and led me into the parlour next door. On the coffee table was a jug of fresh lemonade and glasses. A platter of pâté-topped toast had been left as an afterthought at the end of the table. I watched Sylvia pour me a glass of lemonade with her red, manicured nails. Passing the glass to me, she offered me a smile. Hearing the delicate tinkle of music next door, I thought that Pollyanna must have taken over.

'Chris is away in London at his gallery. He is there a lot these days,' she said, offering me a piece of toast. I took a bite of mushroom pâté and glanced at her. I observed her careful manner of taking small, meaningful bites of her toast mixed with furtive glances meant to observe, but not impose.

'I would like it if you came to visit with Rex more often. We don't need a schedule or anything, there's no need to wait to be asked.' Her hand rested upon her knee.

'Of course, I would like that. I know I'm not good at the friendship business. I'm something of a loner, for other than my parents, there's only ever been Laurence.'

'You have never considered a divorce?'

I lowered my eyes, remembering with pain how close I had come to carrying out my threat of divorce to Laurence. A sob caught in my throat. His visits with us weren't nearly enough.

I wanted much more. I raised my head to look at Sylvia, and to my surprise I saw tears glisten in her eyes.

'I am so sorry, Emily. I never meant to upset you. Sometimes it feels like I have no control over what I am saying. It's as if I am going mad or something.'

I shook my head. 'It's not your fault. It is me, always me; I'm as weak as Laurence in some ways,' I explained, watching her hand move from her knee to take mine. A silence fell in the room, and we didn't say anything for the longest moment.

'It's not abnormal how you feel. It's perfectly natural after what they have done to us. It's what I have been telling you, Emily, the blame doesn't lie with you.'

'They?' I asked, not retracting my hand from hers.

'Our husbands, the doctors, all of them. Sometimes I really hate them and so do you, except you're so bloody calm about everything. If I was more like you then perhaps Pollyanna would be better behaved.'

'She's not that bad,' I said, daring a smile.

'Maybe under your influence she'll get better, but that's not the point, is it?'

'Isn't it?'

'You can't go on like this with Laurence. He's not making you happy, and, Emily you deserve to be happy.'

'What are you saying?'

'There's a chance for you to end all this misery.'

I shook my head before leaning closer to her in my chair.

'That staying with Laurence out of loyalty or some misguided interpretation of love is not doing you any favours. You could divorce him on grounds of his appalling behaviour towards Rex. He'd still have to pay you an allowance for Rex. You could stay with your parents or get a job and find a place of your own with Rex. Wouldn't that be something? I could visit you at your new place and bring Pollyanna with me.' She dropped my hand to take another sip of her drink, allowing me to mull over her idea.

'Are you serious?'

'Deadly, for aren't you sick of being told what to do by everyone? Wouldn't you like a little freedom of your own? Because I know I would,' Sylvia said.

I glanced into her blue eyes, enhanced by thick false eyelashes, and I didn't say anything for the longest moment. I just thought of being alone for the first time in my life. That lump came back to my throat, only this time it wasn't from shock, but from the fear of taking that much-needed leap of faith.

'At least give it some thought,' Sylvia said, squeezing my hand, and with my thoughts whirling in my mind we returned to the dining room and found Rex examining Pollyanna's feet.

'She's got three calluses,' he said, lifting her foot to show us her toes.

'Rex,' I chided, but turning to Sylvia, I was surprised to see her step closer to the children seated on the Persian rug.

'That will go with the bruises,' Sylvia laughed.

'I could bring some remedies over that might help,' I offered.

'Don't encourage her too much. She's supposed to be concentrating on her schoolwork.'

Pollyanna's bottom lip wobbled in protest. 'Next time you come over, Rex, I'll teach you the chords.'

'Mum?' Rex said.

'We'll see, but now it's time to go home. For if I'm not mistaken, Rex, you have some geography homework to be getting on with tonight.'

As he grunted, Sylvia mouthed a thank you, and I rewarded her with a quick hug. It was only as we parted that I caught Pollyanna's pensive gaze at Rex.

'In the end, we only regret the chances we didn't take.'
Unknown

Chapter Thirty-Four

Two weeks passed, and one afternoon as I left school for the day, I found Chris and Sylvia waiting for me at the gate.

'Hello, Emily. We are sorry to turn up unannounced like this, but we have good news to share with you.' Chris offered me a smile as an apology.

I slung my bag over my shoulder and checked my watch.

'Surely we have time for a quick coffee, and I know just the place,' said Sylvia. I followed them towards a street café that, despite its torn leather seats, did serve a good, strong cup of filtered coffee.

'So,' Chris leaned his head to one side. 'I spoke to a publisher in London about your novel.'

Eleven years ago, I had written a romance novel about the British Viceroy's daughter and her affair with a young Gandhi supporter. Set during India's struggle for independence, the story was inspired in part by my mother's childhood in India as the British Viceroy's daughter.

I had recently left the manuscript with Sylvia, unsure whether she would pass it on to Chris.

'Really, I wasn't sure—'

'Emily, you're talented, and you shouldn't let anyone tell you otherwise.' Sylvia took a sip of her coffee, while her aquamarine eyes watched for my reaction.

'What does this mean?' I asked and traced the paisley design on my coffee cup to steady my nerves.

'I could set up a meeting for you with the publisher,' said Chris.

'I don't know,' I said, knowing I would have to leave Rex with my parents for the day.

'My business is in London, so I'd happily drive you to the meeting myself,' said Chris.

I took a gulp of my coffee.

'I could come too,' said Sylvia. 'I know a neighbour who could look after Pollyanna for me. We want to help, because, after everything that has happened, we think you're owed a little luck.'

∗∗∗

The following afternoon, Sylvia and I agreed to meet at the swimming pool. After getting changed into our swimwear, Rex and I sat at the water's edge. We saw the line of Thalidomide boys. They swung their legs over the side of the pool, kicking the water voraciously. A couple of them had armbands camouflaging their stumps, while others wore a rubber ring that teased at their tendrils of flesh.

Rex shuffled on the ledge in a pair of black trunks. His feet dangled over the tiled edge in disappointment.

Sylvia approached us in a black swimming costume, similar to mine; and with Pollyanna at her heels they sat down beside us on the ledge.

Pollyanna was dressed in a pink swimming costume. Rex glanced at Pollyanna and giggled. Pollyanna swung her long legs around to prod Rex in the stomach with her toes.

'Pollyanna!' Sylvia reprimanded. 'I'm sorry.' She turned to me, flushing in embarrassment. 'I had a battle today to get her into the costume. She wanted to wear her old navy one instead.' She raised an eyebrow.

'That's all right. And anyway, it wasn't all Pollyanna's doing, was it, Rex?'

He pouted. 'She just looked a bit different.'

Sylvia offered a rubber ring to Pollyanna, and with her mother's help, slid it over her head and it sat comfortably around her middle. Then, Pollyanna stood and turned to grin at Rex. 'Last one in is a chicken!' At which point she leapt into the water, creating a splash.

'I better keep watch. She's a bit of a daredevil.' Sylvia climbed down the steps and began swimming to the middle, where Pollyanna stood amongst the circle of Thalidomide boys who grappled in the water using their digits of muscle.

'Come, Rex, we'll do it our way.' I slid off the side and helped Rex into the water. With the aid of a rubber ring and long, strong arms, we caught up with Sylvia and Pollyanna.

Sylvia and I remained in the pool for a while longer, watching Rex and Pollyanna bob about in the water.

Later in the café, Rex enjoyed his Bovril. Perched on an ordinary chair, he watched the swimmers below with fascination. Pollyanna leaned her head over the table and sucked at her pink milk through a straw. We caught a few stares, but I threw an arm around Sylvia's shoulder with a sense of indifference.

After a few minutes, Sylvia turned her head towards me. 'Have you given my idea any more thought?' she asked.

I hadn't. How could I? I was certain that Laurence had turned a corner with Rex, and I wanted to give him the benefit of the doubt before making any rash decisions. I took a deep breath.

'I'm still thinking it over,' I said.

'That's good that you haven't dismissed it straight away. Chris and I are looking forward to taking you to London. It's high time you remembered that you have a life, too,' Sylvia said. Her gentle hug full of excitement filled me with trepidation as a fear of failure came rushing back to me. I bit down on my lip. I could handle this, I told myself, and just hoped I was right.

*'No amount of guilt can change the past
and no amount of worrying can change the future.'*
Umar Ibn al-Khattab

Chapter Thirty-Five

At around 9:00, one August morning in 1971, Chris and Sylvia arrived at the house to take me to London. I looked up and saw my mother and Rex from an upper window. I offered them a wave and saw Rex's fingers press on the glass in curiosity. I allowed Chris to guide me to his Rolls-Royce, where Sylvia was in the passenger seat waiting for me. I attempted to convince myself that today was nothing extraordinary, just a chance for me to realise a long-held dream.

'Nervous?' asked Chris, as I climbed into the backseat.

'Yes, a bit.'

A heavy silence fell, and I concentrated on the journey ahead as we left the coast and joined the early-morning traffic heading for London.

Chris drove us towards Waterloo Bridge, a short distance from the publisher's office. We stopped down a side street, and he parked the car to the thundering echo from Waterloo Station.

I clutched my bag to my stomach.

'Do this for yourself and have no regrets,' said Sylvia firmly. 'Meet us afterwards at Southbank.' She scribbled down a meeting point. I nodded and opened the door, still not quite ready for London or what today would bring forth.

✳✳✳

An hour later, Chris, Sylvia and I were strolling along the Southbank, stopping only for me to remove my cardigan. I crept closer to them to enjoy the riverside breeze.

'You haven't told me how you got on,' Chris said as he and Sylvia both stopped to light a cigarette. Chris offered me one, but I shook my head.

'It went well. They want to meet with me once a month for the next six months. There's a lot of editing to be done on the book, but they told me that's normal for first-time writers,' I gushed in excitement.

'They want to publish! That's great news. Well done, Emily,' Sylvia said and took a puff of her cigarette. 'If you're not in a hurry to go home, we could have lunch together; and afterwards, if you like, Chris wants to give you a tour of his famous gallery,' she laughed.

✳✳✳

Chris and Sylvia took me down a narrow alleyway, which didn't appear to contain much more than a few derelict warehouses. The courtyard was situated on the edge of Covent Garden and a short distance from Seven Dials. Walking on, we passed the dairy before stopping outside the blue facade of Neale's Café.

'I am told it is all vegetarian here,' said Chris.

I was surprised to be taken to a vegetarian restaurant, which is pretty much a rarity. I was also shocked that this little yard existed so close to the hustle and bustle of the city. We ordered from the selection of vegetable dishes, puy lentils and alfalfa sprouts.

'I admit we are curious about you, Emily. But that is probably a good thing.' Chris smiled. 'Although you can probably guess, that as Pollyanna's parents, Sylvia and I seem to be failing miserably, so meeting you does seem like a breath of fresh air.'

'He means I am failing with Pollyanna, and that is why, Emily, he was so keen to meet you, and how today is only the start. We hope to get to know you a lot better,' said Sylvia.

The waitress placed our lunch on the table. Their comments made me think that if life was made up of a series of defining moments, which was this one? And how could I allow it to linger for as long as possible?

After lunch, we took a taxi to Grosvenor Square. It was there that they introduced me to Chris' sanctuary of white walls and bare floors. At his gallery, I learnt about his interest in Andy Warhol's pop art, as well as the delight he had in meeting John Lennon and Yoko Ono through art. I imagined, for a moment, a lustrous evening when hundreds of white helium balloons had filled the long gallery. There was even a small plaque commemorating that evening above the doorway.

I moved down the gallery towards a display of land art. I glanced at spiral jetties that reminded me of Brighton.

'What do you think so far?' asked Chris, breaking my chain of thought.

'I am intrigued. Rex is into art. He's pretty good; even Laurence agrees on that.'

'Ah, now I see why you agreed to come here,' Chris chuckled. 'There I was, thinking it was because of our sparkling personalities, hey, Sylvia.'

I felt myself blush, not remembering the last time I had lost control of my emotions so freely.

'I knew you would want to come,' Sylvia said, guiding me on with the touch of her hand on my elbow. We moved forward to examine paintings depicting human anatomy in various forms alongside that of still-life impressions. There was a pink hexagon set against a black background. But my favourite was of a new piece of work that offered splashes of red, yellow, and black that had been created by the artist's own feet.

Feeling weary, I took a seat on the bench with Sylvia just as Chris left briefly, only to return with a glass of champagne for each of us to celebrate my success and toast my visit to his gallery. I took my first sip and felt that at last, after the shock of Rex's birth, I had rejoined civilisation.

That evening, I felt a change in the atmosphere at home. Everything looked the same, but something was different. I went to my little kitchen and found my mother waiting for me there.

'So,' she said, 'how was London?'

'I'm getting my novel published. I can't believe it is finally happening!'

'Going to London with the doctor was one thing.' My mother shook her head in disbelief. 'But this is quite something else. I don't understand. It's not like you are going to earn any money out of it, are you?'

'But I have worked so hard for this,' I said, feeling tears well in my eyes; why wouldn't she give me some credit?

'You're the mother of a disabled child. Your priority is being here for Rex.'

'And I am here for him, but today was about me.'

'Being a mother means putting your child first and yourself second.'

'I haven't done anything wrong, Mummy,' I said, folding my arms under my breasts.

'You've compromised yourself, Emily, by putting yourself in their debt. Whatever they ask of you, you'll have to do. Don't you see this couple has an ulterior motive for their friendship with you? There was nothing coincidental about today, just you wait and see.' She stormed from the room.

Later, I crept out into the garden and found my father sitting on the patio. Upon noticing me, he took a sip of whiskey and chuckled.

'In trouble again, are we?'

✳✳✳

A week passed, and I still hadn't made contact with either Sylvia or Chris. I hadn't stopped thinking of Sylvia, remembering our meetings and missing her. One afternoon, after collecting Rex from school, I found myself leaving Rex with my mother and strolling onto the common. Taking a seat on the bench with my back to the house, I started to think that just maybe she was missing me, too.

I reached inside my bag and took out a copy of Jack Kerouac's *On the Road* and turned the pages until I got to the middle. I sensed footsteps approaching me and looked up into Sylvia's aquamarine eyes, and my heart thumped.

'Good choice,' she said, nodding at my book before taking a seat next to me. 'I hope you haven't been avoiding us, Emily.'

I glanced at her perfect make-up, flared jeans and cowboy boots and felt a pang of envy. 'It's been difficult at home.'

'Mmm,' she mused. 'You don't need to keep away. We had a lovely day the other week. Did you not enjoy it, too? Emily, you've been through a lot with Rex and are more than entitled to experience some joy in your life.'

'One good turn deserves another.'
Russian proverb

Chapter Thirty-Six

One evening after Rex went to bed, I was startled by the sound of tapping on the kitchen door, and creeping into the room, I saw Laurence waiting outside for me. Ushering him inside the house, it seemed like a normal Friday evening when he would drop by the house to see me.

'Distillers is appealing to other families to apply for compensation,' said Laurence, taking a seat at the table. 'Sylvia and Chris have already issued a writ against Distillers, using Pollyanna's health problems as a basis for their case.'

'How do you know all this, Laurence?' I asked.

'I still have contacts there, Emily,' he said, reaching for an apple from the fruit bowl. His eyes looked weary from his busy workweek, and I worried about how these regular visits were putting a strain on his health.

'Promise me you won't get involved in this.' He placed the fruit aside to take hold of my hand.

Without another word we strolled out of the kitchen and headed down the hallway to Rex's room.

'Hello, Dad,' said Rex, still wide awake in bed. 'Will you still be here tomorrow?' he asked.

'Yes, I think I will,' Laurence replied as his hand touched mine.

'And we can go to the park together?' Rex asked.

Laurence gave a nod, and I felt sure that with a little patience everything would get better at last.

✳✳✳

'Why didn't you tell me about Distillers?' I asked as I greeted Sylvia the following afternoon on the common, after Laurence had gone home.

'Who told you about the writ? It was Laurence, our former Distillers man,' she smiled, rather smugly. I felt my cheeks flush in shame.

'I'm sorry,' I said.

'Chris and I have been invited by our solicitor to apply for a writ out of time, as they call it.' She offered a sardonic laugh.

'What does that mean?' I nudged closer to her on the grass and she took my hand. We were silent for a moment.

'The thing is, Emily, our case against Distillers is a weak one. Pollyanna lives with us, and we're pretty well-off.'

'Sylvia,' I whispered, and thought of pulling away, except for some reason I didn't move. I only looked into her eyes and uttered the words I knew she was waiting to hear. 'I'll issue a writ against Distillers myself. If the three of us join together, we could make a difference, couldn't we?'

The next few days I was plagued with a sickness that I hadn't experienced in years. One afternoon after returning home from the doctor's I hurried to my bedroom, removing my coat and shoes. I pulled off my dress to reveal a long white slip. Then I crouched down onto the floor. My hand travelled down to my stomach. I traced my supple skin. I felt for the heartbeat that thumped inside of what I imagined to be a barely formed embryo. Suspended deep inside of me, it absorbed and assimilated every substance that passed my lips from that clump of blood and flesh, the lifeline of oxygen and innocence that connected my body to the baby's, and I felt my tears break.

'There are no secrets that time does not reveal.'
Jean Racine

Chapter Thirty-Seven

My mother was the first person to spot my pregnancy. She pulled me aside one afternoon as I arrived home with Rex from Sylvia's house. I allowed her to wheel Rex out into the garden, and then we sat at the table in my little kitchen, cupping our steaming tea.

'How far gone are you?' she asked casually, as I spooned sugar into my tea to counteract a wave of nausea.

I had anticipated a negative response from my mother about my pregnancy after the way she had reacted to me spending the day with Chris and Sylvia. I felt she had never really accepted Laurence into the family, because of his different views on medicine, so I could only imagine how she felt about me having another child with him, especially since Laurence and I were still separated.

'About six weeks,' I answered finally, taking the cup to my lips as a distraction from her gaze. My mother's beaming smile surprised me. Had it really been that easy to tell her, I thought, swallowing another mouthful of sugary tea? Perhaps being pregnant again wouldn't be so bad after all. This could work out all right. I absorbed what I thought were her usual positive vibes; but as she turned to me, I realised with a growing sense of fear that I had been wrong.

'Well, you'll have to tell Rex. It might be difficult for him when the baby comes. You will need to prepare him for that. And Laurence, you'll have to tell him, too. How do you think he'll feel about being a father again?' My mother's smile had evaporated into one of her icy frowns.

'Actually, I don't know, Mummy. I mean, he was excited about being a father when I was pregnant with Rex, but he's changed since then.'

'Yes,' she replied, sipping her tea, while watching for my reaction. I looked away, thinking how silly I had been to think that talking about my pregnancy would be easy, when my life these last few years had been so difficult.

'So what are you going to do?'

'Laurence will have to move in with us. I won't go back to Richmond. I'll never go back there.' I shook my head, feeling a sense of failure with each word. I shuffled in my chair and looked out into the garden at Rex. Watching him sketch using his new set of pencils, I envied his freedom to be himself. I had never been allowed that luxury, not even as a child, and now this pregnancy meant my freedom was further slipping away.

'I will need to discuss this with your father. The basement was only meant for you and Rex. Will there be enough space for you all down here? Wouldn't it be better for you to move upstairs?'

'We will cope. I'm not moving upstairs,' I said, firmly.

'You are not very flexible about any of this, are you? I never imagined you and Laurence would follow this lifestyle of yours. You wouldn't find all parents being so understanding.'

'Lifestyle?' I shook my head, feeling bile rise to my throat. I poured myself another cup of tea. How I hated being pregnant. I resented all of its restrictions upon my life, but I especially hated having this conversation with my mother.

'I'm just saying there are a lot of matters to consider. First you'll need to tell Laurence about the baby, and this time he'll need to take responsibility for you both and Rex as well.'

'I'll do my best. Laurence has been getting better recently, and his evening visits with Rex are making a difference, I'm sure of that.'

'Good, that's good. You've been very patient, Emily, through all of this,' my mother said, touching my arm gently.

I bit down on my lip, resisting my tears again. 'I'll do what's right. You can be sure of that.'

'Then why have you issued a writ against Distillers?'

'I—I,' I stammered.

'Because when you have that conversation with Laurence about the baby, you'll also need to tell him about your court case against Distillers.'

'I am aware of that.' I released a sigh.

'Because I am wondering what or who motivated you to risk all the good work you have achieved with Laurence so far,' my mother asked, searching my face for an answer which of course I didn't have. I could only look down into my cup in defeat, thinking of the sorry mess I had found myself in and not having a clue about how I was going to get myself out of it.

Later, I went upstairs to see my father, and we sat together in his consulting room. I was reminded of all those years ago, presenting Rex to him and Dr Dhillon.

'So how are you feeling?'

'Scared,' I confessed.

'That's only to be expected after Rex, but if you look after yourself, this pregnancy could work to heal the past. This is the time for forgiveness,' he said.

I inhaled the scent of lavender and stifled another nauseous wave. I felt tears well in my eyes. My hand fell to my stomach, and I rubbed it gently.

'Emily,' he coaxed, 'it doesn't have to be like last time. The forgiveness has to start with you.'

'I can't forgive myself for what I did, not ever.'

He got up and moved his chair beside mine. 'Have you told Laurence about the baby?'

'No, not yet. I will. I just need to find the right moment.'

'With everything happening, there are not going to be many of those for now. Maybe you're having second thoughts about the lawsuit?'

'I have to do that for Rex.'

'It's not really us, is it, going up against the drug companies? For the most part we go through life without making too much fuss, treating patients and offering help and advice where we can. I probably don't need to remind you that being pregnant is a vulnerable time, and makes you more prone to picking up on certain atmospheres.'

'I didn't think back then, I just took it all on blind faith. By the time I realised what I had done, it was too late for Rex. But I love him so much, it's incredible; yet that doesn't stop me from acknowledging that I owe him a terrible truth.'

'We can tell him together as a family, Emily. There's no need to take this to court.'

'In years to come the world will forget about Thalidomide and what Sylvia and I went through with our children. It will be relegated to a blip in scientific history. We can't allow that to happen. The world has to know that a terrible mistake was made, and our children suffered because of it.'

***

The following Friday, having given up on an appearance from Laurence, I drifted to Rex's room to check that he was asleep. I caught the glow of his torch and the odd shape of his body under the blanket. I hesitated for a moment, hearing his concentrated gulps of breath before approaching his bed. Then, I folded back his blanket and sheet to reveal his curled body clasping a copy of *Tom Sawyer*.

'Aw, Mummy,' he whined, 'it's not that late.'

'Rex, it's past nine, and you have swimming class first thing in the morning,' I reminded him. Turning on his table lamp, I sat on the edge of his bed.

Rex pushed himself up the mattress and folded his arms across his chest. I took the book and torch and placed the items down on the bedside table.

'Is Dad coming tonight?'

'You enjoy his visits, don't you?'

Rex's hand reached for mine; his long fingers moulded into my knuckles.

'Yes, but you know, it wasn't that bad at Chailey. I mean I would miss you, and Nanny and Gramps and Pollyanna, too; but don't tell her so.' His eyes widened.

'Rex.' A sob caught in my throat and my hand tightened in his.

***

I flicked on the kitchen light to a loud rap on the door. The clock read quarter to ten.

Laurence had on a black woollen coat and carried his brown briefcase. 'How could you—' he demanded, his eyes reddened from tears and work.

'Laurence,' I said, 'come inside, Rex is still awake if you want to go and see him.' I touched his arm and felt him shudder.

'—betray me like that?' he finished.

'Please, Laurence. There's so much I have to tell you.'

'Why have you issued a writ against Distillers? I didn't shirk my responsibilities as a father, and if you needed more money, you only had to ask.'

'It's not about money,' I said, finding my voice at last.

'You want everyone to think that I'm responsible for what happened to Rex!' he cried.

'It's not like that.' I shook my head. 'I have to do this for Rex because I'm his mother. Distillers had a duty of care to Rex and me, and they let us down. This is not about you.'

'That's where you are wrong. This is exactly about me and what I didn't do!' he yelled.

'It wasn't your fault, Laurence, don't think that.'

I wrapped my arms around his neck and pressed my body to his. I felt his racing heart before he pushed me away.

'Tell that to your friend Sylvia. Good night, Emily,' he said and strode out of the house.

'It takes a strong person to say sorry,
and an even stronger person to forgive.'
Unknown

Chapter Thirty-Eight

My father and I decided to take Rex with us for my first visit to the solicitors in London. I had kept the details of their office in Cheapside safely in my handbag, so I allowed myself the pleasure of relaxing in the backseat of my father's old Rover. It had been awhile since my last road trip with Rex, and glancing at him now, I noticed the changes. His face was leaner than before. His T-shirt clung tighter to his shoulders and stomach. No longer using his artificial legs, he grappled with what nature had given him, little legs that hung limply from his cut-down Levi's. I watched him suck on a lollipop that had been a parting gift from Pollyanna. Then, as usual for our car journeys, he reached for a sketchpad and pencils. In doing so, his hand brushed mine and he offered me a bright smile.

'Where are we heading, Mummy?'

'To the city. I think you'll like it, for there will be lots of tall buildings for you to sketch,' I replied, caressing my stomach. Was it really the baby or my first experience with the legal system that was causing me the most anxiety?

'Who are we seeing?' he asked, choosing a grey pencil from his tin.

I took a deep breath against my beating heart and chose my words carefully. 'I have to see a gentleman to discuss your future. We have to talk about what will happen when you're grown up.' I glanced at him, anxious in case he pressed me for further details, knowing how inquisitive he was.

'Well, that's easy,' he grinned. 'I'm going to marry Pollyanna, and Dad will stay and take care of you and the baby.' He shrugged, making a sketch of a grey, overcast morning.

'If only,' I mouthed at my father in the mirror. He chuckled, which worked to calm my nerves a bit. Turning to Rex, I clung to his childish musing in hope that I could get through the day ahead.

✳✳✳

My father parked the car down Milk Street beside a row of Victorian terrace houses. A gaggle of children flew out into the road dressed in jeans and tank tops. They chased their ball to the kerb before approaching our car with caution. Their small hands stroked the gleaming black paintwork in awe.

My father got out of the car and they scooted away to the other side of the road, loitering instead in front of a development of 1930s semi-detached dwellings. I saw my father reach inside his wool coat and take out a collection of new coins. The children held up their silver with pride, and, approaching our car, they formed a human fortress. Only then did I slide out of the car, and my father went to the boot for Rex's wheelchair. Rex heaved his small body from the car to his wheelchair with relative ease. Then his hands spun the wheels, and the children stood aside and offered us a collective, penetrating stare. I took over from Rex, and with my eyes down we hurried towards the main thoroughfare.

The solicitor's office was situated down the southern one-way street in the Old Jewry. Stopping for a moment, I glanced towards the row of limestone buildings and was impressed by how beautiful the stone reflected the errant sunshine of a winter's afternoon. I wondered about what lay beyond their polished front doors, and if crossing the threshold could really change my life.

The receptionist was dressed in a red suit and sidestepped awkwardly around Rex as all three of us entered the blue-carpeted waiting room. On the table sat a pile of *Home and Garden* magazines and a bowl of boiled sweets. Rex looked around bemused, so I moved some of the chairs, which allowed his wheelchair to fit around the table. Then we took our seats beside Rex and waited for the solicitor to come and greet us.

The solicitor emerged from his office a short while later and greeted my father and me with a firm handshake. He glanced briefly at Rex with a frown before his attention turned back to me.

'Hello, Mrs Alexander, I'm Mr Hardy. I'm the solicitor for the Thalidomide families. Perhaps you would like to accompany me to my office.' He glanced towards my father and Rex.

'Is it all right for my father to wait here with Rex?'

'Of course,' Mr Hardy said. 'I'll get my secretary to find some magazines for your son to read.'

'I can do my drawing,' Rex piped up, taking out his pencils and pad from his rucksack.

'All right,' Mr Hardy said. Leaving my father and Rex in the waiting area, I followed Mr Hardy into his office. The office allowed us a view of the narrow street below, which I focused upon as I waited for our meeting to begin. It had been difficult for me to prepare for the meeting, and as such I couldn't help my heart from racing, worried about saying the wrong thing.

'So, what makes you want to apply for compensation now?' Seated opposite me, his cold blue eyes drifted over my duffle coat that I hadn't attempted to remove. I folded my hands in my lap neatly and took several deep breaths before answering his question.

'Well, for a long time I didn't want anything to do with Distillers. I had my parents, and Rex's father has always supported him financially. But as he has grown, I've come to think differently about Distillers.'

'Mrs Alexander, I admire your courage; of course I do. What you've been through with Rex must have been awful, and bringing him here today was brave. Of course I will advocate on your behalf and that of all the remaining families involved. But I have to warn you that you can only expect to receive 40 percent of the 100 percent figure, and the final figure will be shared between all of the families in a charitable trust fund. If you're looking for some kind of apology, you won't find it with Distillers.'

I looked at him for the longest moment for some kind of emotional reaction to what he had just said, but saw none. Tears rose to my eyes in disappointment. Did our children mean so little to him? I bit down on my lip before nodding my thanks for the support he was offering us. Then without a word of response I hurried from his office and made my way down the corridor to my father and Rex. I shook my head at my father and began to wheel Rex out of the building to the astonishment of both the receptionist and my father. My father rushed behind me and tried to stop me by keeping a steady pace.

'I'm sorry, Emily,' he said, reaching for my hand, causing Rex and me to come to a halt down Milk Street.

'Don't say that, Daddy! It means it's over, and it can't be without a proper fight,' I said, feeling my voice rise with anger. 'I won't let them intimidate me after what they've done, not ever,' I cried.

Rex's eyes widened in surprise as we returned to the car, and my father drove us home in silence.

*'The greatness of a man's power
is the measure of his surrender.'*
William Booth

Chapter Thirty-Nine
November 1971

I chose to wear a tweed suit to the meeting in London, fortunate at that stage in my pregnancy, to be able to camouflage my bump. I took a seat next to Sylvia and Chris amongst the heaving crowd of anxious parents.

As Mr Hardy, QC, approached the podium, Sylvia reached for my hand. 'Don't worry,' she whispered. 'Remember, you have every right to be here.'

I took a breath against my fluttering butterflies. This was about Rex and no one else.

'Ladies and gentlemen, I'm glad to see so many of you here today. On behalf of your solicitors, Kimber Bull, let me reiterate the importance of working together on this, so we can come to a speedy resolution. I appreciate the cost and strain this is placing on all of the families affected by Thalidomide.'

'How can they understand what it's like for us?' Chris questioned.

I took in Chris' weary blue eyes, knowing a little more by now about how having Pollyanna had changed his life.

'It is important that we agree collectively on a settlement. I do have to inform you that this is an all-or-nothing agreement. Once I have gone through the main agenda, I will need a show of hands. Remember, if you decline, your neighbours will want to know why.'

'This isn't the way to do things,' said Sylvia, leaning closer to me. 'You look stunning, by the way. Have you heard from Laurence?' she whispered.

'No,' I whispered back.

'Then have another think about my proposition, Emily.' I sighed, feeling the butterflies in my stomach multiply at Sylvia's demands on top of everything else.

'They are treating us like factory workers, assuming that we don't have the intelligence to work out that we are being cheated left, right, and centre. They'll probably get away with it, too, if no one has the gumption to stand up to them.' Chris shook his head.

'I do have to remind you of your claim to legal aid, should you refuse to sign,' warned Mr Hardy.

'That's it, threaten us with bankruptcy; that's bound to get everyone to sign,' Chris said, turning his attention towards me in curiosity. But I turned my head away, feeling just as angry as I had been at the solicitor's office.

I thought about the Thalidomide children at Chailey and their bewildered faces at being separated from their parents, and a feeling of anger returned. They deserved something better than that. I rushed from the room and headed outside to the toot of car horns from London's rush-hour traffic. A hand on my shoulder made me tremble as my emotions rose to the surface, so turning around I was relieved to see Sylvia and Chris approach my side.

'Don't worry, we are not going to sign either,' said Chris, offering me a tender smile, an assurance of sorts that everything would be all right.

✳✳✳

But the following week, because of my refusal to sign, I was summoned to Mr Nichols' law chambers in London. He had recently replaced Mr Hardy, so I knew little about him as I walked into his office. I took a seat opposite him and felt his scrutinising gaze fall to my thickened waist. This was definitely worse than my last solicitor's meeting had been, as by now people would be able to work out that I was pregnant. So I placed a hand protectively over my stomach as those butterflies returned to frighten me again.

'Mrs Alexander.' He cleared his throat. In that moment, I longed for Sylvia's determination, certain that she would have offered some well-executed remark about how the settlement didn't match Pollyanna's birth defects, and her refusal to sign was the only moral path to choose. But now that I was pregnant, would she still be as supportive as before, if I couldn't go along with her proposition?

'Well,' said Mr Nichols, 'why haven't you signed?'

I blinked back my tears. I was better than that. I took a breath to summon my courage as I turned to the solicitor.

'Mr Nichols, can you guarantee that my son will receive an annual income?'

'No,' he clipped.

'What about a lump sum?'

'No,' he replied. 'A charitable trust fund will be set up for the children by Distillers, from which they will be able to draw money, dependent upon their needs. At present we are looking at a sum of around £3.25 million, to be paid into the fund over ten years. This is the best deal that can be negotiated, Mrs Alexander, and that's why I urge you to sign as quickly as possible.'

'And if I don't?' I waited, hesitantly.

'Mrs Alexander.' He leaned over his desk at me. 'Haven't you listened to anything I've said?'

I shrunk back in my chair, my confidence evaporating with every second that I spent in his awful office. 'If you continue to refuse to sign, we'll be obliged to send a welfare officer to your home to determine your child's needs. Is that what you really want?'

I couldn't speak for several minutes, and when I did, my voice rose louder than ever before from an accumulation of years of silence.

'My son deserves better than this,' I yelled squarely at the solicitor. 'If this is all you can come up with, then Rex might as well get nothing,' I cried as I strode from his office. Hot tears finally broke free and I let out a scream, not caring who heard me. My son had been failed before he was born. I was determined he wouldn't be failed again.

'Patience is the key to solutions.'
Arab proverb

Chapter Forty

The lady barely looked my way as she strolled into the hallway. Dressed in a navy suit, she followed my mother and me down the steps and into the basement. The thump of her stout shoes told me all I needed to know: that she was from the welfare department.

We went into Rex's playroom, and I offered her a seat on the sofa. I grabbed a couple of kitchen chairs for my mother and me. We waited in anticipation for the visit to begin.

'You have a fine home, Mrs Miles,' the lady said, and taking out a notepad from her bag, she began making notes in silence. 'This is where Rex plays?'

'Yes, we have given Rex the space to learn and play. We feel that is vital for his development.'

The lady turned to us. 'Can I be frank with you?' She offered a tight smile. 'You are far better off than most of the Thalidomide families. Your son is a fortunate child.'

'If you can call my grandson being born with shortened legs and never being able to walk as fortunate—'

The lady raised a hand to interrupt. 'Of course, I appreciate your difficulties. I'm just not sure what Distillers can offer you at this point.'

'An apology for what happened,' I said. I crossed and uncrossed my legs nervously opposite the welfare officer.

The lady stared at me with her Biro held in midair for a moment, before shifting on the brown sofa.

'Perhaps it would help if we saw the child's bedroom and garden.'

'His name is Rex. I can show you around and answer any questions you may have,' I said, getting up and accompanying the lady out of the room and down the hallway. With each footstep I felt my heart pound. Anger was all right, but today could mean Rex being taken from us and placed in a care home, and that was enough to make an attempt at least on my part at keeping my emotions in check.

We reached the bathroom and stood inside the room for a moment to glance at the metal bars on the side of the toilet, the low sink, and custom bath seat which my father had installed many years ago for Rex. Then stepping out into the hallway, the woman's eyes darted around as we strode into Rex's bedroom. There she glanced around at the room, taking in his narrow bed, a desk scattered with paper and pencils, while below her feet was a collage of chalky scribbles, old noughts and crosses and hangman games. In silence, she paced the room as if searching for clues amongst the coded messages for evidence in Distillers' defence.

I blinked my eyes, weary from tears and lack of sleep.

'The child—Rex,' she corrected herself. 'He has lived here since birth?'

I bit down on my lip. It was that statement which got to me the most, and I felt the tears escape. I couldn't hold them back nor did I have the energy for anger; years of caring for Rex and being pregnant again had seen to that. I wondered if she could see me cry, but still I avoided her eyes.

'He was in Chailey for a few months when he was seven and we were struggling to find him a school.'

She made a note of that in her book.

I dabbed my eyes with a tissue and saw her look of sympathy. 'I'm sorry,' she said. 'All the Thalidomide mothers cry. I have to tell them it's nothing personal. It's just the questions we have been given by Distillers, that's all.'

I nodded.

'Would you like to see the garden?' I asked, and she seemed relieved when I guided her back down the hallway. Opening the side door, we hurried down the steps and onto the patio.

'He could do with a ramp for his wheelchair,' she said, and wrote that down in her notebook before turning to me with another tight smile.

'Thank you, Mrs Alexander, for showing me around your home. Your solicitor will be in touch shortly.'

'What happens now?' I asked, feeling fresh tears come to my eyes.

'Kimber Bull will advise you on all legal matters concerning your claim.' The lady, sensing I was about to cry again, rushed back inside the house and strode out of the front door with the same determination that she had when she arrived.

'Well, that didn't achieve much,' my mother said, touching my arm in sympathy, before offering me a hug.

'On the contrary, Mummy, it was the first step towards an apology.'

✳✳✳

Later, I met up with Sylvia and Chris on Brighton Pier.

'Have you had the welfare visit yet?' asked Sylvia.

I nodded, sadly.

'Well, I hope she didn't deter you from taking action,' she probed, offering me a fixed stare. I glanced over at Chris and caught his gentle smile of encouragement.

'She didn't.'

'That's good. Now tell us, are you pregnant, Emily?'

I felt Sylvia's eyes fall to my stomach, but a thickening around the middle was the only sign so far of my pregnancy, and one that I had hoped to keep secret for a little while longer. She looked at me with disappointment, knowing that I had left it too late to take her up on her proposition; and worse still, our visits would be interrupted by Laurence, a situation of neither our choosing.

'Congratulations!' said Sylvia, and as an afterthought she offered me a hug. Sylvia pulled away from me and strode ahead to the boom of the amusement arcade, leaving me behind with Chris.

'Sylvia and I contemplated having another child after Pollyanna. But in the end we both agreed that with my job, it wouldn't have been fair on Sylvia to be left looking after another child whilst I was working in London.'

Feeling my sorrow rise after a trying day, I turned from Chris and pressed my hand on the wrought iron. Wordless, I leaned on the railings to gaze at the sea beyond, hoping that would be enough to calm my racing heart. I glanced ahead at a flock of seagulls taking flight.

'What have the two of you been chatting about?' asked Sylvia, nudging herself into a space between us. She wrapped an arm around my shoulder, and all three of us watched the tide creep out in silence.

*'People only bring up your past
when they are intimidated by your present.'*
Unknown

Chapter Forty-One
1972

Sylvia, Chris and I were summoned to appear before the High Court on a bright March morning as representatives of the dissident group comprising six sets of parents who had refused to sign the document of acceptance of Distillers' offer of compensation. I had turned down my father's suggestion of him accompanying me to London, choosing instead to travel to court with Sylvia and Chris.

Sylvia shifted on the bench beside me, awaiting her turn to be cross-examined by Mr Nichols. I felt her take my hand into hers, sensing the fluttering of fear as her ringed fingers kneaded mine. The baby kicked, and my free hand went to my stomach protectively. With the flicker of my eyelashes, I prayed to God for Rex and for the strength to get through the day as fear of losing my son loomed large in my mind.

Mr Justice Clifton turned to address the court. 'Ladies and gentlemen, we are all well aware of the 1968 test case involving the Satherley child, which I believe reflected credit on all concerned. It is therefore my opinion that any resistance to settle is evidence of an unreasonable act on behalf of the parents.'

'I give notice that my clients wish to appeal,' said Mr Matthew Ogdon, QC. He had recently been engaged by Chris to act for the families who had so far refused to sign. Glancing at the young barrister, I felt all of my hopes rested with him. I released a deep-seated sigh, unwilling to consider the alternative outcome of today.

Mr Nichols rose. 'My client, Distillers, has assured me that they will not press for the parents to pay court costs. Of course, my client's generosity would not continue in the event of an appeal. Not that that is a threat—'

'Mr Nichols, if that is not a threat, I don't know what is, and such opinions should be kept to oneself until it can no longer influence a decision about the appeal,' said Mr Justice Clifton.

Mr Nichols reddened and strode up to us, standing before Chris and Sylvia. 'This trial is costing £200 a day, Mr and Mrs Watersmith. How does that make you feel, knowing that unlike yourselves, many of the families won't be able to continue without legal aid?'

'The fact that the families affected by Thalidomide have been left struggling for ten years by Distillers is the reason why we are here today,' said Chris.

'Do you support your husband on this?' Mr Nichols turned to Sylvia.

'Yes, I do; for this is about our daughter, Pollyanna, and all the Thalidomide children that have been let down by Distillers.'

Mr Nichols moved on, and I knew it was my turn to be cross-examined. I was suddenly aware that unlike Chris and Sylvia, I had come alone. I pressed my lips together to summon the courage to face the solicitor. I felt Sylvia's hand squeeze mine, dispelling my fears with her tender touch. I was strong enough to fight for Rex. I really could do this.

'Mrs Alexander, perhaps you would like to share with the court your resistance to sign. Can you assure us it has nothing to do with the fact that your husband was a former employee of the company?'

It was a mild day, but I felt the scorch of a midsummer's afternoon as I faced Mr Nichols' probing grey eyes. A rush of heat burnt my cheeks.

'Mr Nichols, I am fortunate due to my parents' wealth and class. It wasn't money or antagonism that prompted me to seek compensation from Distillers, more guilt at my own lack of thought for my unborn child.' My hand went to my stomach, feeling the baby flutter inside so even the judge raised an eyebrow. Mr Nichols hadn't moved from his spot, clearly mulling over the benefit of further cross-examination, and after a moment or two he returned to his seat.

During the recess, as I took some fresh air on the steps outside the court, Laurence approached me. Rushing towards me, he pulled me into his arms. In silence, there was just the sensation of the baby kicking inside me as a reminder of what had brought us to this point.

As we drew apart, his hand went to my stomach. 'I'm sorry about how I behaved towards you and for not supporting you in court today,' he said and hugged me again, before setting me free.

'It's time for you to come home, Laurence. We are both too tired to fight this anymore,' I said.

'What are you saying, Emily? What do you want me to do?'

'Move into my parents' home with Rex and me. This baby must surely mean it's time for a fresh start,' I said, offering him another hug, and I looked over my shoulder at Sylvia as she stood on the steps behind me.

Returning to the courtroom with Laurence, the judge turned to us. 'It is my opinion that the six dissenting families should be removed from their position of "next friend" to their children, and the official solicitor to be appointed in their place.'

'No,' I shook my head. 'That could mean losing Rex to a care home.'

I doubled over and felt Laurence caressing my back to comfort me as tears ran down my cheeks, and I felt the sensation of my first spotting of blood.

*'Forgiveness does not change the past,
but it does enlarge the future.'*
Paul Boese

Chapter Forty-Two

Laurence took me to St Thomas' Hospital and held my hand as the doctor searched for my baby's heartbeat. With tears running down my cheeks, all I could do was lay still and hope the baby would be all right. Laurence stayed with me most of the time, only leaving to telephone my parents and tell them what had happened.

It wasn't until late afternoon that my mother arrived with Rex. She wheeled him to my bedside before leaving us alone to talk. Lying still as instructed by the doctor, I glanced ahead at a group of nurses hurrying down the ward.

I felt Rex's hand edge towards my stomach as if unsure whether it was safe or not to touch me. I blinked away my tears, frightened more than ever of letting go of my emotions.

'Do you remember going to Roehampton as a little boy for your first set of artificial limbs?' I asked, feeling the baby flutter in my tummy. A sign which I held on to that everything was all right.

'Not really.' He shook his head.

'Well, you were only a toddler then. Dr Donahue took us in his car.'

'I hated those legs.'

'I know.' My hand found his and I felt less frightened. I wasn't alone in this dreadful place I hated.

'This is about me. It's my fault about the baby.' Rex lowered his head, something I hadn't seen him do up to that point.

'No,' I said, turning his face to mine. His eyes watered with tears. It had always been about the two of us, and now Laurence was coming home. I released a sigh. I did so much of that these days. I took his hand and placed it on my tummy. I watched his long fingers spread out.

'It feels funny,' he laughed.

'That's the baby kicking his legs.' A smile came to my lips and I shook my head at such a drastic change of emotion.

'I know the baby won't be like me. Pollyanna and I, we're kind of unique. I understand that.'

'Rex,' I took a deep breath, pushing aside my emotions. 'I think you're old enough to understand the full story of why your legs developed differently from how they should. I have to tell you, because you have a right to know the truth. You remember the children at Chailey?' I paused, wondering how much he had worked out himself. 'And the boys at the swimming pool that we see? Well, their mothers took a pill when they were pregnant.'

He nodded.

I took another deep breath, pacing myself for the hardest part. 'When I was pregnant with you I got very sick, and the doctor gave me the same pill as those mothers. It was called Thalidomide, and although it made me feel better and they thought it was safe and you'd be okay, for some reason it stopped your legs from growing properly. I'm so sorry, my darling, for I'd do anything to go back and never have taken those pills.' Fat tears rolled down my cheeks.

'Don't cry, Mummy, it wasn't your fault,' Rex whispered. He leaned his face on my tummy and his arms stretched up to wrap around my neck. We remained like that for what seemed a long time, waiting for my sobs to subside.

'Come, Rex, your parents need to talk. Let's go and have some supper,' my mother said as she returned to my bedside with Laurence.

Rex disentangled himself from me and slid himself into his wheelchair before turning to his father.

'Dad!' he beamed.

'Hope you've been looking after your mother.' Laurence bent down, his hand grazing Rex's briefly before he pulled away.

'I felt the baby kick,' said Rex.

'That's wonderful news. But your mother and I have some more good news to share with you. I am going to be living with you and your mother from now on at your grandparents' house in Brighton.'

'Really, Dad?' Rex's eyes widened with surprise. He looked to me to see if what Laurence was saying was the truth. I offered him my best smile and reached for Laurence's hand.

'We are going to be a proper family from now on—no more separations,' I promised.

Rex offered me another hug and turned to Laurence with joy. There was a moment when Laurence could have offered a hand to Rex, but instead he shuffled awkwardly on his feet. Give him time, I thought, and it will work out all right.

'Why don't we leave your parents to talk for a bit, Rex?' my mother said. She nodded to Laurence, and without another word she wheeled Rex down the ward and headed towards the corridor.

'I told Rex about Thalidomide, I thought it was time he knew the truth.'

Laurence lay down beside me. His hand reached over to caress my stomach.

'They think I'm an unfit mother.' Fresh tears came to my eyes, causing my head to throb.

'I let you and Rex down. But that is all going to change,' Laurence said. 'I have put in a statement to the court about what a dedicated mother you've been to Rex. We'll do everything possible to stop them from removing Rex from your care.'

'Do you mean that, Laurence? And you will move in with us and try to be Rex's father?'

'Yes, Emily, I'm determined to try harder, starting from today,' he said, pressing his lips onto mine to seal his promise.

*'Just because you fail once
doesn't mean you're gonna fail at everything.'*
Marilyn Monroe

Chapter Forty-Three

I was discharged from hospital the following week to the care of my parents and Laurence. They imposed a strict regime of bed rest and only allowed me to move from my bed to a recliner in the garden for my constitutional fresh air.

My parents took over with Rex, and I was prescribed the homeopathic remedy of Secale by my father to prevent any further haemorrhaging. For the moment with Laurence home, I dared to forget about Distillers as we settled into a new routine of Laurence working until late most weekdays, but spending the whole weekend at home with us. I felt my mood lift and started to believe that we had turned a corner in our lives.

But one afternoon in late March, I was disturbed by the sound of footsteps as I lounged on the patio with a book.

'Emily,' Sylvia said, taking a seat to my right. 'I hope I'm not disturbing you. I'm sorry I haven't been over sooner. Tell me everything's all right with the baby?'

I held my tummy and pushed myself up in the recliner. 'Yes, of course,' I sighed. 'So tell me what's been going on with you?' I forced a smile at her disturbance to my peace.

'We thought you'd want to know,' Chris said and moved his chair to my left. 'We haven't given up. We have the money to lodge an appeal,' he beamed.

'What?' I gazed at him as memories of our day in court flashed through my mind in fear, and I felt myself frown.

'It's not over, Emily, not by a long shot,' said Sylvia from the other side. 'We are going to lodge an appeal on behalf of all the families; that's why we are here now. It's more important now than ever that we have your support.'

I was unsure if I had the strength for that anymore. I had Laurence home, and that had to mean more than any compensation deal.

'Yes, of course, but after what happened last time, do you think we could win?' I held my breath, feeling myself unwittingly drawn into their scheme.

'Emily, we know what you went through with the baby.' Sylvia touched my stomach briefly. 'But we can't give up. We must join together and prove that we were right not to sign and that we only acted in our children's best interest.'

I glanced over at Rex, watching as he sped down the ramp and onto the patio; and everything, including Laurence, that mattered the most was what had happened to Rex through Distillers' negligence. I turned back to Chris and Sylvia. They gazed at me in expectation, and without a moment's hesitation, I nodded my consent. Then my hand reached for theirs, and we formed a human chain of solidarity. It wasn't until my mother approached that we pulled away, and even then we didn't say anything for the longest moment.

'There's going to be an appeal,' I said, turning to my mother. 'And this time we are not giving up.'

I felt my optimism return as a smile broke on my lips. I could do this with Sylvia and Chris, and at the same time I could have Laurence home with us. Everything was changing, and at long last it would work out in my favour, I thought, without realising the long battle I still had ahead of me.

'Do not dwell on the past, do not dream of the future,
concentrate the mind on the present moment.'
Buddha

Chapter Forty-Four
1972

Sylvia arrived at my house during the early hours of a cloudy April morning. Laurence was already up and dressed for work, leaving only Rex and me to be woken from our beds. She strode into my bedroom with my mother at her heels.

'Emily has to rest, and that's on doctor's orders.'

Laurence came into the bedroom.

I reached for my lace-edged gown and wrapped it around myself to camouflage my well-rounded bump. Rex came into the room with a book in his lap, and after a fleeting glance at my crowded bedside, he positioned his wheelchair by the long sash window and opened his book.

'Hello Sylvia,' Laurence said, and seeing Rex by the window, he went up to our son.

'How about us going into the garden and leaving your mother and her friend to talk for a bit,' Laurence suggested.

Rex turned his wheelchair to look at us and gave an emphatic nod. His eyes twinkled with joy at spending time alone with his father.

I felt myself brighten with each passing minute. This was always how I had imagined it to be in my mind's eye, and now there was a chance of it becoming a reality. I felt my biggest smile come to my lips watching Laurence wheel Rex out of the bedroom as they made their way into the garden.

'Hurry up and get dressed. I will take you all out for breakfast.' Sylvia nodded towards the window. From my bed I watched Laurence crouch in front of Rex's wheelchair and talk to him. I saw my son laugh. What progress they were making already.

'Pollyanna and Chris can join us, too,' Sylvia said, interrupting my thoughts.

It had only needed a push from me to tell Laurence he could do it. I turned back to Sylvia.

'What's this all about?' I swung my feet to the floor and approached Sylvia for a hug. She embraced me, and I felt her tremble with excitement.

'Chris and I have won, that's what! The appeals court found unanimously for us! See, we were right not to sign, and the appeal judges agreed. This is a day for celebration. A day that belongs to our children.' She bounced up and down on the floorboards, holding tightly to my hands.

My pounding heart threatened to expel from my chest in exhilaration, even as the baby offered a sharp kick as a warning, if I needed one, to be cautious that such joy couldn't possibly last.

'Emily,' my mother broke in, 'be careful.' She threw Sylvia a stern gaze. 'Or you'll lose that baby.'

I cupped my belly and pulled away from Sylvia.

'Do you know what this means, Emily? It means that we now have a chance of a fair settlement from Distillers for our children. This is the moment we have been waiting for all these years.'

'Freedom lies in being bold.'
Robert Frost

Chapter Forty-Five

Sylvia and I sat on the patio sipping our lemonade during a bright spring afternoon with the promise of summer ahead. Already in the late stages of pregnancy, I rubbed my tummy as the baby somersaulted inside.

'Chris thinks we should try again to get consent from the other families,' Sylvia said. I caught her faraway gaze: a sign of her losing hope. Despite the success of the appeal, her optimism of a fair settlement had been dashed, only to be replaced with a further back and forth between our legal team and Distillers.

'What are our chances?'

'I don't know, Emily, but at the moment our only hope is that with everyone's support, Kimber Bull could negotiate with Distillers for a better deal.'

'Perhaps there is another way.'

Sylvia gazed at me curiously. 'What's your thinking?'

'What if we went to the press with our story?'

'You know we can't do that, Emily.' Sylvia sighed. She was right. We had been advised to keep secret the details of our case.

'With Chris' contacts in publishing, we could break our silence and get our story out to the public.'

'What's this all about, Emily?'

'I look at Rex and see him growing up, and in the years since it happened, nothing has changed. How much longer can we really hold on and wait for our settlement?' I asked and bit down on my lip as sadness welled in my heart from having suffered too many disappointments already.

'I feel the same.' Sylvia reached for my hand. 'But speaking out could jeopardise everything for the other families.'

I nodded.

'I'm impressed, Emily, you have changed. Do you remember when I first told you to fight back?'

'Yes.' A smile formed on my lips, casting aside my sorrow for the moment at the memory of that afternoon nine years ago. 'It has always been about Rex. I had a choice in 1960 and I chose my son,' I brightened.

'Well, if we go ahead with this, it's not going to be easy for any of us, especially Laurence. Do you think you could get him on our side?'

'I don't know, Sylvia, but it's because of you that I have the courage to try. I'm the person I am now because of you and Chris.'

'Courage isn't having the strength to go on.
It is going on when you don't have the strength.'
Napoléon Bonaparte

Chapter Forty-Six

The next afternoon Laurence and I sat on the patio with a pot of tea and a plate of Garibaldis. I caressed my stomach to the sensation of a tight band around my tummy, a symptom, perhaps, of the notorious Braxton Hicks contractions. Although my pregnancy had been difficult, I felt in no hurry to give birth.

'I hear there's been a definite stalemate with the settlement from Distillers,' Laurence said. 'I was wrong to have been angry with you about the lawsuit. You just wanted justice for Rex, and getting to know him better as I have recently, I can see why. But for me it has always been so complicated.' He took my hand in his and wound his fingers through mine. 'You know I love you so much, Emily.'

I nodded, but still I couldn't return his sentiment.

'There's something that I have to tell you,' I said.

'I heard that you have become friendly with Sylvia and Chris.'

'I couldn't have gotten through it without them.'

'I failed you, didn't I?'

'No,' I shook my head. 'It has just taken you longer to come to terms with accepting Rex as he is. I understand that.'

'Emily, I'm not promising to be the perfect father. I know my weaknesses. But I won't let you down again.'

'There is one thing—and I don't want you to be angry with me, Laurence—but I have to tell you this. I want to tell our story, Laurence, and I want you to support me.'

✳✳✳

The following afternoon, Sylvia was waiting for me on the common. Chris drove us to the beach, and daring to take a short stroll by the sea, my heels crunched on the pebbles as I followed them to a row of deckchairs. I took a seat between the couple and regarded them closely, wondering if situations had been different, whether Laurence and I would have led the campaign.

'If you're serious about talking to the press, I have a contact at *The Sunday Times*,' said Chris.

'All right, but they will have to come to the house, for I'm in no state to travel.' I offered a laugh, concerned about how I would juggle the impeding interview with my imminent labour.

Sylvia squeezed my hand, filling me with newfound courage.

'How does Laurence feel about this now that he is living with you?' Chris asked. His blue eyes were tender, with none of Sylvia's intensity.

'I don't expect too much opposition from him because of the baby,' I said, rubbing my huge belly to settle my nerves.

'How did it go with Sylvia and Chris?' asked Laurence as we strolled along the beach the following evening. We found a deserted spot under the pier and felt the sea lap gently against my toes.

'He thinks he can set up a meeting for me with a journalist from *The Sunday Times*.'

'When the baby comes, I hope everything can return to normal again.'

'Life stopped being normal for me when Rex was born.' I sighed. I placed my hand below his, feeling our baby's rhythm of life. I wondered what kind of life we would have with the new baby, and whether Rex was a reminder that too much pain had happened for us to ever feel joy again as a family.

'Believe you can and you're halfway there.'
President Theodore Roosevelt

Chapter Forty-Seven

The following afternoon I waited upstairs for the sound of the doorbell, and managed to waddle to the door before my parents.

'Mrs Alexander?'

'Yes.'

'I'm David Jones from *The Sunday Times*. I was given your details by Mr Watersmith, who is a good friend of mine.' He smiled and offered me a firm handshake.

Glancing at him dressed in a plum shirt and wheat jeans with a brown satchel slung over his shoulder, I beckoned him inside and led him down into the basement and into my little kitchen. I switched on the kettle as David took a seat at the table and combed back his brown hair with his fingertips. He massaged his beard in contemplation and took out a blue Biro and notepad from his satchel.

'Milk and sugar?' I asked. My hand trembled watching the Nescafe dissolve.

'No milk, just sugar,' he replied. 'Would it be all right if I addressed you as Emily? It might make it less daunting for you,' he said gently.

My blue paisley dress grazed my ankles as I moved from the counter to the table.

'Yes, that's fine. Now, can I get you any biscuits? I think we have some Bourbons somewhere,' I said, feeling my nerves rise by the minute. I distracted myself by passing him his coffee before going to the cupboard to search for the biscuits. I listened for the whizzing sound of Rex's new electric wheelchair as he passed from his bedroom to the bathroom.

'No, it's all right. Just a coffee will be fine, Emily.' I nodded and took my coffee to the table, holding on to my mug to steady the flurry of tell-tale nerves from entering my voice; be calm and confident, I told myself.

'How would you like to start?'

'Oh,' I said, stretching out my feet on the cool floor. I admonished myself for not having gathered my thoughts together before his visit.

'What about a little background on your life before Rex was born?'

I took a sip of my coffee and thought back to a bright March morning in 1960 and of feeling awfully sick. I remembered worrying that I wouldn't be able to finish my novel in time. I took a deep breath and bit down on my lip, remembering the row of potted red geraniums on the kitchen step. I blinked away my scalding tears. David gave me a moment's pause. Clearing my throat, I focussed my mind on Rex and began telling my story.

'We were living in Richmond, and in those days we thought ourselves lucky to be so close to the river. Our flat was quite small, even for the two of us, but we didn't care.' Tears rolled down my cheeks. 'We were just starting out in life. Laurence had landed a new job that he was rather good at.' I glanced down at my sticky palms and breathed hard against my reluctance to go on, 'at Distillers,' I released a deep sigh and looked up at David. I saw his eyes water in sympathy for me and thought Chris had been right to send his friend to me.

'When Laurence suggested Distaval, I was desperate to get over my bout of morning sickness. I thought that was the worst thing ever, back then.' I let out a laugh that bounced in the air between us. 'If Laurence said it was safe and his company believed it, too, I thought they had to be right. In that moment I disregarded everything that my parents had taught me about medicine, and was persuaded to believe in the benefit of the biochemical. I was the daughter of a homeopath, but I was fooled by Thalidomide.' I saw David hurriedly scribbling down notes, and another deep breath told me how relieved I felt to have told my story at last.

✻✻✻

I soon learnt through Laurence that while I had been speaking with David Jones, Sylvia had gone to *The Daily Mail* with her story. Laurence presented me the following week with a copy of the newspaper and the headline:

'MY FIGHT FOR JUSTICE, BY THE MOTHER OF HEARTBREAK GIRL POLLYANNA.'

Scanning the article, I read how Sylvia felt that she was being blackmailed into accepting a less-than-adequate compensation deal from Distillers.

Laurence poured me a coffee and we sat together in the garden. 'What did you tell that journalist from *The Sunday Times*?' he asked and took the newspaper from me.

'I told him our story, full-stop.' Pride swelled in my chest that I had been able to talk about it with a stranger.

'This was supposed to be a fresh start. I thought we could move on from this. I am starting to get to know Rex. Why spoil everything, Emily?'

I enveloped my belly protectively. He had been making an effort, but part of the fresh start I had envisioned was acknowledging what had been done to Rex through Distillers.

'What do your parents think about you talking to the press?'

'My parents? Name me a single instance in the last eleven years when you have taken them into consideration.' My voice rose in anger. Had he not changed at all? 'I had to do something; Sylvia was losing hope. I had to prove to her that the fight wasn't over and that we shouldn't give up.'

'And look what she's been doing, Emily. She's been playing you again.'

'No.' I shook my head in denial. 'She hasn't. She has just done it her way; that's Sylvia.' But, brushing a strand of my hair behind my ear, I was reminded of Sylvia on the common a few years back. *'The thing is, Emily, our case against Distillers is a weak one.'*

'I know you did it for Rex. You've been trying to make it up to him since the day he was born. But you don't have to do that anymore. That's why I am here, Emily. I have come to relieve you of your burden,' said Laurence, bringing me back to the present.

'What do you mean, Laurence?'

'You can't be expected to take care of a disabled child and a newborn.'

'I have my parents to help.'

'But they are not getting any younger. Emily, it's time to be practical about this.'

The sound of footsteps halted our conversation as Chris and Sylvia approached.

'Laurence.' Sylvia rushed to greet him by pressing her cheek to his briefly. Chris stood a few paces away from me and frowned.

'What is it?' I asked, looking at the couple in alarm.

'We received a telephone call today from our solicitor. It seems that Distillers has complained to the Attorney General about our article in *The Daily Mail*,' said Chris.

I turned to Sylvia in confusion.

'It means that printing any further articles by the families constitutes contempt of court,' Sylvia fumed. 'Basically, we have been silenced by the law and we're back to square one.'

'A new baby is the beginning of all things.'
Eda J Leshan

Chapter Forty-Eight

I went into labour at the end of May, during a warm afternoon spent drinking lemonade in Sylvia's garden. From the patio, my gaze turned towards Rex and Pollyanna. Situated at a nearby table, Rex shuffled his cards before placing them down in the centre of the table. Pollyanna's feet stretched across the table and after a fleeting glance, she used her feet to grab half a dozen cards, curling them around her toes.

'Snap!' Pollyanna giggled.

'That wasn't even a match. Stop cheating, Pollyanna,' fumed Rex.

'I don't know how Pollyanna would cope without Rex. She's never gotten on very well with her brothers,' said Chris.

I felt a gush of warm liquid run down my thighs, staining my dress scarlet as a sign that the baby was on its way. A wave of panic rose inside me, halting my movements for several minutes. Memories of my day in court came back to me with frightening clarity, replacing my optimism with doubt. There was no lump in my throat this time, but as I gazed at my friends I found myself resenting their presence. I wanted Laurence by my side and to hear him tell me that this wasn't my fault. I hadn't jeopardised my baby's life by my recent activities. Guilt shivered inside me as Sylvia approached my chair and her gentle gaze caused me another flood of doubt for thinking so badly of her.

'What can I do to help?' she asked, kneeling before me.

I breathed hard from the sensation of blood seeping through my underwear. It took me several moments to answer her. 'Look after Rex for me; promise,' I said.

Sylvia and the children gathered around me while Chris rushed inside the house to call for an ambulance.

'Welcome back, Mrs Alexander, and congratulations, for you have a daughter,' the nurse said, as I recovered in hospital that evening, after undergoing an emergency Caesarean section.

My tight face didn't allow for a smile. I could only think of how different the experience had been twelve years ago with Rex. I heard footsteps and saw Laurence approach my bedside.

'It's all right, Emily. We have a healthy baby girl. She is in the neonatal unit at the moment, but the doctor says you can see her later, if you're up to it.'

A wave of nausea hit me, and recognising the tell-tale odour of Milton bleach, I released a shudder. Laurence squeezed my hand.

'There's no need to be anxious, for everything's all right with the baby this time.'

'Where's Rex?' My words, when they came out, seemed an octave too high.

Laurence leaned in towards me. 'I had to do what was right. When your mother called me and told me that the bleeding was bad, I panicked. I thought I was going to lose you both.' His fingers played with mine. That lump came back to my throat, silencing me again.

'Rex is almost a teenager. Think of how difficult it would be for you, having him at home as well as a newborn. In the past I know I wasn't there for you; that's why I acted quickly when I thought I was about to lose you.'

'Just tell me where he is.'

'They have special typewriters at Chailey. I know he is a delicate child, so maybe when he's old enough he can work in an office and carry on with his art in the evening. Please don't be angry, Emily. I had to do what I thought was best.'

'Confront the dark parts of yourself
and work to banish them with illumination and forgiveness.'
August Wilson

Chapter Forty-Nine

The following afternoon, with my having sufficiently recovered from surgery, Laurence got one of the nurses to bring the baby to us. I caught sight of her tuft of auburn hair within her pink blanket. She blinked to reveal green eyes, like my own. The nurse approached my bedside with the baby. But the nearer she got to me, the more I felt a sob rising in my throat.

Laurence stood to the other side of my bed, encouraging me to take the baby with his tender smile. I shook my head just as a shrill cry broke from my throat. The nurse stood only a heartbeat away and was unable to shield the baby from my howl. The baby responded to my distress by letting out a high-pitched bawl and wriggling in her blanket. The nurse struggled to comfort the baby and looked to Laurence in alarm. He took hold of my hand firmly.

'Take it away.' The words slipped from my lips before I had the chance to realise what I had said.

'Darling, it's all right. The baby is okay, look.' He nodded at the nurse, who unfolded the blanket to reveal four perfectly formed limbs. 'See?' he said. 'It's not like with Rex,' indicating for the nurse to come closer, and in doing so the baby's pink cheek grazed mine. This time I felt my body shudder. How could she be mine? I didn't deserve this perfect baby.

I felt my body contort with each fresh sob. Laurence's eyes met mine in fear.

The nurse placed the baby back into its bassinette.

'Mrs Alexander, you are obviously exhausted from surgery. Why don't I take the baby back to the neonatal unit, and we can try again tomorrow after you have had some rest,' the nurse said, whilst wheeling the baby from my bedside.

Kathryn Barnett

'She doesn't belong to me,' I said, and then giving into my fatigue, I closed my eyes and fell asleep.

'With friends you grow wings,
alone you are a single feather in disgrace.'
Rumi

Chapter Fifty

'I blame your mother for this, for not allowing you to get angry about Thalidomide all those years ago,' said Sylvia, as she strode up to my bedside the following afternoon.

'Sylvia,' Laurence reprimanded.

'Can I speak with Emily alone, please?'

'All right,' Laurence replied, and leaning over my bed, he pressed his lips onto mine for a kiss. Sylvia took Laurence's seat and reached for my hand. At the sensation of her touch I blinked away a tear.

'You have got to talk to me, Emily. Tell me how you are feeling, or they won't let you leave here, and I know that's not what you want.'

'I didn't mean to harm my baby,' I said at last.

'Are we talking about Thalidomide? That was a long time ago, Emily. You can't go back to that. You have got to move on.' I watched her reach inside her handbag for a packet of Marlboros.

'He took Rex away from me.'

'Yes, Laurence sent him to Chailey. But if you carry on like this, you won't get to see Rex at all.'

I shook my head. 'I've made many mistakes in my life, Sylvia.'

'You've got Laurence and you have a new baby. Not everyone's so lucky.' She took a cigarette from her packet and pressed it down against the top of my bedside cabinet.

'I'm sorry, Sylvia.'

She reached again for my hand, this time to trace my heart line. 'I think Chris is having an affair.' I reached over to brush her cheek and her lip quivered. I waited for her tears to break, but they didn't. She just plastered a smile upon her lips.

'Laurence has shown me the baby and she looks just like you. Would you like to give it another go?' she coaxed.

'Yes,' I agreed, feeling a dull ache from my stomach to my thighs. Unable to shift my body, I was relieved when she leaned over to offer a kiss on each cheek. I raised my arms to wrap around her neck and inhaled the scent of her jasmine perfume.

'See? You're feeling better already,' she said, her lips inches from mine. She pulled away and straightened herself. 'Let me find one of those nurses and get them to work for us,' she laughed and rushed from my bedside, leaving me with a whiff of her perfume.

Half an hour later, Sylvia returned with a nurse and my baby. Sylvia nodded at me, and I took a deep breath before opening my arms so the nurse could place the baby into mine. I heard the baby gurgle contentedly and turned to gaze at Sylvia.

'Told you that you could do it.' Sylvia took a seat by my bedside. The baby's head moulded into my shoulder. I felt Sylvia's hand over mine, and knew somehow I had to find a way to get back to Regency Square.

*'A flower cannot blossom without sunshine
and man cannot live without love.'*
Max Muller

Chapter Fifty-One

I was discharged from hospital three weeks later. Arriving home to Regency Square, my parents were there to greet me and settle me back into the basement flat. I felt a stab of disappointment at Laurence for not taking time off work to spend with me, and it was with that thought alone that I drifted numbly into the same bedroom with the same white cotton drapes and matching linen and view of the walled garden beyond.

'We have set up a cot in Rex's room for the time being,' my mother said, taking the baby from my arms so I could climb into bed. She waited a moment for me to settle before placing the baby back in my arms and bolstering the pillows behind me. Still plagued by stitching pains from surgery, I nudged the teat of one of my stock of bottles into my baby's mouth and was rewarded with the contented sound of her suckling.

I stared ahead at the magnolia walls, feeling my head droop with exhaustion.

'Have you decided on a name yet?' my mother asked, touching my arm to keep me in the present. I blinked rapidly as my father came into the room with my suitcase. Then, he offered me some Arnica as a post-operative remedy before taking a seat on the opposite side of the bed from my mother. He reached over to touch the baby's head tenderly.

'I'm sorry we didn't come to see you at the hospital. But you know how we feel about such things,' my father said.

I lowered my eyes in fatigue and my mother leaned in close to put an arm around my shoulder to comfort me. 'We are sorry, Emily,' she said.

My gaze fell to the baby, and my mothering instincts kicked in as I wiped milk from the corner of her rosebud lips. Flooded with guilt at my previous rejection of her, my tears broke. She was beautiful. But again, I felt undeserving of her love.

I glanced outside into the garden at the late afternoon sun. 'Clementine,' I said. 'That's what I want to call the baby.'

At the sound of pounding footsteps, a moment of silence fell upon the room. Laurence strode into the bedroom and removed his grey suit jacket and loosened his tie to the expectant gaze of my parents. 'How is she doing?' Laurence asked, reaching for Clementine's tiny fists.

'I have decided to call her Clementine,' I said as Laurence took a seat beside my mother.

'That's a beautiful name,' he replied.

'Tell me, Laurence, when is Rex coming home?'

My parents left the room to give Laurence and me a chance to talk.

'It's what I said at the hospital, you can't be expected to take care of two children. You are not yourself at the moment, I don't think,' he said, touching my cheek.

'That is why it is for everyone's benefit that you focus on Clementine. The doctors were most concerned by your reaction to her birth. They told me that they wanted to keep you at the hospital for further observation, but I explained about Rex. I know you, Emily. I appreciate that deep down you are a good mother.'

I shook my head. 'It's important for Rex to see his sister as soon as possible, for he mustn't think that we are abandoning him for the new baby,' I said, feeling my voice rise in frustration.

'It's what I said, you are not well. You need to rest,' he said, taking Clementine from my arms and placing her down in her cot.

'Now I've got a conference coming up in York. No way to get out of it, I'm afraid.' He pressed his lips together, still regarding me with concern.

I rubbed at my eyes, desperate to rid myself of more tears that worked only to show my weakness, as my courage to speak up against him vanished with each painful stitch of surgery.

'But I will get Sylvia to check in on you. You would like that, wouldn't you?' he asked, with a tight smile.

I nodded. Sylvia, I thought, would know how to help me get Rex home. I just needed to get past my tears, and that was going to take a little more time.

'Life shrinks or expands in proportion to one's courage.'
Anaïs Nin

Chapter Fifty-Two

Laurence was true to his word, and a few days later I was rewarded for my compliance with a visit from Sylvia. Dressed in a navy jumpsuit, she clutched a box of chocolates, and without warning perched herself on the end of my bed.

'How long have you got to rest for?' She broke the seal on the box of Dairy Milk and took one for herself, before stretching over to offer me the box.

'I don't know. The district nurse is due to visit in the next couple of days. Maybe she'll be able to tell me more.'

Sylvia left the box of chocolates by my side. 'Where's Laurence?'

'At a conference in York,' I sighed.

'I thought you were getting better,' she said, rising from the bed and pushing the window up as far as it would go. I glanced at Clementine's navy pram parked on the patio. 'It's four o'clock, Emily, and surely time for her next feed.'

'Can't I have five minutes' peace?' I cried.

'After Laurence sent Rex to Chailey, Pollyanna kicked up quite a fuss at home. She got it into her head that she couldn't go to school without Rex. Chris tried to reason with her, but something inside her snapped. She wouldn't eat, no matter what we offered her, and started playing the piano at all hours of the day. We couldn't live like that anymore, so one morning we got up early and drove her to Chailey. That was two weeks ago, the last time I saw my daughter.' I threw an arm around her neck.

'I'm sorry, Sylvia.'

'It's not your fault; any of it, Emily.'

A tumble of my auburn tresses brushed her cheek. I looked into her aquamarine-blue eyes that held the promise of a better tomorrow. 'Do you think they'll remember Rex and Pollyanna in fifty years' time?' I asked as Sylvia pulled away from me and ran barefoot from the room.

Forced out of my bed at last, I combed my knotted curls with my fingertips before reaching for my dressing gown and following Sylvia into the garden.

She held Clementine in her arms as I saw her first show of tears.

'It's not too late for you to be Pollyanna's mother. Look at Laurence; he's making some inroads with Rex. You have still got that chance with Pollyanna.' Clementine's little fist reached out to me, and she uttered a cry of hunger.

'How you are with Clementine reminds me of my first days with Pollyanna. I didn't know how to love her. But the thing is, you've got to work it out quickly or it's too late.' She put a hand to her chest. 'For that hole in your heart: It just gets bigger and consumes you,' she said and made for the bench.

I returned to the house to warm Clementine's bottle of milk. Staring aimlessly into the garden, it was only the hiss of scalding water that brought me rushing back to the present. I took a moment to clear up the mess before returning to the garden, where I took a seat beside Sylvia and adjusted Clementine in my arms, so my baby was nestled between us.

'They have got to remember our children in fifty years' time. It can't be for nothing.'

'Spread love everywhere you go.
Let no one ever come to you without leaving happier.'
Mother Teresa

Chapter Fifty-Three

It was another six weeks before Laurence waited in the car as I made the slow walk into Chailey, cradling Clementine in my arms. I heard her coo as I strolled through the main entrance and made for Dr Donahue's office. It was a Friday afternoon, and several of the parents had gathered around the junior dorm to collect their children for the weekend.

Navigating my way through the loop of chattering parents, I knocked on the doctor's door. I half-expected him to be with the children, organising the leavers for the long bank holiday weekend, but to my surprise the door opened and Dr Donahue greeted me with a smile.

'Emily.' His outstretched arm indicated that I should step inside his office. He closed the door, and I couldn't help but feel under his control yet again.

'So you've finally made it here.' He leaned over my shoulder and glanced at Clementine. 'Is everything all right with the baby?' he probed gently, stepping away from me to take a seat behind his desk. In that moment, I hoped he would go for Rex's file, any kind of distraction from his close scrutiny of us. But instead, he offered us fleeting glances between sips of his tea.

'She's fine. I wish she slept more, but I can't complain, considering...'

'Um,' he said. 'You haven't been to see Rex in six weeks.'

'That's why I am here today.'

'He has a new friend,' Dr Donahue said, his blue eyes twinkling with mischief.

'I know. Pollyanna.'

'The emphasis now is on his secondary school education.'

'He's growing up. I understand that.'

'You want to show him the baby? Have you prepared him for this?'

'Of course. Perhaps afterwards I can take him home for the weekend.'

'Let's see how he reacts to the baby first, shall we?' he said and rose from his chair to return to my side. Then without another word, he accompanied me down the corridor, and we made our way towards Rex's room.

Gathering inside the room, Rex was sitting on his bed talking to a dark-haired boy with shortened arms and legs. 'You see, if you add all those numbers together, the square root still comes to three,' said the boy, leaning over Rex's shoulder.

'Yes, all right. I get it,' replied Rex.

'Hello, Simon,' the doctor greeted the boy with a tight smile.

'Hello, Dr Donahue,' the boy replied, and after a fleeting glance at Rex, he hopped off the bed and made for the corridor.

'Mum!' Rex beamed, causing that familiar lump to rise in my throat.

I went to his bed and took a seat beside him. 'I'm so sorry, my darling, for keeping away. They kept me in hospital and wouldn't let me see you.' Tears sprang to my eyes.

'It's all right, Mum. I'm not alone anymore, I have Pollyanna now.'

Clementine took a deep intake of breath and Rex reached over to stroke her cheek. 'Meet your new sister, Rex. Her name is Clementine.' I unfolded her pink blanket to reveal her perfectly formed limbs and waited in anticipation for his reaction.

Rex's long fingers curled around Clementine's toes curiously. 'Hello, Clemmie,' he greeted her with a smile, and that was a name that stuck in the family. I turned to Dr Donahue and was surprised by his glistening blue eyes.

Then I lifted Clementine and placed her into Rex's arms, showing him how to support her head in the nook of his shoulder. By that time a crowd of teenage Thalidomiders, some with four-limb deficiencies, had either hopped or crawled over to us, curious to meet Rex's little sister.

'Have enough courage to trust love one more time,
always one more time.'
Maya Angelou

Chapter Fifty-Four

We gathered around the font for Clemmie's christening on the coolest day of September. I wore a black silk dress imprinted with pink and red flowers. The three-quarter-length sleeves barely kept the chill away, so I was glad of the warmth from Clemmie's tiny body.

In my arrangements for the christening, I had managed to persuade Rex to wear a suit and his artificial legs for the ceremony. Also, I had chosen Sylvia and Chris to be Clementine's godparents.

As I stood at the font, Clemmie wriggled in my arms. I contemplated a future ahead, when Rex was grown up and Laurence and I were left with Clemmie to raise as our daughter: a time when all three of us would finally live apart from my parents. For some reason that thought made me glance expectantly towards Sylvia. My friend gave me an encouraging smile. I took a deep breath and convinced myself I could do this.

'I turn to Christ,' said Laurence, breaking my chain of thought. I searched his brown eyes, to determine whether I could trust him at last. 'I repent of my sins and renounce evil,' said Laurence.

His hand brushed mine, but still I needed more time and progress from him with Rex to be convinced of his conviction.

'I believe and trust in him,' we chorused, and I surrendered Clementine to the Church.

'I baptise Clementine in the name of the Father—' said Father Fitzgerald, pouring water over her head.

Clemmie howled.

'—the Son and the Holy Ghost,' Father Fitzgerald concluded.

And with the final sprinkling of water, Clemmie managed to squeeze out a cry that echoed into the eaves. As the priest passed her back to me, I did my best to console her, before handing her to my mother in exchange for a lit candle.

'Shine as a light in the world to fight against sin and the devil,' Father Fitzgerald said.

'Amen,' we said in unison.

***

Later, we gathered in my parents' house to wet the baby's head with champagne and eat canapés that my mother had ordered from Selfridges. Taking glasses of champagne, Laurence and I mingled with the guests in the upstairs dining room. Sylvia and Chris soon approached us. The two men glanced at each other in silence before Sylvia spoke up.

'Allow me to take Clemmie for a bit. Godmother duties,' she said with a smile.

Rex waddled over to Pollyanna. He glanced around at the stream of guests and proceeded to huddle into a tight corner with her. I placed Clemmie in Sylvia's waiting arms, and reaching for Laurence's hand, I let him guide me to an alcove by the long bay windows with a view of the square below.

Our hands looped as we watched the guests ascend the front steps for their first glance of Clementine.

'I've been thinking about how much I miss Rex now that he is at Chailey and how I'm happy for him to come home at weekends,' Laurence admitted.

'You are?' I rewarded him with a smile.

'Rex is my son. It's time the world knew that, too.'

I offered him a brief kiss as thanks, thinking how strangely it was that everything was starting to get better, just when I thought things were bad again. I turned around to catch Sylvia's conceited smile and scooped Clemmie back into my arms as Chris, Sylvia, Rex, Pollyanna and my parents gathered around for the official christening photograph. The flash hit my eyes, and trying not to blink, I sensed Laurence's hand touching my side.

'Success is simple. Do what's right,
the right way at the right time.'
Arnold H Glasgow

Chapter Fifty-Five
September 1972

I was giving Clemmie her morning bottle when Laurence strode into the bedroom clutching a copy of *The Sunday Times*. He spread the broadsheet across the bed and nudged in beside me. I cradled Clemmie between us and helped her to hold her own bottle. Then with my other hand I edged towards the newspaper and the headline that caused a smile to break on my lips.

'OUR THALIDOMIDE CHILDREN:
A CAUSE FOR NATIONAL SHAME'

Reading the black typeset, I was distracted by my own joy that at long last our story was being told to the world, and felt Clemmie slip in my arms. She let out a cry and I adjusted her bottle, listening to the sound of her gurgling on her milk, before reaching again for the paper.

'Hey, that's our Rex,' said Laurence, pointing out a grainy black-and-white photograph of our boy with his wide grin and cut-down trousers. Together, we scanned the rest of the three-page article, shaking our heads at the frightening statistics of the drug. We followed the commentary with interest, and it was only when we had both finished reading that we began to talk.

'If I had supported you from the start, you would have had a better case.' He reached over to stroke Clemmie's hair.

'It wouldn't have made any difference. They just want us to settle, full stop. There's no room for questions or debate. That's why we have to fight on, regardless.'

'How are you going to do that, Emily?'

'I have to carry on refusing to sign, until they present us with a proper deal. It's not easy, but I can do it because I'm not alone. I have people who love me.'

'Where do you get your strength from? I couldn't have done what you have.'

'From Rex, I suppose. He's not your average child, and over the years he's offered me little clues to show that it's all right and that I'm not alone. But one day, he will have to find his own way in the world, and I need to know that if he needs help, it will be there for him.'

I glanced down at Clemmie. She had let go of her bottle. I watched it roll onto the quilt by the side of the newspaper with the separate editorial headline:

'CHILDREN ON OUR CONSCIENCE'

Laurence leaned in closer to me, and I wondered what he was thinking at that moment as his eyes scanned the editorial, which talked of the plight of the Thalidomide children that shamed society, the law, and Distillers.

It was then that I heard him whisper, 'I'm so sorry, Rex,' and clinging to me, he didn't move for the longest moment, not until I felt Clemmie shift as she slipped into a deep sleep.

'Scared is what you're feeling,
brave is what you're doing.'
Emma Donoghue, from Room

Chapter Fifty-Six

Following the Thalidomide spread in the previous month's *Sunday Times*, I sat down at my typewriter on a bright October morning in 1972 with little more than a cup of coffee and a rough idea of a letter. With Clemmie asleep, I had a spare hour or so to compose my letter before she was due her next feed.

I took a sip of my coffee and thought back to September 1960, when I had first held Rex in my arms. Once again, I swallowed that knotted ball of fear, as Laurence's scream resounded in my head. Despite the years that had since passed, I found myself shuddering at the memory.

It took me a few moments to compose myself. I bit down on my lower lip, telling myself not to give up. I could do it, and with my fingers poised on the keys I struck the letter 'D.' I surprised myself at how quickly my letter came out as follows:

Dear Editor,

I am writing in response to your Thalidomide campaign as the mother of a child affected by the drug. I gave birth to my son Rex Elliot Alexander on September 21st 1960, after a long and painful labour. On hearing that I had a son I was duly excited, knowing that my husband would also share in the joy of our first-born child together.

Like most new mothers, I had high expectations for Rex: One of which was of him taking his first step. But Thalidomide had left my son's legs terribly deformed, rendering him disabled. Yet that wasn't the worst of it for Rex. His father rejected him at birth, and even twelve years later, he has yet to touch his own son.

Trust Me On This One, Emily

My son has suffered the repeated trauma of limb-fitting to make the abnormal normal, but worst of all, he has never known a father's love. He is almost a teenager now and is in need of a father more than ever. This is my plea to Distillers: Don't forget your promise to us. Don't leave us in limbo for too much longer, please.
Yours sincerely,
Mrs Emily Alexander

Tears moistened the keys, and I had to force myself to stop. I hugged my knees and felt a shooting pain in my abdomen. I held myself back from sobbing as punishment for Rex dwelling in Chailey, and it wasn't until I heard Clemmie's cry that I took a deep breath and went next door to my daughter. Scooping her into my arms, I rocked her to and fro and went to the kitchen to warm her milk. Waiting for her milk to heat on the hob, I resolved to post my letter to *The Sunday Times* and to ask my father for a lift to Chailey. I had to see Rex, and the rest of it I would work through at my own pace with a little help from Sylvia.

'The price of success is hard work,
dedication to the job at hand,
and the determination that whether we win or lose,
we have applied the best of ourselves to the task at hand.'
Vince Lombardi

Chapter Fifty-Seven
April 14, 1973

That evening, I turned on the television to catch the BBC news. The cameras turned towards Sylvia and Chris in the London studio. Holding Chris' hand, Sylvia offered the world a jubilant smile before uttering the words we had been waiting to hear for the past eleven years.

'It's over. Our fight is at an end.'

The reporter cut in to inform the viewers that an historic settlement had been made between Distillers and the remaining sixty-two Thalidomide families. The amount of £6.8 million was to be paid into a charitable trust. The sum would be protected by inflation, bringing the total up to £26 million.

'Are you sure this is it, no last-minute demands on your behalf to Distillers?' asked the reporter.

'Well,' Chris cut in, 'we do have a couple of demands, don't we, Sylvia?' I saw him squeeze her hand and felt my heart pound in anticipation, thinking that even at this late stage it could all fall through and we'd be back to square one again.

'They know us by now, and after all, it's for the children. Everything we have ever done has been about them,' said Sylvia.

Tears streamed down my cheeks at pride for my brave friend. I was amazed how after everything she had been through with Pollyanna that she could speak with such clarity. Laurence, thinking it was shock and nothing more, pulled me into his arms for a hug. I looked away from the TV for a moment.

'Do you have any regrets?' the reporter asked.

I turned back to the TV and held my breath. Both Sylvia and I could have told that reporter so much more about how Thalidomide had affected our lives over the years. Sylvia must have been thinking the same because she appeared thrown by the question and turned instead to Chris. He gripped her hand.

'None whatsoever,' replied Chris. 'When we discovered the cause of Pollyanna's horrific birth defects, we knew that we had to right a wrong, and not just for us, but for all the parents out there struggling to deal with the shock of their Thalidomide children.'

'For all the mothers, today justice has been done,' Sylvia finished.

I released a deep breath. Today was a day for our children and nothing more.

Laurence drew me back into his arms; and as his lips pressed on mine, I was sure that tomorrow would start with new hope, because the worst was over.

PART THREE

'I've learned that people will forget what you said,
people will forget what you did,
but people will never forget how you made them feel.'
Maya Angelou

Chapter Fifty-Eight
1973

'Hold Clemmie for a moment, Rex,' I said, passing her wiggly body to him. Rex was parked to my right at the kitchen table with his maths book tucked down the side of his wheelchair.

I switched on my typewriter and fed in a sheet of crisp white paper. Then I took a moment to focus my mind on the right words to conclude a series of short stories, which I had been commissioned to write by a well-known woman's weekly.

Rex's arms enveloped Clemmie's waist. I caught sight of her chubby thighs as she turned to gaze at him in wonder. A smile broke on her lips and I started to relax. Laurence's initial fears about how I would cope with the two of them had been proven wrong. I relished the weekends when he came home and was on hand to help me with Clemmie.

She let out a cry at being reined in by Rex's strong arms. I tapped away at the keys and waited for her to settle.

'Sshhh, it's all right, Clemmie.' I turned around as Rex let out a laugh. 'Stop tickling me, Clemmie,' he reprimanded gently.

'Do you want me to take her, Rex?'

'No, it's all right.' He smiled. 'What's your story about?'

'A couple who meet every morning on the commuter train, but don't realise they are in love until the very end.'

'Why's that?' He held Clemmie against his chest. She pulled herself up onto his knees and looked at me with interest. Her little hands made a wave, and getting up to approach her, my hand went to her auburn ponytail.

'Through a series of misunderstandings they are unable to acknowledge their feelings for each other until the very end.'

'Sounds all right,' he said.

I went to my bedroom and found Clemmie's blonde-haired doll. I returned to the kitchen and offered it to her. Her fingers curled around the flaxen hair, and she slipped down onto Rex's lap. Occupied for the present, Rex leaned his chin on her head and reached for his maths book.

I turned back to the typewriter and tapped away.

Louise couldn't believe she had ever doubted her feelings for Jack after hearing him speak of his father's death, and with such genuine emotion that she felt compelled to offer him a hug. He wasn't the arrogant man she first thought him to be. They now had an hour, at least, to talk and decide the next step in their friendship.

✳✳✳

Later, after I put Clemmie down for her afternoon nap and left Rex to his homework, I slipped away to my bedroom. From my handbag I took out my packet of contraceptive pills that I had collected from the pharmacy earlier. I sat on the bed holding the box in my lap, turning it over in my hand as a moment of childhood guilt stabbed at my heart. I felt sure that I couldn't tell anyone about this. I just knew without a doubt that I couldn't have another baby. But it took me several moments more before I went into the kitchen for a glass of water. I glanced at Rex busying himself with his fractions.

'All right, Mum?' he said.

'Yes, my darling,' I smiled weakly and went back to the bedroom.

I pushed out a single pill and held it in my palm for a moment longer. No regrets, I promised, tossing it to the back of my throat and washing it down with my glass of water.

✳✳✳

A few weeks passed, and I was in the kitchen just as Rex offered Clemmie a crayon and held down the colouring book with his left hand so she could make her first blue squiggle. Laurence sauntered into the kitchen, dressed for work.

'So,' he coughed, turning to me, 'I've been offered a new job as sales manager for the south. It will mean more travelling and nights apart,' he said, switching on the percolator.

I went to the fridge for milk, lingering there longer than necessary.

'I know that you were hoping for me to help out more with Clementine, but at least it means we can think of moving out sooner and getting a place of our own. Surely it's time for that.'

I passed him the milk bottle in silence. The more I trusted him, the more I felt him backing away from Rex rather than stepping forward to take on the responsibilities which he had promised.

'Look at what Clemmie's done. Pretty good, isn't she?' Rex grinned, holding up the colouring book for us to see. We both stared at her patchwork of tiny marks, and as Rex flashed a smile, I leaned heavily against the refrigerator and felt a deep sigh rise from my chest as a sign of my growing sense of disappointment in Laurence once again.

There was a tap on the kitchen door and I looked to see Chris waiting outside with Pollyanna. They walked into the kitchen, and I remembered that Rex was due at a swimming class with Pollyanna that day.

I went to my bedroom to get changed and found my mother waiting for me there.

'Emily—' she began.

'Please, Mummy, I have to get dressed, Chris and Pollyanna are here to take Rex swimming.'

'Emily, it's your father. He's had an accident and has been taken to hospital.'

After much debate it was decided that my mother and I would go to the hospital to see my father. Chris offered to take us in his car, and a tender smile from him managed to lift my mood slightly. But as I approached the front door, Laurence pulled me aside.

'I'll wait for you in the car,' my mother said, reaching for her handbag before following Chris out of the house.

'I know what you're trying to do,' Laurence said.

Rex and Pollyanna had caught up with us in the hallway. Rex's brown eyes flew from Laurence to me in sorrow. He still had Clemmie nestled in his lap, and by now she had started to suck her thumb.

'My father has been injured. Please, I can't think of anything else,' I cried.

'Why won't you let me take you?' he yelled.

'I have to go now,' I said, rushing to Rex and Pollyanna. I kissed them each on the cheek. I sensed Laurence behind me and straightened myself.

He took hold of my arm. 'We haven't finished yet.'

I snatched my arm back as all three children gazed at me in fear. 'Yes, we have, Laurence,' I said, beckoning for Rex to come forward. He pushed down the control on his chair, and inches from my feet I scooped Clemmie into my arms. Reaching for the door, I came face-to-face with Sylvia. She raised an eyebrow at Laurence before turning to me.

'I thought you could do with some help with the children.'

Sylvia took Rex and Pollyanna to her house. With Clemmie in my arms, I climbed into the back of Chris' car. My mother turned to me sternly, but I held Clemmie tighter. I blinked as my lips teased Clemmie's soft curls, offering me an inhalation of Johnson's Baby Shampoo. Then I leaned back in my seat and shut my eyes as tears scalded my cheeks.

My mother went in first, leaving Chris and me alone with Clemmie between us.

'Sometimes I wish we had found the courage to try for another baby,' he said, as Clemmie let out a yawn. 'Maybe it could have made things right between Sylvia and me.'

Clemmie stirred in my arms, and I adjusted her on my lap as my mother returned. She took Clemmie from me and I went in to see my father.

I sucked in my breath as I took in my father's splintered leg. I took a seat in a chair by his bedside. I caressed his bruised and cut cheek.

'Emily.' He took my hand from his cheek and held it tight.

'Daddy.' My tears flowed easily.

'It's all right. The car took a bit of a battering, but nothing that can't be put right, and my leg will heal in time. Everything mends eventually, Emily.'

I shook my head, feeling the sensation of my wet cheeks.

'You must go home and talk to Laurence.'

'I can't offer him what he needs without feeling a betrayal that runs too deep—' I thought of Sylvia and Chris, just like Laurence and me, struggling to come to terms with Thalidomide.

'You're just feeling overwhelmed after everything that has happened, none of which was your fault.' He patted my hand. I leaned over his bed and planted a kiss on his forehead.

'What was that for?' He smiled weakly.

'For telling me exactly what I needed to hear.'

✳✳✳

Chris dropped my mother and me at home. I settled Clemmie into her playpen in the lounge and handed her favourite doll to her. My mother had already disappeared upstairs to sort out clothes to take to the hospital for my father. I went in search of Laurence. I found him on the patio with his head in his hands, tapping his foot to the sound of Marvin Gaye's 'Let's Get it On' blaring from his transistor radio. I took a seat at the table and folded my hands in my lap. Then I cleared my throat. Laurence, upon noticing me, reached over to switch off the radio.

'I understand why you got angry before, and I'm sorry,' I said.

Laurence offered me a soulful gaze. 'I was naive,' he admitted. 'I thought we could just pick up where we had left off and nothing would have changed. But everywhere I look I see either Sylvia or Chris lingering around you, and ready to claim you as their own, which makes me feel the outsider in your life.'

'That's not true, Laurence. Are you taking this job to run away again?'

'I'm not,' he said, gripping my hand.

'Then what are you doing?' I asked.

'Trying to win back your trust, and I know that's hard after everything that has happened and how I am still struggling to be a proper father to Rex. But, I am trying to change all that with this new job, which might not be one you totally approve of. But it will get us to the place we need to be.' His hand stroked my cheek, tantalising me with the thought of a different future ahead, when at last Laurence would prove to be the father that Rex had been waiting for all his life.

'Well, you still owe Rex and Pollyanna an apology for your behaviour today.'

'I know.' He kissed me, and I filed away any feelings of doubt to a dark crevice in my mind, to be reviewed at a later date. He pulled me up from my chair. I took his hand and he led me inside the house. We stopped by the lounge to check on Clemmie, but hearing her contented chatter, we went into our bedroom and shut the door.

'In the midst of movement and chaos,
keep stillness inside you.'
Deepak Chopra

Chapter Fifty-Nine

My father was discharged from hospital a few weeks later, and one Saturday afternoon as he took a nap in the garden, I invited Sylvia for tea. She had Pollyanna home for the weekend, so the two of them were happy to join me in the garden. I poured us tea and watched Rex and Pollyanna from a distance.

Rex had positioned himself at the end of the garden. He had with him a sketchpad and a set of watercolours. Pollyanna had on a cornflower-blue dress. She sat against the wall with a backdrop of creeping honeysuckle, and turning her head to one side, her blonde hair fell beautifully over her narrow shoulder, almost resembling a golden mane.

'I remember that pose,' said Sylvia.

I glanced away from the children to regard my friend closely. A tender smile played on her lips, as if in remembrance of happier times, before Thalidomide had cast its shadow on all of our lives.

'What was it like, being a model in those days?' I asked, taking a sip of my tea.

'It was exciting. There was an optimistic feeling of change ahead, and being young, of course, I felt no fear or anxiety. I was eager to embrace the future,' she beamed. 'I met Chris and everything just got better for me. He was so good-looking that I fell for him very quickly. I think I needed to be in love because my life had been quite nomadic up to that point, with no place to call home.'

I nodded. 'But still you must miss that life sometimes.'

'I never really had a home life as a child. My mother died when I was very young, and I wasn't particularly close to father, so escaping to Paris at the age of sixteen felt right; and to be honest I can't ever remember feeling freer.'

I turned my attention back towards Rex and Pollyanna, watching my son's brown eyes dance over the nape of her neck.

'I kind of envy you, having your parents as a support. Without Chris or the children I'd be completely alone in the world.'

'I'll always be your friend, Sylvia,' I promised, taking her hand in mine. 'They are doing so well, considering,' I said, watching Pollyanna change position on her chair. Then with her bare feet she picked a daisy and held it between her toes.

'She would have made the perfect model,' said Sylvia, sadly.

'Any chance of a cup of tea?' Asked my father, from across the patio. I raised an eyebrow at Sylvia to the sound of her laughter. Then I poured some tea into a china cup and took it to him.

I glanced at his box of cigars on a nearby table and frowned. 'Daddy, have you been keeping up with your remedies? How about your doses of Arnica and Symphytum?'

'Who is the homeopath here?'

'Daddy—'

'Your mother has been acting as chief prescriber in my absence, although I'm not sure how long I can remain laid up like this. I do have a practise to run.'

'Dr Dhillon has offered to oversee your list in the interim. Now you just need to concentrate on your recovery.'

'When's Laurence due home?'

'He's not due back until the middle of next week.'

'You must be missing him.'

Rex was busy washing his brushes. The gentle breeze had picked up, causing Pollyanna's skirt to flap against her knees.

'It doesn't matter how long it takes, you just have to be patient and wait, my darling girl.' His hands heavy with the scent of tobacco held mine, leaving me with the promise that the time for truth and reconciliation was at last within our reach.

✳✳✳

On Rex's fourteenth birthday, Laurence presented our son with the gift of a 'grown up' adapted bicycle. The blue hand cycle had three wheels and an upright seat.

'What do you think, Rex? I've been told that the bike will allow you to go at a fair speed, and Dr Donahue has assured me that it will be excellent for toning your upper body.' Laurence beamed.

Rex edged closer to the bike in his wheelchair and examined the handles with interest. Pollyanna stepped forward and circled the metal fame, tracing the thick wheels with her toes.

'Shall we give it a go?' I suggested and helped Rex slide onto the bicycle.

He gripped the handlebars in contemplation before reaching for the handle by his seat, which slowly powered the chain and wheels and propelled him down the ramp and onto the patio, still damp from the morning's downpour. Gravity took over and with another turn of the handle, Rex gathered speed, circling the garden and forcing Pollyanna to chase after him.

Watching from the sidelines, a smile formed on my lips in pride. But as I turned to Laurence I saw his deep frown, and thinking his old doubts about being Rex's father had slipped back into his conscience, I offered him a hug; yet to my shock he pulled away.

'Laurence,' I said, 'what is it?'

'It's me, Emily,' he lowered his head solemnly.

'Why? I don't understand. You've been doing well with Rex.'

'I gave up on him all those years ago, and that was my biggest mistake.'

'So it's about you again?' I shook my head. 'You really have to make everything about you and those stupid pills of yours.'

'Why not? I did wrong, at least I am willing to admit that now.'

'None of us knew what to do back then. We didn't have a clue about how to raise our Thalidomide children. We just did what we thought was best,' I said, wistfully reminded of when I had first held Rex in my arms all those years ago. 'But I was lucky enough to find the people that got me here today.'

'I haven't been the father I should have been with Rex. Even now living here with you, I find myself struggling because of his disability. I have moments when I think of leaving again and of how Rex would be better off without me.'

'He didn't do so well without you, Laurence. You saw how he was coping from the outside because it is easier that way. When

I had Clemmie, I didn't cope as well as I thought I would,' I paused, feeling a sob rise in my throat from not being able to love her enough.

Laurence pulled me into his arms, and I leaned my head against his chest for support.

'I'm still getting there. I'm not perfect; none of us are. We just try to learn a little more about being a parent each day. You could leave and I wouldn't even try to stop you, but you can bet that walking out after all the promises you made to us would hurt Rex as much as it would hurt you. You are getting there, Laurence. It may not feel like it today, but you are—you just need faith, and I need you to help me get there with Clemmie. So maybe it's time we helped each other.'

'Can I ask you something? I know how close you are with Sylvia and I try not to feel jealous, really, I do; but what are we doing? Do you still love me? Or are we together for the sake of the children? Over the years there hasn't been anyone else but you. Do you still feel the same way about me?'

'Rex!' squealed Clemmie. Lifting my head, I watched Clemmie escape barefoot into the garden. She took up the chase after Rex, but her small feet caused her to lag behind Pollyanna.

'I love you—really I do, Laurence, but Sylvia,' I paused, feeling my chest swell with emotion, 'she sees into my soul and no one has ever done that before, so for us to have a future you've got to be able to do the same.'

'Action is the functional key to all success.'
Pablo Picasso

Chapter Sixty
1974

One afternoon, after putting Clemmie down for her afternoon nap, I drifted into the kitchen to make a cup of tea before getting down to writing, when I heard the kitchen door open abruptly. I turned and saw Sylvia stride into the room. She paced the floor for a bit before coming to a stop by the counter.

'I had a call today from Chailey about Pollyanna.' Her hands gripped the melamine top between Clemmie's dirty plate and cup.

'They found Rex in her room last night.'

I shook my head in denial, but the fluttering of fear in my chest told me that deep down there was every chance that what Sylvia was saying could be true.

'She's only fourteen.' Sylvia's gaze turned towards the window.

'I'm sure it was innocent. They are still so young, how can it be anything more than two friends comforting each other?'

'Don't be so blind, Emily. They are both teenagers now. All this self-affirmation and hugging has clouded your judgement. You can't know what goes through his head when he's away in an institution.'

'I know Rex, and he's innocent,' I said, but still I kept my distance from Sylvia.

'You still think of him as your special little baby, but time has moved on. You need to face up to the present, stop making excuses for everyone and take responsibility or—'

'Or what, Sylvia?' I stared at her firmly.

'I could take what happened with Pollyanna further. Chris and I are not without influence.'

'What happened, exactly?'

'They kissed.'

'All right,' I stepped up to her. 'Let's both go to Chailey and talk to them together,' I said.

Sylvia turned to me and nodded. I saw a tear escape from her eyes before she turned towards the kitchen door and hurried up the steps.

✳✳✳

'I have done my best for fourteen years. Whatever they think, they can't say I didn't try with Pollyanna,' said Sylvia the following afternoon, as we waited outside the headmaster's office at Chailey.

'This is not about our capabilities as mothers. I think even Dr Donahue knows better than that.'

'What are you going to do when Rex has finally grown up, Emily? What kind of life are you going to make for yourself?'

'If this is about what happened yesterday, Sylvia—'

'Emily, I worry about you. You don't think enough about yourself.'

'I still have Clemmie, remember?'

'Clemmie won't replace Rex to you.'

'Laurence and I will work something out. It will be all right.'

Sylvia raised an eyebrow just as the headmaster's door swung open.

'Ladies,' the grey-haired gentleman greeted us with a tight smile. 'Perhaps you'd like to step inside my office.'

Sylvia and I entered his office and took a seat opposite the headmaster's long desk.

'So,' said the headmaster, 'try not to worry too much, this isn't the first time we have experienced this type of incident amongst our disabled pupils.'

Sylvia glanced awkwardly around the office; and as her hand brushed mine, I reflected upon the future with a feeling of sadness at not sharing these moments anymore because Pollyanna and Rex had grown up.

✳✳✳

As Sylvia and I left the headmaster's office, we wandered down the hallway and found Laurence in deep conversation with

Dr Donahue by the corridor that led to the junior dorm. Upon noticing us, I caught the doctor's frown. Collectively, they strode up to Sylvia and me.

'Perhaps we should talk more about what happened?' Laurence suggested.

'Come into my office. We can speak more privately there.' The doctor offered an outstretched arm, and without another word, we followed him down the long corridor and into his office.

Once we were in the doctor's office, Laurence sat between Sylvia and me.

'Right,' said Dr Donahue, pulling out their files from the cabinet and placing them on his desk. 'Are you aware of how close they have become recently?'

'They've always been close.' I turned to glance at Sylvia with a smile. 'Whatever he has done, I'm sure we can resolve it,' I said, turning to the doctor.

'Rex is a fine pupil and a nice-natured boy; this is not a reflection upon your parenting style, Emily. But as he matures, there will be certain aspects of himself that he will struggle to have control over.'

Sylvia coughed.

'Is this about Rex's understanding of the birds and the bees?' asked Laurence.

'He knows about that, Laurence. My father told him when he was ten, by way of teaching him the natural sciences. I've done everything I could to teach him what it means to be a human being. But what he needs now is his father.' I watched Laurence hang his head in shame. Instinctively, I reached to take Laurence's hand in mine.

'It's time Rex knew what it means to be a man, and I believe you will find in yourself the right words to tell him.'

✳✳✳

I couldn't be certain whether Laurence had found the right words to say to Rex, as he returned to the office and pressed his lips together to offer Dr Donahue and me a pensive gaze.

Sylvia went to talk to Pollyanna, so Laurence took me to the common. We strolled for a while in silence, allowing the breeze to tickle our cheeks and cast our worries away. He wound his fingers through mine, and his hand whipped against my hip as we strode through the grass. I stopped to allow Laurence to crouch down, then slowly I knelt down beside him in the long grass and leaned my body into his, feeling him shudder in remorse from not having got to know his son sooner.

'I told Rex that being a man takes courage. It is about staying true to your convictions, and being tender and respectful to those you love. Never walk away from a girl without good reason, and even then you have to be absolutely sure that you won't have regrets years later. It is about learning to open your heart, without fear. I told Rex that to be a man you must be strong but gentle, and that can be hard at times. I told him not to be afraid, for experience would teach him what youth cannot, and I thought he was growing into a fine young man and that he should be proud of himself.'

Tears streamed down Laurence's cheeks and I held him to my breast, my lips brushing his golden-brown hair. 'I told him that I loved him, despite how I had treated him over the years—I loved him every day of my life,' he confessed. His shoulder heaved with a sob and I held him closer, inhaling the scent of his sweet sandalwood-soaped skin.

It took several minutes for us to pull away.

'We should go and speak to Sylvia and Chris,' I suggested.

He pulled me up, and I was reminded of years ago watching Rex as he crawled through the dew-speckled grass free of his artificial legs. Rehabilitation begins with the tiniest of steps, and Laurence had started today.

✻✻✻

Laurence pulled up outside Chris and Sylvia's house, and entering the hallway, Chris and Laurence went ahead to the lounge whilst Sylvia took me upstairs to her bedroom.

We sat upon the crushed velvet quilt, and I glanced towards the window at the way the cotton drapes cast a misty hue on the garden below. She had on a blue floral dress that reached her ankles, and for a moment she ignored me to reach for her mirror and to apply a layer of red lipstick.

'Laurence spoke to Rex. He gave him the talk about being respectful to Pollyanna. I think he understands about proceeding with caution.' I glanced down at her pink nails. She discarded her mirror for my hand.

'It didn't go so well with Pollyanna. We had a terrible fight. She asked me why I took Thalidomide, and the worst of it was that when I really looked at her, deficient of arms with no hands to hold or comfort, I didn't have an answer.'

'There is real magic in enthusiasm.'
Norman Vincent Peale

Chapter Sixty-One

One afternoon, my mother and I took Pollyanna and Rex to the lido at Black Rock, near Brighton Marina, offering us a view of the dotted high-rise buildings which had sprung up in the town. We sat on the upper terrace and gazed at the swimming pool below. The place had been more spectacular during my childhood, when its art deco architecture had been fashionable; but gradually over the years the building had fallen into a state of disrepair. I sipped my lemonade, positioned with my mother to one side and the teenagers on the other. Rex and Pollyanna still caused a few fixed stares, but they had long grown accustomed to that. During that sultry afternoon with a gentle sea breeze, the two seemed more content to play cards than worry about what others thought of them.

My mother drew her chair closer to mine. I lapped up this moment of freedom, watching as Rex leaned over the table at Pollyanna. His lips brushed against her ear to whisper something that caused her to laugh. The table quaked from excitement, and she spilled her cards from her feet onto the table between them.

'Do you think Pollyanna is right for our Rex?' asked my mother. My trepidation set in as she directed my gaze to hers: brown eyes that didn't dare to hold back on emotion.

'Yes, I do. Look at how happy they are together.'

'That doesn't mean they are right for each other. Pollyanna, despite her disability, could well meet a strong and healthy man. Her beauty is quite exquisite.'

'Sounds like you think Rex is not worthy of her.'

'That's not what I meant. Rex is a good, kind boy without a fault. But if they ended up together, my concern is that Pollyanna might not be in it for the long term.'

'You're worried she's taken after her mother—or is it Chris who bothers you the most?'

'You know at some point you'll have to cut your ties with them.'

'Not if Rex and Pollyanna end up together, I won't,' I grinned.

'I wish you saw things more from my point of view,' my mother said.

I sat back in my chair, offering a glance at Rex and Pollyanna. This time her foot was grazing his cheek.

'I take everything you say into consideration, really I do. It's just that I'm an optimist, so imagine if they did end up marrying? That would mean all our hard work had paid dividends, and we had remained true to your intuition.'

'That must be the Rex effect. You have developed into an extraordinary woman, another reason for me to be proud,' my mother said, smiling in satisfaction.

I allowed my mother to think that she had won that battle, and with the lure of the summer's afternoon, I got to my feet, still feeling hope was within my grasp. 'We should go for a swim,' I suggested.

'Oh, not for me. You should take the children, though, it's good for their health.'

'Teenagers, Mummy, that's what society calls them at their age.'

Half an hour later, I was sitting by the pool's edge between Rex and Pollyanna. 'What were you talking about with Nanny?' asked Rex.

I took his hand. 'We have been talking about the two of you,' I said and awaited their response.

'Oh.' Pollyanna's lips curled in contemplation. She rested her chin on my shoulder.

'I think that what the two of you have together is very beautiful; never let anyone tell you otherwise. But for the serious stuff, you should wait until you're sure you'll have no regrets.'

I felt two sets of eyes penetrate mine for clarity. But today wasn't about lectures, it was about pure unadulterated joy as I leapt into the pool and shivered from the shock of the cool water. I turned to offer my arms to Rex and Pollyanna.

'Told you it would be cold,' said Pollyanna, seeming content to just splash the water with her feet.

'Tell me you're not scared of a little cold water?' I challenged.

Pollyanna pushed herself into a standing position, and without hesitation she jumped into the water and bobbed along beside me. We got Rex to slide into the pool, and, floating as one, we gazed up at the sun. I thought how marvellous it would be if the future was just as golden as the summer of '75.

✳✳✳

'Have you thought about the future—about what you are going to do now that Laurence seems to be a permanent fixture? The basement is becoming a little crowded,' my mother noted the following afternoon as we walked together by the marina.

'It's what I told you before. We are happy in the basement flat. I never expected to have another child after Rex, but in some strange way it has worked out well for both of us. Laurence and I have been helping each other to be better parents,' I said, looking ahead at the stark coastline and edge between two quite different worlds that were now coming together.

My mother pushed my hair behind my ear. I stopped on the pavement and turned to her anxiously. 'It's still all about Laurence, isn't it? You can't trust yourself to love him fully,' she hinted.

I glanced down at the asphalt, searching for the tiniest of cracks. 'Do you want us gone? Has our tenancy expired?' I asked plainly.

'Of course not, Emily. I just worry that your friend across the square is enough to cast aspersions on the state of your marriage.'

'My marriage must remain my personal concern. But I'm more certain than ever that Laurence will stay. This time, there is hope.' I glanced ahead at the sight of a small ship in the distance, making me wonder what the future held for my family in the years to come.

'Hope is all any of us have. Welcome to the real world,' she chided me gently. Then I allowed her to loop her arm through mine and guide me along the rest of the promenade in silence so worries of any kind could be left to another day.

'There are better things ahead than any we leave behind.'
C S Lewis

Chapter Sixty-Two
1975

One early autumn morning, a few days before Rex and Pollyanna were due to return to Chailey, my mother and I left the house with the children and headed for the seafront promenade. Rex rode ahead with Pollyanna, snaking beautifully between the blue metal frame and thick spinning wheels of his bicycle. Her head bobbed to and fro as she maintained a steady pace. Clemmie strolled between my mother and me, pulling on my hand and seeming desperate to be within reach of her brother's bicycle. I glanced at my mother and was surprised by her rare smile. We walked on until all I could see ahead was the tiny figure of Rex heading towards the beach and the shadow of the armless Pollyanna.

'Emily,' my mother said, still with the same tender smile. Her gentleness today was as infectious as Rex's newfound independence. 'What are your plans for the winter?' I slowed down and was rewarded by Clemmie's pout.

'Laurence will be in New York after Christmas. The basement will be quiet for a time, especially as I have been commissioned to write a new series of short stories on the theme of the sea. I imagine long walks on the beach for inspiration.'

'I miss them too, when they are away at Chailey,' my mother said. I nodded and my chest heaved with sorrow, for acknowledging that fact didn't make it any less painful.

'I was thinking of us taking a trip abroad this winter,' she said.

I gazed at her in surprise. 'I'm not sure. Wouldn't it be difficult with Rex?' I guided Clemmie over to the railings.

'But not impossible,' she added, coming to stand beside me. 'We could take Clemmie, too. She's young enough to enjoy the culture without it having too much of an effect on her education. It would be good for Rex to have time apart from Pollyanna. I would call it a healthy separation.'

'I don't know.' I shook my head, not sure about another separation from Laurence just as we were making a breakthrough in our marriage.

'I see this trip as an extension of Rex's education.'

'Where did you have in mind?' I asked, knowing that in this mood nothing would stop her. I also wondered contrarily if there was still a spirit of adventure lurking inside me somewhere.

'I want to go back to India. It's been a long time since I've been home.' My mother's lips quivered in memory of the past that she hadn't spoken to me about.

'What about Laurence?' Could the opposite of what we were doing be what was needed for us to move ahead in our marriage?

'It would just be the two of us and the children. Think of it as a journey of self-discovery.'

'Very modern, Mummy,' I smiled. 'So who is going to break the news to Pollyanna?'

'It will only be for a month at the most, and I won't allow myself to be intimidated by a fifteen-year-old.'

'Um,' I said, as Clemmie climbed onto the railing between us. We breathed in lush mouthfuls of salty air. I couldn't help but contemplate what it would be like for us in India; and of the ones left behind, whom would we miss the most?

'Friends can help each other.
A true friend is someone who lets you have
total freedom to be yourself.'
Jim Morrison

Chapter Sixty-Three

Sylvia stopped by the house to see me the following week. My mother had already been to Sylvia and Chris' to discuss the India trip. But I didn't know if they had broken the news to Pollyanna yet. So Sylvia and I walked to the pier in silence. Leaning over the railing at the waves below, I thought of another time with Sylvia at her house on Regency Square, memories that were now rather distant, but appeared all the more poignant that afternoon.

'So you're going to India?' Sylvia said. Her bare arm grazed mine, creating a mosaic of freckles and goose bumps. A chill in the air warned us of the changing season and of sporadic weather, which we had no control over.

'My mother sprang it on me yesterday. I had no idea she felt so strongly about India.'

'I don't think that's the reason why she is doing this. I see it more as a way of determining her grandson's future. The dilemma of old or new money must be a tough one,' she said.

'Don't be like that,' I said, glancing into her cool eyes.

'You're very brave to take Rex to India. The chance of picking up a stomach bug will surely dissipate much of the holiday feeling.'

'I'm thinking of it as more of a cultural trip for Clemmie and Rex to learn about India.'

'A month with Mummy, I'm not sure if I envy or pity you.' She paused. 'I wish I could get away from everything. You must know that this month away will do little to cure Rex of his friendship with my daughter. Life is rarely that simple.'

'I know, but my mother hasn't figured that out yet. Which,' I bit my lip, 'makes it all the more gratifying for us.'

'So you're not running away then, Emily?'

Sylvia turned her blue stare upon me. I looked out to the sea, because that was my way of dealing with things in those days.

'Of course not,' I shook my head. 'Why would you say that?'

I still wasn't looking at her.

'Because, Emily, it wasn't all that long ago when you were seriously thinking of leaving Laurence for good. And what's more, you would have done it if you hadn't fallen pregnant with Clemmie. That's why you feel the way you do about her, and it is okay to feel that way. It's not your fault. It's just the way it happened. So now you're going to India, and I'm guessing that is without Laurence, which makes me think that you haven't completely dismissed my proposition. You are still drawn to the idea of an independent life. But I am disappointed that you are willing to be that far away from me when nothing in our friendship has changed, as far as I am concerned, that is,' said Sylvia.

I felt myself blink away my tears. Her intuition felt almost frightening. She reached for my hand but I didn't turn to her, thinking how infuriating it was that she was right about everything—yet again.

'It had better be just a month you're gone for, or I might have to fly out to see you and bring you home.' The lightness in her tone encouraged me to turn to her at last, and a smile beckoned at my lips, thinking how much I would like her to do just that, but most of all how I wished she were coming with us. A month without Sylvia—could I cope with that? I took a deep breath, convincing myself that I would just have to try.

*'Life is not a problem to be solved,
but a reality to be experienced.'*
Søren Kierkegaard

Chapter Sixty-Four

I wasn't looking forward to breaking the news of the India trip to Dr Donahue, and delayed my visit to Chailey until just before the Christmas holidays. Stepping inside his office, I took a seat opposite his desk and cleared my throat a couple of times to find the courage to break the news to him.

'Is everything all right?' His blue eyes regarded me gently, but I remained silent. 'Rex has not been as talkative as usual. From what I have been told, he has been distracted in most of his classes. Pollyanna hasn't been much better, either. I would like to think that over the years, I have gotten to know you pretty well and understand when something is troubling you.'

'It wasn't my idea,' I said. 'It's important you understand that.'

'I see,' he said, pouring a cup of tea and passing it across the desk to me. I shook my head. 'Please, it doesn't taste that bad,' he promised with a smile.

I took the cup and saucer into my hands and enjoyed a small sip of warm milky tea.

'I haven't travelled much in my life,' I confessed. 'I went to university; that was where I met Laurence. He studied the sciences while I was occupied by the arts—English literature, to be precise.'

'Right,' he offered me another warm gaze.

'After university we got married, and a couple of years later Rex was born. The rest you could probably well guess.'

'Indeed.'

'My mother has proposed a trip for us to India. I can't leave Rex behind at Chailey. He has to come with us. I think you can understand why.'

'Are you aware of how much schooling he will miss in the process?'

'Couldn't we put it down to a cultural trip for Rex? A chance to demonstrate that disability isn't a bar to worldwide travel?'

'He will need permission from the headmaster before he boards his flight.'

'My mother is quite insistent about us going.'

'Mrs Miles is the grandmother, but you are Rex's mother. What do you think?'

'I think Rex has missed out on a lot in his life and has earned the right to an exotic holiday. As for his education, we can take some books with us. Rex is a bright boy, like his father.'

'His mother more, I would say.' I felt heat rise to my cheeks. 'Save your blushes, Emily. I know why you came to me rather than the headmaster.'

'I'm sorry?' I said.

'My wife wasn't able to have children, so I have always had a bit of a soft spot for Rex. I'll speak to the headmaster on your behalf; but knowing Rex's academic record, I'm sure that we can come to an arrangement about him keeping up-to-date with his studies whilst abroad.'

'I don't know how to thank you, Doctor.'

'Just take good care of his health and your own. We will expect him back in February fit and well, and ready for class.'

'Yes, of course,' I said, returning my cup and saucer to his desk. I rose from my chair, and Dr Donahue stepped out from behind his desk and stood next to me.

'So what does Laurence think about all this?'

'If you're looking for an ally, you'll find him a weak one. He has always been thought of by my mother as more of a guest than an authority figure, I'm afraid.'

'I can imagine. Tell me, though: How did the two of you get through the shock of Thalidomide and remain married?'

'I have no idea. I think we are still working through it, even now.'

'Then trust me, you're doing well,' he said, offering me another smile before we parted ways for the time being.

'Nothing on earth can help the man
with the wrong mental attitude.'
Thomas Jefferson

Chapter Sixty-Five
January 1976

Laurence was folding his shirts into his suitcase for his trip to New York when I walked into the bedroom, a few days into the New Year. I found the legacy of Thalidomide lingered most strongly in our painful goodbyes, and sitting down on the bed beside him did little to ease the sharpness of our separation.

I watched Laurence reach for a pair of steely-grey trousers to pack. He didn't look at me for several minutes, and when he did, I saw dry eyes and taut cheekbones and reflected that subconsciously he had already departed from my life—yet again.

'I haven't explained properly the reason for the Indian trip,' I said, handing him a bundle of blue and grey ties.

'There's no need, really, Emily,' he said, finding a space for the ties amongst boxes of prescription pills.

'Even so, you will come home to find us gone, and that warrants some explaining. You know my mother has always been determined that Rex be raised like any other child with the same opportunities for love and education. Our trip to India is part of that plan.'

A glance at Laurence told me that I was looking at a confident salesman, and like any other pharmaceutical deal, I sensed him weighing up the merits of my conviction in his mind.

'Rex is not a normal child, regardless of your mother's sugar-coating.'

'Hardly,' I scoffed, reminded of my first trip to the park with Rex. I trembled, remembering the painful stares. 'You have no idea what it was like for me in the early days. My mother has mellowed somewhat with age.'

Laurence stared at me. I remained silent, playing instead with the zip on his suitcase.

'If you want to know the truth, I wish I was going with you. I've spent years in the drug industry, and I still can't predict which way it will go or if the stain of Distillers will ever leave me. There are times when I envy you, Emily.'

'Really?' I shuffled closer to him, so that just a pile of starched white shirts separated our hearts.

'Do you know what a rarity you are in the circles that I move in?' I shook my head. 'You are pure in heart, but the same cannot be said of me, for I am characterised ultimately by my past.'

'You're not that person anymore. Forget New York and come with us.' I bit down on my lip and grabbed his hand in mine. I was putting Laurence first for a change, but to my disappointment, he pulled away from me to concentrate again upon his packing.

'I would, if I could come with you. I love Rex, and do you know why, Emily? It is because he is you, everything good about you went into him, and in some strange way, he's more complete than I am. I cannot go with you because this job has got me tied in so tight.' He lowered his head in defeat. 'But I will wait for you to come home. I'm not running away anymore. I'm determined to be the husband you need,' he said, leaning over to cup my cheeks. I clung to his kiss as a bittersweet goodbye and the promise of a brighter tomorrow.

'To travel is to live.'
Hans Christian Andersen

Chapter Sixty-Six
January 1976

On the day of our departure to India, my father invited us for drinks in the upstairs dining room. My mother and I had a glass of sherry to toast our safe journey, while Clemmie and Rex sipped on their lemonades. It was hard to believe that in a matter of ten hours we would be in India.

'A penny for your thoughts.' My father smiled.

I glanced into his green eyes and found myself trembling in anticipation at the thought of being away from home for a month.

'I'm going to miss you. I hope I am doing the right thing.'

'Of course you are, Emily. The moment you can't bear to be away from home is the time to look beyond your horizon and see something more of the world.'

I looked at him sceptically.

'Your mother's ideas may be a little different, but she knows what she's doing, and trust me, you will enjoy Kerala.' He offered me a hug just as my mother approached to tell me that it was time for us to go.

My father drove us to Gatwick, and relaxing in the back seat of his old Rover, I watched Brighton slip away. I held tight to Clemmie and Rex, only hoping that the India of my imagination would live up to the reality of my first glance.

We said goodbye to my father outside the southern terminal and took our first step towards India. Later, after settling onto our British Airways flight, I watched Rex's eyes widen in excitement as the jet engines screeched on take-off. I felt my heart race, for apart from my father's neatly packed homeopathic travel remedies, I had prepared myself little for the culture shock of India.

We changed planes at Delhi, and, still dressed in our winter jumpers, we watched in wonder at the golden sunrise of southern Asia. A dozen fleeting birds soared through the misty sky, eager to escape the rising heat, which even through the Plexiglas, threatened to engulf our English bodies in a sweaty fever.

My mother reached into her handbag and offered us a homeopathic remedy. Chewing on the sugar pill, I glanced at her.

'Arsenicum,' she said, 'to help protect our English tummies from the bugs.' Rex looked to me for an explanation, but I shrugged my shoulders, knowing that from now on I was at the mercy of my mother's timely wisdom.

The flight from Delhi to Trivandrum, the capital of Kerala, took four and a half hours. Disembarking from the plane to board the bus to the terminal resulted in something of a military exercise, with Rex crawling and hopping between a tightly packed crowd of sari-clad women in hues of tangerine, mustard, and emerald, all of whom clung helplessly to each other under a fierce Indian sun. It wasn't until we had Rex back in his wheelchair, with the help of an Indian gentleman dressed in a sarong, that I was able to make my first impression of India. It was steamy and frantic, but despite the hurried atmosphere of the place, I was relieved to note that the adventurer in me was back to life.

During our taxi ride to the hotel, I glanced at the dotted palm trees as we snaked through the concrete centre to head towards the white colonial buildings. Thinking that must have reminded my mother of her childhood, I reached over to squeeze her hand. She looked at me in return, now free of my woollens.

'I hope you will like it here, Emily. It is close to the beach. The sea air has always been good for Rex's health.'

I glanced at Rex curled up next to a sleeping Clemmie. The driver's eyes flickered away from Rex in shame and focused instead on the garlands of brightly coloured lotus flowers which dangled from his mirror.

The car stopped just before the curve of a narrow backstreet. I had to crane my neck to make out the red-tiled gabled houses. The driver slammed his door and went to the boot for Rex's wheelchair. The scene was familiar to me by now, but not for the driver, who probably knew so little about Thalidomide. I caught his look of horror as he unfolded Rex's wheelchair and glanced at me in pity. My mother took charge with Rex, leaving me to carry Clemmie inside the guesthouse.

Our suite opened into a high-ceilinged veranda decorated with hunting trophies and rosewood furniture. We showered and took a nap. Falling asleep, I saw the driver's tormented eyes; except when he turned around properly, he had changed into Laurence. I trembled, feeling my body drench in sweat, at the thought of my old fears returning. Hours later, I forced my eyes open to the midday sun and the inhalation of a dozen spices and found that travelling had left me feeling ravenous.

'Wherever you go, go with all your heart.'
Confucius

Chapter Sixty-Seven

The following evening on the cusp of sunset, Rex and I left the guesthouse together and clambered onto the back of an auto-rickshaw bound for the nearby beach. His folded wheelchair rattled beside us as we bumped along the road. I inhaled the aroma of deep-fried batter from the dozens of stalls which lined the street, causing me to feel a wave of nausea, unsure if my body had quite adjusted to the shock of India yet.

I blinked to the sound of Indian pop emanating from the roadside vendors. This was mixed with the vibration from several motorcycles revving up for the evening's entertainment. Rex's fingers brushed against the edge of my cotton skirt in apprehension, and I thought of my mother back at the guesthouse with Clemmie.

'I hope they will be all right,' I said anxiously as our vehicle came to a sudden stop.

The driver jumped out of his cab and glanced at us. I pulled Rex into my arms. At fourteen he now weighed about six stone. The driver grabbed Rex's wheelchair and unfolded it quickly. He offered me a casual gaze as I settled Rex into his chair before I handed over several rupees in exchange.

Our struggle was rewarded with the sight of a golden sunset as we strolled around the perimeter of the beach. The sand beneath my feet was a welcome change from the shingles of Brighton. But as we continued farther, we found ourselves surrounded by a group of Indian children in bright cotton prints. One of the young girls swished in a tangerine-and-white spotted dress and was adorned with a golden choker at her throat. They danced around us in fascination, and their dark eyes widened at the sight of Rex's legs. Two of the older children stepped forward to gaze at him more closely. I placed my hand on Rex's shoulder and we remained silent, glancing ahead as the horizon turned a vivid pink.

I shuddered to the echo of clapping hands as a gentleman in a long white shirt and printed sarong shooed the children away, before turning to us in shame.

'I am so sorry for that.' He placed his palms together in prayer. At dusk his eyes shone with tears. 'Please accept my apologies.'

'It's all right. We are used to the stares, aren't we, Rex?'

'I just wish I could explain to the children why I am like I am,' said Rex, squeezing my hand.

'Please, you must come to my café for tea. I want you to have good impression of Kerala.'

I clutched the handles of Rex's wheelchair and glanced at the grey-haired gentleman. He seemed genuinely sorry about what had happened, so I followed him up the beach and to the seafront café.

At the café we found ourselves the last remaining customers and seated beneath an auspicious painting that depicted a cage of fighting tigers. I took a deep breath as a young woman dressed in a turquoise sari placed a platter of dosas down on the table in front of us. A glass of steaming tea sat to our right. I don't know which one of us was more surprised that evening by our courage; but as we enjoyed our first taste of Indian pancakes, I was glad that, of all the places in the world to begin our travels, we had brought Rex here to Kerala.

We stayed at the café for another hour, trying our best to explain Thalidomide and how it had caused Rex's birth defects, before hurrying back to the street to hail a rickshaw back to the guesthouse. By that time it was dark, and my heart thumped as our vehicle sped away from the beach and headed back towards the narrow side streets of the city.

Once back at the guesthouse, I helped Rex to shower and toilet in the small, dank, wet room, before my mother took over with the last of his dressing for bed. I heard the sound of Clemmie's snore and made for the outside veranda for my last breath of fresh air of the day. My mother joined me outside with the offer of a tipple of local whiskey as a nightcap.

'How did you do tonight?'

'Pretty well, I think.' The whiskey burned at my throat.

'That's good, Emily, ideal preparation for the future.' She stood close to me, without us touching. 'You should finish your drink and get a decent night's sleep. We'll be on the move first thing in the morning,' she said, and before I had the chance to ask anything further, she had disappeared back inside the bedroom.

'We travel not to escape life,
but for life not to escape us.'
Anonymous

Chapter Sixty-Eight

We left the city early the following morning after a breakfast of egg masala and spiced tea. Leaving the guesthouse, I took a quick stroll of the garden, looping between the potted palms and golden oleanders before feeling beckoned away by my family. I wheeled Rex along the main street, while my mother held Clemmie's hand. Then we scrambled onto the bus bound for Kovalam Beach. Juggling Rex and his wheelchair with a sleepy Clemmie clinging to my hip, I thought momentarily of home and of Laurence and Sylvia and wondered how they were coping without me. But I cast that thought aside as I pushed through the throng of travellers to claim the last remaining window seat. Rex shuffled onto my lap and my mother pulled Clemmie onto hers. I took a deep breath and was rewarded with the aroma of coconut oil and the whiff of a substance, which I later learnt, was hashish. The bus pulled away and we disappeared into the crowd, swaying from side to side as the bus began its descent through the village. Clemmie slunk onto my shoulder, seeming more lethargic than usual. Her bright cheeks I put down to a change in altitude.

We entered a lush oasis of towering palms and moist paddy fields, before reaching the first of several beaches. The sight of rich golden sand caused Rex to press his nose upon the misty glass for his first view of the tropics. The bus screeched to a halt. I saw a red-and-white lighthouse in the distance. We clambered off the bus and I turned to my mother.

'While you were out yesterday evening, I secured our accommodation here,' she said, pointing to a hotel at the end of the beach. My mother lifted Clemmie into her arms and my little girl buried her face into my mother's breast. I sighed, hoping that Clemmie's change in behaviour wasn't the sign of anything more sinister than traveller's fatigue.

Rex spun his wheels and we made our way along the concrete path to the hotel ahead. The hotel was surrounded by coconut palms, the breeze of which eased my thumping head. Our room had a balcony overlooking the sea. I put Clemmie down for a rest before my mother, Rex and I sat on the balcony, cupping our glasses of fresh lime juice.

'How long are we staying here for, Mummy?' I asked.

'I've booked us in for a week. It might be a little hectic here at night, so we will see how it goes,' she said, while fanning herself with her straw hat. The beach was filling up with tourists, all sporting various interpretations of Flower Power, while closer to the sea stood several fishermen in sarongs and white shirts, pulling in their fishing nets.

I leaned back in my chair, absorbing the heady atmosphere. I had come to India, like most of the travellers, to discover a little more about myself. I was aware that as Rex steadily grew into a man, I would have to make a decision about my own future, with both Sylvia and Laurence weighing heavily on my mind.

Later, Rex and I decided to go for our first swim. He crawled along the sand, gazing up at my black-and-pink printed swimming costume as we made our way into the sea, but it wasn't long before the waves thrashed us about wildly.

'Mum,' said Rex, 'I think Pollyanna would like it here, too.'

I smiled. 'Yes, I think she would, although I'm not sure your father would approve. It might be a bit too rustic for him.' I laughed, swallowing a mouthful of salty water. I held Rex in my arms and struggled to carry him back to the shore. We rested on the sand, and as little ripples passed over our bodies, I couldn't remember the last time I had felt this much at peace. Staggering back to the hotel to towel ourselves off, Rex crawled beside me; but as we climbed onto the balcony, I sensed a suspicious silence from our bedroom. Rex rested on the balcony, drying out his black trunks, while I wrapped a sarong around my waist and went into the bedroom. There, I found my mother pacing the room anxiously.

'Mummy?' I trembled.

'Where's Rex?'

'He's outside drying off,' I said.

'It's Clemmie. She started being sick while you were out.'

'No!' I cried. 'Where is she?'

'She's in the room next door to stop the spread of infection.'

'Infection?'

'We are in India, Emily. The hotel called a local homeopath who has given her some remedies and left us a flask of boiled water, ginger and honey to administer to her every two hours.'

'Right,' I said, although I didn't really understand at all. I felt my heart pound with worry that my little girl could fall seriously ill so far from home and admonished myself silently for having not been able to persuade Laurence to join us on our trip.

'I will sit with her, if you'll look after Rex,' I said, rushing next door to be with my little girl. I saw her curled up in bed surrounded by vials and flasks of traditional medicine, making me think that if ever there had been a test of my mothering instincts, this was it.

I stayed with Clemmie for the afternoon, massaging her back as she vomited into the bucket. My mother came in periodically to offer us both cool drinks, and for me she offered rice from the hotel buffet. I forked at the sticky grains, seeing only my daughter's pained expression and flushed cheeks. It wasn't until the evening that I could be persuaded to sit on the balcony with Rex. I was relieved to see that, so far, he hadn't fallen ill with Clemmie's horrible bug.

A crowd had gathered on the beach and began swaying their sarong-clad hips to the Indian beat. They each bore a single red dot in the centre of their foreheads as a symbol of their recent visit to the temple. I thought of Clemmie. When was the last time I had prayed for her health? Had I been too preoccupied with Rex to notice her vulnerability to disease?

'It's not your fault, Mum. We all ate the same food. It could have been any of us.' Rex squeezed my hand.

I nodded. Rex's kind words did little to dissuade my feelings of guilt. Her infancy should have been reason enough to have kept her at home with my father. 'I wish your dad was here now.'

'You think he could have helped us with his medicines?'

'Probably, but more than that I wish for his support. I have always thought of him as being more knowledgeable than me; maybe that was my weakness,' I sighed.

'I look up to Pollyanna, and not just because of her height, but because of her beauty. She could choose any of the arm-deficient boys from the swimming club, yet she seems to want me—and do you know why?'

I shook my head.

'She thinks I'm the best of the wheelchair boys.' He grinned and a smile broke on my lips.

'I'm glad I had you, Rex. You make my world a brighter place.' I kept my hand in his, feeling a transference of strength.

'How is she?' I asked my mother as she came out to join us.

'Still the same,' she said, and touched my shoulder. I felt my stomach knot and ran inside to the bathroom to vomit what little I had eaten of my lunch.

There was a party that night on the beach. I heard the twang of the Indian sitar before the sky exploded with a shower of red, yellow, and green fireworks. I had been sick half a dozen times since learning of Clemmie's condition. I stopped by her room every so often to hear her pained groans, causing my stomach to twist tighter in guilt. Why had I brought her here?

I sat on the balcony and sipped on a concoction of water, ginger and honey, the local remedy for bad tummies. With the party in full swing, I caught sight of a young couple sharing a cigarette, which let off a sickly smell as potent in scent as my tender stomach. I thought of Laurence and Sylvia back home drifting through their ordinary lives, and reflected how travel allowed us to slip into the skin of someone else. Perhaps that was what made travel such an appealing pursuit.

My mother came out to offer me a quilt to wrap around my bare shoulders, but feeling feverish, I shook my head.

'Clemmie has clearly inherited my weak stomach,' I smiled, through another knot of pain.

'How are you doing, Emily?' She touched my forehead. 'You should stay with Clemmie tonight as a precaution,' she said, helping me to my feet.

I squeezed her hand tighter than I should, and felt my insides fall away as we reached the sanctuary of the cool-tiled bathroom.

✳✳✳

I awoke the following morning and found myself on a makeshift mattress at the foot of Clemmie's bed. My sheet was drenched in sweat and I had a dull ache in my stomach. I reached for the bucket to vomit and heard a reassuring sound.

'Rex,' said Clemmie from above.

'Clemmie, sweetheart, how are you doing today?' I pulled my body up and onto the side of her bed. Strands of her auburn hair were stuck to her cheeks, which I took as a sign of her broken fever.

My mother came in to offer Clemmie yoghurt as her first food to break the fast, and seeing her lips curl around the spoon, I gripped her small hand in mine and prayed for her recovery.

'Peace comes from within.'
Buddha

Chapter Sixty-Nine

We left Kovalam Beach two weeks to the date of our arrival and took the bus back to Trivandrum, where we caught a train bound for Kollam on the Malabar Coast, situated at the heart of the old spice trade. The train journey took us about an hour; and although Kovalam had intrigued me with its party scene, it felt good to be escaping the air of sickness and hashish. I was excited to journey farther into the exotic Kerala backwaters.

Exiting Kollam railway station, we found ourselves in the centre of a town built between the sea and surrounding lake.

'We will find a hotel first to shower and relax,' said my mother, gazing at Clemmie.

My daughter was looking better than she had during the last few days. Her green eyes now shone with vitality, which I took as a sign of her recovering health. But still I held her hand protectively, while my mother wheeled Rex towards the waiting taxi. The driver glanced at us in curiosity, and we probably looked a strange sight to him as we clambered into the backseat to the stares of a growing crowd.

During the drive into town, we bypassed the bazaar with its tiled wooden houses and patchwork of winding backstreets. I felt a little disappointed by the place, for other than the groups of fishermen weaving through the market and sporting their day's catch, the town had little to hold my attention.

I turned to Rex and he, too, seemed a little downcast. With my thoughts turning to home, I decided it was time for postcard writing and lunch.

The hotel room in Kollam bore smudged white walls and a view of the beach. I had to carry Rex up to the rooftop garden for a view of the sea. We settled down to a lunch of steamed rice, various vegetable dishes, lime pickle, plantain chips, and curd—all served on a banana leaf—before getting down to my writing. My first postcard was to Laurence. I wrote of our safe arrival and of the beaches and sea. It was only as I signed my name that I realised how distant he had become, and thinking of our different interweaving paths, I wondered where mine would take me next.

✳✳✳

The following morning we took the bus to the jetty at Ashtamudi Lake for the morning cruise to Alappuzha. Standing on the jetty, I looked ahead to the lush greenery and red-roofed bungalows dotted along the shoreline. We boarded the double-decker boat carved from dark oil-wood with a plaited canopy of palm and coil. Barefoot and fashioning the regional sarong, the crewmen helped Rex and his wheelchair board the boat, while I carried Clemmie, whose body felt lighter than it had before the start of our holiday. Taking a deep breath, I resolved to give adequate attention to both of my children, but felt that caring for Clemmie through her sickness had shown me that my feelings for her ran a lot deeper than I thought.

The next days passed easily, and we glided along the serene waters with the help of the gondolier-like boatmen and their long poles. This proved to be my own personal highlight of a difficult decade. There was just the lapping of water against the side of the boat as I enjoyed coconut pancakes and caught up on my sleep. Between naps, I watched Clemmie plait the blonde hair of her doll. Rex had his wheelchair positioned beside me. He kept himself busy by sketching the passing scenery, taking an interest in the coconut trees and curved bridges, which sprouted out from the velvet-green bed of the lagoon. I closed my eyes in peace and opened them again as our boat pulled into another stop along the way: this time beside the jetty where a row of wooden houses stood perched at the water's edge.

✳✳✳

We stayed on the houseboat for five days before pulling into Kottayam, the gateway between mountain and forest. From there we took the bus into the Cardamom Hills, close to the Periyar Wildlife Sanctuary, renowned for its elusive sightings of tigers and leopards and the spice trail. Our bus chugged into a rather scruffy bus stand in the village of Kumily. We clambered off the bus, with Rex crawling and hopping down onto the gravel road. While an American couple helped Rex get back into his wheelchair, I held Clemmie's hand and my mother went to fetch our bags. We headed for the roadside bazaar, and I bought some herbs and essential oils to take home to my father. Then we made our way into the village.

We found a red-roofed bungalow in which to spend the night. The bungalow was situated with lush green plains on one side and the blue-hued mountains in the background. The owners were a young couple in their thirties with two young daughters. The husband proudly boasted of the bungalow's bucket hot water and a balcony with a view of the point where the mountains caressed the clouds.

Upon settling into our room, my mother decided that she needed rest and offered to watch Rex and Clemmie, leaving me free to explore the village alone. The proprietor, dressed in western clothes, offered me a ride in his car to the local spice gardens. During the short car journey, he chatted incessantly about the points of interest in Kerala. But feeling weary from my travels, I found my attention drifting away from the present and back to Brighton and my life there.

Arriving at the gardens, I thanked him but was glad for the freedom to explore alone, and upon paying the entrance fee, I wandered inside. I stood to the back of a group of Americans learning the finer details of the nutmeg. I quickly slipped away unnoticed and found shade under a rubber tree. It was there that I took out a postcard of the backwaters, depicting a scene of several long wooden boats moored to a coconut tree. I sat on the dusty ground and took out a blue pen and wrote:

Dearest Sylvia,

It is truly beautiful here. This place is paradise. Your tender smiles and courage are with me in India. I wish only for your company to share this stunning place with!

Missing you dearly,
Love and kisses,
Emily x

I hugged my knees and placed the postcard to one side. I hadn't realised how long I had been daydreaming, until a blonde woman in Indian dress approached me with a frown.

'Are you okay?' she asked, with what I recognised as an American accent.

'Yes,' I said and reached for the postcard before accepting the offer of her hand. Pulling me up, I brushed away the wood chipping from my skirt and adjusted my handbag on my shoulder.

Her grey eyes fell to the postcard clutched in my right hand.

'Must be to someone special.' She smiled. 'Do you want to see the rest of the gardens or are you ready to go? If so, we could share an auto-rickshaw back to Kumily.'

'I'm ready to go. I've left my children with my mother in the village.'

She nodded and walked alongside me. The breeze from the spice trees made me gaze up at the sky, the same one that covered Sylvia and Laurence in Brighton.

'You're English? Where are you from, London?' she asked as we passed through the gates and found several auto-rickshaws touting for business. We clambered into the first one, and I was relieved when the driver switched on the engine.

'Brighton, actually. I have a son called Rex, and he's disabled because of Thalidomide.' I watched her lips form an 'oh,' and she fell silent.

When our rickshaw pulled outside the site of several red-roofed bungalows, I was surprised by her offer to pay the fare and of her parting words.

'Good for you for raising him yourself. I hope you enjoy the rest of your trip.'

'Thank you,' I said, and hopped down to catch the swish of her green scarf as she headed for the bungalow adjacent to ours. I hoped to see her again before we journeyed farther into the mountains the next day.

*'Use everything as an opportunity to understand,
grow, and expand.'*
Unknown

Chapter Seventy

The cluster of corrugated iron indicated that our bus was approaching the hill station of Munnar. I glanced downwards at the leafy slopes of the tea plantations. The gardens were broken only by the gables from the old colonial-style bungalows. As we stumbled from the bus, our lungs were rewarded with a breath of crisp air from the Anamudi Peak Mountain. Under a perfect blue sky, I felt a sense of rising nausea after the crisscrossing mountain road. So we headed towards a roadside café for a cup of sugary tea and pondered the next stage of our journey.

'I think we should spend a few days here,' suggested my mother. 'There are some lovely walks to be had, and the opportunity for writing or sketching.'

My writing had come to a halt since coming to India. If I was to keep to my deadline, I would have to make a start soon; but for some reason I felt compelled to take a breath and observe everything that India had to offer. I couldn't remember the last time I had relaxed and taken life at such a slow pace.

We ventured into the town surrounded by beautiful mountains, streams and random buildings, all centred round a hectic market. Our accommodation for the next few days was a British-style stone bungalow nestled in the tea gardens and perched on the hillside of Munnar. The front terrace had a flower garden with views of the Anamudi Peak.

In our bedroom little stars and moons had been stuck to the ceiling, in celebration of the town's popularity with honeymooners. That night I fell asleep under the illusion of a night's sky, allowing me the rare privilege of not having to consider a single regret of my life.

The main excursion from Munnar was a visit to the tea plantation, but the effort it would take for Rex to join us convinced me that our time here would be better spent soaking up the calm, gentle air, surrounded by the peace of the mountains. Rex didn't seem to mind all that much and retreated to his art by collecting samples from the wild gardens to examine and sketch in detail. In between this activity, I pressed his schoolbooks on him as part of my promise to Dr Donahue. With something of a scowl he retreated inside the bungalow to study.

My mother had brought along chalk from home and drew out an outline of hopscotch on the patio. I thought of Pollyanna dangling from the monkey bars as my mother rolled a stone and Clemmie's fair legs hopped from one number to another.

I sat down with a glass of tea to write and tried to imagine the wild Arabian waves crashing onto the sand, the revellers dancing barefoot into the night, and a sky lit by a festival of colour. Then my mind turned back to Brighton: casual saunters amongst the shingle, the taking of the water under a continental sky. The sea had set the rhythm of my life, and as I picked up my pen, I was bobbing on the waves with Rex, without a single care.

Sometime later, I looked up and saw the American lady from the spice gardens, still clad in Indian dress.

'We never introduced ourselves properly. I'm Jennifer Lewis.'

'Emily Alexander.' I smiled as she took a seat beside me.

'You are alone again,' she observed with interest.

'Not quite.' I nodded towards Clemmie and my mother, a few yards away and still engrossed in their game.

'Your daughter is very beautiful. You must be proud.'

'I am,' I said, feeling her glance at me to see if what I said matched up with how I felt inside.

'Where is your son; Rex, isn't it?'

'Inside studying, or at least I hope he is.' I gave a little laugh, feeling somewhat unnerved by her conversation.

She nodded. 'After you told me about him, I hoped to see you again. You looked so wistful in the spice garden, and your confession all added up.'

'Really?' I said, forgetting my nerves to draw closer to her in fascination.

'I work at a Catholic school here in India, helping all kinds of disadvantaged children. India is a very spiritual place. I can understand why you brought Rex here.'

She got to her feet. 'You're a writer, which makes you something of an educated woman. You're married, but you didn't bring your husband with you, and that postcard wasn't addressed to him, either. Am I right? If you're looking to change your life, then consider taking the first step. I run a school in Kochi, and I'm looking for teachers.' Jennifer scribbled down her contact details, but before I could utter a response to her question, she had disappeared inside the bungalow.

'He travelled in order to come home.'
William Trevor

Chapter Seventy-One

A few days later, we departed Munnar and headed north to the peninsula of Kochi at the point where the backwaters meet with the Arabian Sea. Upon arrival in town, we took a taxi to the oldest church in India. I glanced at the white stone façade and triple bell towers of St Francis' Church. The sight of the cross propelled me forward, and I wheeled Rex inside. He slid himself into a pew next to Clemmie at the back of the church.

As my mother and I walked down the aisle, the wood and cloth fans, which operated from the ceiling, offered us a refreshing breeze from the heat. I crossed myself in the nave and cast a glance at Clemmie, who sat wrapped in Rex's arms. My mother placed a hand on my shoulder and guided me towards a pew close to the wooden carved altarpiece.

'Emily,' she whispered, 'I saw you talking to Jennifer in the garden.'

'You know her?' I asked.

'I saw how happy you were in the backwaters. You have come a long way since the day you brought Rex home to us. In that time you have grown into a confident woman and able to achieve many great things, one of which was leaving Laurence behind in England, and taking the children on this trip with me. So now is the time to think about your life and decide what you want to do next. Where is your heart? India is good as any place to work that out.' My mother touched my shoulder, giving me much to ponder during the last day of our glorious holiday.

I went to light a candle.

Later, we took a taxi to the fort, bypassing the spice market and stopping a short distance from the beach. There, my mother had secured our night's stay in a suite with a large wooden bed and teak floor. We had a view of the fishermen in their bright hues, busily unhooking their large Chinese fishing nets onto the golden sand.

That night I left the hotel alone and wandered onto the beach. I threw a pebble into the sea and thought again of Jennifer's proposition. Did I really need to start again, when everything I wanted in my life could be found in Brighton? Was it just a matter of accommodating my love for Laurence with my friendship with Sylvia to live the life that I want? I returned to the hotel and crawled into bed beside my mother, Clemmie, and Rex to contemplate the idea further still as I prepared myself for the start of our journey home in the morning.

✳✳✳

Clemmie sat on my lap during the train ride back to Trivandrum. The barred windows allowed for a shrouded view of the dusty villages, interspersed between the larger towns. Our train trundled through the southern Indian plains at a steady pace that made my head nod from exhaustion after our four-week travels. Had it really been that long since I bid my father goodbye? Was I really not tempted by Jennifer's offer of a fresh start without the need for any concessions to be made?

I turned to my mother and watched her play Scrabble with Rex. She gazed at me blankly. Clemmie snuggled in my lap and stuck her thumb in her mouth. I glanced down at her without the nerve to correct her babyish ways.

'Chai!' sang a small Indian gentleman pushing a metal trolley. He was dressed in a white jacket speckled with grease. His weary eyes regarded me with hope. Sharing his fatigue of life, I nodded. He offered me black tea in a small clay pot.

'Be careful what you drink,' my mother warned.

I took a gulp of sugary tea and cupped the pot protectively.

'You never told me how you knew Jennifer Lewis,' I said. Opposite me, Rex spelt out the word *tenacious*.

'Emily, my family was in India for a long time before independence.'

I traced the lip of my cup in fascination. 'What do you think about Jennifer's proposition?'

She shrugged nonchalantly. 'That's not up to me, but for you to decide. In the end the decisions you make about the future are your responsibility, not mine, or that friend of yours.' She raised an eyebrow.

I sighed because for a whole month she hadn't mentioned Sylvia. It was with a feeling of dread that all the tension went to my stomach, causing my nausea to return at the thought of the conflicts which lay in wait for me at home.

That evening we returned to the same guesthouse in Trivandrum, but to a changed atmosphere. Rex positioned himself as far from me as possible on the balcony. He refused to leave the guesthouse for dinner, content only for Clemmie to crawl onto his lap and scribble into her colouring book. It was left to my mother to arrange for our take-away curries from a local restaurant. We spooned our vegetable biryani to a shared silence, and I was relieved that my mother had us booked on to an early-morning flight home.

'To live happily is an inward power of the soul.'
Aristotle

Chapter Seventy-Two

The following evening, when we returned home, Laurence was waiting in the basement flat ready to offer a hug. I shivered in our lounge from the shock of an English winter's night, and wrapped my arms around Laurence's neck, not pulling away until my mother came in with Rex and Clemmie. Then he let go of me and picked up our daughter, holding her high in the air so her small hands grazed the cornice. She let out a cry of excitement.

'You're as light as a feather. Tell me your mother fed you in India,' he teased, planting a kiss on Clemmie's cheek.

'She was sick, we both were. Somehow Rex and Mother evaded the bug. I'm not sure how,' I sighed.

'But you're both all right now,' he said with a watchful gaze.

'Yes,' I smiled.

'Mum got offered a job in India as a teacher,' Rex piped up.

'Really?'

I nodded.

'I see.' He cleared his throat and set Clemmie down onto the floor. She ran to Rex and clambered onto his lap.

'I'll leave you to it,' my mother said, and I heard the click of her retreating footsteps down the hallway.

'So,' he pursued.

'I can't take the job, Laurence. It would mean splitting up the family, and that's the last thing I want to do.'

'Are you sure? I mean, we never sat down and made plans for the future.'

'Absolutely. Clemmie's too young and you have your job here. Brighton is the place for us. This is home, and that's the way it is going to stay,' I said, placing one hand on Rex's shoulder and the other on Laurence's in jubilation of being home at last.

'I missed you all so much when you were away,' his eyes were still on me and the tension returned to my stomach, making me feel that it was all too much at times, with too many expectations placed on me. I wished for a moment to be back in India. But how could I have stayed there with Clemmie so small? I focused on Laurence. I was here for him, and he had been so good about our trip in the first place that I felt a stab of guilt about wanting to be somewhere else.

'No more separations, and we must mean it this time, Emily. We have come so far, that must count for something surely?'

I nodded, knowing it would be a long while before we would ever be separated again.

Laurence drew me away from Rex, and we hugged each other tightly to convince ourselves that what we said, we meant.

I had missed him, of course I had, but my short experience of freedom had taught me that I was more than capable of being separated from both Laurence and Sylvia; and now that I was back with them, a sense of independence had been borne in my heart. I needed a more fulfilling life—one that involved me taking back control of my life, starting from this day.

'One day I will find the right words,
and they will be simple.'
Jack Kerouac

Chapter Seventy-Three
June 1976

Rex was home for the weekend when David Jones from *The Sunday Times* came to the house. Sporting the same long haircut and brown satchel, he offered me a jubilant smile as I ushered him into the hallway.

'Emily, I had to see you personally to show you the article that I couldn't have done without your help.'

For a moment, I stood wishing he had a coat for me to take. I was thankful to hear the whiz of Rex's wheelchair as he joined me by the door, followed shortly by the pounding of Clemmie's footsteps. My father came out of his study and looked from David to me curiously.

'Please, allow me to introduce myself, I'm David Jones from *The Sunday Times*. As of today, we are free from legal inhibition and are finally able to publish our full article on Thalidomide. I was so impressed by Emily's courage to speak out against Distillers that I wanted her to be the first to see the article in full.'

'Then you had better come into my study,' my father said, glancing at David with interest.

'Thank you,' David replied, and as we assembled in my father's study, Clemmie was quick to climb onto Rex's lap.

'Can I get you a coffee?' I asked, taking a seat on the leather sofa beside David and feeling a lot less nervous than I had been when I gave him my interview on Thalidomide a few years back. But still I felt on tenterhooks about seeing his article in print.

Crossing his legs, David's interest turned to Rex, watching as his arms reached around Clemmie's waist to hold her in place.

Clearing his throat, David reached inside his satchel for a leafed copy of what must have been the article, still in its rough version.

'I thought you might like to have a read before it goes to print,' said David. 'The Thalidomide story really stuck with me. I can't remember the last time a story has made me so angry. That's why I pushed my editor for it to go public. I felt action had to be taken to make sure this never happens again. Future generations have to be made aware of the facts of Thalidomide and of the simple truth that, as a rule of thumb, if they say a drug is non-toxic and safe, it probably isn't.'

'Rex doesn't have any thumbs,' Clemmie blurted out. A silence fell on the room until Rex spoke up.

'Can I see your article, too?'

'Yes, of course,' said David. Clemmie climbed down from Rex's lap and ran to the window seat to retrieve her favourite doll. Releasing the lever on his wheelchair, Rex sped over to us, and David opened the front page of his tightly bound article entitled 'Thalidomide: The Story They Suppressed.'

My father joined us, and together we read how Thalidomide was the greatest drug tragedy of our time, and that it could have been avoided altogether.

I reached for Rex's hand and squeezed it tightly, confident that having some of the answers to our questions would be enough to help us to forgive the past and take a positive step forward in our lives.

'Fortune favours the brave.'
Virgil

Chapter Seventy-Four
May 1977

'Mrs Alexander,' said the headmaster, as I put the phone receiver to my ear.

'Is everything all right with Rex?' I asked, just as Laurence came through the door with Clemmie. I indicated for him to stand by the telephone.

'I'm afraid that Rex has gone missing from Chailey; so has Pollyanna.'

'Missing?' I felt my voice rise with panic. 'How has that happened? Aren't they supervised at school?'

'We do allow the pupils a certain amount of freedom at Chailey, Mrs Alexander, and as part of his upcoming graduation from school, Rex has been learning life skills such as cooking, cleaning, and using public transport to do shopping. But of course we are doing everything we can to locate them and bring them safely back to school.'

I had heard through Rex about his practical life training with another boy called Simon, who I had met briefly in the boys' dormitory when I had first taken Clemmie to Chailey to introduce to Rex. This left me wondering how Pollyanna would react to Rex spending time with another friend. Sylvia had never said how Pollyanna had handled Rex's month-long absence during our India trip last year, so I surmised that she had stored up these feelings of jealousy and had quietly planned their escape today.

'Do you know of any special place that they like to go to together?' I felt Clemmie press a collage on me that she had made from various cutouts from the Kays Catalogue.

'Mummy!' She pulled on my arm to force my attention towards her.

I covered the mouthpiece. 'Yes, darling it's beautiful.' I suppressed a feeling of frustration from the current demands of both my children and turned to Laurence for help. 'Rex and Pollyanna have gone AWOL,' I said.

'What? Okay, I'll settle Clementine upstairs with your mother, and I'll be back shortly.' He squeezed my hand as a gesture of support.

I breathed calm into my lungs.

'Have you contacted the Watersmiths?' I asked.

I heard the chime of the doorbell. 'Sorry, there's someone at the door, I'll have to call you back.' I placed the receiver back in its cradle and was about to answer the door when my father descended the staircase with a middle-aged female patient.

'You've got your remedies, Mrs Lewes. Any problems, do telephone,' he said, opening the door to let her out, while at the same time ushering Sylvia and Chris into the hallway.

'There you are, Emily, I have been trying to call you. Have you heard about—'

'Yes, Rex and Pollyanna. So what are we going to do?'

'I think we should start with the beach. You know how much Rex likes going there,' said Laurence, approaching Chris and Sylvia by the foot of the staircase.

'Do you need a lift there? I know the place where we took Rex as a child,' my father said, and without any further discussion we left the house together and headed towards his black Rover in haste.

My father found Rex and Pollyanna on the pier, and by the time the rest of us had caught up with them, they were sharing an ice cream with Rex spooning soft whip into Pollyanna's mouth. He had discarded his wheelchair on the beach and had managed to hop along the pier with the aid of his crutches.

Rushing up to the pair, I stood a few paces away and reached inside my handbag for a tissue to dab at my eyes.

'Rex,' I said, 'you didn't have to do this! The two of you could have spoken to us if you were worried about being separated at school.'

'Please, don't be angry with us,' Rex spoke up and put a hand on Pollyanna's shoulder protectively.

It was at that point when Chris left Sylvia's side and stood with Laurence in solidarity, whilst Sylvia pushed past me to pull Rex's hand from Pollyanna. 'My darling!' cried Sylvia. 'Tell me what happened. What did he do to you?'

'Sylvia,' I implored. 'They are just teenagers.' I glanced towards Laurence, only to see his eyes dart from mine, seeming to understand more than me about what might have happened between the two of them.

'I warned you this would happen, Emily,' Sylvia retorted.

'Nothing happened, Mum,' Pollyanna interjected. 'Rex and I, we just wanted to be alone, to be away from the others. We had enough of Chailey.'

Chris strode up to Pollyanna and took a seat beside her. 'You know you can't just leave without telling anyone where you're going.'

'It doesn't matter. We have to leave there soon, anyway,' said Pollyanna.

'Now, let's talk about this rationally,' my father interjected. 'It's not all bad. It must have taken a lot of courage for the two of them to get to the beach on their own.'

'We caught the bus,' said Rex. 'I can do that by hopping on and off. I just need help with my wheelchair.'

'That was a lot for you to do by yourself,' agreed Laurence.

'Exactly my point. They are not children anymore; they've come a long way in a short time. And if I remember rightly, Emily, at their age you had started going dancing. Remember?' my father said.

'So you're saying that we should overlook this incident? Pretend it's nothing more than an act of teenage rebellion when, in fact, it is an example of Pollyanna refusing to follow rules? She's at Chailey for her own protection. Just answer me this: When they leave school this summer, are we are going to be faced with this kind of problem again? What are we going to do then?' said Sylvia.

'Tackle it together as we always have done, Sylvia,' I said.

My father cleared his throat as he returned with Rex's wheelchair. 'Why don't I drive Rex and Pollyanna back to school and leave you to discuss the matter further yourselves?'

'Maybe it's time I helped out more with them both,' Laurence said. 'I have a responsibility towards Rex and Pollyanna. The connection Rex has with Pollyanna reminds me a little of you and me, Emily.' A smile crept to Laurence's lips as Rex slid back into his wheelchair and my father wheeled him down the pier and towards the beach, with Pollyanna close to my father's heels.

'That's very thoughtful of you, Laurence,' said Chris. His gaze went from Laurence to me in admiration.

'We should be the ones to help,' said Sylvia. 'We like Rex, but we don't want Pollyanna to get hurt; and if they were both living with us, we could make sure that didn't happen.'

'I don't know. Can we think about this?' I said.

'Please do, and remember, we're only across the square, day or night.'

Sylvia took my hand and squeezed it tightly, and it was in exhaustion that while Laurence and Chris became better acquainted, I leaned my head onto Sylvia's shoulder, relieved as ever of her unwavering support.

'Duty makes us do things well,
but love makes us do them beautifully.'
Phillips Brooks

Chapter Seventy-Five
Summer 1977

We gathered in the school hall at Chailey for the prestigious Seymour Overmore Prize that recognised a child's ability throughout their education: not only academically, but also in their spirit to embrace the difficulties imposed upon them by their disability.

Laurence and I took our places in the middle row. I glanced over at Sylvia and Chris at their crossed legs and touching shoulders. Like us, this was the first time they had attended an awards ceremony at Chailey. Our children had been latecomers to the school, so we felt privileged to have been invited.

Already the hall was filling up with Thalidomide children, some displaying four-limb deficiencies. I held my hands together, feeling that those children were more deserving of the prize than Rex or Pollyanna, who had at least been blessed with two good limbs.

A brown-haired girl with shortened arms and legs received the Seymour Prize, and we rose to offer our applause. I looked over at Sylvia and she smirked, but not thinking anything more of it, I sat down again.

The headmaster offered the crowd a smile and cleared his throat. 'Ladies and gentlemen, this year we have a couple of other prizes that are not just about practical life, but are to be awarded to a couple of pupils who, during their time with us, have demonstrated special skills that override the limitations of their disabilities. It is with great pride that I would like to offer the first award for Contribution to the Arts to young Rex Alexander.'

The headmaster offered an outstretched arm, and Rex wheeled himself onto the stage to receive his silver prize cup.

Laurence shot up and applauded. It took me a few minutes to take in what I had just heard: Rex had won a prize. But as I got up to join in with the applause, it wasn't long before the other parents joined in, too.

'Well done, Rex, and I look forward to seeing your future work.' The headmaster lowered the microphone, and Rex spun around in his chair to address the audience.

'Thank you, Chailey, for my education. But I would especially like to thank my family, for without their love and belief in me, I wouldn't have had the courage to achieve great things.' He grinned.

My heart swelled with pride. Who would have imagined that my strange bundle of joy would have turned out like he had? And for a split second upon seeing him at the hospital, I had my doubts that were quickly proven wrong.

We sat down to a hushed silence as Rex left the stage, and the headmaster raised the microphone.

'Good luck, Rex,' he smiled. 'Now for the second and final award. As you know, the Thalidomide children presented us at Chailey with unique challenges in terms of care and education, and none more so than Pollyanna. She came to us as a shy twelve-year-old, but what she lacked in confidence, she certainly made up for in unique talent. I was as surprised as the rest of the staff when I first heard her play the piano.' He paused to smile again. 'That's because, ladies and gentlemen, she was playing the piano with her feet. So I am awarding the prize of Outstanding Performing Arts to Pollyanna Watersmith.'

We waited a moment in anticipation before turning to see Pollyanna approach the stage. She had on a beige chintz double skirt and bodice. It was belted and bowed in black with matching suede shoes. Her blonde hair swished as she approached the headmaster.

'Congratulations, Pollyanna. I look forward to hearing more of your music in the future.'

Pollyanna unbuckled her shoe with her teeth and offered her foot for the headmaster to shake. In exchange, he offered her a mounted award, which she held in her mouth. Then, slipping her shoe back on, she made her way into the audience. She took a seat beside Sylvia and Chris. Sylvia took the award from Pollyanna. There was a moment when Pollyanna looked towards her mother, and I wondered if, in Pollyanna's mind, she felt that this was what she had to do to win her mother's love.

Later, Laurence and I went for tea with the headmaster. We formed a huddle in a side corner of the auditorium.

'It's been a great honour to have Rex at our school, for he is such a gifted young man,' the headmaster said, shaking our hands in rotation.

I glanced over at Rex and Pollyanna. She eased herself onto his lap, and he spun her around the room in his wheelchair to the excited cheer from a growing crowd of Thalidomide-impaired teenagers. Some of them drew close to Rex and Pollyanna on their artificial legs, while others gave chase in their wheelchairs by pushing themselves forward with the aid of their crutches.

A smile formed on my lips, and I couldn't have been prouder of my little boy. Laurence touched my arm tenderly, forcing my attention back to the headmaster.

'I will schedule an appointment for you and Mrs Watersmith to initiate their discharge from Chailey. The future is theirs now,' the headmaster said; and feeling dazed, I struggled to take it all in. Rex was leaving school. It didn't seem possible that his childhood was up; but more importantly, without Rex to care for, what direction would my life take now?

'To give anything less than your best
is to sacrifice the gift.'
Steve Prefontaine

Chapter Seventy-Six
Autumn 1977

Rex and Pollyanna both agreed upon Hereward College in Coventry as a suitable place for continuing with their education. The college catered to students with disabilities and had a good programme of extracurricular activities. But Sylvia and I had one stipulation of our own. We wanted them to do well in life and got them both to enrol in a business course, alongside their general music and art classes. Yet helping pack their boxes and cases that summer did little to prepare me for the heartache of parting from Rex once again.

The day of their departure turned out to be a sunny interlude after a rather wet August bank holiday. My father offered to drive us to Coventry, but in the end it seemed more practical for us to go in Chris' Rolls-Royce.

So whilst Chris helped pack the car, my family got down to the business of saying goodbye to Rex. That afternoon Laurence stopped by Rex's room. Feeling at a loss myself, I hung around the hallway and saw Laurence's tight smile as he knelt before Rex's chair.

'I know I haven't always been around for you, and I wish there was some way of making up for all those lost years,' Laurence said, on one knee.

'It's all right, Dad, really.'

I edged closer to the doorway and felt tears well in my eyes at the love Laurence felt for Rex; if only he could find a way to let go of his fear.

'I know you'll do well at college. That you will put your heart and soul into everything you do.'

Rex nodded.

'Promise you'll phone every week?'

'Yes, Dad.'

'And you'll be careful when it comes to Pollyanna?'

Rex laughed and Laurence joined in, too. For a moment, Laurence's eyes lingered on Rex, making me wonder if, like me, it was during times like these that it didn't matter that Rex had no legs.

Laurence and I met on the common for a final breath of air before starting the long journey north. Clemmie asked Rex for a final go in his wheelchair. Wrapping his arms around Clemmie's waist, Rex's fingers hit the controls, and we spread out on the grass watching their full-speed tour of the common. As Rex edged closer to us, Clemmie screamed in delight, and I was relieved when my parents came out to join us.

My father nudged in between Laurence and me and threw an arm around my shoulder. 'How are we doing?' he asked as Rex nearly missed an unsuspecting female dog-walker.

'Perhaps we should get Rex to stop,' I said.

'Allow him his last moment of freedom,' my mother said. I saw her eyes glisten with tears, not realising until then how much Rex meant to her, and contemplated breaking free from my father to give her a hug.

It wasn't long afterwards that Chris and Sylvia approached us with Pollyanna to bid goodbye to Laurence and my parents. Feeling that we could delay the departure no longer, we made our way to Chris' car. There was a moment when I wished Laurence was coming with us. He could have left Clemmie with my parents. I wondered if it was his fear of hugging his son that kept him rooted at home.

Filling the car with bodies of all shapes and sizes, we waved to Laurence and my parents. Laurence held Clemmie on his shoulders, and as his eyes met mine I saw his tears of regret. I bit down on my lip and continued waving until they were out of sight, and it was just the coastal road between us and the journey ahead. Glancing in the mirror, I saw Sylvia already reaching for a stack of tissues from her handbag, and I wondered if she would hold out crying at least until we reached the M1.

I glanced at the low-slung building visible from the main road through the avenue of trees and read the sign that stated 'Hereward College.' This time I had no doubts about sending Rex away for his education, for it seemed the next sensible step towards him gaining independence.

Chris drove around the college car park before choosing a spot to park near the main entrance. Then he left us to go inside the college to find out about the arrangements for settling Pollyanna and Rex in to their accommodations. A single glance at Rex and Pollyanna told me that they weren't children anymore, but still their eyes darted around at their new green surroundings with a look of apprehension.

Sylvia clambered out of the car and went to retrieve Rex's wheelchair from the boot. After sliding himself into his chair, we all made a straight line along the rear of the car. Sylvia and I stood at either end and looked at each other. A horrible lump came to my throat, and I felt my first sob break free. Sylvia reached into her handbag to offer me a tissue.

'Thank you,' I croaked.

'It's all right.' Her hand squeezed mine. I wiped away my tears and turned to Rex and Pollyanna hesitantly.

'Told you I was right,' Pollyanna grinned.

'About what?' Rex frowned.

'About your mum being the first to cry.'

✻

I took Rex to his room and busied myself with unpacking his clothes, which consisted mainly of T-shirts and shorts, with a few shirts and jumpers slipped in. His room had been decorated in turquoise and furnished with a single bed and wardrobe. It had a view of the surrounding countryside, making me realise that it had been a year since our last trip out of Brighton.

Rex had gotten out of his wheelchair, and his small body occupied the centre of the bed in the lotus position. Stacked against the wall were a series of boxes still to unpack. The room, although more welcoming than Chailey, struck at my heart as a barricade between Rex and me.

'Won't you sit down, Mum?' Rex asked tenderly. His hand reached for mine.

I was glad that much had not changed. I climbed onto the bed. It felt comfortable enough. Perhaps once the room was decorated with a few of Rex's things from home, the place would come alive with his spirit.

His hand lingered in mine, and I turned to glimpse his familiar smile. 'I'm going to miss home, too, Mum,' he said at last. I leaned in for one last hug. 'But I have to do this. I have to prove to you that your time and dedication to me was worth it. It's time to make you proud.' His eyes shone with unshed tears.

'You've already made me proud in so many ways, Rex.' I paused, feeling tears run down my cheeks. 'My dedication to you was out of love, and I have never regretted it, not for a single moment,' I took a deep breath. 'From the time I first held you in my arms, I knew I had been given a very special baby, and that faith would show me the way forward.'

With my cheeks wet with tears, I was grateful for the strength of his arms to hold me tight; but I was reminded that despite his size, he had matured into a man, and it was time to let him go.

I pulled away from him and watched him reach inside his rucksack and produce a drawing of Laurence, Clemmie, and myself on the beach. Gazing at the picture, I felt the lapping waves calming my trembling body.

'I forgot to give this to Clemmie. It should go in her room now.' Gone were the watery eyes, only to be replaced by a cheeky grin.

'Thank you, Rex,' I said, wiping my eyes with a tissue.

'Look after yourself, Mum, and tell Dad that it's okay; everything is all right.'

I nodded. 'Always the man of the house.'

We were silent for a moment, allowing me to gather my emotions back together again, before I cleared my throat. 'Clemmie's going to miss you.'

'And I her, but I will study hard. When the time's right I will come home again,' he promised, and I was determined to hold him to that.

'There is no greater agony
than bearing an untold story inside you.'
Maya Angelou

Chapter Seventy-Seven
1977

One afternoon I was in the lounge flicking through a copy of my novel, *The Last Indian Summer*, when I heard the sound of footsteps from above. My father, even in his later years, still maintained a steady practice, which made me think about what I should be doing with my life now that Rex was settled at college. Sylvia would probably pop over later, for with Rex and Pollyanna away at college, our homes had become unnervingly quiet. I had Laurence home for a couple of days before he went off to another conference. He would probably collect Clemmie from school. So I had some time to myself for a change and thought of my next writing project: more freelance work for the magazines, or something more challenging? I turned my novel over in my hand and considered the struggle I had encountered in getting it published in the first place. Had it really been worth it? My thoughts, as they so often did, turned to Rex. Was it possible that I had an even greater story to tell, if only I had the courage to begin?

I went to my bedroom and opened the bedside drawer. I took out some notes that I had scribbled down from years ago on a similar afternoon, only then Sylvia had distracted me with news of an incident between Rex and Pollyanna at Chailey. But now it was different. I had time every afternoon to write. Time to think of my life back then, when during the first weeks of my pregnancy with Rex, my aspirations, other than becoming a mother, had been for me to become a published author.

I closed my eyes and pictured that tiny flat in Richmond. The small kitchen and the overriding smell of garlic from last night's bolognaise. On the kitchen table stood an empty bottle of red wine with a melted candle poking out from the top, and the neck coated in hardened wax. Laurence strolling in for a kiss at the end of the day, his hand reaching for my stomach with closed eyes.

Tears streamed down my cheeks before I managed to write a single word. I rubbed my eyes and thought of going to see Sylvia. A cup of tea with her was sure to soothe my tender heart. I was about to rise from the bed when the door opened and Laurence strode in. He removed his coat and dumped his briefcase by the wardrobe. Then he took a seat next to me on the bed. Amongst the strewn papers was a copy of my novel.

'I remember that book.' His fingers grazed the front cover, tracing the gold and turquoise lettering with interest. 'Are you thinking of writing another? I know we have never talked about your writing career, but I am proud that you got a book published. In my mind that is quite an accomplishment.'

'I do want to write another book, except I don't know if I can, Laurence. What if the process is too painful for me?' I said, and as he held me close to him, I felt desperate for him to convince me that it was the right thing to do.

'Of course you can, Emily. We all believe in you. What happened to Rex was never your fault. Take the plunge and start writing, and you'll surprise yourself,' Laurence said, and I thought perhaps he was right. I could find the right words within me to tell the story which I felt the world needed to hear.

*'Take every opportunity that comes your way
and most importantly, have fun with it.'*
Cody Simpson

Chapter Seventy-Eight
One Year Later

Sylvia and I went to Brighton Station to meet Rex and Pollyanna for the summer holiday. With them approaching their eighteenth birthdays, I expected this to be a memorable summer. But feeling a degree of trepidation at their coming of age, I reached for Sylvia's hand and was rewarded with a gentle squeeze.

The crowd tumbled out into the ticket hall. We caught sight of the railway guard approaching us carrying two suitcases (the rest would come separately in a large trunk). Alongside the guard, I caught sight of Rex's wheelchair and the figure of a tall, blonde girl who I recognised as Pollyanna.

'Rex!' I called out with a wave and the group finally reached us. Pollyanna was dressed in a sleeveless white frilly blouse teamed with blue flared jeans. Her long hair had been braided, and this was the first time I had seen her wearing pink lipstick. Rex was in a tight black Star Wars T-shirt and his usual cut-down jeans. Glancing at them both in excitement, I rushed over to Rex to offer him a hug and a kiss on the cheek.

'Mum.' He wriggled in protest.

'Sorry, you're all grown up now. I keep forgetting,' I explained to the guard and pulled away from Rex.

Sylvia and Pollyanna stood a short distance apart from each other. Sylvia's attention was drawn to the middle-aged train guard, who stood watching us in curiosity. 'Thank you for all your help, we'll take it from here,' she smiled.

The guard nodded. 'Just pleased to help. Such well-behaved youngsters, considering everything,' he remarked, before finally leaving us alone.

Sylvia threw an arm around Pollyanna's waist and drew her into her arms. 'Look at you! You've grown so pretty, sweetheart. I've missed the pair of you, so much. Now tell us that you're going to study closer to home this autumn. Trust me, Brighton has plenty to offer in terms of education, not that I'd know much about that. I never even managed to pass my GCE's, but the two of you are going to make us proud,' she said, giving Pollyanna a squeeze.

'Mum.' It was Pollyanna's turn to protest.

Sylvia set her free and reached inside her handbag for a handkerchief. 'Well, that's me done embarrassing you both. Now let me drive you home,' said Sylvia, and we followed her out of the station and into the car park.

With Rex and Pollyanna snuggled in the back of Chris' Rolls-Royce, I watched them in the mirror, taking note of the way his hand stroked her cheek, making me worry about just how close they had become this past year.

'So,' said Sylvia, turning into the main road and heading towards the lanes. 'I suppose the real question is, your place or mine?'

✳✳✳

It was Rex and Pollyanna who came up with the idea of them going between the two houses and spending a week at each. At that point they hadn't given us any indication of their future plans, so what better way for them to enjoy their summer? They started off by staying with Laurence and me in the basement flat, which had changed somewhat since Rex left for college last year.

Clemmie had taken ownership of his old bedroom, and a vibrant pink now embraced the walls. The low shelves were now crowded with her collection of dolls and paraphernalia. All that remained of Rex's time there was a single easel and his collection of floor art that had once fascinated the welfare officer on her visit to us all those years ago.

The playroom had changed, too, for Rex's old toys had been set aside for him in boxes in one of the spare rooms upstairs. Laurence had built a wall to separate the lounge from a small guest room that I had decorated in a sea-blue colour, thinking it would suit Rex's taste. I had furnished the room with his old desk and easel facing the sash window and with a view of the walled garden.

Sylvia dropped us off outside my parent's house before heading for the Regency Square car park. Entering the basement through the kitchen, we soon got to work sorting out the sleeping arrangements.

'Is it all right for you to share with Clemmie?' I asked Pollyanna. Her braids swished from side to side, surveying Clemmie's bright bedroom with horror.

'Who did your hair?' asked Clemmie, glancing at Pollyanna's sleeveless blouse.

'Clemmie,' I reprimanded.

'I went to the hairdressers, of course. I will keep them in for a few weeks.' Pollyanna explained, 'Rex likes my hair that way.'

'I could plait your hair for you, if you like. I do all my dolls' hair,' Clemmie replied, pointing at her neat row of dolls, all fashioning Heidi plaits.

'Yes, I'd like that,' Pollyanna grinned.

I watched in fascination as Clemmie helped Pollyanna unpack her case, by unfolding and folding her clothes and placing them in the chest of drawers. Both my children were growing up in a hurry, I thought with disappointment.

I took Rex to his room. He slid his body from chair to bed and looked out into the garden, where my mother was busy pruning the roses.

'I know it's different from what you had before, but your father and I thought you might like it still. I don't know what your plans are, and whether you and Pollyanna intend to go back to Coventry.'

'How's Dad?' Rex asked, patting the bed. I took a seat beside him, marvelling at how grown up he had become this last year.

'He's still here. He's not going to leave this time, and in his own way, he's looking forward to seeing you both,' I said. He squeezed my hand and I offered him a hug in exchange.

'I'm glad, Mum, I really am,' said Rex.

I was in my little kitchen by the time Laurence returned home from work. I heard the hum of the television and set about preparing dinner.

'I want to sit on Rex's lap!' yelled Clemmie.

'Well you can't, for once,' replied Pollyanna.

I threw a handful of chopped onion into the frying pan and marched into the lounge. I folded my arms under my breasts as Pollyanna and Clemmie encircled Rex's wheelchair.

'Right. This is what happens. Rex, out of your chair and on the sofa. Clemmie and Pollyanna, pick which side you want to sit on.' They nodded in unison as the theme music from *Happy Days* rang out.

'Or the television goes off.'

I waited a moment as Rex slid himself onto the sofa and the girls shuffled up beside him.

'Thanks, Mum,' he said, and smiling in satisfaction I returned to the kitchen to Laurence's shocked stare.

Laurence had changed over the years. He had settled into the basement with us. But there had been other changes, too. The daily commute from Sussex to London had caused the lines under his eyes to deepen. A few grey hairs had started to mingle harmoniously with his brown ones. But as he swept me into his arms for a kiss, I felt relieved that some of my feelings for him hadn't changed since we first fell in love all those years ago.

'You're very good at this,' he said, pulling away to uncork a bottle of white wine. He poured us each a glass and set aside the rest for dinner.

I added chopped pineapple and spring onions to the pan before reaching for my glass to take a small sip of wine. 'I've just had more experience, that's all,' I shrugged.

'I don't know how this is going to work out, us all living on top of each other,' he laughed between sips of his wine.

'I don't know either, but let's give it a chance, hey?'

That evening, we dined on vegetable stir-fry. Laurence, Pollyanna, Clemmie and I managed to fit around the table. I fixed a tray on Rex's chair, and he parked himself between the girls.

Pollyanna had mastered a new trick. She could now curl her toes around a glass of wine and was able to join in with our toast for a glorious summer of '78. Taking a sip of my wine, I wondered, *who'd have thought the day would ever come when Laurence would join us around the same table?*

At the end of the week, we each packed a case and headed across the square to Sylvia and Chris' house. There we each had a room of our own. The one I shared with Laurence had a view of the sea beyond, filling me with hope that at long last we had every reason to be happy.

***

The next few weeks were busy helping Rex and Pollyanna to make plans for the future. Rex had already decided upon the art school in Brighton. After a perusal of his portfolio, the principal was satisfied with the standard of his work and offered him a full-time place on a three-year course as a student of fine arts. This meant some adjustments on part of the college, but they were eager to meet those challenges just to count Rex as one of their students.

Next came Pollyanna. She had decided not to continue with her education, wanting to have a go at finding a job instead. This led us to search for office jobs in the area; and with her business course behind her, Pollyanna started to apply for some administration work within the government, albeit with some help from Sylvia and me, which resulted in her landing an interview for a data-input clerk position at the local hospital. It wasn't what Sylvia and I had planned for her, but on the sly she had enrolled in a couple of music classes in the evenings, and had even managed to land herself a couple of gigs: one for a birthday party in the church hall and another as part of a pop group at a local pub.

On the morning of the interview, I combed her hair and chose a red suit for her to wear. She allowed me to help her with the buttons rather than rely on her dressing sticks. I hugged her for luck, and Rex, having passed his driving test in Coventry, was now the proud owner of a specially adapted Mini nicknamed 'Boris.' He gave Pollyanna a lift to the interview, and we all awaited the outcome with a sense of deep anticipation. Despite her physical disability, I wanted them to overlook her difficulties and see her as we did, as a beautiful and courageous young woman.

That evening, our wait was rewarded with a kicked door and a flood of tears. Rex helped Pollyanna to change her clothes and dried her eyes. Then he took her out to her evening gig at the pub. She returned home late with Rex and smelling of tobacco and beer. I didn't ask any questions, I just retreated to my bedroom and gave her space.

The following week she had another interview, this time with the council as an information officer in the children's department. We didn't think too much about it, but when Pollyanna returned home this time, she skipped into the kitchen.

'Well?' I asked, tentatively, as I sat with Clemmie, going through her spelling book.

'They offered me the job!' she grinned.

Rex did a peace sign. 'That's great news,' I said.

'They have one condition, though,' she said, and knelt down to Clemmie's level to snuggle in beside my daughter. 'They think I will need help with certain things.' She stared at Clemmie's looped letters.

'Oh?' I replied.

'It's nothing bad, Mum,' said Rex. 'It just means helping her to the toilet and things, girl's things. That's why they want either you or Sylvia to go to work with her.'

'Really. Well, I think between us we could manage that.'

'That's what I said to Pollyanna.'

On cue she raised her head to offer us a beaming smile.

'We should celebrate your good news,' I said.

'Will you come out tonight and see me play?' Pollyanna asked.

'I'd love to. I'll get Laurence to babysit Clemmie. I could do with a night out,' I smiled.

That evening I wore a blue denim skirt and cotton blouse and joined the packed crowd inside the church hall. Pollyanna was dressed in khaki, and took her position on a special stool that allowed her to raise her legs so her toes could tap out her rendition of 'Moon River.'

'Mum,' said Rex as his hand touched mine. 'I'm in love, I truly am.'

***

At the end of the summer Sylvia and I organised a joint eighteenth birthday party for Rex and Pollyanna at our local church hall. We filled the hall with balloons and streamers and swayed to the beat of Abba's 'Waterloo.' Rex exchanged his usual casual attire for a suit and wore his artificial legs.

At the end of the night, the floor cleared and he took Pollyanna into his arms for a final slow dance. She had chosen a pink dress with a sweetheart neckline, and I couldn't help but notice the gold chain and ring around her neck.

As the music finished, Rex and Pollyanna approached the DJ together, I turned to Laurence in curiosity, only for him to shrug and throw an arm around my waist, drawing me close to him.

The DJ handed the microphone to Rex. Then Rex put his hand on Pollyanna's shoulder and turned to face the audience. 'First of all, I want to thank everyone for being here tonight, but especially our wonderful parents.'

'It is with great pride that I can share my news with you. I have asked Pollyanna to be my wife.'

There was a general hush in the crowd as Sylvia and Chris came to stand by our side. The microphone squeaked, and leaning in to Rex came Pollyanna's booming reply.

'And I said yes!'

✳✳✳

'Well, I didn't see that coming just yet. They are too young, of course,' said Laurence that evening, as he strode into the bedroom behind me and closed the door.

'We weren't that much older ourselves when we got engaged at university,' I said, pulling off my dress. Then I sat on the bed, watching Laurence unbutton his shirt. I wanted to savour the memory of tonight for just a little bit longer.

'That's true,' Laurence agreed.

I hugged my knees. 'Do you think?' I asked.

'What?' He unbuckled his trousers and reached for a packet of painkillers from his jacket pocket. He pressed out a single white pill and cast it to the back of his throat, before gulping down a mouthful of water from the glass on the bedside cabinet.

'They could have what we did once?' I said.

'I don't know, Emily.' He massaged his temples before turning his back on me. His spine pressed rigidly against mine.

'I hope so,' I said.

I rose to push open the window. It was a cool late summer's night without a drop of that awful humidity which we had suffered during July.

'Got to admire Rex, he's got courage to even contemplate marriage,' said Laurence as I climbed back into bed. I curled up to Laurence, but feeling a sudden wave of apprehension for our son, I stayed awake long into the night.

*'Sometimes letting go is an act of greater power
than defending or hanging on.'*
Eckhart Tolle

Chapter Seventy-Nine

That autumn, Rex started art school, and on his first morning, I helped him pack his car with canvases and paints. I brushed away a tear as he slid himself into the driver's seat. I had promised myself I wouldn't cry. I had him back home for a while, but he wasn't a little boy anymore, and the effort of letting go brought back all those horrible emotions that I had felt when I first had him. That lump rose in my throat, fearing that pretty soon he wouldn't need me anymore. He had Pollyanna now.

'Mum,' he reprimanded with a smile.

'I'm sorry, my darling, you know I am so proud of you getting into art school. I have every faith in you, knowing you work so hard and never complain.' My hand touched his long fingers that I had known since his birth. I allowed my hand to linger in his to cherish the last of our in-depth moments together. I thought back to our early plans for his education that my mother and I had drawn up together. Surely Rex was proof that our theories about disability had been right?

'I'm the lucky one. I get to do what I love every day. I think of Dad, feeling so sad about what had happened to me and still doing his job without complaint,' Rex said, breaking my chain of thought.

I leaned inside the car and took pleasure in stealing a kiss from him.

'Mum,' Rex protested.

'Sorry,' I said and stepped away from the car. He started the engine and pulled away from the kerb. I offered him a wave before retreating inside the house to find Laurence and Clemmie munching on their cornflakes in our little kitchen.

'Has Rex gone?' Clemmie asked, disappointed.

'He'll be back later,' I promised, but still I stood at the window and imagined the scene from across the square as a car door was flung open and Pollyanna got in. His yellow Mini would probably remain stationary for a few minutes as they shared a kiss. But wasn't that how it was supposed to be?

'Emily, are you all right?' Laurence asked and I spun around. He had gotten up from behind the table, and tasting milk mixed with cornflakes from his kiss, I closed my eyes, wondering about the love Rex would soon share with Pollyanna.

My gaze fell to Clemmie. I still had a child who needed me.

'You've got him for a while longer,' Laurence reminded me. My mind returned to the probable exchange between Rex and Pollyanna, and I knew it was now only a matter of time before he left home for good.

'We should be focusing on Clementine. Remember how I promised to help you bond with her if you helped me to do the same with Rex?'

I nodded, admonishing myself for my own selfishness.

'Why don't we take Clementine swimming on the weekend? Wasn't that something you used to enjoy with Rex? Clementine needs to learn these things, too, and afterwards we could always go out for lunch together as a family.'

It was his hand that I took this time; and while Clemmie's green eyes lingered upon us, I felt relief that she was intrigued, but too young to guess what was going through our minds.

'I do love you, Laurence and in some ways you understand me as much as Sylvia does,' I said, reminding myself of that conversation I had with him a few years back: *She sees into my soul and no one has ever done that before, so for us to have a future you've got to be able to do the same.*

'You just don't show it as much as Sylvia does, but now is the chance to prove yourself,' I said, drawing him close to me for a hug. We had just a moment together, before the real world caught up with us, meaning Laurence had to go to work and I was forced to take a reluctant Clemmie to school.

But as I approached the school gates with Clemmie that morning, I hugged her longer than usual before bidding her goodbye with a kiss and watching her race across the playground to join her friends as I repeated silently to myself my promise to love my children equally.

'Creativity takes courage.'
Henri Matisse

Chapter Eighty
1979

One evening Rex arrived home with a large black portfolio balanced on his lap and disappeared into his bedroom through the lounge. Since his starting art school the year before, I had been curious about his latest pieces of work, so I followed him into his bedroom with an armful of clean laundry. I found his narrow bed covered in sketches: graphite portraits, pastel still-life and watercolour urchins. They had been scattered together, resembling the inner workings of a muddled mind. Rex picked up the graphite drawing of what appeared to be that of a young woman and gazed at its careful contours with a frown. Then he turned his wheelchair from his bed to the window in a short spin.

I busied myself sorting out his laundry, arranging his underwear into the appropriate drawers and hanging up several pairs of denim shorts and T-shirts in the wardrobe. I lingered longer than I should have, keen for an in-depth study of his drawings.

'Mum,' he said, looking up at me, while still attempting to shield the drawing from my view. I stepped forward and stood by his side. It was then that I identified the nude figure as Pollyanna.

'Rex!' I exclaimed and crouched down beside his wheelchair to inspect the monochrome life drawing of Pollyanna. Feeling heat rush to my cheeks, I turned to Rex for an explanation of what exactly the two of them had been up to behind our backs.

'She models at the university to earn extra money,' said Rex, not quite answering my question.

'I don't understand.' I shook my head in disbelief. Why would they need money when they were both offered a reasonable allowance from their parents?

'It's not about the money. Pollyanna says it helps her feel more confident about her body; to her it is like a form of psychology. It's not bad, Mum, what she does. The students are respectful of her body. She's not like other girls, and if this helps her to feel better about herself, then it can only be a good thing, eh?'

'Does Sylvia know about this?' I demanded.

Rex shrugged. 'Probably not. Pollyanna says this is as close as she can get to following in her mother's footsteps.'

I gazed at the sketch and at the curve of her neck. Slowly, my eyes went down to the swell of her breasts, feeling a mixture of curiosity and shame.

'Rex.' I felt my voice rise in anger. He touched my hand, but I pulled away only to gaze at his lean jaw in disbelief. I thought I had brought him up well. I blinked away another glance at the sketch. He reached across to place the drawing on his bed alongside the other ones of ripened fruit and exotic jellyfish.

'I've embarrassed you, haven't I?' he apologised with a weak smile.

'I don't know what to say, Rex.'

'You don't approve. You think Pollyanna has been exploited in some way because of her disability. What people don't get is that her body is just as free as anyone else's. How she chooses to interpret it is for her to decide. I'd never force her to do anything she wasn't comfortable doing.'

'We brought you up to accept your body freely and to be proud of yourself, so I should be the last one judging you. But you must understand that not everyone sees things the same.'

'You're talking about her parents. Her mother will feel I have taken advantage of her again.' He sighed and lowered his head in defeat.

'That's possible.' A second glance at the drawing, and I saw Pollyanna's crossed legs and the way her eyes appeared to look up to heaven. Was it so wrong what she had done, and would I think differently of them both if they weren't disabled?

'Perhaps we should keep this drawing a secret between the three of us for the meantime,' I said.

***

My mind was still occupied by the thought of Rex's sketch as I went to bed that night, and I felt myself shudder at the thought of Pollyanna's tender body untouched yet by age.

'Laurence,' I said.

'Mmm.' His lips brushed my hair and his hand went down to rest on my thigh.

'I saw one of Rex's drawings today.'

'Oh, yes.'

'Of Pollyanna—naked.' The words fell from my lips, and I trembled at how quickly I had broken my promise to Rex. Laurence pulled away from me. I turned to face him, seeing the darkness of his eyes in stark contrast to the mesmeric blue of Pollyanna's.

'You want me to talk to him about this,' he said, firmly.

'I don't know, unless we shouldn't think of it as anything more than art. But I admit I am a little scared, Laurence.' Drawing me back into his arms, he held me tight as I shuddered and his kisses caught my tears.

'I don't know how Sylvia will react when she finds out.'

'Is that all?'

'No,' I cried. 'I'm scared of them growing up and not needing me anymore.' He slipped down the strap of my negligee and kissed me from my neck to my shoulder as a solution to my fears, just as I wondered if the life I had with Laurence was enough.

'It is such happiness when good people
get together, and they always do.'
Jane Austin, Emma

Chapter Eighty-One

A few months passed, and Rex and Pollyanna's attention turned back to their engagement as they grew eager to set a date for their wedding. Wanting to help, we gathered one afternoon in the basement flat to put forward our ideas for the wedding.

'Something small, perhaps,' shrugged Rex.

'Yes. You will want the ceremony to be held at our church, and for the reception there's the church hall. Unless, of course, you want to hold it at a pub.' I had the scene already planned out in my mind. Perhaps Rex had his friend Simon from Chailey lined up to be his best man. And there was Laurence, who had to be involved in the wedding somehow.

'Are you sure about that, Pollyanna?' Sylvia asked and moved closer to her daughter on the brown sofa to place a hand on her shoulder.

'Maybe we could do something different,' said Pollyanna. 'What do you think, Rex?' Her eyebrows furrowed in contemplation.

'Sure,' Rex said.

'What about inviting some of your friends from Chailey to the wedding, Rex? I bet you haven't seen them in a while,' said Chris, seated in the armchair opposite.

I bit my lower lip in frustration. This wedding wasn't about grand gestures, more of a celebration of how far they'd come already as young adults. 'What do you think, Laurence?' I asked.

'I think we should leave it up to Rex and Pollyanna to decide what they want. This is their wedding, after all.'

Sylvia took out a brochure of the Brighton Grand Hotel from her handbag and spread it across Pollyanna's lap.

'What about bridesmaids?' I interjected. 'I was thinking of Clemmie.'

'Yes, of course, Emily,' Sylvia smirked.

Rex turned to me and mouthed a 'Sorry.' But as Pollyanna glanced at the glossy photographs of the hotel, I knew the decision about the wedding had already been made.

✳✳✳

A few days passed, and it was early Saturday morning when I heard a loud rap on the kitchen door. I filled the kettle for a cup of tea and saw Sylvia waiting outside. I ushered her into the kitchen. She took a seat at the table and I switched on the kettle.

'How's Pollyanna?' she asked casually. I took in her trouser suit and the scent of her perfume and anticipated an impromptu visit into town.

'She's watching TV with Rex,' I said. It was their turn to stop with us that week, offering me a rare advantage over Sylvia. A glance at her darting eyes told me that she knew it, too.

'Don't worry about making any tea, because I've come to take Pollyanna into town to help her choose a wedding dress.'

I nodded to confirm a point to myself: that a crack in the veneer of our friendship had just started to emerge. I could only imagine how hurt she would feel if she discovered Rex's sketch of Pollyanna.

'No, you don't, Emily.' She reached for my arm, only for me to pull away.

'Let me get Pollyanna for you.'

'I want you to come with us. I'm asking for your support here,' she said with a fixed gaze.

'Oh, I just thought—'

'I know you did. That's why I had to set the record straight.'

'About what?'

'I'm not trying to undermine you, Emily. I know what you're trying to do with Rex and Laurence, because I'm trying to do the same with Pollyanna.'

✳✳✳

An hour later Pollyanna, Sylvia and I were clambering into Chris' car. I always found it surprising that Chris allowed Sylvia the use of his car. That was another mystery about the couple.

Pollyanna had on a pair of blue dungarees and a grey T-shirt. I wondered if that was a sign of rebellion against her mother, or just the girl reverting back to her tomboy ways. Sylvia took a puff of her cigarette and offered me furtive glances as a test of our friendship.

'So, I know a couple of bridal shops in North Laine. Shall we have a look there first, sweetheart, before venturing farther afield?' Sylvia and I turned around to gaze at Pollyanna. The girl nodded her approval.

I looked out of the window as we headed towards the train station. It was moments like these when the world seemed to close in on me, and feeling I couldn't breathe, I wound down the window for a gulp of fresh air.

'Are you all right?' Sylvia asked, touching my arm.

'Yes,' I lied; and as our car headed towards the city's main shopping area, I felt my stomach somersault, and I wished for a cup of sugary tea to remedy my rising nausea.

Sylvia parked the car at the station and we made the short walk to North Laine. Already, much of the city's residents were up and about, skirting around us as we hit the winding alleyways and found ourselves amongst the centre of the Saturday market.

The loud cries from the fruit and vegetable barrows assaulted my ears as I followed Sylvia onto the asphalt. We weaved through open van doors and moving rails of colourful cottons. Sylvia wound a protective arm around Pollyanna's slender waist, propelling her forward and forcing me to hurry after them in pursuit.

Continuing onwards, we strode past dilapidated buildings and bright awnings until we entered a wider lane. It was blessed with façades in varying shades of sun-bleached pastel that promised, amongst other things, fish and chips and bohemian fashions. I glanced at Sylvia with relief when she finally stopped to take a breath.

'It will be worth it, I promise,' she grinned. Pollyanna's lips curled in contemplation, as sandwiched between the modest shops, we stepped inside a thickly carpeted store. It was packed floor-to-ceiling with white gowns of organza, silk and satin, separated only by a shelf of sparkling tiaras.

The manageress approached us, and I immediately regretted my worn jeans and green T-shirt, sensing her gaze of disapproval. She bypassed me to approach Sylvia and Pollyanna and extended a hand in welcome, then, taking in the armless Pollyanna, she retracted her hand in exchange for a look of horror.

'Mrs Watersmith,' she said after a moment's silence. 'And this must be the lucky girl, Pollyanna. Please take a seat, and we can have a discussion about your requirements for the big day.'

Sylvia, Pollyanna and I took a seat on the velvet couch.

'I don't want to wear a tiara,' said Pollyanna as the manageress sat down beside us.

'There are other options to consider. Have you thought about a veil?'

'I don't know,' said Pollyanna, glancing down at her pink toenails that peeked out from her brown sandals.

'Well, what kind of bride do you see yourself as?'

'I can't hold a bouquet except with my feet. I'm not like other brides.' Pollyanna shuffled closer to me. Her tightly wound braids whipped against my cheek in agitation. I fought back the urge to give her a hug.

'She just needs to find the perfect dress,' said Sylvia.

'Yes, of course,' the manageress said, flashing a look of exasperation at me.

Raising her head, Pollyanna's attention turned to the rail of white silken dresses that stretched as far as her eyes allowed. Each dress promised a day to remember.

'How about trying on a couple of gowns? That will give us a better idea about your preferences,' the manageress coaxed.

Pollyanna nodded slowly.

Sylvia and I glanced at each other, and we both released a deep breath in anticipation.

'Come on, my darling, let's get started. It will be so much fun, I promise.' Sylvia gave Pollyanna a hug. Pollyanna's head turned to rest on her mother's shoulder, allowing her to regard me closely without exchanging a word.

'Whilst mother and daughter have a browse, perhaps we can have a chat about the groom's requirements.'

'Of course,' I replied. I turned to glance Sylvia's way, but already she had an arm around Pollyanna, and was busy pulling dresses from the rail and struggling to hang them over her spare arm.

'If you need any help,' the manageress called over to Sylvia, 'just give me a shout.'

But Sylvia had already guided Pollyanna into the changing room and pulled the curtain behind them.

'Mum,' muttered Pollyanna.

'It will look lovely on you,' replied Sylvia.

'So,' the manageress said, forcing my attention back to her.

'Rex's legs didn't form properly. His suit must allow for that,' I said, biting down on my lip because, even after all this time, talking about his disability with a stranger brought tears to my eyes. I heard a yelp from behind the curtain and marvelled at Sylvia's perseverance.

'I have a tailor who can design a suit to match all sorts of body shapes. We could schedule a meeting for next week.'

'All right,' I said, taking a deep breath.

'I appreciate that the wedding must bring up certain feelings for all concerned,' she said.

'Yes, it does,' I agreed, lowering my eyes and feeling myself hit by another wave of emotion. 'But after everything they have been through in their short lives, they deserve a perfect day. So if you can work a small miracle with Pollyanna, it will make the experience easier for everyone concerned.' I flashed a smile, just as I heard the sound of footsteps approaching us from behind.

I turned around and saw Pollyanna dressed in satin overlaid with organza. Her lips curled in disgust. Sylvia brushed her fingers through her blonde hair and straightened her back. 'Doesn't she look stunning? My little girl. See, Emily, it was worth the time and trouble. Tell me you're glad you came with us.'

'I am,' I said, and my tears finally broke just as Pollyanna offered us a twirl. The manageress passed me the box of tissues. 'Happens all the time,' she said, sympathetically.

Sylvia wound an arm through mine and I felt my tears subside. In the end we managed to persuade Pollyanna to try on a dozen dresses, before she settled upon the one of her choice. With only a couple of minor alterations needed, it seemed as if we had taken a big step towards guaranteeing an unforgettable day; and for once I was right.

'Right actions in the future are the best apology
for bad actions in the past.'
Tryon Edwards

Chapter Eighty-Two
1980

On the morning of the wedding, Laurence took Rex into the garden. I had been up for hours, unable to sleep. I settled upon a navy and yellow suit and matching shoes to wear. There had been a storm the night before, and the patio was still damp with raindrops as I ventured into the garden. I remained by the garden door as Rex and Laurence gathered on the patio.

Both were dressed in their wedding suits, steely-grey with white roses in their lapels and maroon cravats. Gazing towards Rex, it was hard to place him beside the boy I knew in signature T-shirts and cut-down jeans. But today was different, and as I leaned against the doorway and glanced at father and son, I knew this to be especially true.

Laurence parked Rex's wheelchair under the arboretum interwoven with pink and white roses that had been constructed in celebration of the wedding.

Creeping closer to where they stood, I inhaled the heady scent of the roses with pleasure, while curious about what Laurence had to say to Rex.

'Dad,' said Rex, looking at Laurence squarely.

A smile played on Laurence's beautiful lips. His hand went to his combed-back hair, and I held my breath in anticipation, hoping he would find the right words to say. 'Rex, I have thought long and hard about this moment, played it out in my mind how I would execute it because I wanted it to be right.'

Rex's fingers played with the petals of his white rose, a symbol of his eternal love for Pollyanna.

'I wanted to take you to Richmond, to where it all began, to explain my part in everything; to try and demonstrate how sorry I am that you've had to suffer all these years.'

'Dad, you don't have to do that. You just have to be with Pollyanna and me today to give us your blessing.'

Laurence's hand moved to rest on Rex's wheelchair, and he crouched down on the patio. I found myself edging closer to them, only a heartbeat away. 'But what I have to say can be said here—what better place than where you spent your childhood and I watched you grow up from a distance—to ask for your forgiveness. Rex, as my son, can you forgive me for my part in Thalidomide? For everything I didn't do, and my neglect of you as your father?'

Rex's hand rested on Laurence's, but this time Laurence didn't pull away. 'Dad, I love you with all my heart. There is nothing for me to forgive.'

Rex's hand wound into his father's and their eyes met. My lip quivered as, without warning, Laurence leaned into Rex's chair and wrapped his arms around his son to give him his first-ever hug.

Rex's arms went around Laurence's neck, and I saw their bodies tremble. When Laurence finally pulled away and straightened, I saw his cheeks were wet with tears and heard him whisper, 'Thank you, Rex.'

'No, thank you, Dad. See you at church.'

Laurence nodded and strode away. Noticing me at last, I caught his hand and pulled him close to me. After all these years of waiting for him to touch our son, when the moment arrived, I found myself lost for words. We could only gaze at each other in wonder with a longing in our hearts to go back in time to 1960, but as that wasn't possible, we drew apart from each other and disappeared inside the house to get ready for the wedding.

✳✳✳

Pollyanna's brother Mark entered the church first. Now fully grown, he strode up the aisle to the opening melody of 'Ave Maria.' Mark, who had once teased his sister for struggling with her utensils, now took his place at the altar as one of Rex's groomsmen. Her elder brother, Edward, soon joined him.

Rex entered next, wobbling up the aisle on his artificial legs. He walked beside his friend and Best Man, Simon, who positioned his wheelchair beside Rex at the altar.

The bridesmaids marched up the aisle, led by Pollyanna's three grown-up cousins, in pastel pink dresses with puffed sleeves. Their hands clutched posies of white roses and tulips. Clemmie was the last to enter, and at age eight, her head darted from side to side, searching for Laurence and me.

'It's going to be all right,' said Laurence, as my fingers wound through his. The choir reached the high octave, causing an echo of joy to resound around us, and with my free hand I traced my gold cross and waited.

There was a pause in anticipation as Chris' hand rested upon Pollyanna's shoulder and she made her way down the aisle. Hers was a tentative approach, as she wore a veil supported by a crown of cream-coloured tulips and white roses. Her two-inch heels clicked against the stone floor as each step brought her closer to Rex at the altar.

Wearing a wide-brimmed hat, I was forced to twist my neck for a view of Pollyanna's silk and lace-embroidered dress. I was reminded of how she had chosen the dress with Sylvia and me and felt a smile tease my lips in pride.

Shifting in my pew, the brush of Pollyanna's pointed sleeve beckoned a concerted gaze. Her skirt rustled against the blushed peonies tied to the end of each pew, a methodical task that I had completed myself yesterday evening.

When at last Pollyanna's eyes met mine, I was rewarded with a wide grin. I beamed my encouragement at her rare show of enthusiasm, which caused her to stop for a moment by my pew before Chris' hand guided her forward. With a nod in my direction, she made her final steps towards Rex at the altar.

Chris and Rex met and embraced each other. We all held our breath as Chris patted Rex on the back, and their eyes met in silence before Chris pulled away and took his place on the front pew with Sylvia.

Rex and Pollyanna stepped up to the altar. There was a pause as Rex adjusted the lever on his legs, and then they both knelt before Father Fitzgerald.

'Rex and Pollyanna, have you come here freely and without reservation to give yourselves to each other in marriage?' asked Father Fitzgerald.

'We have,' they replied in unison.

Laurence's hand found mine and he squeezed it tightly, as events of an hour earlier played in my mind, still struggling to convince myself that it had really happened: Rex and Laurence had hugged.

'Will you honour each other as man and wife for the rest of your lives?'

'We will,' they answered.

I gazed at Laurence and found my hand still clung to his, which told me that a bright future was still possible for us.

'Will you accept children lovingly and bring them up according to the law of Christ and his church?'

'Yes,' replied Rex. There was a pause before Pollyanna said, 'Yes.'

'Since it is your intention to enter into marriage, join your right hands and declare your intention before God and his church.'

There was a murmur from the crowded nave as everyone awaited Rex and Pollyanna's adjustment to the usual ritual. It was remedied quickly when Rex placed a hand on her shoulder and their noses touched.

'I, Rex, take Pollyanna to be my lawful wedded wife. For better and for worse, in sickness and in health, I will love and honour her for as long as we both shall live.'

I reached inside my handbag for a tissue, and my gaze drifted along the pew and met with Sylvia's, her cheeks already streaming with tears. Chris put an arm around her shoulder and gave me a steady gaze that took me back to our many shared moments during our long fight for compensation. It took me a few moments to return my attention to Laurence.

'I, Pollyanna, take Rex to be my lawful wedded husband. I promise to love him for better and for worse, in sickness and in health, and forsaking all others, for as long as we both shall live.'

'Rex and Pollyanna have declared their consent to be married, and it is with God's blessing that what God has joined together, let no man put asunder.'

I wrapped my arms around Clemmie and she squirmed on the pew. Her hands still gripped tightly to her posy of white tulips and roses. 'When can I give Pollyanna the bouquet?'

'Later,' I whispered. I kissed her on the cheek and held her tightly in my arms for a moment.

Rex fastened a gold chain around Pollyanna's neck.

'I take this ring, as a sign of my love and fidelity, in the name of the Father, the Son, and the Holy Ghost.'

Then Simon edged his wheels between the couple and opened his palm to Pollyanna. She bowed her head and took the ring between her teeth to pass to Rex. He slipped it onto his finger and she repeated the same vow to him.

'You may kiss the bride,' Father Fitzgerald concluded.

It was with a wobble that Rex leaned over to kiss Pollyanna, cupping her cheeks to the sound of Mendelssohn's 'Wedding March.'

✳✳✳

'One, two, three!' Pollyanna spun around and kicked her bouquet into the crowd that had gathered around the spiral staircase in the hallway of Brighton's Grand Hotel. We felt a spray of tulip and rose petals scatter around us. A young cousin of Pollyanna's in a dusty pink dress grabbed the bouquet from the floor and claimed it as her own.

The wedding party spilled out into one of the banqueting rooms, which had been set up with one long table and a series of smaller ones, under a canopy of pink and silver balloons. We dined on vegetable paella and rich chocolate mousse.

Later, Rex and Pollyanna took to the floor for their first dance and swayed gently to the love notes of Lionel Richie's 'Three Times a Lady.' I caught sight of Dr Donahue watching in fascination as Rex wrapped his arms around Pollyanna's neck and held her close to his chest. I resolved to find time that night to speak to the doctor alone.

Meanwhile, the dance floor had started to fill with guests, including a group of ex-Chailey Thalidomiders who managed to manoeuvre their wheelchairs under the glare of the disco lights.

Laurence and I, having left Clemmie in the care of my parents, found the party in full swing as we finally took to the dance floor.

Laurence's lips brushed against my cheeks as the music switched to the soulful sound of Leo Sayer.

'I'm so proud of you, Laurence,' I said, gently swaying my hips. 'What you did this morning took a lot of courage.'

'No more than raising Rex alone,' he said, with his hand on the small of my back. We moved slowly, just inches from Rex and Pollyanna, allowing me to watch as Rex's lips found Pollyanna's. I glanced away and met the doctor's gaze again.

'I had my parents, remember?'

'You chose Rex above everything else, and that took courage. But after today I really feel that I am Rex's father.'

'Yes, you have passed the final hurdle. From now on you get to enjoy the best bits.' My lips brushed his, and closing my eyes, we shared a tender kiss.

✳✳✳

It was around midnight when I wandered outside onto the balcony and found Dr Donahue, nursing a whiskey. Ahead was the view of the seafront with just the odd car passing by on the road below, while in the distance glowed the sparkling lights from the pier.

'Beautiful night,' he said, taking a sip of his whiskey.

'Thank you for coming, Doctor, it meant a lot to us.'

'It was my pleasure to see Rex and Pollyanna doing so well.' He smiled and his face took on a faraway expression, as if lost in a moment from the past. 'The beauty of life,' he said, 'was never more evident than with Rex and Pollyanna tonight.'

I nodded. The cool breeze, although chilling my body, made me feel hesitant to return back to the party.

'Are you still at Chailey?' I asked, leaning over the balcony and catching a glimpse of a young couple below with their hands looped together. I looked out to the sea. There was still so much for me to experience in life, but from now on I would be doing it without Rex.

'No, I'm afraid my work ended there last year with the last of my Thalidomide children.'

I caught a glance of the couple again, crossing the road. As they turned I saw her thickening waistline and took a gulp of sea air. 'What now for you?' I asked.

'Research into new drugs, and in particular their teratogenic potential. That's the future for me now, Mrs Alexander. We have to make sure that the Thalidomide tragedy never happens again.'

'Do you think that's possible?' I thought of that young couple again. Was there a way of changing the course of history to prevent them from going through what Laurence and I did? 'Perhaps we could find a way for both systems of medicine to work hand in hand,' I mused.

'I'd like to think that, too,' the doctor laughed lightly, 'because just maybe Pollyanna's child's life could depend upon the safety of the drugs of tomorrow.'

*'Opportunity often comes disguised
in the form of misfortune and defeat.'*
Napoleon Hill

Chapter Eighty-Three

The following morning, to ease my aching head, Laurence took me for a walk on the beach with Clemmie. By mid-morning a crowd had gathered to enjoy the late summer sun. They sprawled on deckchairs and paddled in the sea with their children.

Laurence and I kept our distance and chose to saunter in silence. After a few paces, Clemmie pulled my hand so that she could collect pebbles in her bucket. The sun glistened on the lapping waves, clearing my head of last night's champagne. We took up a steadier pace, and my arm brushed against Clemmie's as we headed towards the pier.

'I saw you disappear with Dr Donahue last night,' said Laurence, coming to a sudden stop that jolted Clemmie and me, and caused several of her pebbles to tumble from her bucket.

'They are for Rex!' she shouted, 'for his bathroom mosaic.' She bent down to retrieve them.

'Sorry, Clemmie,' I said.

Laurence unfolded his sunglasses and put them on.

'Dr Donahue has a new job, working in medical research. It is his job to make sure all new drugs undergo certain tests to exclude dangerous effects on unborn babies. He works to oversee such tests.'

I had barely finished explaining before Laurence stalked away, disappearing into the crowd at the shoreline. Clemmie looked up at me, her green eyes widening in shock. 'Is Daddy mad at me for shouting?'

'No, my love, he is mad at himself. It has nothing to do with you or me,' I sighed, fearing I was expecting too much from him again, despite his success with Rex yesterday. Perhaps I had been naive to think that some things would change. I pressed my lips together as my thoughts turned to Sylvia, wondering what she was doing today.

'Why? That's a bit strange.' Clemmie said, bringing me rushing back to the present with a jolt.

'Yes,' I let out a nervous laugh. 'He wishes he had known something a long time ago that could have prevented a lot of tragedy for everyone.'

'Oh, is it to do with Rex and his funny legs and toes?'

'Yes, that's right, Clemmie, you're such a clever girl. I forget that sometimes.' She held my hand and her bucket of rocks.

Laurence returned and hugged us both as a way of apology. 'Why did you need to tell me that?'

'I see a way out for you, Laurence; a chance for you to make a difference yourself.'

'Doing what, exactly, Emily?'

'Scientific research, to make sure the drugs we take tomorrow have been tested sufficiently to be as safe as they can be.'

Laurence crouched down into the pebbles, and I bent down beside him, removing his sunglasses so I could look at him properly. Our glistening eyes met, understanding each other too well.

'What about working with Dr Donahue? Isn't it time for a change?'

'I haven't done anything else all these years. What if being a salesman is all I can do?'

'You won't know if you don't give it a chance. What have you to lose?'

'A good job and respectability,' he said with a smile.

'I know it's not what you expected to hear from me, but Rex and Pollyanna marrying has made me think that we need our lives to change, too. This job could be it.'

'So how do I go about changing jobs? Have you thought about that?'

'Yes,' I said, pulling out a piece of paper from my handbag. 'I got Dr Donahue to give me his work number. He could set up an interview for you, if you make the call.'

'Why would he want to help us?'

'Because of his commitment to the Thalidomide children; but more than that, I think it is because Rex touched his soul. That was the reason for his reluctance to let him go from Chailey.'

'You really have turned into your parents with your philosophical views.'

'They have served Rex well though, haven't they?' I grinned in satisfaction of knowing I was right. 'Say you will at least give the job some thought.'

'You really want me to do this? I don't know about an office job. I hadn't reckoned on that, but then look at my family. If someone had told me years ago' he shook his head sadly, perhaps reminded of the scene at the hospital soon after Rex's birth, 'how it has worked out these last few years, I wouldn't have it any other way. All I want now, Emily,' he wound his fingers through mine, 'is for us to be happy together.'

We stood up and he planted a kiss on my forehead. I clung to him longer than normal, parting only to glance at Clemmie squinting in the sun. I took her hand and led her towards the shade under the pier.

'I owe you again, Emily, don't I, for believing in me? What would any of us do without your faith?'

*'It takes hands to build a house,
but only hearts can build a home.'
Anonymous*

Chapter Eighty-Four

On a cloudy Monday morning, Rex and Pollyanna returned home from their honeymoon in Florida to an empty three-bedroom bungalow in Hove. They brought with them three suitcases of clothes, Rex's trusted easel and Pollyanna's piano. Watching Pollyanna's feet skip from room to room in excitement, I felt this house to be the beginning of something rather profound for all of us.

But there was still a lot of work to be done in turning the house into a comfortable home for the couple. We started off by shopping. Sylvia had compiled a list of what the couple would need, and it began something like this:

Sofa (Pollyanna's choice was a green one). Coffee table, plus dining room table and chairs (my choice), pots, pans, cutlery and especially wine glasses (Sylvia's choice). Double bed with blue and white linen to match (Rex's choice).

There was, of course, one final purchase of a single bed; for in all the excitement of setting up home, came the practicalities of being a Thalidomide-impaired couple. They would require the assistance of a community service helper, and that was how nineteen-year-old Natasha entered their lives.

I noticed her long brown hair and agile movements as she walked through the front door and bent down to offer Rex her hand. Then, straightening, she touched Pollyanna's shoulder before greeting Sylvia and me.

'Hello, everyone, I'm Natasha and I'm your CSV helper.' She smiled. 'I like gymnastics, art and music, and I'm here to help, not hinder.'

Sylvia raised an eyebrow.

'Perhaps you can help set up my studio room for me?' Rex said.

'Yes, I'd love to help,' Natasha gushed. 'Afterwards, perhaps I could sit with Pollyanna and we could go through how she'd like us to work together.'

'Sure,' said Pollyanna, narrowing her eyes.

Rex took Natasha into the spare room, while Pollyanna, Sylvia and I went into the garden. The weather had started to warm up a little. Barefoot, Pollyanna's tanned legs hopped onto the long grass, interwoven with dandelions. I saw an avenue of fruit trees close to the garden fence.

'I hope you'll like it here,' said Sylvia, looping her arm around Pollyanna's waist. Pollyanna didn't shrink away, and I took that as a sign of improving relations between mother and daughter.

'I'm not sure about Natasha. She seems a right know-it-all,' Pollyanna grumbled. Bending down, she knelt into the grass and rested her chin upon her knees.

'Give her a chance, she's probably just as nervous as you are,' I said, and crouched down next to her.

'Will you bring Clemmie over next time?' Pollyanna said, turning to me wistfully.

'Yes, of course. She'll love the garden.'

'You don't blame me, do you, Mrs Alexander?' Pollyanna asked. I looked to Sylvia as her lips parted in astonishment. 'For taking Rex from you. I know how much you love him,' Pollyanna finished with a hesitant gaze.

I thought of the sadness I had felt on Rex's first day at art school, feeling he didn't need me anymore; but then watching him happy with Pollyanna, a smile came to my lips, knowing that without my love he would never have gotten to this point.

'Firstly, now that you are married to Rex, you should call me Emily. And I just want to see Rex happy. That's all I have ever wanted for him and for you both.'

Pollyanna nodded. 'This bungalow was bought on Distillers money, wasn't it?'

'That's true, Pollyanna, but that doesn't make it any less your home, nor does it mean you can't be happy here,' Sylvia interjected.

We turned as Rex and Natasha entered the garden, deep in conversation. It was only as Rex mounted the ramp and his wheels cut through the grass that Natasha turned and disappeared inside the bungalow. I hoped more than anything for Sylvia to be right, and for this to be Rex and Pollyanna's time at last.

'Even the darkest night will end and the sun will rise.'
Victor Hugo

Chapter Eighty-Five
1981

A year passed, and by the following summer came the news that Pollyanna was pregnant. I greeted her news with the same sense of enthusiasm that I had done throughout much of Rex's life, by offering my help where I could and by being a support to the couple. By now, Rex was busy working to put together an exhibition of his work at the university. Pollyanna was also busy at work, and I anticipated little change in her work and social pursuits, for the first few months of her pregnancy at least.

That September, with Rex's twenty-first birthday looming, we were keen to organise a party to celebrate him reaching this milestone in his life. We had so far kept quiet about Pollyanna's happy news. So this seemed the perfect opportunity to announce her pregnancy to her circle of friends and work colleagues. After a discussion with the couple, it was deemed that the easiest place to hold the party was their bungalow.

On the afternoon of the party, I joined Natasha and Sylvia in decorating the living room with balloons and bunting. We also undertook the catering ourselves. So by the time the guests arrived at five, the dining room table had been laid with platters of sandwiches, quiche, and various salads. Sylvia had bought a Marks and Spencer chocolate cake, and we had champagne on ice for the occasion.

I helped Pollyanna into her red-and-black spotted cocktail dress. The guests started to pull up outside, and with Laurence sorting drinks, Sylvia and I were left responsible for the buffet. But, in the crowd of their young and eager friends, I lost sight of Pollyanna. I glanced out into the garden and saw Rex giving his guests a tour of the garden, pointing with pride at the several types of lilies that he had planted in the centre plot that spring.

Inside, the guests were given a blast of Diana Ross, but Pollyanna wasn't among the group of women from her office. I frowned, knowing that despite her social ineptness, she would still have wanted to be here.

'Have you seen Pollyanna?' I turned to Sylvia.

She shook her head. 'Don't worry, she's probably around somewhere. She won't let Rex down.' Not convinced by my friend, I hurried away to find her.

In the hallway, I found Natasha chatting with Chris. 'Have either of you seen Pollyanna lately?'

'She went into the bathroom,' Natasha said, eying me cautiously.

'When was that?'

'I'm not sure, about twenty minutes ago.'

'That long ago and you haven't been in to check on her? You're her CSV, and she's pregnant.' I shook my head in disbelief.

'I'm sorry,' she said. I pushed past her to knock on the bathroom door.

'Pollyanna, are you all right in there?' I heard her cry, and my heart thumped in fright as several possibilities went through my mind.

'Mrs Alexander?' Natasha touched my arm.

'Emily,' Chris stepped forward. 'Can I help at all?'

I turned to them in anger. 'I think you should get her mother,' I said, pulling on the door handle and stepping inside the bathroom.

I found Pollyanna leaning over the bath with smudges of blood at her ankles.

'Sweetheart,' I knelt down beside her on the floor as she winced in pain. My heart raced, feeling helpless about what to do, knowing my father would be able to handle the situation far better than myself. A tear dripped down her cheek. I pressed my lips together, holding back the urge to panic, and with my hand on her back, I supported her gently as she doubled over in pain.

'When did it start?'

'About half an hour ago. I got a stomach pain and started bleeding!' she cried.

'All right, I'm going to help you as best as I can,' I said, wrapping my arm around her waist. Her body shuddered, and I looked at the trail of blood dripping down her legs. Finding the strength to act, I reached for a towel and slid it on the floor beneath her.

'There, there,' I soothed, crouching down beside her to stroke her hair tenderly.

She bore down and let out a cry, and out slipped a large clot of blood: a sign of the baby that was never to be.

The door was thrust open and in wheeled Rex with Sylvia close by. Rex almost sent Sylvia flying to the floor in his haste to get to Pollyanna's side.

'Pollyanna,' he wept. She leaned heavily over my shoulder. Sylvia looked around helplessly at the trail of blood and caught sight of her daughter's soiled black lace knickers by the side of the bath.

'Get away!' she shouted at Rex, kneeling down before Pollyanna. I passed Pollyanna to her and she gathered her into her arms, raining her cheeks with kisses. 'My darling, my poor darling,' she whispered. She rose, pushing past Rex and me to carry her daughter out into the hallway. It was there that the guests crowded around us in alarm. Sylvia turned tearfully towards Chris.

'Send everyone home,' she ordered, trembling.

Chris nodded sadly and gathered the guests into the living room. Someone, possibly Natasha, switched off the tape recorder.

I followed Sylvia and Rex into the bedroom. Sylvia laid Pollyanna down onto the bed. Sylvia turned her head, and with fresh, unshed tears, fixed her gaze upon Rex.

I stood beside Rex's wheelchair, watching him bow his head over the metal bars of his chair in silence. 'Somebody needs to call the doctor. We have to make sure Pollyanna's all right,' I said, numbly.

Rex lifted his head to gaze at me blankly, before Sylvia got up and went to the back of his chair.

'We can do that,' Sylvia said. 'If you look after my Pollyanna,' and teary-eyed she wheeled Rex from the room.

Pollyanna had curled up in bed, and it didn't take much persuasion from her for me to crawl in beside her. I wound my arm around her waist, and at seeing her distress, I had to breathe deeply against the urge to cry. Pollyanna let out a wail that didn't seem to belong to her, so I held her tighter, holding all my sorrow inside. She started to bleed again, only this time a little more heavily, soiling the cotton sheet beneath us.

Sometime later, I heard the door open again as Sylvia returned with Rex. By that time, Pollyanna's head had slumped to one side and she had passed out.

Rex went with Pollyanna in the ambulance, leaving Laurence, Chris, Sylvia and me to stand in the living room and gaze at the trail of crumbs and empty fizz in silence.

I waited until the following afternoon before getting Laurence to drop me off at the hospital. There, I sat at Pollyanna's bedside, watching her chest rise and fall. With my fingertips, I combed her hair back behind her ear, and with my other hand I gripped Rex's and felt a prayer slip silently from my lips. Sylvia positioned her chair against mine, lost for words to say to make us all feel better.

'When you encounter unexpected situations, don't panic.
Close your eyes take a deep breath and pray.'
Lailah Gifty Akita, Pearls of Wisdom, Great Mind

Chapter Eighty-Six
1982

One afternoon, as Sylvia came over to the house to visit, I prepared a tea tray and took it out into the garden. We sat together on the patio under the shade of the arboretum. It was a bright September morning that gave the illusion of an Indian summer ahead.

'I had a call yesterday evening. I probably should have come over last night, but something else came up.' Sylvia frowned.

'What is it?' I took her hand in mine and gazed into her aquamarine eyes that normally held a clue as to what was troubling my friend.

'It's Pollyanna; she's pregnant again.'

'That's wonderful news!' I exclaimed and began pouring tea into our little china cups. The rising steam warmed my cheeks, and I couldn't resist a smile. 'I can't wait to tell Laurence.'

'She's about two months gone, I think. I promised not to tell too many people yet because of what happened last time, but I had to tell you because of Rex, and for another reason too.' I reached over and hugged her, feeling an impulse to squeeze her more than was necessary.

Upon parting, our eyes lingered upon each other for the longest moment.

'We are going to be grandmas, I'm sure of it this time,' I said.

'Yes,' Sylvia smiled and brushed away an escaped tear from my cheek that must have slipped out unnoticed in my excitement.

'It will be all right. Pollyanna will have every test possible. They will look after her.' I nodded, confident of her good care.

'Sweet Emily, always thinking of others. You were always the kind one, which makes this all the more difficult.' She took my hand in hers, but the gesture felt final.

'Tell me, Sylvia, for nothing can ever be that bad again. We've been through the worst already.'

'Chris and I are going away for a few months to New York. He has to oversee an exhibition there, and he's asked me to go with him.'

I stared at her in disbelief.

'I hope for us to be back in time for the birth. Don't look at me like that, Emily. You knew it was bound to happen at some point. Please try and understand.'

'I just thought—' I shook my head.

'You've got Laurence. This is your time now; grab life with both hands.'

'But why now?' I wondered aloud.

'I need you to look after my little girl and make sure she's all right. It's going to be tough for her in the months ahead, but I trust you with my life. I know you will do the very best for her. She's in safe hands with you. You've always been good with them, and that's what made you special to me. If only I could be you, Emily. But I can't.'

'Don't go! They will need you more than ever now. This is your chance,' I pleaded.

'Chris and I: We need to work on us,' she said, looking to me for support.

'Yes, of course,' I said, offering her a cup of tea at last, pretending that I understood her decision when deep down I couldn't fathom it at all.

✳✳✳

The following afternoon I resolved to go and visit Rex and Pollyanna. I packed my handbag with the remedies that I had taken during my pregnancy with Clemmie: little pots of tissue salts, Calcarea fluorica for bone development, Magnesium phosphate for nerve and muscle development, and Ferrum phosphoricum to aid oxygenation of the blood.

Feeling positive about Pollyanna's pregnancy, I passed Laurence on the stairs as he made his way up to see my father.

He had an armful of papers to share with Father. Reaching my side, we gazed at each other for a moment in exhaustion before he leaned over to plant a kiss on my cheek.

'Is it all right for you to collect Clemmie from school today? She can do her homework with my mother, if you're feeling a bit tired.' I glanced into his weary brown eyes.

Dr Donahue had him working hard, and from what I had gathered it was long, laborious work that kept Laurence searching for answers late into the night. But for once I couldn't be happier for him.

'Yes, of course darling; are you off to Rex's?'

'I'm taking some remedies for Pollyanna. I'm not sure how she is coping with everything, what with Chris and Sylvia going away.'

'I know.' His hand went to my cheek. I closed my eyes, clinging selfishly to the sensation of his caress, when all I could think about was how cruel it seemed for Sylvia to desert us for Chris.

✳✳✳

I took the bus to Hove and had to walk a couple of streets before reaching the bungalow where Rex and Pollyanna lived. I unlatched the gate and strode up the path, admiring their show of hollyhocks and geraniums, before walking up the ramp to ring the bell.

Rex answered the door, and his beaming smile dispelled any fears I had about Pollyanna.

'Mum.' He reached out for my hand to give it an emphatic squeeze, ushering me inside. 'How are you? And how's Dad's new job? Will he be making any important discoveries soon?' He fired the questions with such zest that I released a laugh of pure relief.

'He's snowed under with paperwork at the moment, but your grandfather has been able to help. This new job could be the making of this family, alongside other things, of course,' I grinned.

Inside the hallway, I heard voices from the kitchen and my thoughts turned to Sylvia. I had to be the mother that Rex and Pollyanna needed right now. I had come too far to let them down.

'How's Natasha?' I asked casually, for after Pollyanna's miscarriage, I had my doubts about her suitability as their carer.

'They're coordinating lunch today,' said Rex, with a wink. 'Better go into the lounge and wait.'

I followed Rex's wheelchair through the wide double doors and into the beige lounge. Natasha was already placing platters of sandwiches onto the glass-topped coffee table.

'Emily.' Her brown hair swished as she straightened to greet me with a smile. 'It's good to see you again. Pollyanna will be in shortly, so unless there is anything else?' she turned to Rex, but he shook his head.

'Then I'll leave you to it,' she said, dashing through the double doors to her room.

'I hope everything is working out all right,' I said. The door was thrust open and Pollyanna entered, wearing a pair of blue leggings and matching tie-dyed T-shirt. A single glance at her paler-than-usual complexion was the only sign of her pregnancy so far. I gazed at her waif-like figure, wishing that held a clue as to the state of health of her growing baby.

'Emily!' She raced over to me and threw herself into my arms for a hug. I wrapped an arm around her waist, protectively. 'Careful, Pollyanna, you're in a delicate condition now,' I warned.

'My mum told you.' She scrutinised my face for an instant reaction.

'Congratulations, Pollyanna and Rex.' I indicated for him to come over. 'I'm so happy for you both,' I laughed and felt tears streak my cheeks in joy.

Rex's hand touched my back, and I was determined to remain in this pose for the longest moment. When we did finally pull away, I gazed at the young couple and anticipated all kinds of complications ahead. Yet I felt positive that I had the strength to help them through whatever came their way.

'I know your parents are going away.' I glanced at Pollyanna. 'But Laurence and I, we can help with whatever you need. As a starting point, I've brought over some tissue salts for you to take, Pollyanna, as you'll need to think of minerals and vitamins for a healthy baby.' I glanced at them both, anxiously awaiting their reaction.

'That's good, because we've already been to see a homeopath and have our own supply of remedies.' Pollyanna grinned and I sighed in relief. The worst part was over.

'We know it's going to be more difficult for us, but we want to be good parents, and with a little help from you we think we can do it,' said Rex, his brown eyes full of optimism.

'And I believe you can, for there were just as many challenges when I had you, Rex, but I managed to cope all right,' I said, and my heart seemed set to burst with excitement.

The following week, I organised a small farewell party in the garden for Sylvia and Chris. Clemmie skirted between the guests to offer iced fairy cakes, which she had baked that morning with my mother. On the table were an assortment of little crust-less sandwiches, a jug of freshly made lemonade, and a tray of glasses.

Laurence, Rex, Pollyanna, and my parents had crowded onto the patio, looking at the food between furtive glances at Sylvia and Chris, who held hands as they stood in the centre of the circle.

I surveyed the scene from a distance, holding a pink-iced cake between my palms. I realised a fact that must surely have been evident for a long time. Over the years, I had been slowly collecting people to surround myself with. As a result, I had experienced few moments of true loneliness, and much of that had come about because of Rex.

'We are sorry to be leaving Brighton, if only for a few months, because we've long considered this place home.' Chris glanced towards me. 'But when I received an invitation to oversee an exhibition of Impressionist work at New York's Metropolitan Museum, I couldn't resist.' My father filled his glass with lemonade. 'And Sylvia decided at the last minute that she wanted to come, too,' He raised his glass. It was several seconds before his attention turned towards Rex and Pollyanna. We watched as Rex broke off a piece of sticky cake to tenderly slip into Pollyanna's mouth.

'Emily.' I felt a hand squeeze my shoulder and turned to face Sylvia. She beckoned me to the other side of the garden, where we stood together beside the garden wall. She had her hair piled atop of her head with just a couple of loose tendrils. I couldn't escape those aquamarine eyes that were filled with tears.

'I don't want to go, not really,' she explained.

'Then don't.' I took her hand in mine, feeling the ridge of her silver jewellery push against my skin.

'I have to, Emily, for it's a matter of no choice.'

'Why? Is it Chris? Is he making demands on you?'

She let out a sardonic laugh, and I felt heat rush to my cheeks in shame.

'Sorry,' she said, with the same playful gaze. 'No, Chris is not like that. You should know him by now. He's very free about everything.'

I turned away briefly to see Laurence deep in conversation with my father.

'Then what is it? We've known each other too long for secrets, please.' I crept closer to her, even as I caught my mother's puzzled gaze from the patio.

'I have to see if there is another life out there for Chris and me away from everything that has happened here.'

I glanced away, desperate to understand why she would want to go when she had everything she needed here.

'Why would you want to do that?'

'Call it a sabbatical,' she smiled.

'Are you coming back to Brighton?' I asked, turning to her as tears spilled down my cheeks at the thought of not seeing my friend again.

'The time is always right to do what is right.'
Martin Luther King Jnr

Chapter Eighty-Seven

'Here,' Rex pointed to the pebbled place with a view of the sea below.

Pollyanna tripped along beside him, while my mother paid for the loan of a couple of deckchairs. It was a bright but breezy September afternoon, and the excursion had been a last-minute decision on our part.

My mother and I helped set up Rex's easel, while he shifted in his wheelchair for a view of the bobbing boats in the distance. I handed him his palette and brushes from his canvas bag attached to his wheelchair, and waited for him to pull on his sun hat and stretch out his arms. Pollyanna brushed past me and crouched down amongst the shingle to take her position as his model for the afternoon. She was fully clothed for this session, much to my relief.

'Well, that's those two occupied for the afternoon. What are you going to do?' asked my mother.

'Some work on my memoirs.'

Mother leaned in closer. 'Emily,' she probed, gently.

'It's something I have wanted to do for a long time.'

'I thought you had gone through all that years ago with that journalist of yours,' she said.

'Not everything, not about what we tried to achieve with Rex and Pollyanna. I want people to understand that amid the tragedy of Thalidomide, my life has been one of love, hope and inspiration,' I said, out of breath.

'Of course it has.' My mother looked to me with pride. 'You have more courage than I thought. But what of Laurence; isn't it enough that he had to live through this scandal? Does he need to be reminded of Distillers with this book?'

'He's the reason I'm doing this. I want to help him through this so he can finally accept that it wasn't his fault; that he, too, was a victim of Thalidomide, just like the rest of us,' I said, glancing towards Pollyanna and Rex for a moment.

'But is this the right time, Emily?' My mother drew my attention back to her.

'I won't know unless I try. Maybe we are all ready for closure, to forgive ourselves and move on. Look at Rex and Pollyanna—they're having a baby together. There was a time when they weren't expected to reach adolescence. They have a future together because of us. And perhaps, with the gift of truth, we can finally be exonerated of the past.'

I felt confidence swell in my heart, for at last I knew what I was doing with my life.

Rex turned around then and glanced at my leather-bound notebook. A smile curled on his lips as if he knew what it contained. I sensed the time for action was upon us, but for once I wasn't afraid.

'Volunteering is at the very core of being human.
No one has made it through life without someone else's help.'
Heather French Henry

Chapter Eighty-Eight

One afternoon during Pollyanna's fifth month of pregnancy, after arranging to meet under the pier, we took a stroll along the beach together. I was now able to ascertain subtle changes in her body, as her dungarees showed evidence of a small rounded bump, adding weight to her otherwise slender figure. I had heard through Rex that she had stopped playing the piano, probably because her body, unique at the best of times, had yet to adjust to her growing baby inside.

That afternoon I placed my hand on her shoulder, a reminder, if I needed one, of similar walks with her mother. I thought of Sylvia and my eyes filled with tears, wishing that she was here to share these moments with her daughter.

Pollyanna leaned her head towards mine, and we took several tentative steps on the shingle. I imagined the pulsating heart of the baby inside her. We carried on walking for a while before coming across a vacant deckchair for Pollyanna to rest on. I took a breath of restorative sea air and we fell into silence.

It wasn't just Pollyanna's pregnancy that had taken us by surprise. In fact, changes had occurred all around us. Craving a sense of adventure, Laurence, Clemmie and I had settled in over the road at Chris and Sylvia's to house-sit until their return. I had thrown myself into writing my memoirs.

'Rex tells me you have started a new book,' Pollyanna said, adapting a cross-legged position on the chair. I saw her wince in pain and felt a stab of motherly concern, anticipating that at her stage of pregnancy the baby had probably started to kick.

'Yes, that's right. I needed something to take my mind off everything else,' I said, reaching across to caress her stomach.

Feeling the baby's tiny kicks caused a smile of joy to form on my lips. I looked into her eyes and caught her frustration. I pulled my hand away, realising with remorse that I hadn't asked for her permission to touch her. I wondered how often during her time at Chailey her silence had been taken for consent.

'I'm sorry,' I said.

'It's all right, really. I don't mind you touching my tummy, Emily. I always liked you from the start.' She nodded to indicate that it was all right for me to touch her stomach again. My hand reached over to her tummy, but to my disappointment I couldn't feel any movement this time.

'I'm sorry about my mother,' said Pollyanna, offering me a casual glance. 'She wants your adoration, and once she's got you worshipping her, it's as if that gives her the right to have complete control over your life and to dump you at will. Because she is so beautiful you kind of let her get away with it, even though it hurts like hell. I know.'

I dropped my hand from her stomach and gazed at Pollyanna's wet cheeks. Moving closer to her, I hugged her tightly, causing my own tears to drip onto her neat braids. When I did finally let go of her, we sat side by side.

'I've been thinking that now I'm on maternity leave, I'm free to help you.'

'Of course, Pollyanna, whatever you'd like to do.' I gazed at her in curiosity.

'I want to help you type your manuscript. Together we could get your book done in half the time.' She grinned, and feeling a smile return to my face, I thought she was probably right.

✳✳✳

The following morning, I heard the beep of a car horn from Rex dropping Pollyanna off at the house. I waited a few moments and listened for her tap against the door. I ushered her inside. Her rounded belly grazed my side as she followed me upstairs to the drawing room and hopped onto a chair. She used her teeth to pull down the zip of her calf-length boots. She tiptoed on her red-lacquered toes across the room to the dining table, where I had set up the typewriter with a view of the square below.

'So where do I start?' she enthused, her head darting back and forth in excitement. I found myself surprised by the new Pollyanna and especially by her commitment to my project.

'Would you like a drink first?' I asked.

She shook her head vehemently. 'Rex gives me too much tea in the morning, my bladder can't take any more.' She giggled, and considering that she had suffered a miscarriage only the year before, I thought she had recovered extremely well.

'Right. Well, is there sufficient light for you?' I asked, as she adjusted herself on the velvet-backed chair. Appearing at ease, she lifted her feet onto the typewriter. Her toes got a feel for the keys, while I stood watching her in amazement.

'It seems all right to me,' said Pollyanna, curling and uncurling her toes in rotation. I placed a cushion behind her back. Her bump seemed to have grown an inch since yesterday, which I took as a sign that all was well with the baby.

'He kicks between seven and nine in the morning and then rests until eleven o'clock, leaving us with a couple of hours to work before I need to rest again,' she said, flicking on the switch to the typewriter with her big toe.

'Of course,' I said and offered her a bundle of handwritten notes. On the top of the first page was the sentence: *Trust me on this one, Emily.* Pollyanna used her tongue to lick the first page and I watched her eyes scan the opening chapter. I held my breath, admonishing myself for not preparing her properly for this moment. She should have been aware that the book was no work of fiction, but the story of my life, our story.

Over the years I had learnt to predict her moods. But as she turned to me with tears caressing her rosy cheeks, I stood, held to the spot and needing something to hold onto, pretty sure that otherwise I would fall.

'Emily,' she said, and we looked at each other as strangers meeting for the first time. I cleared my throat of dryness, but was still unable to get any words out.

'I'm sorry for what you and my mum had to go through. The shock of Rex and me, it belonged to you two, solely.'

I nodded. She beckoned me over with her toes. I knelt before her and sobbed at receiving the forgiveness of a generation.

It took another half an hour for Pollyanna to start tapping away, and as I watched her in fascination, I felt my chest swell with admiration. I came in and out of the room to offer her glasses of water and remedies of Rhus toxicodendron and Arnica for her hardworking toes. Pollyanna managed only an hour and a half of work before the baby's kicks caused her to wince in pain. I got her to lie down on the sofa and offered to massage her feet with peppermint lotion.

'Have you told Rex about the subject of your new book?' she asked with a relaxed gaze that meant the baby had probably stopped kicking.

'No,' I sighed. 'I haven't told Laurence, either. Perhaps we can keep this between us for the time being. I know that's a lot to ask of you, keeping it from Rex.'

She curled her lips in contemplation. 'Rex goes off to his studio every morning, and he doesn't show me his work until he's ready. It could be the same with the book,' she beamed.

I relaxed at her calm attitude. She lowered her feet to the floor and returned to the table, eager to get back to work, and I thought with relief that everything was working out just as planned.

*'A baby fills the place in your heart
that you never knew was empty.'*
Unknown

Chapter Eighty-Nine

'Aunty Sylvia!' shrieked Clemmie, dropping her trowel into the rose plot. She ran towards the patio where Sylvia stood dressed in a long black-and-white wool coat and shiny heels, looking remarkably fresh despite having just arriving home from New York.

We had received a telephone call from Sylvia a couple of days ago about her imminent return home, and had moved back over the road to my parents' house, and it was there that Sylvia found us busy in the garden.

I approached her tentatively, just as Clemmie threw her arms up to Sylvia for a hug.

'Look at you!' Sylvia ruffled Clemmie's auburn hair. 'All muddy—when did you get into gardening?'

'Whilst you were busy shopping at Macy's,' I countered, and immediately I hated myself for such petty jealousy.

'Emily.' Sylvia arched an eyebrow. 'I had hoped you wouldn't still be holding a grudge about New York.'

I stood only a few paces away from her and saw her pursed lips, reminding me of the last time we had met, when we had stood together beside the garden wall. I thought back to my show of tears. But this time I reverted back to my old ways of holding my arms at my sides and diverting my gaze to the damp flagstones beneath my feet.

I caught sight of Laurence wandering into the garden. He took one look at Sylvia and hastened back inside the house.

'What was New York like?' asked Clemmie, gazing up at Sylvia in awe.

'Cold and frantic,' Sylvia laughed. Her eyes twinkled in exhilaration. It was a relief to note that we were still a curiosity to her. I turned to Clemmie with a forced smile.

'Daddy's home. Why don't you go and wash your hands, and then you can watch TV with him for a bit?'

'Really? No homework on Friday?'

'You can catch up tomorrow, before we go to Rex's.'

'Sure,' she beamed and ran inside before I could change my mind.

'So how's Pollyanna? She must be huge by now,' said Sylvia, throwing an arm around my shoulder and guiding me around the garden.

'Due any day. I was planning to pop over later with Laurence, to drop off some labour remedies for her.'

'Thinking of Pollyanna giving birth fills me somewhat with dread,' Sylvia sighed, and leaned her head to one side. Sensing her closed eyes, my hand reached over to caress her cheek.

'Pollyanna's been working for me,' I said.

'Has she?'

'Yes, she's been busy typing up my new book.'

'So the job didn't work out for her then.'

'She's on maternity leave at the moment. But I'm not sure if she will go back to the job once the baby's born. Not that I mind too much, for I've enjoyed her company, and being pregnant has certainly matured her. I think you'll notice the changes when you see her next.'

'I think I will.' She lifted her head, and there was that same self-satisfied grin which I had come to know and love.

'I don't doubt that you haven't done a good job with Pollyanna in my absence.' Sylvia took my hand in hers as a thank-you.

'Did you enjoy New York?' I asked, as we neared Rex's old swing.

She let go of me and ran towards the swing to hold the seat between her hands. 'I never thought they would grow up, our Thalidomide babies. And now look at us: redundant at last! The boys and their wives are with Chris in New York. I suppose I'll have to make do with Clemmie.'

'Oh, she'd like that.'

I watched Sylvia's fingers slide through the safety bars. For a moment, I thought of Dr Donahue strolling into the garden, desperate to help Rex learn to walk.

'We've been through so much, Emily. It's no wonder we feel confused and have no idea which path to take next,' Sylvia said, and came to stand by my side.

'The square wasn't the same without you.' She glanced ahead to where the garden wall ended. 'I'm glad you came home.'

✳✳✳

The telephone rang the following evening after dinner, and I answered it in the lounge, while Laurence and Clemmie did the washing up.

'Mum!' Rex said, excitedly.

'Is everything all right?' I said, keeping the phone close to my ear.

'Pollyanna's waters have broken. Natasha's about to drive us to hospital.' His voice trembled.

'I'll get your father to drop me off at hospital. Rex, you're going to be a dad!' I breathed.

'I know, Mum, and I can't wait!' he laughed down the line. My only thought then was for Pollyanna and for everything to go all right with the baby. She had suffered enough in her life already, and it was with that thought alone that I went into the kitchen and broke the news to Laurence and Clemmie.

Hours later, Sylvia and I were seated outside the labour ward, watching as the anaesthetist rushed past us through the swinging doors into the delivery room.

'They should give her a caesarean,' said Sylvia, 'after the problems she had with her heart.'

'Yes, but Pollyanna probably just wants to feel as if she is doing her bit.'

Sylvia turned to me with a teary gaze. 'Sometimes you just have to let go,' she said, tapping her fingers upon her knee in anticipation. 'I missed you when I was in New York.'

'Really?'

'If I'm honest, I hated every minute of it. But we all like to think that we have travelled a bit in our lives, don't we?'

'Yes,' I smiled, remembering my time in India with fondness. The sound of muffled voices coming from the delivery room made me think that perhaps they had followed Sylvia's advice and were performing a caesarean. In that case it would be over soon.

'You haven't asked how things are between Chris and me,' she reprimanded gently.

I bit down on my lip. I cared about her, of course I did, but she could be exhausting at times.

So as she shuffled closer to me and leaned her head on my shoulder, I was happy to close my eyes and fall asleep.

A firm hand on my shoulder jolted me awake. I prised myself from Sylvia. The doctor beamed at me, and I shook Sylvia awake. We straightened ourselves before glancing at the young doctor in expectation.

'How is she? How's my daughter?'

'Congratulations, for you have a healthy grandson, and I'm relieved to say that mum is doing fine, too.'

I rose to my feet and pulled Sylvia up with me. 'Can we see them?' I said, hardly able to contain my excitement.

'Yes, of course. Come this way.'

We followed the doctor into the delivery room. Pollyanna appeared to be between two states of consciousness and had a tube attached to her neck, pumping painkillers into her bloodstream. Rex sat at her bedside with his arms cradling my grandson.

The baby was wrapped in a blue blanket, yet I could still make out his tuft of auburn hair. But thankfully this baby was a completely different little boy altogether.

'A bridge of silver wings stretches from the dead ashes
of an unforgiving nightmare
to the jewelled vision of a life started anew.'
Aberjhani

Chapter Ninety

I went to see Pollyanna in hospital a couple of days later. Creeping into her room during the afternoon, I expected Pollyanna to be having a rest, so I was pleasantly surprised to find her awake. She had the baby in an infant carrier strapped to her front. A few cushions had been left scattered at her tummy. On the tabletop to her left were a packet of Pampers nappies and a tub of Sudocrem. I took a seat at her bedside and listened to the sound of the baby suckling at her breast.

'Emily!' Pollyanna's eyes brightened at seeing me. 'Look.' She pulled back the blue cover of the carrier with her teeth, and I saw the baby's pink lips gorging on her nipple. Her normally svelte figure had swelled to accommodate her milky breasts. I stroked the baby's auburn curls in pleasure, and he let out a tiny whimper in fear of missing out on a single drop of sweet honey milk.

'This is the first time he's latched on properly.' She beamed with pride.

'Well done, Pollyanna. You're doing everything right.'

'Do you think so?' She looked hesitant. 'My mum's employed a maternity nurse for when we leave the hospital next week.'

'The first weeks are the hardest.'

She looked at me with sincerity. 'I want you to be part of it. I couldn't have gotten through my pregnancy without you,' she said, as tears pooled in her eyes.

I smiled and wiped away her tears with a tissue.

'Try and keep me away,' I replied. The baby closed his eyes and with his lips still parted, he rested on Pollyanna's breast.

I heard the sound of Rex's electric wheelchair.

'You're supposed to be resting at home,' Pollyanna reprimanded. His reddened eyes told me that he hadn't slept much since the birth.

'Pollyanna's right, you won't get much sleep when the little one comes home,' I said, as his wheelchair came to a stop at my ankles.

'I don't care much for sleep.' He shrugged, scooping the baby into his arm for a cuddle.

'Have you thought of a name yet?' I asked.

A nurse entered the room to check on Pollyanna's drains. She smiled at the baby. Rex kissed his son's ruddy cheeks, before holding him over the bed so Pollyanna could do the same. The nurse looked at the three of us in amazement.

'We thought the name Lucian sounded all right,' said Rex, and with a nod from Pollyanna, the nurse scooped the baby from Rex's arms and took him back to the nursery.

'That sounds perfect to me,' I agreed and turned to Pollyanna. With her head tilted to one side came the sound of her steady breath.

'She's exhausted,' said Rex. 'She lost a lot of blood with the birth. I don't like to leave her alone for too long.'

I squeezed his hand. 'I know, but trust me: Everything is going to be all right this time.'

✳✳✳

A couple of days passed, and one afternoon Chris dropped by the house as I was busy packing my bag with homeopathic remedies of Arnica, Calendula and Hypericum to take to the hospital for Pollyanna. I cast my bag to one side and we went into the garden and sat under the arboretum.

'I had to see you personally to explain what happened in New York between Sylvia and me,' said Chris, crossing his legs as he took a seat at the table.

'There's no need, Chris. I understand how it has been for the two of you over the years, and I hope I am not partly to blame for that,' I said, glancing ahead at the first show of daffodils which had sprung up by the garden wall.

'You shouldn't,' he said, forcing me to look into his blue eyes. 'The blame always lays with me. Sylvia was the driving force behind our fight for justice for Pollyanna. But the money won't ever make up for the lost time, will it?'

I thought of Laurence and all he had missed because of his guilt about Thalidomide and shook my head.

'New York was an attempt to rekindle some of the earlier flame between us, before Pollyanna was born,' he confessed. 'Please, don't reproach yourself for anything. You've always been a good friend to both of us, and I hope that never changes,' he said, with a look that spoke of a bond between us that could never be broken.

'Sylvia is an intense woman, I'm sure you can agree with that.'

I smiled. I couldn't argue on that.

'I have no idea where we go from here. Travel seems to allow us to evade the reality of tomorrow,' he mused.

'Yes, but reality does have a way of catching us up,' I said.

'So you and my wife?' He arched an eyebrow.

'Sylvia and I are the greatest of friends. I couldn't have gotten through the shock of Thalidomide without her. I don't have any more answers than you do, Chris. All I know,' I paused, 'is that after everything we have been through with our children, now is the time for living.'

'There's nothing half as pleasant as coming home again.'
Margaret Elizabeth Sangster

Chapter Ninety-One

The following week, Chris came to the hospital as Pollyanna and Lucian were discharged home. Pollyanna and Rex, with baby Lucian, plus Sylvia and I, happily clambered into Chris' Rolls-Royce. We placed Lucian in his carrycot on the backseat with Sylvia and me on either side of the couple. My fingers stroked the centre of Lucian's forehead, sending him off into a peaceful sleep.

'Lucian, eh,' said Chris, making a turn towards Hove. 'It sounds very posh.' He winked at us in the mirror.

'We like it,' said Pollyanna, leaning her head onto Rex's shoulder in fatigue. But privy to Laurence's plans, I knew she wouldn't get much sleep when we arrived home at their bungalow.

As we pulled into Rex's driveway, I saw a string of blue 'Welcome Home' balloons. By the time Chris had turned off the ignition, Laurence, Natasha and a young woman who I assumed to be the maternity nurse were waiting for us on the front path.

While Sylvia helped Pollyanna out of the car and towards the bungalow, I wheeled Rex up the ramp with Chris following close behind me holding Lucian in the baby carrier.

Laurence gave everyone a hug, and we inhaled the scent from dozens of bouquets of roses, which had been arranged around the bungalow in large ceramic vases in celebration of the birth. Natasha offered us each a glass of champagne (all except Pollyanna, who due to breast-feeding had to contend with a glass of orange juice instead) to officially welcome Lucian into the family.

Laurence then stepped aside so we could all view his handiwork, which turned out to be a series of intercoms that he had set up around the bungalow to assist Pollyanna and Rex in caring for the baby. I took a seat on the sofa as Lucian started to stir.

'Would you like to hold him?' asked Pollyanna, relaxing next to me.

I nodded and scooped him into my arms, gently rocking him to and fro. 'How about we go and see the nursery?' I suggested, while Laurence and Chris stood to one side and each picked up a sandwich to try. Rex joined Laurence and Chris to discuss the finer details of electronics.

I followed Pollyanna and Natasha into the nursery, where the same young woman from outside the bungalow was waiting for us. Her blonde hair was tied back into a ponytail.

'Hello, I'm Evie, and I'm the maternity nurse. I am here to help to settle Lucian into a routine and to help you bond with your baby,' she said with an Australian accent.

On the wall of the sky-blue room, stencilled in yellow, were images of lions and towering giraffes. I slipped out of my shoe and curled my toes around the springy beige carpet and took in the pinewood cot, above which was a dangling mobile. Nearby was the changing table made to Rex's specifications.

My hand swung the rail of my old rocking chair positioned not too far from the low shelf of toys upon which sat Rex's old basket of rattles. This room was a place of joy and inspiration, just as it should be.

Lucian wriggled in my arms, and I soon realised that a nappy change was in order. Evie stepped forward to take Lucian from me, and I couldn't help but notice Pollyanna's eyes cloud with disappointment, knowing that nappy-changing wasn't something that she would be able to do herself because of her disability. So I guided her towards a seat by the window.

'I should get back to Rex,' Natasha said, leaving us alone to talk at last.

The nursery offered a view of the garden. A string of pink and blue lanterns hung from the roof of the lean-to, beyond which stood a border of daffodils and crocuses. Under the arch interwoven with passion flower was a baby swing and sandpit, waiting in expectation for Lucian to explore when he was ready.

'Thank you, Emily, for everything you've done for Rex and me.' Pollyanna leaned her head upon my shoulder, and I felt her body tremble from exhaustion.

'You need to rest. You've been through a lot with the birth.'

'Not as much as you did when you had Rex,' she said and raised her head.

Our eyes met for a moment in silence.

I hadn't talked to anyone about my early days with Rex, except Sylvia. There was now a move towards counselling for traumatic events, but I hadn't received anything like that; just a few homeopathic remedies and the love of my family.

'It was difficult,' I admitted, breathing slowly to allow my tears to flow freely, feeling no shame at all. 'But how can you not love your child when he is placed in your arms? Not feel something for the baby you've carried for nine months? That's how I got through it.' I paused. 'It wasn't easy at times, but Rex gave me so much love in return, and that made up for the missing pieces of the jigsaw of my life.'

I glanced at Pollyanna to see that she had tears, too. I hugged her tightly, loving her every bit as if she was my own daughter.

'I want to be just like you, Emily,' Pollyanna said at last.

I shook my head. 'No, Pollyanna, you must be yourself. Love who you are and Lucian will latch on to that, and won't be able to resist loving you in return.'

As I was still hugging her tightly, Evie approached us with Lucian, fresh with the scent of Sudocrem. He let out a cry, this time eager for his next feed. I took him from Evie as she knelt at Pollyanna's feet and unbuttoned her top before unclipping her bra. I handed Lucian back to Evie, watching in fascination as she held the baby to Pollyanna's breast. Latching on, he suckled at her milk greedily, just as Pollyanna closed her eyes in surrender to her fatigue.

I wandered from the room, feeling tears of joy that day, and found Laurence waiting for me in the hallway. He clasped my hand in his, and as Rex wheeled himself into the nursery, I heard the door close behind us and knew that my work here was done.

*'For every minute you are angry you lose
sixty seconds of happiness.'*
Ralph Waldo Emerson

Chapter Ninety-Two

A month after Lucian's birth, Rex held an exhibition of his work at Chris' gallery in London. This was an opportunity for him to present a selection of work that best represented his development as a young artist. It was an eclectic mix. Amongst the new pieces were those from his art school days depicting images from under the sea, as well as his earlier works including *The Wave* that he had painted as a young boy. Spaced between the paintings hung a couple of sketches of Pollyanna. One was set against the background of our garden, while the other was the life drawing of her, which up to this point had been kept secret from Sylvia and Chris.

On that summer's evening, I wore a coral wraparound silk dress and held Laurence's hand as we stepped onto the polished floor. A white-gloved waiter offered us each a glass of champagne, and taking a sip, I scanned the crowd nervously for Sylvia and Chris.

A blonde woman in a paisley floral dress, tight above the knee, spun on her heels. I quickly recognised her to be Sylvia. Chris stood to her left and had on a black dress suit. Upon noticing us, he offered a warm smile, seemingly glad that we could make it. My hand looped with Laurence's, feeling the absence of Clemmie who we had left back home for the evening with my parents in Brighton. I tugged Laurence forward to approach our friends, and it was then that we circled the nude drawing of Pollyanna in apprehension.

Sylvia's fingers grazed Chris', not quite touching. Laurence flinched at the sight of his naked daughter-in-law, represented in the drawing as a delicate nymph on the verge of womanhood.

I searched for Rex, but he was busy pointing out the finer elements of *The Wave* to a crowd of eager spectators on the other side of the gallery. A baby's cry echoed nearby, and I caught the wisp of Pollyanna's white cotton dress as she wound her way through the crowd to analyse her husband's art. Watching her closely, I ascertained her favourite to be that of the Brighton Pier with its white-domed amusement arcade and, poignantly, the site of their teenaged escape from Chailey.

'Who knew about this?' Sylvia nodded towards the sketch, breaking my chain of thought with a sense of uneasiness.

A glance into her cool eyes stunned me into silence.

This was going to be as awkward as I thought it would be. I paced myself by taking several deep breaths. We could get through this just as anything that we had faced in our long friendship so far.

'You know Pollyanna, she's always been the adventurer,' Chris said, offering me a tender smile.

'That's our daughter we are talking about, Chris, not one of your paintings in this bloody gallery of yours,' she fumed. Her hand moved to her chignon for fear of an escaped lock of hair.

'I'm sure she had her reasons for doing this. After all, it was done before she was married. Must have been one of those foolish things we do when we're young,' Laurence said, offering me the best encouragement he could muster.

'You knew about this, didn't you?' Sylvia turned on me. 'Your precious son could never do any wrong in your eyes. But Rex wasn't enough for you, was he? You had to have Pollyanna, too.'

'That's not fair, Sylvia, after everything Emily has done for you,' Laurence interjected.

'This has nothing to do with you, Laurence, but everything to do with Emily. She likes to play the martyr rather than be honest about her feelings. But take a look at yourself, Emily, still dependent upon your parents at your age. Ask yourself: How far have you really come in all these years since Rex's birth? Have a good long think about that one. Do you have the courage to make that final leap and live the life you want?'

Before I had a chance to respond to her questions, she marched over to the spot where Pollyanna stood with Lucian strapped to her front. I watched her lead Pollyanna towards a red velvet couch, and under her mother's fixed gaze, Pollyanna lowered her head in submission.

I looked at Chris and Laurence, both of whom I knew well.

'Emily, I'm so sorry about Sylvia. Take no notice,' Chris apologised.

'Don't let her upset you, Emily,' said Laurence, slipping an arm around my waist. 'You don't need her anymore, not after everything you have achieved through your own strength of character. Whatever decision you make, let us make it together.'

Feeling overwhelmed by the demands of others, I pushed through the crowd and stumbled out of the gallery and into the fresh, dark August night. I found a bench to sit on, needing to take breath to quell my trembling body. Hearing Pollyanna's footsteps, I waited for her to take a seat beside me and rest her head upon my shoulder.

'All that fuss over one sketch.' Her chin nestled against my hair. 'Are you okay?' she asked.

'Not really.' I shook my head. 'But give me some time and I will be. It was a fine sketch,' I said. 'And Sylvia won't abandon me. She can't —we've been through too much together.'

*'The most important thing is this;
to sacrifice what you are now
for what you can become tomorrow.'*
Shannon L Alder

Chapter Ninety-Three

On a bright October afternoon, three months after the scene at the gallery, the family gathered in my parents' upstairs dining room to celebrate Lucian's christening. Upon the lace tablecloth were several trays of long-fluted glasses, ready for a toast to Lucian's health. I placed platters of caviar-topped crackers and a variety of filled *vol-au-vents* that my mother and I had prepared earlier. At the end of the table sat a blue-fringed christening cake waiting to be cut later.

I wore a dusty-pink dress and matching jacket for the occasion and lingered close to Laurence's side, needing to persuade him now more than ever of my enduring love for him.

I glanced at Rex and Pollyanna from across the room. Pollyanna had Lucian strapped to her front. I smiled at the thought of little Lucian snug against her red short-sleeved dress. Rex's wheels were close to her ankles, but as he was positioned to one side, he was able to offer the crowd of well wishers his usual broad smile. His long fingers reached up to slip inside the baby carrier and pet Lucian's head, gently.

Clemmie ran into the room in a blue-and-pink ra-ra dress. At the age of ten, her long freckled legs skipped easily between the guests. She approached Rex and Pollyanna and pulled back the hood of the baby carrier to expose Lucian's white silk christening gown to the curious crowd.

'They will come,' Laurence whispered into my ear and tenderly squeezed my hand. I shuddered from the sound of footsteps on the landing.

Pollyanna's brothers entered the room first. In grey silk suits they proceeded to crowd around their sister to offer their congratulations. They hung on the arms of their pretty blonde wives and lingered only long enough to catch a fleeting glance of their sleeping nephew.

Chris strode into the room in a midnight-blue suit and brown shoes. He turned to us with a dazzling smile, and a few confident strides brought him to our side with handshakes and hugs. Daring to look over his shoulder, I saw Sylvia. She had on a classic black dress, nipped in at the waist with a bias neckline. I pulled away from Chris to the reverberation of her clicking heels. Her eyes offered no malice; they only glided over my body in tenderness.

I saw Laurence slip away with Chris and head towards Rex and Pollyanna. The crowd spilled out onto the landing, leaving us alone on the parquet floor. My mind flooded with memories of Sylvia when, dressed in beige tweed and red kid boots, she had approached me in the Regency Bookshop. Her welcoming smile had been her way of accepting me into her life. Little had I known, back then, that had been my initiation act for surrendering my soul to her.

We sauntered across the room and stood by the mahogany glass cabinet.

'I'm sorry about what I said at the gallery,' said Sylvia. Her hand brushed mine, and my heart thumped in response.

'I had no intention of ever abandoning you, Emily. It was a spur-of-the moment reaction to the sketch. I probably gave you reason enough to walk away from our friendship. I'm not an easy person to understand or love.'

'I never thought they would display that sketch. I hadn't meant to deceive you.'

She waved the matter aside with her delicate hand. 'Let's put it behind us and think of the future instead.'

'Yes, of course.' I glanced at her, yet everything about her kept me rooted to the spot.

'So what have you been up to?' She led me to the window. I gazed towards the square and at the figures dancing on the lawn below.

'Well, I have been busy with a number of things.' I offered her a copy of my published memoir from the nest of tables. She scanned the front cover, before flicking it over in excitement. 'Also, I have been arranging the christening party and finding us a new home.' I returned my gaze to hers.

She hugged me without another word.

'Well done, Emily, for being braver than I could ever hope to be.' As we finally pulled away, I caught sight of her tender smile.

'So where's the new place? Near here, I hope.'

'It's in Hove and not far from Rex and Pollyanna.' I glanced at her, searching for her response to what I had just said.

She clasped my hand. 'We will always be close, Emily. You don't let go of those you love, not without a fight, at least,' she laughed.

We held onto each other for a moment longer before parting. And then to my relief I realised that everything was as it should be, and that the bright future I had prophesied in the summer of '75 was finally falling into place.

✳✳✳

Later, the remaining guests spilled into the upstairs lounge and filled up the two blue sofas. In the centre of the room, Rex spun his wheelchair and addressed the crowd.

'Thank you. Thank you for coming here today to celebrate the birth of our beautiful son, Lucian.' He touched Pollyanna's shoulder before continuing. 'He has come from two parents who were taught the precious gift of love from their parents. Thank you, Mum, Dad, Sylvia and Chris, but most importantly of all, Nanny and Gramps.' We all turned to glance at my parents seated on the opposite sofa and still holding hands in their seventies.

'I was Lucian's age when I first arrived at this house, wrapped in a blue blanket, in my mother's arms. Nanny and Gramps welcomed me into their home and hearts. Thank goodness they did, for otherwise my life could have taken a very different turn. Please raise a glass with me to baby Lucian, the newest member of the Alexander and Watersmith family,' said Rex, lowering his glass to clink against Pollyanna's glass that she balanced between her toes.

'To family!' we exclaimed against the echo of clinking glasses. I turned to Rex and remembered the little baby who had once clung to my breast. I had a choice back then, and although it had meant a difficult journey for us both, looking at him now convinced me that I had made the right decision.

The guests scattered around the lounge as the sun set on Brighton, presenting us with a golden-hued horizon. Pollyanna offered Lucian to me, and scooping him from the baby carrier, his tiny fists grasped at my satin dress in urgency.

My father set up the piano with a stool for Pollyanna, and upon positioning herself comfortably, she began to tap out with her toes her own rendition of 'Over the Rainbow' to the astonished crowd. My father nudged in beside me and squeezed my hand.

'They're quite a couple, aren't they?' My father had been right after all to believe in Rex, and to show me the beauty of homeopathy. Now Laurence and I really could enjoy the best years of our lives.

'What I went through raising Rex, it was worth it to see him now,' I said and meant it.

My father got up and sat beside my mother again. Clemmie shuffled closer to me on the sofa. I brushed a stray lock of her auburn hair from her face, and reflected upon my vow in India to give equal attention to both my children.

Pollyanna's melody came to an end, and as she spun on her stool to face us, Rex wheeled himself to her side, and his hand reached up to rest upon her shoulder.

'I want to thank everyone, too, for coming here today to celebrate the birth of my little boy, Lucian—the reason, I'm sure, to be excited about the future,' said Pollyanna.

It was then that Dr Donahue stepped up to Rex's wheelchair and smiled.

'I hope you don't mind my intrusion, but as some of you are aware, I had the privilege of knowing Rex and Pollyanna as Thalidomide children at Chailey. Seeing them now as parents themselves gives me great pride. In fifty years' time, perhaps no one will remember Thalidomide and the effect it had on our lives; but those children have grown up, and their lives have headed in many different directions. It is true that their bodies developed differently from ours, but the heart of what makes them living and loving beings can be celebrated today. So please raise a glass to the future of our extraordinary Thalidomide children.' The doctor beamed and raised his glass in celebration.

I brushed away a tear and turned to glance at Laurence, noticing his gentle smile of peace at last. Sylvia and Chris were seated not too far away from us and held hands. No one could predict the future or who we would love or lose, but a gaze at Rex and Pollyanna convinced me that as long as the family remained together, the future at last was a bright one.

References

Abram, D, (2007) *The Rough Guide to South India*.

Medus, L, (2009), *No Hand to Hold & No Legs to Dance On*, Accent Press Ltd, Mid-Glamorgan.

Moriarty-Simmonds, R, (2009), *Four Fingers and Thirteen Toes*, Authorhouse, Milton Keynes.

Mulvagh, J, (1988), *Vogue History of 20th Century Fashion*, Penguin Group, London.

The Sunday Times Insight Team, (1979), *Suffer the Children: The Story of Thalidomide*, André Deutsch Limited, London.

Printed in Great Britain
by Amazon